## A Night To Surrender

"Please let me go," Joanna whispered to the handsome Indian warrior.

Windhawk drew Joanna closer to him, fearing that he had frightened her with the overwhelming love he had displayed. "I have not the words to say to you in English. If you could understand my language, I could tell you how I feel."

Joanna felt his lips brush her forehead, and she felt a weakness wash over her. He lifted her chin and gazed deeply into her eyes.

"I want you for my woman, Jo-anna. I believe that it was meant for you and I to be lovers."

Joanna closed her eyes and felt his lips softly touch her eyelids. She wanted to leave, yet she wanted to stay. She was experiencing a new feeling so consuming it pushed all other thoughts out of her mind. She could feel his warm breath upon her flesh and it sparked a deep pain of longing within her. Her young body yearned for something from him, but she didn't know what it was. As he lowered her to the ground, she cast all doubts and fear to the wind. He was her destiny, the man of her dreams — her sweet savage lover . . .

# Savage Autumn

## CONSTANCE O'BANYON

**ZEBRA BOOKS**
**KENSINGTON PUBLISHING CORP.**

*This book is dedicated to John and Beatrice, whom I lovingly call Mom and Dad. You gave the gift of life to my husband, you gave the gift of love to me. This is also for my friend and secretary Jean—for the times we laughed together and the long hours you labored tirelessly without complaining. I thank you.*

Fort Union, which is mentioned in this book, was built by the American Fur Company in what is now known as North Dakota. It is not to be confused with Fort Union which was built by the United States Army in New Mexico Territory in the year 1851.

## WINDHAWK

He came down from the north with the swiftness of
    the wind,
With a noble spirit that would not break nor would
    it bend.
He is not of my world and not of my kind, yet he
    touches my
Heart and troubles my mind.

With his hair black as ebony and dark eyes flashing
    and bold,
I love him, yet I fear him, for I know he seeks my
    soul.

Constance O'Banyon

# Introduction

It was a time when America was young. The white man had recently landed on her shores with his eyes moving restlessly westward. He was cutting down her forests to build his villages and farms. He would take from her bounty without giving back to her. America's plentiful resources would be loaded onto great cargo ships and transported across the seas to be sold to the highest bidder.

It was a time when America was old. On her lands the mighty Blackfoot Indians had coexisted with Nature long before the first white man had sailed the uncharted oceans.

The Indian took from Nature only that which he needed to survive, without upsetting Nature's delicate balance.

The Blackfoot was undisputed gladiator of his vast domain. His territory stretched from the Saskatchewan River in the north, and south to the present day Yellowstone National Park. The Rocky Mountains formed the western border, and the mouth of the Milk River was the eastern limit.

The white man would soon become greedy for the land that by birthright belonged to the Blackfoot, but that time had not yet come.

Journey back with me in time when the mighty Blackfoot was lord of these vast prairies and mountains. Walk with me in the savage autumn of time.

# Chapter One

## Philadelphia, 1838

It had begun to sleet. A strong wind swirled the frozen particles into Taggart James's face, stinging his cheeks like the prickle of tiny needles.

Taggart felt his sister, Joanna, tighten her grip on his hand and he looked up at her, wishing he could cry, but knowing he must be strong for her sake.

A strong gust of wind lifted the black veil that Joanna wore and he saw that there were tears on her face. He swallowed a lump in his throat when he felt her hand tremble.

Taggart James was twelve years old. He was trying to be grown up, but he felt very much like a young boy who needed comfort. Joanna's arm slid around his shoulders and he looked into her face. He could read in her eyes the same pain and confusion he was feeling and somehow it comforted him.

11

He heard the sleet hitting against the wooden coffin that contained his mother's body and he shivered. It was the first time in his young life that he had experienced the death of a loved one and the tears he had tried so hard not to shed spilled down his face. The pain in his heart was so intense that he no longer felt the cold.

As the preacher spoke glowing words about his mother's goodness, Tag's mind transferred itself to another time and place. His heart ached for the time before his whole world had come crashing down around him. He remembered sunny afternoons and picnics in the park. He thought of winter sleigh rides and snowball fights at his boyhood home back in England.

There were very few people who had come to his mother's graveside services, but then they knew so few people here in America. If only his father were here, Tag thought miserably.

Tag blinked his eyes in astonishment. The people had begun to leave. Was that all there was to it? he wondered. He stared down at the coffin, wanting to cry out at the injustice of it all. He would never see her again. Death had robbed him of his mother.

Tag felt Joanna lead him toward the carriage that would take them back to the house. He was reluctant to leave, feeling that he was abandoning his mother.

Tag and Joanna were silent on the ride home. He leaned back against the black leather upholstered seat and closed his eyes as Joanna tucked a wool coverlet about him.

Their home was located in the more fashionable part of Philadelphia. As the buggy pulled through the iron gates and stopped in front of the huge, three-story brick mansion, he could see the housekeeper, Franny, standing on the steps. Her husband, Simon, the coachman, opened the door and helped Tag and his sister out of the buggy.

They were home, and the terrible ordeal was over. How quiet the house seemed. The servants talked in whispers, and all the curtains were drawn, making the dark, dismal day seem even more depressing.

Joanna removed Tag's coat and handed it to Franny, then led him into the huge sitting room where a bright fire was burning in the marble fireplace.

Tag sat down on a stool before the fire, staring into the bright flames without really seeing them. The warm fire did nothing to remove the chill in his heart.

Joanna handed him a cup of hot apple cider and then sat down beside him, placing a comforting arm about him. Neither of them spoke. It was somehow comforting just to sit together silently, feeling a kinship in their shared loss.

Joanna had removed her black veil, and her red-gold hair spilled down her shoulders to her waist. The reflection of the burning fire fell on her hair, and it almost seemed as though her hair was on fire. For the first time Tag realized that his sister was beautiful. Her violet-colored eyes were sad as she placed a kiss on his cheek.

"Everything will be all right, Tag. Before too

long Papa will be home, and besides, we still have each other."

Tag leaned his head against her shoulder. Somehow her words gave him comfort as nothing else could. Through all the long weeks of their mother's illness, and finally her death, Joanna had always been there for him. Sometimes he had felt closer to her than he had to their mother. He knew that he and Joanna shared a special bond that time and distance would never destroy. He felt her hand cover his and he closed his eyes, feeling drowsy.

Joanna stood at the window, staring out on the front lawn which was now snow covered. It was late March, but winter retained its grip on the land. She sighed as she looked at the mound of paperwork that was stacked on her father's desk. He had been gone for almost a year. Tears gathered in her eyes. He would be so devastated when he learned of her mother's death.

Russell James had left on one of his cargo ships last spring, heading for Oregon Territory. His ships often sailed to Oregon taking men and supplies to the new frontier. Joanna wished he had been with her mother at the end. Althea James had always been in fragile health, and in January, she had developed the lung sickness, and within a month had died.

Joanna was only seventeen, but at the moment she felt much older. It was as if she carried the weight of the world on her shoulders. There were so many things that needed attention.

They had very few friends here in America for until two years ago their home had been in England. Her father had decided that he would move his headquarters to America, since it was where most of his trade was located. Joanna hadn't minded the change; it had been exciting for her and Tag. She had known, however, that her mother had not been happy about the move, although Althea James had never complained.

Joanna walked over to her father's desk and sat down. Picking up a sheet of paper and a quill, she tried once more to write to her father about her mother's death.

She crumpled up the piece of paper and threw it into the fire. It was so difficult to tell her father about her mother's death in a letter.

The truth was that she hardly knew her father. While they had lived in England, more often than not, he had been in America. Joanna knew the only reason her mother had consented to move to America was with the hope of seeing more of her husband, but that had not been the case. He had installed them in the great house in Philadelphia and had sailed away.

Joanna stood up and walked over to the huge portrait which hung above the mantel. It had been painted but a year ago, and to the naked eye it seemed to portray a happy family. Althea James's blond beauty complemented her husband's handsomeness. Russell James had bright red hair and Joanna and Tag had a combination of both their parents' hair coloring. Joanna couldn't help but smile at the portrait where Tag stood so straight and proud beside his father. Both she and Tag had their father's blue eyes. Joanna looked at the likeness of herself, and thought that the artist had flattered her. She felt no kinship with the lovely girl in the portrait who had such a wistful look in her eyes. The artist had painted her as she had always wanted to be, she thought, and not as she actually looked.

If you had asked Joanna if she was pretty, she would have said no. Her hair was a golden color until the sunlight hit it, and then it seemed to come alive with fiery red highlights. Her eyes were such a deep blue that they seemed violet in color, and she thought they were too big for her delicate features. Joanna thought she was much too tall for a girl. Most of her friends in England had been petite and pretty, while she had always felt very awkward, towering above them. Sometimes she had even been taller than her gentleman acquaintances.

Joanna's mother had been a bit of a snob, and had not wanted her children to mix socially with the "colonists," as she had called them, so Joanna had never had a young gentleman tell her that her face was breathtakingly beautiful. No one had ever told her that her hair was a glorious curtain of fiery spiraling curls. No one had said to her that her violet eyes with their long silky eyelashes were a startling combination with her creamy white skin. She had no idea that her sweetly curved body had disturbed many young men's thoughts.

She had been only fifteen when they had moved to America, and they had lived such a secluded life for the past two years that Joanna had no idea that she had blossomed into a lovely young woman.

There was a tap on the door of her father's study, and Tag poked his head into the room.

"Are you busy, Joanna?"

"Never too busy for you," she smiled.

He ambled into the room and plopped down on the window seat. "I don't think winter will ever be over. I detest staying in the house all the time," he said, staring out the window wistfully.

"If you would like, you can bundle up warmly and go out and play for a while."

"It's no fun playing alone. Why don't we have any friends like we did in England, Joanna?"

Joanna was thoughtful for a moment, wondering how to answer him. When they had first moved into the house they had been visited by their neighbors and sent many dinner and party invitations, which her mother had always declined. Soon the invitations stopped coming, and the James family was all but cut off from their neighbors.

Tag had been the one who had suffered most, Joanna thought. It wasn't good for a young boy to have no friends to play with. "How would you like it if I read you a story?" Joanna suggested.

"I would like that," Tag said with little enthusiasm.

Joanna took a book from the bookshelf and sat down beside Tag on the window seat. Soon they were both lost in the world of make-believe, as Joanna read *The Last of the Mohicans,* by James Fenimore Cooper. It was a book about Indians and the early days of the American frontier. The story seemed to come alive for them both.

Joanna glanced down at Tag and noticed he was

absorbed in her reading. She felt an almost maternal love for her brother. In the two weeks since their mother's death he seemed to look to her for guidance. There were times when Joanna was frightened about what the future held, but she had to put up a brave front for Tag's sake. She couldn't let him suspect that she was every bit as lost as he was. She only wished their father would come home soon.

It was but a week later. Joanna had climbed up a ladder and was dusting the books on the top shelf in the library.

Franny, the housekeeper, came bustling into the room with a disapproving frown on her face. She had been with the family since before Joanna was born, and had sailed with them to America. Joanna loved the stern-faced housekeeper whom she had relied on so much lately.

"Miss Joanna, you won't believe who just showed up on our front doorstep. With your permission, I'll show her the door without hesitation," Franny said, looking as if she would be able to do just that.

"To whom are you referring, Franny?" Joanna asked, climbing down the ladder.

"That woman, Margaret, your father's sister, that's who."

"Aunt Margaret's here?"

"In the flesh. Says she just arrived from England three days ago. She's got that no-account husband with her. I think you should allow me to tell her you aren't receiving guests."

Joanna tried to remember all she had been told about her Aunt Margaret. Joanna had never met her, for her mother hadn't allowed her into their home.

Joanna's mother had come from the British gentry, and her family had all but disinherited her when she married Russell James, for at the time he had been a struggling shipbuilder. Her mother's family had looked down on anyone who was in trade.

All Joanna knew about her Aunt Margaret was that there had been some kind of scandal when she had joined a traveling acting group and had married one of the actors.

"Where are they, Franny?"

Franny sniffed. "I left them in the hallway. I told them that your mother had died and you weren't up to seeing anyone."

Joanna smoothed her hair into place. "Send them in here. I am curious to know what they want, and after all, she is my father's sister."

"That don't make you obligated to her. If your father were here, he wouldn't see her. Mark my word, that woman means nothing but trouble."

Joanna gave Franny a stern look. "My father isn't here, and I feel we should at least see them since they have come so far."

Franny looked as if she would have liked to object, but she clasped her mouth shut and left, shaking her head and mumbling to herself.

Shortly afterward the door opened and a pudgy, round-faced woman rushed toward Joanna. "My dear child, I was just told about your tragedy," she said, gathering Joanna into her arms and hugging

19

her tightly. The woman reeked of cheap perfume, but Joanna suffered the ordeal in silence. "Don't you worry, your Aunt Margaret's here now and I'm going to look after you."

Joanna was finally able to step back a pace, and she studied the woman who in no way resembled her father. Margaret Landon looked years older than her brother. Joanna had never seen anyone who wore makeup, but she was sure the bright red cheeks and the white, powdery look on her aunt's face must be artificial. Her gown was of bright red satin, and was too low-cut for daytime wear.

"I am pleased to meet you, Aunt Margaret. I have heard about you."

Her aunt poked Joanna in the ribs with her elbow and winked. "I can just imagine what you heard." Her laughter was lewd and high-pitched. "Come, you must think me rude. I want to introduce you to your Uncle Howard."

For the first time Joanna noticed the man who accompanied her aunt. He was tall and heavy-set and wore a bright purple coat with a lemon yellow waistcoat. He looked every bit the stage actor with his overstated clothing. His eyes were small and beady, and Joanna felt uncomfortable at the way he was staring at her.

"So this is my little niece," he said, taking her hand and raising it to his lips. Joanna had the strongest urge to jerk her hand free of his grasp. "Margaret, you never told me your niece was such a beauty," he drawled through thick lips.

Margaret looked Joanna over. "She ain't too bad. Looks a lot like her mother. Now me, I wasn't so skinny when I was her age. Had the bulges in all the right places, and all the gentlemen noticed, including yourself, Howard."

Joanna felt her face flame at her aunt's salacious remark. She was already wishing she had taken Franny's advice and refused to see them. Never had Joanna met anyone like her aunt and uncle, and she was at a loss as to what to say to them.

"I heard that you have a brother. Where is the little mite? I would like to meet him, too," Margaret said removing her gloves and fanning her face with them.

"My brother's name is Taggart. Simon, our coachman, has taken him on a sleigh ride around the park. He will be sorry that he missed you."

"Hell, sweetie, he ain't gonna miss us," her aunt said, slipping into bawdy language. "Me and Howard don't have any intentions of deserting you and what's-his-name, in your hour of need. We're staying right here, ain't we, Howard?"

Howard looked into Joanna's eyes and spoke in a voice she was sure he had perfected on the stage. "I wouldn't dream of leaving you at a time like this. Your aunt and I will stay and look after you until your father returns. When do you expect him home?"

Joanna would have liked to say that he was expected home at any moment, but it was not in her character to tell an untruth. "I don't know when my father will return. He has been away for almost a year."

Joanna saw the glance that her aunt and uncle exchanged. It was almost a smirk, she thought.

"Well, dearie, you aren't to worry about a thing. Your Aunt Margaret is here to look after you now."

Some inner instinct told Joanna that these people were evil, and she knew that she must not allow them to move into her home. "I thank you for your kind offer, but I am perfectly capable of looking after my brother and myself. I will offer you lunch, and then when Simon returns he can drive you to wherever you are staying."

Her aunt sat down and buried her face in her hands. "That's just the trouble, Joanna. We ain't got no place to stay or no money. It took all we had for passage from England. You can't just throw us out to freeze."

There were tears sparkling in her aunt's eyes. Joanna was later to learn that Margaret Landon was an actress and could turn the tears on and off on cue. Now, however, Joanna's heart softened and she felt pity for their plight.

"You are welcome to stay in one of the guest-rooms until you can find a place of your own, or I could lend you some money if you would rather."

Her aunt's face brightened. "You are a good and kind-hearted girl, not at all like your mothe . . ."

"What Margaret means," Howard broke in, giving his wife a warning glance, "is we would be grateful for your kind hospitality. Mind you, we aren't looking for a handout, but I could sure use a loan until I get on my feet."

Joanna rang for Franny. "I will have the house-keeper show you to your room. Did you bring your baggage with you?"

Howard reached out and drew her into his arms.

22

Joanna felt revulsion as his sweaty hands moved up and down her arm. "I'll take care of you, pretty girl," he whispered, and his breath reeked of cheap rum. Joanna pushed him away and he smiled, but the smile never reached his eyes.

Franny appeared and looked sternly disapproving when Joanna told her to show her aunt and uncle to one of the guest rooms. After they left the room, Joanna sat down, feeling as if she had been drained. She hoped she had done the right thing in inviting them to stay with her and Tag. She suspected her mother would not have approved, and she knew her father would object had he been home. She felt very uneasy. There was something about her aunt and uncle that troubled her. Oh, well, she thought, perhaps they wouldn't stay more than a day or two, and she hoped her father would be home soon. He would know how to handle the situation.

It had been two weeks since Joanna's aunt and uncle had moved into the guest room. Joanna had already had many occasions to regret her hasty invitation.

Her aunt spent most of the day in her bed, telling Joanna that as an actress she never got out of bed until long after the noon hour. She insisted on having one of the servants bring all her meals to her room, which didn't exactly endear her to Franny.

Joanna stood before her aunt's bedroom door hesitantly. She had already given her aunt a great deal of money, but she was now prepared to give her a substantial amount so she and her husband could find a place of their own. Joanna could hear her aunt's voice coming through the door, so she rapped lightly.

The door opened and Margaret Landon motioned for her to enter. "I would like to talk to you, Aunt Margaret," Joanna said, noticing that the bedroom was in a shambles. Discarded clothing was scattered on the floor, and the room reeked with an unpleasant odor of unwashed bodies.

Her aunt grabbed her chest and slumped down upon the bed in the worst display of play-acting Joanna had ever witnessed.

"Oh, dearie, I have a terrible misery in my heart. It's painful for me to even move. The doctor said I could go at any time."

Joanna had learned that Margaret was not given to telling the truth. She was determined that by tonight she would have her aunt and uncle out of her home.

"I was told by Simon that he took you shopping today. You must have become ill after he brought you home," Joanna said, looking at all the packages and boxes which were scattered across the bed.

Aunt Margaret's face became distorted and her eyes narrowed. "I had nothing to wear and I didn't want to embarrass you with my shabby appearance should any of your friends come by. I hope you don't mind my spending the money you gave me on a few needed items of clothing."

"No, of course not," Joanna said, eyeing the brightly colored gowns, and wondering why her aunt would buy clothing that would be more suit-

24

able for a young girl.

"You are a dear child, nothing at all like your mother. She always looked down her nose, thinking she was better than me."

Joanna stiffened her back. "I will ask you not to refer to my mother if you have nothing nice to say about her."

Aunt Margaret sniffed. "I meant no disrespect for the dead, but she never allowed me to visit my brother. How would you feel if you were restricted from ever seeing Taggart?"

Joanna was thoughtful for a moment. She saw no reason to tell her aunt that her own brother had also forbidden her entry into his home. Joanna remembered a time when she had overheard her parents discussing a letter they had gotten from her Aunt Margaret. Evidently she had asked for money because, at the time, Joanna's father had angrily declared that he wouldn't send her another penny. It had been at her mother's urging that Russell James had finally consented to send his sister money.

"I was wondering if Uncle Howard had found employment yet?"

Margaret shook her head. "It's mighty hard when one gets old, and no one wants to hire him. My poor Howard is beside himself with worry, wondering where he will get the money to live on."

Joanna sat down on a chair and folded her hands in her lap. "That's what I wanted to speak to you about. I'm sure if he were to go to the shipyard, the manager would hire him since he is my father's brother-in-law."

Margaret lay back on the pillow and sniffed, dabbing at her eyes with a handkerchief. "My poor Howard could never stand up to manual labor; he is a gentleman."

Joanna stood up grasping at straws. "I am prepared to give you and Uncle Howard a substantial amount of money if you would like to find a place of your own. I know how hard it must be not having your own home."

Margaret's eyes narrowed. "That would be most kind of you, dearie. You give me the money and I'll talk to Howard about it tonight."

Joanna walked to the door. "You talk to him and *then* I will give you the money."

Once outside the room Joanna leaned against the wall to breathe in fresh air. No wonder Franny objected so strongly to cleaning her aunt's room. It was like a pigsty, she thought. She felt guilty that she wanted to be rid of her aunt and uncle, but for some reason she had begun to feel fear whenever she was alone with Howard. It wasn't anything he said, for he was always polite. It was more the way he watched her, and sometimes he would brush up against her and then act as if it had been by accident. She hated it when he touched her.

Joanna went downstairs, and when she passed her father's study, she noticed the door was ajar. She entered the room and saw that her uncle was sitting behind her father's desk. Her anger was boundless as she saw him going through her father's papers.

"May I ask what you are doing in my father's study?"

He smiled and propped his feet up on her father's

cherrywood desk. "Get used to seeing me here, my dear, because as of this morning I became your and Taggart's legal guardian."

Joanna felt like the wind had been knocked from her body. "What are you saying? My father will never stand by while you commit such an atrocity."

"Sit down, Joanna. I am afraid I have some bad news for you."

"I prefer to stand, and I will ask you to do the same. I invited you and my aunt for a visit, not to take over as if my home belonged to you. I want you to go upstairs and pack your things and I will have Simon drive you into town immediately."

Howard's eyes narrowed. "You think that your aunt and I are just scum under your satin slippers. I have seen how you look down your nose at us. Well, missy, the shoe's on the other foot now. I am in charge and you had better learn to be nice to me."

Joanna sank down in a chair and gripped the arms until her knuckles hurt. "What are you saying?"

He stood up and walked toward her. "This is what I'm talking about, missy," he said, thrusting a letter at her.

Joanna took the letter and saw it had been addressed to her mother. "How dare you open my mother's mail? I will have Simon throw you out right now!" She started to rise, but he put a restraining hand on her shoulder.

"I think you had better read the letter, Joanna."

She resented his high-handed manner and wanted to throw the letter in his face. There was something in that letter that made him think he could take charge of her life, and she had to know what it was. She opened it and began to read.

Dear Mrs. James,

You don't know me, but I was a friend of your husband's and it has fallen to me to tell you some unfortunate news. I am grieved to inform you that your husband took ship, heading for Philadelphia, and the ship went down just off the Oregon coast. Although an extensive search was made, we found no survivors. I know it is a cruel way to learn of the passing of a loved one from a letter, but I had no choice. Your husband often spoke of you, your daughter, Joanna, and your son, Taggart. I will soon be in Philadelphia and I will call on you at that time to express my sympathy in person.

Yours sincerely,<br>Richard Land

Joanna didn't know how many times she re-read the letter, but when the tears had dried on her face, she still clutched it tightly in her hand. "Oh, Papa," she cried, "it can't be true. There has to be a mistake!"

Howard took her hand, drawing her up beside him and put his arms about her.

For the moment her grievances with him were all but forgotten. He had become merely someone to lean on in her time of sorrow.

"How is it possible?" she cried. "How will I ever

tell Tag?"

She felt her uncle's hands move up her arm and over her shoulder. Suddenly she felt him caress her breast and she pushed him away angrily. "How dare you! You are a despicable man, and I want you out of my home this instant!"

He merely smiled and shook his head. "I have been with a lawyer all morning, Joanna. I am now your legal guardian and there is nothing you can do about it."

Joanna's mouth flew open in protest, but he held his hand up to silence her. "You are under my control now, fancy piece. You don't breathe unless I say it's all right."

Joanna backed toward the door, too stunned to think clearly. When she reached the door, she fled into the hallway. She had to find Tag! First she had the heartbreaking task of telling him about their father, and then the two of them would go into town to speak to her father's lawyer. There had to be some mistake. She would never submit to her Uncle Howard's domination.

Joanna and Tag sat in Mr. Barker's office, trying to digest all he had told them. They were still too stunned by the news of their father's death to think coherently.

"I'm sorry, Joanna, but I feel I was acting in your best interest when I handed your guardianship over to your uncle. When I talked to him this morning I was very impressed with his good business sense. I think you and Tag can depend on him to look after you."

Joanna stood up and took Tag's hand. She knew it would serve no purpose to tell Mr. Barker that her uncle was a lecherous old man who couldn't keep his hands off her. He would never believe her anyway. Apparently Uncle Howard had impressed Mr. Barker with his great acting ability. She and Tag walked to the carriage and got in. Neither one was aware that the snow had begun to fall and a cold wind was blowing from the east. Tag laid his head over on Joanna's shoulder.

"Why did they both have to die, Joanna?"

"Perhaps it was a blessing in a way, Tag. You know how much they loved one another. Each of them died without knowing that the other had . . . died. I know Papa hadn't gotten my letter telling of Mama's death. Just think of them as being together now."

Tag looked up into her face. "What about you and me, Joanna? I don't like Uncle Howard and Aunt Margaret. Do they have to live with us?"

"It won't be forever, Tag." She tried to smile. "We still have each other and no one can ever separate us."

His arms went around her waist. "Don't worry, I'll take care of you, Joanna," he said earnestly.

She hugged him tightly, "We will take care of each other, Tag."


Winter was slowly releasing its grip on the land. The bleak snow-filled days turned to bleak rainy days.

Joanna and Tag were sitting in the morning room, quietly reading a book, when Franny appeared. "That man wants to see you and Tag in the sitting room," she declared. "He thinks you are at his beck and call."

Joanna laid her book aside and took Tag's hand. "Whatever he wants it's best to find out now," she said.

When they entered the room Aunt Margaret smiled triumphantly, as if she were privy to information that pleased her. Uncle Howard was standing by the window, and he motioned for Joanna and Tag to be seated on the settee, but they both remained standing.

How pompous he looked, Joanna thought. Now that he had access to her father's fortune, he had changed his appearance. His outlandish clothing was now of a more expensive cut, but still in bad taste.

"I was told by Franny that you wanted to see me," Joanna said, raising her head defiantly.

"That's right, missy. It galls you that I call and you must come to me, doesn't it?"

"It galls me that you think you have the right."

He smiled, "Oh, I have the right by law, as you have already found out."

Joanna clenched her teeth together, knowing he was right. "Tag and I are here. What do you want?" she demanded.

He walked toward her with a satisfied smile on his face. "I have made some plans for your and Tag's future. Would you like to hear what they are?"

"What more can you do to us that you have not

already done?" Joanna said, staring into his little beady eyes with contempt. She felt his foul breath on her face. "I could show you, fancy piece, if your aunt weren't present." He pressed his body against hers and Joanna felt afraid. Seeing her eyes dilate in fright, he gave her a satisfied smile. He then forced her to sit down, and placed a heavy hand on her shoulder.

"I will tell you what I can do. I have decided that it's time for Tag to become a man. What better way for a boy to grow up than to go to sea?" he replied, watching Joanna's face closely.

The color drained from Joanna's cheeks as she stared at him in disbelief. "Never! I will never allow you to separate Tag and me."

"You think not?" her aunt asked, popping a chocolate bonbon in her mouth and looking at her husband. "Tell Joanna what our plans are, Howard."

Howard crammed his hands in his pockets and propped his foot on one of Joanna's mother's gold velvet chairs. "As I said, Joanna, I want Tag to take ship as soon as possible."

"Never!" she cried, looking at her brother fearfully. "I would die before I allowed you to take him from me."

"Oh, you won't die, Joanna, but Tag might," her aunt said with an evil grin on her face.

Howard Landon frowned. "Hush, Margaret."

Joanna clasped her trembling hands together to still their quaking. "What are you talking about? Do you dare threaten me with my brother's life?"

Howard smiled humorously. "Of course not. That would be unlawful. I am merely looking out for the boy's own good. I am well acquainted with the captain of the *Sea Witch,* and he has consented to take Tag on his next voyage as a cabin boy."

Joanna looked at her uncle suspiciously. "That's not one of our ships. Tag is the legal heir to my father's shipping line. Why would you want him to sail aboard . . . unless . . ."

"I think you get the picture, Joanna," her aunt squealed with delight. "Howard tells me that accidents happen all the time at sea. One could be lost at sea, never to be heard of again. Didn't that very thing happen to your pa?"

Joanna looked from one to the other, wondering what kind of monsters they were. "Do you think that I would just sit idly by while you threaten my brother?" Joanna asked, as her eyes blazed dangerously. "I will go to the authorities and tell them what you are planning to do."

Her uncle threw his head back and laughed. "I don't think you will, missy. You see, you and Taggart will be locked in your rooms until such time as he sails next week. Should you try anything so foolhardy, you will never see your brother again."

Joanna felt as though an icy hand had touched her heart. She was trapped, and her uncle knew it.

Tag ran to Joanna and she placed a protective arm about him, but her uncle grabbed him by the shoulders and lifted him up as if he weighed nothing.

"Put him down!" Joanna demanded through clenched teeth. "If you harm Tag, I will see that you pay."

"My, my, she does have a temper," her aunt said

through fits of laughter.

"You will see how I can fight when my brother's life is at stake. I will see you both damned to hell!" she cried.

Her uncle released his hold on Tag, then turned to strike Joanna a stunning blow that knocked her back against the settee.

Tag went flying at Howard, pounding him with his fists. His uncle picked him up once more and carried him toward the stairs. "From now until the day he takes ship, your brother will be locked in his room, Joanna, as will you."

Joanna wiped the blood from her cut lip and watched helplessly as Howard Landon took Tag away. For now she could do nothing. But her uncle and aunt had made one fatal mistake. They had threatened her with the life of her brother. She would fight like a tigress defending her young. If she was to save Tag and herself she must pretend to be beaten, but she wasn't; she would find a way to save them both, she vowed.

## Chapter Two

Joanna felt as if she were living in a nightmare.
Three days had passed since she and Tag had been
locked in their bedrooms. There was no one she
could turn to for help. Franny came to her room
three times a day to bring food, but she was always
accompanied by Joanna's uncle, who was watchful,
giving her no chance to speak with Franny alone. If
Joanna was going to save Tag she would have to
come up with something soon, because time was
running out. She paced the room trying to think of
a plan.

Suddenly there was the sound of a key grating in
the lock, and Franny came in, flanked by Uncle Howard. Franny's eyes were bright as she placed the
tray of food on the bedside table.

"Miss Joanna, if you will just set the tray by the
door when you are finished eating," Franny said,
winking at Joanna.

"Of course," Joanna agreed, wondering why Franny was acting nervous and fidgety.

"You can go now, Franny," Joanna's uncle said, dismissing her with a curt nod.

Franny sniffed haughtily and raised her head, sailing out of the room.

"Look at me, Joanna!" her uncle commanded.

She raised her violet-colored eyes and he could read the defiance in their bright depths.

"You haven't fooled me. I know you aren't one to sit idly by doing nothing. If I know you, you are at this moment hatching up some scheme, thinking you can thwart me. You are probably thinking that something will happen at the last minute to save you. Let me assure you, that will not happen. I can handle you, little girl."

Joanna's red-gold hair swirled about her as she raised her chin proudly. "You have a very high opinion of yourself."

He smiled and took her hand while he arched his eyebrow, daring her to pull away from him.

"I would do anything to possess you, Joanna," he said in a silky-smooth voice.

"I would rather die than have you touch me," she said, jerking her hand free.

He seemed unconcerned by her rejection and merely shrugged his shoulders. "There is no rush I have plenty of time. When I decide to take you to bed, you will squeal in delight and beg for more."

Joanna couldn't resist a shudder. "I would kill myself before I would allow you to touch me."

His eyes sparked dangerously. "I have taken more from you than I would ever take from anyone else, missy. Just count yourself lucky that I am a tolerant man."

She laughed insultingly but did not reply.

"I would give it all up in a moment, Joanna, if you would have me. You have gotten into my brain, and I can't seem to do anything without thinking about you. If you would only be nice to me, life would be more pleasant for you and Tag."

Joanna looked at him in disgust. "I have no desire to be nice to you. You have stolen everything that belonged to my brother and me. If my father were alive, he would have you jailed."

Howard looked at her in speculation. "Well, missy, I think you and I understand each other. I would have gladly given you anything you asked for, but now you will rue the day you tried to defy me." He removed his watch from his pocket and twirled it around. "If you had said yes, Joanna, Tag would have been allowed to remain here with you, but since you refused, he sails in three days. Barring any unforeseen accident, he should be back home within two years."

Joanna felt tears of helplessness well up in her eyes, and she tried to keep him from seeing her weakness. If she was to save Tag, it would have to be tonight, and she had no idea how that could be accomplished.

"I am very tired. I wish you would leave now."

He nodded his head, knowing he had finally humbled the proud Joanna. His eyes gleamed brightly as he crossed the room and left, locking the door after him. He actually felt more satisfaction from piercing the calm that always surrounded her than if she had consented to his proposition.

Joanna sat down on the bed and buried her face in her hands. It all seemed so hopeless. What could she do? Was she some weak little mouse that she couldn't outsmart someone with her uncle's limited intelligence? She would never allow him to win — she would fight to the bitter end. The determined light in her eyes slowly faded. How? What could she do to help Tag while she was locked in her room?

Suddenly Joanna remembered Franny's words, and she knew that the housekeeper must have placed something under the lunch tray. She glanced at the door and quickly lifted the tray. She gasped when she recognized her father's handwriting on the letter that Franny had hidden for her. It was as if he had reached out from his watery grave to bring her courage and comfort, she thought. She quickly broke the seal and began to read.

My dearest Joanna and Tag,

I was sorely grieved to get your letter and learn about your dear mother's death. I cannot tell you how sorry I am that I was unable to be with you at such a time. Be brave and try not to grieve.

Joanna closed her eyes. He had known about her mother's death before he died, but how?

I blame myself for not being with your mother when she needed me. I know that you will be shocked to hear from me since Richard told me he wrote you of my death.

Tears of joy washed down Joanna's cheeks. It had all been some horrible mistake. Her father was alive! Joanna's hand trembled, and she had a hard time reading since her eyes were swimming with tears.

How you, my dear ones, must have grieved, thinking you had lost both your mother and father. I was on the ship when it went down, but was able to drag myself upon the broken mast and the waves washed me ashore. I have not been well. I suffered a broken back or I would have come to you instead of sending you this letter. I am doing the next best thing, however. I have made arrangements for the two of you to come to me in the spring on the *Althea*.

Know in your hearts that I love you and await the time when we can all be together again.

Your loving father

Joanna was overcome with joy. She wanted to shout her happiness to the world. What should she do? Demand to see her uncle and tell him that her father was alive? No, he was a desperate and dangerous man. He might yet harm Tag even if he knew that their father was alive. She lay down across the bed, trying to think what to do. Suddenly an idea came to her. It was just daring enough to work. She got up quickly and rummaged in a drawer until she found a paper and quill, and began to write.

Franny, I have a plan, but I will need your cooperation. When everyone has gone to sleep, go into the study and look behind the portrait. There you will find my mother's jewels. Give them to Simon. Have him saddle two horses and wait in the stable for me and Tag. Pray God that I am able to carry through with my plan.

Joanna wrapped the note in a napkin and set the tray beside the door, knowing Franny would not be allowed to come to her room until she brought the evening meal. What she would have to do now was wait.

Walking over to the window, Joanna looked at the giant oak tree with its branches spread wide. Yes, it just might enable her to reach Tag's room and then they could both climb to safety. After they were free, they could then find a way to reach their father.

The sun was almost down when Joanna heard the key grating in the lock. She tried to act normal, but her young heart was pounding with fear and excitement. Franny entered, and her eyes sought Joanna's.

"Franny, I am not at all pleased with you. You gave me a soiled napkin at lunch. You must be more careful in the future."

Franny nodded and ducked her head. "I will, miss. I'll see to it." She picked up the tray and rushed out, leaving Joanna alone with her uncle, who made no move to leave.

"What do you want?" she asked in a shaky voice, fearing he had discovered her plan.

"I want to talk to you. I hate to end the day with bad feelings between us."

Joanna could feel her heart drumming in fear. "I have nothing more to say to you," she told him, hoping he would leave.

He advanced on her, and she cringed as he reached out and grabbed a handful of red-gold curls. "I have been bewitched by you ever since the first day I saw you. I have decided I will have you, with or without your consent."

Joanna could smell the liquor on his breath and she knew he had been drinking. She tried to think of some way to save herself as his hands ran caressingly down her back.

"If you don't release me, I'll scream, Uncle Howard."

"Don't call me uncle. I am no kin to you. I would rather be your lover." His thick wet lips fastened on hers, and Joanna thought she would be sick. She struggled to get away from him, and turned her head away when he tried to nuzzle her ear.

"I want you, Joanna. The money means nothing to me if I can't have you."

Joanna had forgotten she had stuffed her father's letter down the front of her gown, until her uncle's hands wandered to the neck of her gown.

He grunted questioningly. "Huh. What is this?" he asked, withdrawing her father's letter from the bodice of her gown.

Joanna drew in her breath. "It is nothing, merely

41

an old letter from my father."

He shoved her away and walked over to the candle and began reading. Joanna stood as if frozen until he turned to her. His face was a deep purple color and he stumbled toward her.

"You bitch! You think you have won, do you? I will show you a thing or two." He threw her onto the bed and pinned her beneath his body. "Do you think you could somehow reach your father? I would have had every ship searched until I found you, you little slut. I will never let you go. Your father may be alive, but when he comes home, he won't find you."

"Please, you are hurting me." Joanna tried to move away but he was too heavy for her.

"I'll give you what you have been asking for," he said angrily.

Joanna felt him fumbling with his trousers, and she bit her lip, trying not to cry out.

"What's the meaning of this?" Joanna heard her aunt's voice and was overcome with relief.

Howard moved off the bed quickly and straightened his trousers. "I found this," he said, thrusting the letter at Margaret.

"What does it say? You know I can't read. And don't try to take my mind off what I just saw. I know why you were in Joanna's room. I have seen you watching her, don't think I haven't ."

"The letter is from your brother. He's alive!"

Margaret's face lost its color. "I told you we should have made sure Russell was dead. He will have us jailed for sure."

Howard looked past his wife to Joanna. "He

won't do nothing because we will have his daughter and son."

"What do you mean?" his wife asked.

"I think in the morning both Joanna and her brother will go aboard the *Sea Witch*."

Joanna hid her face in the pillow, knowing she would be watched closely from now on.

Margaret gave her niece a malignant glare. "I'm going to lock this fancy piece in and *I'll* keep the key."

Joanna looked up in time to see Howard's face flush with anger. She could almost read the frustration in his eyes. He had thought he would have his brother-in-law's fortune and dispose of his niece and nephew as he saw fit.

"If I were the two of you I would try and find some place to hide before my father returns. He will see you both swing from the gallows."

Howard frowned angrily. "If and when your father does return, you will not be here to greet him, missy."

Margaret took her husband's arm and pulled him toward the door. "Let her talk. It will be small comfort to her in the morning."

Joanna watched them leave the room and she waited impatiently for the sun to go down and the house to become quiet. At last, after what Joanna considered an eternity, she dressed in her green velvet riding habit and put her matching fur-lined cape on.

She opened the window carefully and climbed onto the ledge. She caught hold of a strong branch and swung up into the tree. Easing herself slowly along the ledge, she soon came to Tag's window. Joanna knew that this would be the most critical part, for her aunt and uncle's room was next to Tag's. Bracing herself against the tree, Joanna tapped on the window. She got no response, so she tapped harder. At last her efforts were rewarded when Tag's face came into view. Seeing his sister he quickly raised the window.

Joanna placed her finger to her lips to silence him. She spoke softly. "Dress warmly, Tag, and hurry! Simon is waiting for us in the stable."

In no time at all Tag was dressed, and he climbed out the window into Joanna's waiting arms. She hugged him tightly, then motioned for him to climb to the ground. She watched until he hit the ground, then she hurried after him. Joanna pulled Tag into the shadow of a laurel bush, and they both waited for a moment to see if their movements had been detected. Joanna's heart was pounding loudly. They weren't out of danger yet; they still had to get to the horses and get safely away.

Joanna pushed Tag forward and looked over her shoulder as he disappeared into the stable.

When they reached the stable, Simon was waiting for them. "Thank the good Lord you made it. I didn't hold out much hope. I half feared you wouldn't be able to get away."

Joanna threw her arms around Simon. "Tag and I want to thank you and Franny for all your help."

"Saints preserve us, Miss Joanna, me and Franny aren't about to let you and Master Taggart strike out on your own. You had better get on the horses and ride out nice and quiet. I'll meet you past the grove of apple trees. Me and Franny put our heads together and got a room for all of us at an inn on the other side of town."

Joanna hugged Simon once more. "I don't have the words to thank you. Tag and I could never have gotten away without your and Franny's help."

"We don't want no thanks, Miss Joanna. Now you and young Master Taggart here had better leave," Simon told her. He picked Tag up and placed him on his horse while Joanna swung into the saddle from the mounting block. She kicked her horse Fosset in the flanks and she and Tag rode away into the night.

Joanna was too relieved to be free to have any regrets about leaving her home, but Tag halted his horse and looked back at the big three-story mansion. He vowed silently that someday he would return and claim what belonged to him.

Joanna glanced out the second-story window of the inn, watching the people scurrying by. She and Tag had been staying at the Wellmore Inn with Simon and Franny for three weeks now.

Tag had been overjoyed to hear that their father was still alive. He pestered Joanna each day, wanting to know when they would be going to Oregon.

Simon had discreetly inquired at the docks about a ship that would carry them to Oregon. But Joanna's uncle had foreseen that they would try to make their way to their father, so he had alerted the authorities about her's and Tag's disappearance and the docks were alive with men searching for them.

There would be no way for them to board a ship without their Uncle Howard finding out about it.

Joanna hadn't known what to do until she saw a notice which had been posted in the paper. There was a wagon train that was headed for Oregon Territory, and when it left Philadelphia, she intended for her and Tag to leave with it.

When she had first told Simon and Franny her plans they had protested loudly, but in the end they had agreed that the situation was desperate enough to call for reckless measures.

Joanna was overcome with relief and gratitude when Franny and Simon insisted on accompanying her and Tag on the long and dangerous journey.

To Joanna's surprise, Franny had somehow managed to smuggle much of her and Tag's clothing out of the house before she left.

Some of Joanna's mother's jewels had been sold to buy a wagon, horses and supplies.

Tomorrow morning before sun up, the train would be heading out, and Tag was a bundle of excitement. He looked on the excursion as an adventure, while Joanna looked upon it with fear. She had heard all sorts of tales about the brutal Indian attacks on the wagon trains. If she weren't so desperate she would never have decided to go overland to Oregon.

Howard Landon stood beneath the portrait in the study and gazed at the likeness of Joanna with a grim expression on his face. His eyes were blurry from too much wine, and he raised his glass in a salute to the flaming-haired beauty.

"I got to admit you were the clever one, but I'll find you, and when I do, you will pay, Joanna." Her violet-colored eyes seemed to mock him, and Howard threw the wine glass at the picture and the red-colored wine looked like blood as it ran down Joanna's face.

"Damn you! Some day I'll make you pay."

He slumped down in a chair and stared at Joanna's face once more. "You are so beautiful. You make a man forget many things, but he can never forget you."

One thing was certain; Joanna might get to her father but he would be dead by the time she arrived. Howard had sent a man ahead to see that Russell James wasn't in any condition to cause him any trouble. The man would remain behind to wait for Joanna and Tag when the deed was done. One day he would have her back.

# Chapter Three

*August*

Joanna sat beside the river with her back braced against a cottonwood tree, trying to concentrate on the book she had been reading. She sighed in exasperation when she realized she had read the last sentence over several times without comprehending its meaning.

She closed the book and laid it down on the grass beside her. It was such a beautiful day, she couldn't keep her mind from wandering. A warm breeze was blowing, and she could smell the sweet scent of the blossoming wild flowers.

She lay down on the sweet-smelling grass and rolled over on her stomach to observe a bumble bee as it buzzed from buttercup to buttercup gathering nectar to make honey.

It was so peaceful beside the river that Joanna

felt she was the only human being within hundreds of miles.

She trailed her hand in the river water, which felt icy in spite of the fact that it was late August.

What was she doing in the middle of this no man's land? she wondered. Closing her eyes, she allowed her thoughts to drift backward. She remembered the night she and Tag had been forced to flee from their home. Her anger was still smoldering just below the surface. When they reached Oregon their father would take care of his sister and her husband. Joanna's violet eyes flashed. Someday her aunt and uncle would pay for what they had done to her and Tag. She thought of her father and hoped he was recovering from his injury. What would he do when the *Althea* docked in Oregon and she and Tag were not on board? Had she known about all the delays, she would have found another way of reaching Oregon. She shook her head, knowing she had done the right thing. At the time there had been no other alternative.

The journey had been ill-fated from the start. They were traveling with ten other families, and the plan had been to meet up with a larger wagon train at Independence, then continue on to Oregon. They had been plagued with broken equipment, sickness, and flooded rivers. By the time they reached Independence, it was to find that the main wagon train had left a week earlier. Captain Thatcher, who was in charge of the small train, had been confident that they could overtake the larger wagon train, but he hadn't counted on the bad luck that still continued to hound them.

It was now late August, and everyone was resigned to the fact that they would never overtake the other wagon train, and they couldn't continue the journey with so few men to protect them.

The wagon train was now camped near a trading post beside the Platte River. The families were laying in winter stores with the intention of wintering at Fort Leavenworth, which was yet another four weeks journey.

From her vantage point, Joanna could see the wagons which were drawn into a small circle, their white canvas tops gleaming in the bright sunlight. How long ago and far away England seemed. She stood up and gazed at the bright blue sky that seemed to stretch across this desolate prairie. This land was so alien to her. With the exception of the trees that grew along the Platte River, the prairie was nothing but a never-ending sea of grassland. Would the Oregon Territory be anything like this? she wondered. This land had no name; it stretched from New Orleans up to Canada, and was called the Louisiana Purchase.

Her attention was suddenly drawn to the bottom of the incline leading away from the river, and she saw Tag waving his arms as he ran toward her. When he reached her side, his face was flushed with excitement and he was gasping for breath. His red-gold hair was tumbled in his face, and with a careless sweep of his hand he brushed it aside.

"Guess what? You'll never guess what Mr. Clifford just told me and Bobby! " he blurted out.

Joanna took him by the shoulders and turned him around, tucking his shirt into his trousers. "You have ruined your best shirt, Tag. Look at the rip on the sleeve," she scolded.

Tag ignored her reprimand. "I saw a real live Indian this morning, and Mr. Clifford, who runs the trading post, told me and Bobby that two tribes of Blackfoot would be arriving tomorrow."

"Slow down, Tag, and tell me what you are talking about," Joanna said, smiling fondly at him. "We saw several Indians from the barge on the Missouri River. Thank goodness they were on land and showed very little interest in us."

Tag gasped in a breath of fresh air and started to speak again, this time more slowly. "Mr. Clifford told Bobby and me that the Indians were coming to do some fur trading and to have horse racing and games. I didn't know Indians played games, did you, Joanna?"

Joanna's eyes widened with apprehension. "Mr. Clifford was only teasing you and Bobby, don't you think?"

"No, it's true, Joanna. An Indian rode right up to the trading post. Me and Bobby saw him. I ain't never seen anything like him before."

"Don't say ain't, Tag. I have told you repeatedly that there is no such word," Joanna said, trying to discount her brother's announcement as foolishness. "Are you sure the Indians are coming here, Tag?" Joanna asked in alarm.

"Yes, that's what I've been trying to tell you. Mr. Clifford told me the Indian was a Blackfoot."

"I heard Mr. Phillips and Captain Thatcher talking, and they said the Blackfoot don't like the white race, and wouldn't come within a hundred miles of us unless they were on a raid. I have cautioned you before not to believe everything that someone tells you."

"But I saw the Indian with my own eyes," Tag argued.

"I don't doubt that you saw an Indian, Tag, but it wouldn't have been a Blackfoot. They live too far north. Captain Thatcher said that this is Pawnee territory. Chances are, the Indian you saw was a Pawnee."

"No," Tag insisted. "He was a Blackfoot. That old trapper Crazy Farley was at the trading post and he was talking to him in Indian language, and when the Indian left, he told Bobby and me that the rest of the tribe would be arriving just before dark tomorrow. They are going to camp on the other side of the river."

Joanna remembered overhearing Captain Thatcher telling Simon that the Blackfoot were the most fearsome of all Indian tribes, and she had a feeling of dread deep inside. Tag saw the fear in his sister's eyes and smiled at her confidently. "You don't have anything to worry about, Joanna. I'll take care of you."

She smiled in spite of her fear. Tag was trying so hard to be a man, but he was still so young. She hated that his life had been touched by tragedy and ugliness. "How could I be afraid with such a brave brother to look after me," she said, hugging him tightly.

As they both stared westward, Joanna glanced at Tag and caught the most wistful look in his eyes. "Don't worry, Tag. We will reach Oregon, and when we do, Papa will go back to Philadelphia and deal with Uncle Howard and Aunt Margaret."

"I know, Joanna, but we won't see Papa until next summer and that's a long time away."

Joanna tried to divert Tag's attention, knowing the bitterness he felt against their aunt and uncle. "Let's just look on this as an adventure, Tag. How many of your friends back in England will ever get the chance to see the sights and wonders you have seen? Just think, you will be spending the whole winter at an army post."

He grinned up at her. "Not to mention seeing the Blackfoot that will be arriving here tomorrow night. I always wanted a tomahawk. Do you suppose one of the Indians will trade me one for my knife?"

Joanna raised her eyebrow. "No, because if the Blackfoot really are coming, you are not to go anywhere near them."

"Aw, Joanna, I won't be in any danger. Mr. Clifford said so, and Crazy Farley agreed with him."

Joanna pulled Tag's ear playfully. "Don't refer to Farley as crazy, Tag. It isn't proper."

"That's his name, Joanna. He told me so himself."

"Nevertheless, since you don't know his last name, you will simply call him Farley."

Looking at the position of the sun, Joanna saw that the day was slipping away. Taking Tag's hand, she led him toward the wagon train. Her mind was filled with visions of fierce-looking Indians with brightly painted faces, and she shivered.

The heat from the afternoon sun beat down on the peaceful valley with a punishing force. There was a slight breeze blowing, and it stirred the leaves on the cottonwood trees that grew beside the winding Platte River. A doe and her fawn were grazing on the sweet green grasses that grew in abundance in the valley.

The only sound that could be heard was the cooing of the mourning doves that nestled in the branches of the tall cottonwood trees. It was a peaceful world, somehow untouched by the hand of man. Here, nature was the supreme ruler.

Suddenly the stillness was broken by the sound of thundering hooves. Man had intruded on this wondrous paradise.

The doe raised her head and became alert and watchful. With a powerful leap into the air she bounded up the hillside, followed closely by her young fawn. The mourning doves took flight and soared into the cloudless blue skies.

A lone Indian topped the hill and surveyed the surrounding countryside, searching for anything that could represent danger. His keen eyes were alert and watchful. Raising his hand, he signaled that all was well and the others should join him.

There were fifty fierce-looking Blackfoot warriors who rode down the hill toward the stream to water their thirsty horses. When they reached the river, all but one dismounted. He was chief of the mighty Blood Blackfoot tribe. Although he was no more than twenty-seven summers old, his warriors followed him with blind obedience. There was something about him that set him apart from his companions. Perhaps it was his dark eyes that somehow seemed to reflect a deep sadness as if he had seen too much—felt too much.

He sat so still that it seemed as if he were carved of stone, but his eyes were watchful and alert. It had been seven sunrises since he and his warriors had started out on this journey, and he had been plagued with a feeling of unrest. He felt somehow that something was about to happen to him that would change his life completely. He knew not if the omen bore him good or ill. He knew only that he could not prevent it from happening. The time was drawing near—he could feel it in the very depths of his soul. Soon, very soon, he would meet his destiny.

A sudden gust of wind ruffled his long ebony-colored hair, and still he didn't move. Around his head he wore a leather headband from which hung five eagle feathers that fell down his back. His face was deeply bronzed and handsome.

He dismounted and led his mount forward to drink from the river. His movements were graceful for one so tall. Fawn-colored buckskin trousers hugged his long legs like a second skin. His wide, muscular chest was bare but for the twelve bear claws which dangled from a leather strap that was tied about his neck.

He had been named for the mighty predatory bird that soared through the sky on the breath of the wind. His name was Windhawk!

Windhawk became aware that his warriors had remounted and were silently waiting for him to do the same. He drew in his breath, wondering what the future held for him. If the omen foretold his death, he would meet the event with courage and daring. Windhawk had never felt fear until now. He faced the unknown, and he knew he could not battle destiny.

He swung onto his horse, and without a backward glance urged his black steed forward. Riding swiftly eastward, the Blackfoot warriors soon disappeared from view, leaving no sign that man had intruded on the peaceful valley. The mourning doves returned to their perches in the cottonwood trees and all was quiet once more.

Joanna and Franny had just finished the dishes and put them away in the wooden crate while Tag read a book by the light given off by the campfire. Joanna had insisted, in spite of the adverse conditions, that he continue with his daily lessons, much to Tag's displeasure.

Joanna was lifting the heavy kettle which contained the deer stew, when Crazy Farley came ambling by.

"Here, now, young lady, you shouldn't be handling anything so heavy." He took the pot from her and sniffed. "My, my, that do smell good. I ain't even ate yet."

Joanna smiled. "Would you like some stew? I was about to throw it out, Mr. . . ."

"Call me Crazy Farley, everybody does."

Again she smiled. "Farley, I'll get a bowl and dish you up a generous helping."

He grinned. "That would be right kindly of you, young lady."

Tag laid his book aside and sat down beside Farley on the wagon tongue. "Do you live around here, Farley?" Tag wanted to know.

Farley took the bowl Joanna handed him and took a bite before answering. "Nope, I don't call no place home. I travel, mostly in Blackfoot country."

Farley finished his bowl of stew. The juices from the stew had dribbled down his snow-white beard, and Joanna watched in horror as he took his fingers and cleaned out the last remaining scraps of stew from the bowl and licked them from his fingers. He was an awesome figure, with long shaggy white hair and beard. His filthy buckskin clothing gave off a repugnant odor. His eyes were a funny color that she could not put a name to. They were somewhere between a gray and a brown.

He smiled, showing a surprising number of white teeth. "That were mighty good, young lady. I ain't had nothing half so good in many a long year."

"Thank you. Would you like more, Mr . . . Farley?"

"Well, seeing as how you were gonna throw it out anyway, I'll save you the trouble," he said, smiling once more.

At that moment Joanna looked into his eyes and knew for a certainty that he was not crazy as he claimed to be—his eyes were alive with wit and intelligence.

When Farley had finished the third bowl of stew, he reached into his buckskin shirt and withdrew a plug of tobacco and offered it to Simon, who had just joined them. Simon refused with a shake of his head. Farley bit off a large chunk and then slipped

57

the remainder into his shirt pocket.

"I once had me a wife, and she could sure cook up a mighty fine pot of deer stew. She were full-blood Blackfoot, a beauty too. Never had me no younglings though. She Who Sings were taken by the pox nigh onto ten years back. Ain't never been inclined to take me another woman."

"Will you tell us about the Blackfoot?" Tag asked enthusiastically.

Franny poured her husband a cup of coffee, then she too sat down. Her eyes were wide with fright and Joanna clasped her hand, understanding what she was feeling.

"I 'spect you are wondering if you will be in any danger when they get here?"

"They are coming then, are they? I had hoped Tag was mistaken," Joanna said.

"Yeh, they'll be here all right. There will be two tribes of them—the Blood and the Piegan. You will be among the few white folks who has ever observed the Blackfoot close up." Farley laughed, "Leastwise, you will be among the few white folks what have seen the Blackfoot and lived to tell about it."

"I have heard tales about the ruthlessness of the Blackfoot. It is said that they have no love for the white race. Is there any truth to the rumor?" Simon asked.

"Take everything you ever heard 'bout the Blackfoot and multiply it ten times over and you still won't have the right of it. They are the most fearsome, bravest, meanest of all the Indians in my estimation. They been wronged by the white man and

58

it's true they ain't got no love for any of us."

Joanna studied the old man closely. "I'm wondering how you got the name Crazy Farley? If you are crazy then we all are."

Farley roared with laughter. "Acting crazy has saved my hide more than once. The Indians think that anyone who's crazy is touched by the Great Spirit, and to harm them would bring the wrath of the spirits down on 'em."

"You say you were married to a Blackfoot woman. Does that mean you have been welcomed into their village?" Joanna wanted to know.

"Yep, I am one of the few white men they do tolerate."

"Tell us more about the Blackfoot," Tag urged excitedly.

The old man let out a stream of tobacco juice and then leaned back against the wagon. "That would take some telling, boy. There are three tribes of Blackfoot: the *Sik-si-kau,* which means the Northern Blackfoot; the *Kainah,* which means Blood; and the *Pikuni,* meaning Piegan. I mostly been with the Piegan Blackfoot. I like them better than most folks I knowed. They've a code of honor that we could all benefit by. Don't get me wrong; ifen they's ever crossed, they strike with a vengeance. They have several chiefs, but the head chief is chosen for his wisdom, bravery and generosity. They break up into small groups during the spring, then come together again before winter sets in. Right now the Piegans, the tribe my wife come from, are led by a chief that's meaner than sin. Name's Running Elk. He kills just for the fun of it, I been told. I think the

Piegans would just as soon not follow him, but he holds on to them somehow. I don't reckon he will be chief too much longer though."

Joanna swallowed a lump of fear. Tag's face held a look of excitement, and Franny's eyes were filled with concern.

"Tell us about the Blood Blackfoot, Farley," Tag urged.

"Ah, yes, the Bloods. They be the ones I knows the least 'bout. They have them a young chief who they follow blindly. I don't know too much 'bout this young buck—he's surrounded with mystery. His own people is in awe of him. I ain't seen him but once. He's a handsome devil with the strangest eyes I ever seed. He walks around like some young god, and his people almost thinks he is one."

"What's his name?" Tag asked, caught up in Farley's stories.

"Name's Windhawk," Farley replied, chewing on his tobacco.

"Will he come here?" Tag wanted to know.

"I kinda doubt it. He don't show himself that much, leastwise to white men."

"Tell me more about him," Tag urged.

The old trapper closed his eyes in thought, and when he opened them, he smiled at Tag. "Like I said, I don't know much. I heard something once but I don't know as it's true. I'll throw it at you folks and you can judge for yourself."

Joanna noticed that other people from the wagon train had gathered around, and they all listened intently as the old man started to speak.

"I heard tell he ain't no more than twenty-seven

summers. Don't know if he's married or not. Them Blackfoot sometimes take more than one wife, especially if they be considered wealthy, which Windhawk be. They count their wealth in horses, and I heard tell he has over five hundred. Don't know if it's so or not, don't know if it ain't. He lives in a big lodge in the middle of the village. Some say his lodge is big enough to hold fifty men. Don't know if that's true neither." Farley scratched his head. "The tale I'm about to tell you was told me by a Blood Blackfoot. It was said in the winter of eighteen-thirty, the Blackfoot was starving to death. They sent out scouts far and wide to find the great herds of buffalo, but they all returned without never sighting nary a one of 'em. It was said that Windhawk was but twenty summers then. He went to the great chief, Running Wolf, who was his father. It's said the old chief was dying at that time. Windhawk told his father he'd seed a vision of a *Tomeksih-siksinam,* which means white buffalo, and in his vision he were shown the way to find that there animal."

Farley stroked his beard. "The Blackfoot put great store in their visions. Every young buck will go off by himself and fast 'til he has a vision. They make what they calls a medicine bag, which is said to have very powerful medicine. The young warriors will never go on a hunt or raid without their medicine bags. Anyway, it was said that Windhawk saw this vision about the white buffalo, so the old chief told him to take many warriors and find this buffalo. Now the white buffalo is sacred, and not too many Indians have ever seed one. I doubt any white man ever had the privilege. The Blackfoot will never eat its meat, but offer it to Napi, their God. The story goes," Farley continued, "that it took many weeks and the Blackfoot covered many hundreds of miles before they found them a small herd at the foot of the Rocky Mountains. And sure 'nough, among the herd was one of them albino buffaloes. They tell that Windhawk got off his horse and walked among them great beasts until he came to the white buffalo. The animals moved apart and made a path for him. When he reached the sacred beast, he raised his spear and plunged it into its heart without no trouble. The others watched in awe as the young Windhawk cut out the albino's heart and ate it. You know good and well that no Indian would ever dare to eat any part of the white buffalo, fearing what might happen to them.'"

Tag's eyes were glued to Farley's face, taking in the old man's every word. "What would happen to someone who ate the meat of the white buffalo, Farley?" he asked.

Farley looked at the eager young face, happy to have such an interested audience. "Who can say, boy? Nobody but Windhawk ever ate the forbidden meat, far as I knowed."

"Was Windhawk harmed because he ate the heart of the white buffalo?" Tag inquired.

"Not so far as I knowed, but then Windhawk ain't no ordinary man, or so they say."

"What did he do with the remainder of the white buffalo?" Joanna wanted to know. "Did he eat that, too?"

Farley smiled at the beautiful young girl. "The remainder of the white buffalo was hung in the branches of a tree as a tribute to Napi. The next morning Windhawk told the others that they would return home where they would find them a large herd of buffalo grazing near their village. If any of them braves doubted his words, they soon found out he was right, 'cause when they come within shouting distance of the village, there was the largest herd of buffalo ever seed. It is said that it took from sunrise to sunset just for them to pass. The old chief declared that Windhawk would be chief when he was gone, and there weren't none who disputed his right after that. Now I ain't saying it's true, and I ain't saying it's not. All I know is that he has been the greatest chief the Bloods has ever knowed. Like I said, they be in awe of him. I knowed that for a fact. It's been said that his enemies fear him and his people love him. I've seen that for myself."

"It sounds just like a tale from a book," Tag said.

"Oh, Windhawk ain't no imaginary person. He's real flesh and blood all right," Farley spoke up.

Joanna tried to imagine what the man Windhawk would look like. Was he just a figment of Farley's imagination, or did he actually exist? She tended to think Windhawk couldn't possibly be a real person.

"Do you think there will be any danger to the people of the wagon train?" one of the men asked, thinking the old man must be crazy after all.

"Can't say for sure, but I kinda doubt it. Windhawk don't like for his Bloods to drink the white man's liquor, or so they say. The Indian can't take liquor like a white man. It makes them crazy. Clifford at the trading post has made sure all his liquor is locked up. He ain't taking any chances with so many women and children about. Besides, as you knowed, it ain't lawful to sell spirits to the Indians, though I knowed plenty of traders who aren't above it."

The old man stood up and ambled off, mumbling to himself. He left without even saying good-by. Joanna watched him until he was swallowed up by the night shadows.

Each person was caught up in his own thoughts. They would be hopelessly outnumbered by the Indians, and they wanted to believe that Farley had spoken the truth when he said they wouldn't be in any danger.

Later, as Joanna and Franny were spreading their pallets inside the wagon, Franny spoke up. "Well, Miss Joanna, the fat's in the fire now. Seems to me that the road we have been forced to travel has been a bit bumpy lately."

"I know, Franny. I'm sorry to have involved you and Simon in my and Tag's problems."

Franny had been spreading a quilt to make the pallet softer, and she stood up and placed her hands on her hips. "What are your troubles if they aren't mine and Simon's? Haven't we been a part of this family since long before you was born?"

Joanna smiled fondly at the older woman. "So you have, Franny. I can wager you never thought your loyalty would take you to Indian territory."

"Humph, maybe I prefer an Indian to that aunt and uncle of yours." Franny handed Joanna a pillow and climbed out of the wagon. "I'll make Master Taggart's and Simon's bed under the wagon. You'd best get some sleep. Tomorrow will be here soon enough."

Joanna smiled to herself. What would she have done if it hadn't been for Simon and Franny? As she pulled on her long white nightdress, Joanna felt a prickle of fear run like icy fingers down her spine. Her thoughts were troubled, and she feared for the safety of the wagon train.

Tag popped his head into the wagon. "Joanna, do you think we will see Windhawk?"

"Let's hope not, Tag. I want you to stay near the wagon for the next few days."

"Can't we watch the games, Joanna?"

"No! I want you to promise you will not disobey me. These Indians are dangerous. You heard what Farley said."

Tag yawned and turned away, thinking he would find a way to see the horse races. He just had to.

Joanna picked up her brush and began brushing her red-gold hair. She was tired, but doubted she would sleep a wink, for fear that the Indians would swoop down upon them in the night. Soon, however, her eyes closed and she drifted off to sleep. She wasn't even aware when Franny lay down beside her.

Quiet settled over the wagon train as all the campfires went out one-by-one.

That night, Joanna's dreams were disturbed by nightmares. She dreamed of a wild, beautiful Indian who rode with the swiftness of the wind. She never quite got a clear glimpse of his face, but he seemed to beckon her to follow him. In her dream he told her his name was *Windhawk!*

# Chapter Four

Windhawk stared at the darkened skies. There would be no moon tonight, and the thousands of stars lent no light to the darkened shadows.

His keen hearing picked up the sound of footsteps, and he knew his boyhood friend, Gray Fox, was approaching. The two men stood silently for a long while, until at last Gray Fox spoke.

"I sense about you an uneasiness, my friend. Are you troubled?"

"You know me very well, do you not?"

"I know you as well as any man can. You are a man of deep secrets and mystery."

"You are mistaken. There is nothing mysterious about me. I am a man like any other."

"No, my chief, you are like no other man. I believe that Napi saw in you a man of great power and wisdom, and he has chosen you to guide our people through these troubled times. I am not alone in this

66

belief, for it is shared by all your people."

Windhawk placed his hand on his friend's shoulder. "If that is so, then you and the others put too much faith in me. I am but a man who has feelings as you do."

"If that is the truth, my chief, why, then, do you not take unto yourself a wife? I have two wives, and you have not even one, yet we are of the same age. Have you found no maiden whom you favor?"

"No, I have not yet found the woman whom I would choose to walk beside me and bear me sons. Until I find her I will have no other."

"I have heard your mother say that you are too selective. There are many who would walk beside you should you make the offer."

"I will not allow my mother to speak of this, nor will I talk with you about it. I search for the woman I could love, but I have not found her." Windhawk's voice was but a whisper, and Gray Fox could almost feel the pain in his words. He decided it would not be wise to pursue the conversation so he changed the subject.

"What is troubling you, my friend?"

Windhawk was silent for so long that Gray Fox thought he wouldn't answer. At last he spoke.

"How can I tell you of this feeling that is deep inside me when I do not myself understand it. It is a feeling so strong that it is with me all day, and awakens me at night so I cannot sleep."

"What kind of feeling?" Gray Fox asked, puzzled.

"I do not know. It is as if I am waiting for something to happen."

"Waiting for what?" Gray Fox asked, not understanding Windhawk's words.

Windhawk raised his face to the heavens. "I know not what it will be. I only know it will not be long in coming."

"Do you think it will be bad?"

"I know not." Windhawk turned to his friend. "But I would ask something of you. Should anything happen to me I would wish you to see that my mother and sister are cared for. I would ask this of no one but you."

Gray Fox was disturbed by Windhawk's words. He loved him as a brother and honored him as he had never honored another man. Although they had been boyhood friends, Gray Fox was still in awe of his chief.

"Should anything bad befall you, I will treat your mother and sister as if they were my own," he vowed solemnly.

Windhawk reached out and rested his hand on Gray Fox's shoulder. "I know why I have chosen you as my friend. Each time I have asked something of you, you give without question."

"I only gave back what you have always given me. I love you as I do my brother. I honor you as my chief."

Both men lapsed into silence. Windhawk raised his face once more to the heavens, and Gray Fox stared at his profile. Here was a man that others looked up to. They heeded his words and followed wherever he led. Never had there been a man such as he. If anything happened to him, no one could replace him. Gray Fox felt fear in his heart. Windhawk seemed to sense his friend's thoughts and turned to smile at him.

"All rests in the hands of Napi. It does no one good to predict the future. We can do no more than wait."

"It is as you say, this I know."

"We will reach the trading post tomorrow," Windhawk said, changing the subject.

"I am surprised that you consented to come to the games. You have not done so before."

"I would not have come this time, but my destiny awaits me. I could do no more than follow."

Gray Fox watched as Windhawk walked over to where the horses were tethered and patted the neck of his great black stallion. Although Windhawk had many horses, *Puh Pom,* * was his favorite. Together the two of them defied nature and raced the wind.

"Come, my friend, it is time to get some sleep. Tomorrow will soon be here," Windhawk told him.

That night Gray Fox's thoughts were troubled. What destiny awaited his chief? What force had persuaded him to attend the games? It was well known that Windhawk didn't like Running Elk, the chief of the Piegan Blackfoot, and he liked the white man even less. Windhawk's pallet was not far from where he lay, and Gray Fox could sense that he too was having troubled thoughts.

Joanna made her way through the camp. She

*The Lightning

smiled and waved to several people. She had grown to know the other families of the wagon train very well. They had been through many hard times together. Joanna had formed a strong bond of friendship with most of them. As she passed the Phillips's wagons, Amanda Phillips fell into step beside Joanna.

"If you are on your way to the trading post, I'll walk along with you," Amanda said.

"Good, I welcome your company. I am searching for Tag, and if I know him, he's sitting around listening to Farley weave his Indian yarns."

"Joanna, are you scared with all those Indians descending on us tonight?"

"I'm terrified. Simon told me that Captain Thatcher is taking every precaution by posting extra guards day and night."

"Speaking of Captain Thatcher, I know something about him that you don't suspect."

Joanna looked sideways at Amanda. "I know that he is to be stationed at Fort Leavenworth, and only agreed to lead the wagon train as far as Independence."

Amanda giggled. "That has nothing to do with what I know. Do you think the captain is handsome?"

"Yes, but I am not alone in that. I think half of the young girls on the train are enamored of him. I suspect that Claudia Maxwell has captured his heart though."

Amanda stopped in her tracks and gave Joanna a disbelieving glance. "You can't see what's right before you, can you? Everyone but you knows that

Captain Thatcher can't keep his eyes off you."

Joanna was astounded by Amanda's statement. "That's not true. I have hardly spoken two words to Captain Thatcher since I first met him."

Amanda smiled and linked her arm through Joanna's. "I know. The captain told my brother Frank that he was afraid to approach you."

"Why?"

"He said that you were so beautiful that you must have many beaus back in Philadelphia."

"Now I know you are teasing me, Amanda. I am neither beautiful, nor do I have any beaus back in Philadelphia."

"Anyone can see you are beautiful, but are you telling the truth about having no gentlemen friends?"

"I can assure you it is the truth," Joanna said looking at Amanda who was petite and pretty. Her coffee-colored hair enhanced her soft gray eyes. "Since we are handing out compliments, I think you are the pretty one, Amanda."

Amanda's face lit up. "Do you really mean that? You wouldn't say it if it weren't true?"

"I can assure you, it's the truth. Tell me, are you perhaps one of Captain Thatcher's admirers?"

"Goodness no! I think he's handsome, but I would be frightened to death of him. He's so . . . manly. No, I have my eye on Robert Gorden."

"Yes, he's nice. Do you think he likes you?"

"I think so," Amanda blushed. "He says he does."

By now they had reached the trading post, and

just as Joanna suspected, Tag was inside with Farley. Amanda gave Joanna a sideways glance as Captain Thatcher walked over to them.

He removed his hat and placed it under his arm. "Good morning, Miss James, Miss Phillips. It looks to be a fine morning."

Joanna assessed the captain closely. He was tall and indeed very handsome. His hair was blond and his eyes were a clear blue.

Harland Thatcher had wanted many times to speak to Miss James, but he always felt like a fool when he was around her. She was so lovely, and miles above any woman he had ever known. He, like the others on the wagon train, knew very little about her background. All he knew about her was that she was from England and was traveling with her brother and two servants to join their father in Oregon.

Taking his courage in hand, Harland blurted out, "Miss James, I wonder if you will be going to the dance tonight?"

"I don't know, Captain. I thought the dance might be canceled because of the Indians?"

"No, ma'am. I thought it would be best if we were to carry on as normally as possible."

She smiled, and Harland felt his heart racing with hope. "Yes, I believe you are right, Captain. I shall surely come to the dance tonight."

His face lit up. "I wonder if you might honor me with a dance, Miss James?" he dared to ask.

"I would be delighted to dance with you, Captain. Now if you will excuse me, I need my brother's help to lead the stock down to the river for water.

72

Do you think there will be any Indians arriving this early?"

"No, ma'am, but if you would like I would be glad to accompany you to the river."

"I wouldn't dream of asking you to do such a thing. Tag and I can manage quite well."

Joanna didn't see the stricken look on Harland's face, but Amanda did. She wondered how Joanna could be so blind. Couldn't she see that the captain was in love with her?

Joanna and Tag led the stock toward the river. There were seven horses in all; four that they used to pull the wagon, Joanna's gelding Fosset, Tag's pony, and Simon's bay. Joanna's father had given Fosset to her for her sixteenth birthday. He was a beautiful solid white animal, that was sometimes wild and unpredictable, but Joanna was an excellent rider and could easily control him.

Against her better judgment, Joanna had given in to Tag's pleading and allowed him to lead Fosset to the river.

It was late in the afternoon, and as they neared the river Joanna looked about carefully to make sure there were no Indians. It was too quiet, and somehow eerie. There wasn't the usual noise of the scolding birds in the branches overhead. Joanna glanced at Tag, but he didn't seem to notice anything out of the ordinary, so she dismissed her feeling of foreboding. She didn't suspect that Tag was having trouble with Fosset until the horse had already dragged him into the water.

73

Rushing forward, she tried to grab hold of the trailing rope that was tied about Fosset's neck, but the animal shied away, taking Tag along with him into the swirling current.

"Turn loose, Tag! Let him go!" Joanna yelled.

Tag tried to do as she asked, but by now his legs had become entangled in the long rope. With each movement Fosset made, he drew Tag into deeper water.

Panic raced through Joanna's mind when she saw Tag being pulled under water. Forgetting about her own safety she plunged into the river. Her gown and shoes seemed to pull her under, and she struggled to reach her brother. She grabbed his arm and tried to pull his head above water, but his legs were so entangled in the rope that she couldn't bring him to the surface. Joanna clawed and tugged at the rope, knowing if Tag didn't get some air he would soon drown. After many futile attempts, Joanna realized she would never be able to free him without help. She was whimpering as she surfaced to take another breath of air. Tag was going to drown! she thought, diving under the water with renewed determination. Just when she thought her lungs would burst from lack of air, she felt a firm hand about her waist pushing her above water. The man removed his knife and sliced through the ropes, then pulled Tag to the surface.

It flashed through Joanna's mind that the man was an Indian, but she was too grateful that he had helped Tag to be frightened of him. The Indian swam toward the bank with Tag, and by the time Joanna reached them, he had turned Tag over on his stomach and was pounding on the small of his back. Tag started coughing, and expelled the river water he had swallowed. Crawling over to Tag, Joanna hugged him tightly to her, thankful that he was alive.

Windhawk stood up and watched as the young girl cried and sprinkled the boy's face with kisses. He had not seen her face, but he was staring at her hair. Never had he seen hair that color. Even wet, it resembled the dying rays of the sunset. He held his breath as she turned to look at him, and he felt as if his heart had stopped beating. Her violet-colored eyes seemed to look right into his heart. He wanted to look away, but he could not. Her face was beautiful and unlike any other he had ever seen. In that moment Windhawk knew he had met his destiny. This white girl was what he had traveled so far to seek! It was not his death that he had come to find, but his life. This was the woman who was fated to walk beside him. He felt no regret that she was white—it did not matter. She had been created for him. He wondered if she also knew that their destinies would be intertwined.

Joanna's eyes were misty with tears, and she couldn't see the Indian's face very clearly. "I am so grateful to you for saving my brother's life. How will I ever be able to repay you?" She smiled and Windhawk's heart felt as if it had taken wings. He understood English very well although he had never spoken to a white woman. He knelt down and touched the boy's head noticing that his hair was the same glorious color as his sister's.

"It is not good, little brother, that the horse lead

75

the warrior. The warrior must always lead the horse."

Tag was too awestricken to speak, and could do no more than nod his head.

Joanna was now assured that Tag was going to be all right so she stood up, and Windhawk's eyes followed her. He noticed the way her wet gown clung to her sweetly curved body. He stood up also, towering above her. Looking into his face, Joanna felt a lump come to her throat. Never had she seen a man of such power and strength. His face went beyond handsome. His dark eyes seemed almost liquid. She felt somehow as if she had known him forever. If there were other lives, as some people believed, perhaps she had known him in another time and place. It was such a strange feeling, that Joanna shook her head to clear it.

Windhawk watched silently as her cheeks became lightly flushed. Her skin was a soft ivory color, and he resisted the urge to reach out and touch her. He wished her hair were not wet so he could see its true color.

Joanna shyly offered him her hand. "How can I thank you for giving my brother's life back to me? I will always be grateful to you." Her voice was soft and musical. She even made the grating English language sound beautiful, he thought.

Windhawk hesitated before he took her hand. When their hands touched, Joanna felt a tingling sensation racing through her body.

"I . . . do not wish the thanks." He stared at her so long and hard that Joanna felt uncomfortable. Windhawk saw her discomfort, and he released her hand and turned back to Tag.

"Are you a Blackfoot?" Tag asked.

"Yes." Windhawk nodded.

"Have you got a tomahawk?"

Windhawk smiled. "Yes."

"I'd rather have a tomahawk than anything else in the world."

Windhawk touched Tag's head. "First become a man, little brother, then you can have the tomahawk."

Windhawk turned and plunged into the river where he gathered up Fosset's reins and led the horse from the water. He handed him over to Tag, and then walked away, soon to be swallowed by the thick bushes and trees that grew along the river bank.

Joanna might have thought she had imagined the whole thing, but for Tag's enthusiasm. "Did you see how tall he was? I bet he could throw a tomahawk better than anyone else."

"I don't doubt it," she replied, staring at the place where he had disappeared. Somehow she felt a loneliness, as if she had lost something very precious. Joanna thought she had either been out in the sun too long, or else she was losing her mind. Perhaps her strong reaction to the Indian had been because he had saved Tag's life. Yes, that was what it was, she reasoned.

Joanna began rounding up the other horses, and this time she put Tag in charge of the team animals, while she led the reluctant Fosset back to camp.

Windhawk watched Joanna from among the bushes. What was her name? he wondered. He knew that he would see her again. Their paths were destined to cross, and one day she would belong to him. Had she felt the oneness between them as he had? He turned away and mounted his horse, riding back across the river, and downstream, where his warriors had already set up camp. For the first time in days his spirits were light. For the first time in his life Windhawk felt love in his heart for a woman. He had found the woman who would one day belong to him!

Before nightfall everyone in camp knew about Joanna's and Tag's adventure. Tag hadn't wasted any time spreading the word that he had been rescued from drowning by a Blackfoot Indian.

Franny had scolded both Joanna and Tag over their misadventure. She demanded that they remain in camp until the Indians had gone. The Indians would be leaving in three days, and the wagon train would be pulling out the day after that.

The music from the fiddles filled the air when Joanna and Amanda walked into the circle of light, where several couples were already dancing. Joanna had put on a pretty blue and white print gown and tied her hair back with a blue ribbon.

The first person Joanna encountered was Claudia Maxwell. From the beginning of the trip, Joanna had known that Claudia didn't like her, and although she couldn't understand the reason for her dislike, it hadn't bothered her overmuch.

Claudia now favored Joanna with a poisonous glare. "You sure know how to get yourself noticed, Joanna," she said spitefully. "Who but you could set the whole camp up in arms with her escapades?"

Joanna's temper was rising, but she just managed to hold it in check. "Oh, you know how it is, Claudia. When I want a little attention, I just ask my brother, Tag, to try drowning."

Claudia's face became distorted with anger as Joanna and Amanda walked away. She jealously stared at Joanna's gown, wishing she had a gown half so nice. Claudia had been trying to capture Captain Thatcher's attention ever since she had first met him, but he always seemed to be watching Joanna.

"Goodness, you know how to go for blood, Joanna. Many's the time I've wanted to put Claudia in her place, but you did it with such style," Amanda said.

"I know I was horrid, but she makes me so mad sometimes."

"I don't like her at all. She's a pretty girl but her actions make her unlikable," Amanda said thoughtfully.

"I suppose we should pity her," Joanna said.

"You pity her if you like, Joanna. I just plain don't care for her."

Captain Thatcher saw Joanna approaching. He straightened his blue dress jacket and smiled at her. "I half feared you wouldn't come tonight after the incident at the river, Miss James."

"I received no more than a good soaking, Captain," she said, smiling up at him.

The fiddle was playing a lively jig, and Captain Thatcher asked Joanna to dance. The two of them danced until they were breathless. When Joanna wanted to sit out a dance so she could catch her breath, Captain Thatcher sat beside her.

"I am wondering if you just came over from England, Miss James?" Harland asked, wanting to find out more about Joanna.

"No, as a matter of fact, we have lived in this country for some time."

"In Philadelphia?"

"Yes, we lived on Beacon Street."

"You don't say! I was born and raised on Carlson Street just one street over. Strange we never saw one another."

Before long, the two of them were talking about music and books. It seemed they shared the same tastes in many things.

Joanna was having fun and was unaware that other eyes watched her. One pair of eyes stared at her jealously. Claudia felt as if Joanna had stolen Harland Thatcher from her. The other eyes that observed her were dark and brooding. Windhawk watched from the distant shadows, hating the long knife soldier who dared touch his woman. Was the man her husband? he wondered.

"I thought I saw you walk in this direction, my friend," Gray Fox spoke up. His eyes followed the sound of the music. "It is strange, the white man's dance, is it not?"

"I do not like it," Windhawk answered. "It is not good for a man to hold in his arms another man's woman."

Gray Fox looked more closely. "Do they dance with someone's woman other than their own?"

"Do you see the young maiden with hair the color of flames?"

"Yes, I see her. She is dancing with the long knife with the yellow hair."

"She is not his woman."

"How do you know this?"

"She is the one I told you about."

"You said that she was very beautiful, but I cannot see her face from here. Her hair is a wondrous color, though. Are you sure she is not the woman of the yellow hair?"

Windhawk turned away, not wanting to watch any more. He felt betrayed because the flaming-haired one danced with the long knife. He was angry with himself for caring.

Joanna allowed Harland to accompany her to her wagon. As they walked along she could tell he had something on his mind.

"I had a lovely evening, Captain Thatcher," she said, offering him her hand.

"I . . . have never enjoyed myself more than I did tonight, Miss James. I wonder if you would allow me to call on you again sometime?"

"I suppose so," she told him. "Yes, that would be nice."

He smiled and his eyes lit up. Harland had always had his share of beautiful women, but this time was different. For the first time in his life, he had met a woman for whom he would gladly give up his freedom.

"Good night, Captain," Joanna said, turning

81

away.

Harland's thoughts were happy ones as he made his way to his wagon. He would have all winter to woo Miss James at Fort Leavenworth.

Windhawk stared across the river, wondering which of the many wagons the flaming-haired one slept in. What was she doing now? Was the long knife her husband? Was she now lying in his arms? Was he touching her, making love to her? He felt an ache deep inside.

"You are my woman, and I will have you," he whispered. "No one can take you from me, not even Napi himself."

# Chapter Five

Taggart lay on his stomach peering through the thick growth of some evening primrose bushes. He could hear the sounds of laughter coming from the other side of the river. Even though he had been cautioned by Joanna and Franny not to go near the river, he had conveniently forgotten their warning. More than anything, he wanted to catch a glimpse of the Indian who had saved his life.

Tag's friend, Bobby, was hunched down behind the trunk of a cottonwood tree, his eyes wide with fright. He wished Tag would tire of gazing across the river so they could return to camp.

"Come on, Bobby, you are acting just like a silly old girl. There isn't anything to be afraid of," Tag told him.

"I ain't coming out from behind this tree. Them Indians won't like you spying on them."

"These aren't bad Indians. You know about the

83

one who saved me from drowning. Besides, if they wanted to, they could have already raided our camp. Mr. Clifford says that there are over a hundred Indians camped on the other side of this river. They outnumber us, and yet they haven't done us any harm."

"Ma would give me a licking if she found out I had come to the river. I ain't about to let them Indians see us spying on them." Bobby said, hunkering down lower.

"I can't see anything from here," Tag said, standing up. "I think I'll cross the river so I can get a closer look."

Bobby blinked his eyes in disbelief. "You can't do that! Them Indians will scalp you for sure!"

"If you are afraid, stay here," Tag said, rolling up his trouser legs and wading into the river.

Bobby jumped to his feet. "You ain't going to cross the river! You're crazy!"

Tag hesitated. He was afraid, but he didn't want Bobby to know it. "I got me a good knife, and I want to see if I can trade it for a tomahawk."

Bobby's eyes brightened with admiration. He wished he could be as brave as his friend. He had visions of Tag being scalped, and he shuddered. Nothing on this earth would persuade *him* to cross that river.

"I'm gonna tell your sister on you, Taggart James. She'll give you a licking," Bobby threatened.

"No, you won't," Tag said, wading into deeper water. He felt the taste of fear, and wished he hadn't made such a big show of bravery. He couldn't back down now, though. He thought about the tomahawk he could trade for, and that gave him the courage to continue.

"Tag, come back!" Bobby realized he had raised his voice, and he held his breath, expecting any moment to see a group of wild Indians bearing down on him and Tag. He hit the ground hard, and then crawled behind the tree trunk to hide. Peering carefully around the tree, he watched as Tag waded out of the river on the other side.

Tag ducked behind a tree, thinking how foolish he had been to cross the river. His heart was drumming in his chest. It had been easy to act brave with the river between him and the Indians. If he went back now, Bobby would still think he was brave. With that intention in mind, Tag started back to the river but he had only taken a few steps before he was grabbed from behind and someone clamped a hand over his mouth. Tag was too paralyzed with fear to put up a struggle. The Indian threw him over his shoulder and carried him toward his camp.

Bobby had witnessed his friend's capture. He buried his face in the grass and covered his head with his arms, fearing any moment the Indians would cross the river and discover his hiding place. After a few moments he decided he was safe, so he jumped to his feet and ran back to camp as if the devil himself were chasing him.

Windhawk, and Running Elk, the chief of the Piegans, were standing in front of a tipi when one of Running Elk's warriors brought Tag forward and tossed him to the ground in front of them.

Tag scrambled to his feet and looked about him wild-eyed. He recognized the Indian who had saved his life and gave him a nervous smile.

"What is the meaning of this?" Windhawk asked the brave who had captured Tag.

"I found this boy hiding behind a tree," came the reply.

"Were there others with him?" Running Elk asked.

"No, my chief, I watched him cross the river alone. There was another boy, but he did not cross."

"What shall we do with him?" Running Elk asked.

Tag could understand nothing that was being said. His knees were shaking so badly he was sure the Indians were witnessing his cowardice.

The man who had saved his life knelt down beside him and placed a hand on his shoulder, giving him a reassuring smile. "Why have you come among us, little brother?" he asked in English.

"I wanted to watch the games, and I wanted to trade my knife for a tomahawk," Tag replied, sounding braver than he felt.

Windhawk stood up and spoke to Running Elk. "I know this boy. He is the same one I pulled out of the river. I will allow him to watch the games."

"He is white!" Running Elk challenged.

Windhawk drew Tag closer to him. "I saved his life, therefore, I am responsible for him. He will watch the games."

Running Elk looked as though he would like to disagree with Windhawk, but he didn't. No one ever challenged Windhawk!

"Come with me," Windhawk told Tag.

Tag no longer felt fear. His eyes sparkled brightly as he walked beside the tall Indian. Bobby was going to be sorry he didn't come with me, Tag thought. His mind was racing ahead to the stories he would tell his friend when he got back to camp.

Tag watched several horse races, and showed his excitement by clapping his hands. The tall Indian explained to him that the one who won the race also won his opponent's horse.

The Blackfoot were superb horsemen and performed many tricks while on horseback. Tag particularly enjoyed the race where an Indian on a pinto was matched against an Indian on a big roan horse. The man on the pinto pulled into the lead, then turned around backwards on his horse and taunted his opponent by motioning for him to try and catch him.

Tag laughed delightedly into the eyes of the tall Indian.

Windhawk smiled. The small boy was very brave. He placed his hand on the red curls, thinking how like his sister the boy looked.

When Bobby reached the James' wagon, he was so out of breath he could hardly speak. Joanna was peeling apples, and she smiled at him, but her smile quickly vanished when she saw his face.

"Come quick, the Indians have got your brother! I watched them take him away. I think they were going to scalp him!" Bobby blurted out.

Joanna gripped his shoulders tightly.

"Where! Where is my brother?"

By now many of the women had heard the commotion and had gathered around Joanna.

"The Indians got him. I told him not to cross the river, but he wouldn't listen to me!" Bobby cried.

Joanna tried to swallow her fear. Without stopping to think about what she was doing, she bounded onto Fosset's back.

"Merciful heavens," Franny cried, wringing her hands. "What will they do with my boy?"

Joanna looked at Franny. "Don't worry. I'll bring him back." She whirled Fosset around and rode off in a cloud of dust, heading for the river.

"Joanna, you come back here right this instant!" Franny cried, but her cry went unheeded. With Fosset's great strides, Joanna had already neared the river. She didn't slacken her pace as she entered the river, but forced Fosset onward with an urgency. She didn't give a thought to the danger she might be riding into. All she could think of was that Tag was in trouble and she must help him.

As Joanna rode up the bank on the far side of the river, she was immediately surrounded by half a dozen fierce-looking Blackfoot warriors. Fosset reared on his hind legs and pawed at the air, but one of the Indians grabbed his reins and easily subdued him.

Joanna felt great fear and trepidation as they led her away from the river toward their camp. She took a deep breath, ready to face what lay ahead. Holding her head high, she tried not to look at the half-dressed savages.

Silence fell over the crowd of Indians as she was led to a large tipi. One of the Indians pulled her roughly from the horse and shoved her forward. She stumbled and fell at the feet of the man who was obviously the chief.

If she judged correctly the man would be somewhere around her father's age. His dark eyes rested on her flaming hair, then he looked into her violet-colored eyes.

Joanna stood up slowly and faced the man defiantly. She had once heard that Indians admired bravery, and she was not about to allow them to see how frightened she really was. Tag's life might depend on the way she handled herself.

"I have come for my brother," she said, fearing her courage would desert her.

Running Elk looked Joanna over from head to toe. Never had he seen a white woman of such beauty. He judged by the color of her hair that she was related to the boy, and he knew she had come to take him back. He admired her courage, for it would take a woman of great bravery to face danger alone. In that moment Running Elk knew that he must have this woman. There would be trouble with the whites at the trading post, but the Blackfoot greatly outnumbered the whites. Yes, he would fight for her if he had to.

"Take this woman to my tipi," he said, nodding to one of his braves.

Joanna was grabbed roughly by the arm and shoved none too gently inside the tipi. She landed hard on her stomach, and it took her a moment to catch her breath. She stood up slowly and walked over to the opening. When she tried to leave, an Indian blocked her path and motioned for her to remain inside the tipi.

She now realized how foolhardy she had been to ride into the Indian camp alone. The Indians now had two captives. Where was Tag, and what were the Indians planning to do with her? she wondered. Joanna tried not to think of all the stories she had heard about white women who had been captured by the Indians.

Sitting down, she buried her face in her hands. She had not rescued Tag, but had become a prisoner herself. Surely Simon and Captain Thatcher would come for her and Tag. But what could they do? They would be badly outnumbered. If only she could see Tag and know that he had not been harmed.

Gray Fox had seen the white girl as she was being led into camp by Running Elk's warriors, and recognized her as the girl Windhawk had told him about. He knew that Windhawk would not be well pleased that the girl was being held captive by Running Elk.

"What will you do with the white girl, Running Elk?" Gray Fox demanded.

"She is mine. I will keep her."

"Windhawk will be angry if you harm this girl. She is the sister of the boy he pulled from the river," Gray Fox threatened.

"She belongs to me. My warriors took her."

"I would reconsider if I were you. It is not wise to defy Windhawk."

Running Elk knew that Gray Fox spoke the truth. Only a foolish man would go against Windhawk. There would be another time to take the girl. Soon Windhawk would return to his lands, and then no one would stand in his way. It did not please him that he must back down in front of his warriors, but later he would have the girl.

"Take her," he said sourly. "It seems to be your lot in life to walk in the shadow of Windhawk."

Gray Fox didn't answer the insult. He moved to the tipi and flung the flap aside. His eyes fell on the girl with the flaming hair, and her beauty touched his heart. He saw the fear in her eyes, and he wanted to assure her that he would not harm her.

"Come with me. I will take you to my chief. You have no cause for fear," he told her in perfect English.

Joanna stood up and eyed him suspiciously. "I want to see my brother."

"I will take you to him." He reached for her hand and led her out of the tipi.

Joanna blinked in the bright sunlight. She expected him to lead her to the man whom she thought to be the chief. She saw the chief watching her with something in his eyes that frightened her.

Gray Fox saw her look of inquiry. "No, that is Running Elk, chief of the Piegans. He is not my chief."

Joanna felt overwhelming relief when the Indian took her away from the frightening man. She received many startled glances as Gray Fox led her through the crowds. She felt the taste of fear like a bitter pill in her mouth. The crowds parted, and suddenly Joanna saw Tag. He was standing beside the man who had rescued him from the river!

Tag saw his sister and ran to her. "I have been

91

watching the games, Joanna!" he said excitedly.

Joanna was too relieved to see that Tag was safe to scold him. That would come later. For now she placed her arms about him and hugged him tightly. "You are going to be the death of me, Taggart James," she said, wanting to shake him thoroughly.

Tag lowered his eyes. "I'm sorry, Joanna. Are you very mad at me?"

"I believe I will allow you to stew about that. You deserve to be punished, don't you think?"

At that moment a sudden gust of wind caught Joanna's bonnet and sent it sailing through the air, and it landed at Windhawk's feet. He picked up the bonnet and walked slowly toward the flaming-haired girl.

Joanna watched his approach, and she felt his dark eyes burn into hers. Her heart was racing, and it had nothing to do with fear.

When he reached her, his eyes traveled over her red-gold hair. It was windblown and curled about her lovely face, then cascaded down below her waist. Napi had done his best when he created this woman, for Windhawk could see no flaw in her. It must have taken a great deal of courage to ride across the river to find her brother, he thought.

Looking deeply into her violet eyes, he could see his own reflection, and it startled him. Her eyes were like the water reflecting an image. In that moment he wished that his image would always be reflected in her eyes.

Without taking his eyes from hers, he extended the bonnet to her. Joanna took it and her fingers brushed against his. She felt the sparks of electricity

92

as she had the other time he had touched her.

"I want to apologize for coming to your camp uninvited. I came for my brother."

"Bravery is in the sister, as it is in the brother," Windhawk told her.

"May I know your name?" Joanna asked, almost shyly. She now knew that she and Tag were in no danger. This tall Indian would never harm her; she could see it in his eyes.

"My name is Windhawk," he answered her in a deep voice.

Joanna and Tag exchanged startled glances. Here before them stood the legendary chief of the Blood Blackfoot that Crazy Farley had told them about.

"You are the chief of the Blackfoot," Tag spoke up.

"I am chief of the Blood Blackfoot. What is your name, little brother?"

"My name is Taggart James, but my friends call me Tag."

"Then I shall call you Tag, as well." Windhawk's eyes moved to Joanna. "What is your name?" he asked her, hoping her name would be as beautiful as her face.

"I am called Joanna," she answered him breathlessly.

"Jo-anna," he repeated, thinking he had never heard such a strange and wondrous sounding name. He stared at her with such intensity that it touched her deeply. Joanna found she could no longer look into his expressive dark eyes. His eyes spoke to her from beyond the language barrier. She read things in the dark depths that frightened her.

93

"Jo-anna, I would not like you to punish your brother. Bravery should be rewarded and encouraged."

"I . . . he has disobeyed me by crossing the river. He must learn discipline."

Windhawk looked down at Tag. "Your sister is right, little brother. It is hard to know what to do. You were wrong to disobey your sister, but you were also brave. I shall leave your punishment to your sister, while I shall reward your courage."

Windhawk motioned for Gray Fox to come to him. He spoke to him rapidly in Blackfoot language, and Gray Fox disappeared for a short time. When he returned, Tag saw that he carried a tomahawk. Windhawk took the tomahawk, and smiling, he handed it to Tag.

"I see in you a brave warrior. I give to you this tomahawk to seal our friendship."

Tag's eyes gleamed with excitement. He turned the weapon over, examining it carefully. It had images carved on the handle, and several feathers from a hawk had been attached to the handle with a leather strap. Tag could hardly believe that Windhawk had given him that which he desired most.

"I have nothing to give you but this knife," he said, removing the small knife from his pocket and offering it to Windhawk.

Windhawk took the knife and slipped it into the leather belt he wore about his waist. "If we never meet again, little brother, I will remember you by this knife."

Joanna was touched by Windhawk's kindness. "I

thank you for allowing a young boy's dream to come true. You have made my brother very happy. I owe you a great debt which I can never repay," she said, looking into his dark eyes which were dazzling and bright.

"I want no thanks. It is reward enough to look upon your face." The words were spoken softly, and Joanna thought she must have misunderstood him.

"Are we allowed to leave?" she asked hurriedly, wanting to put the river between her and this man who disturbed her peace of mind so greatly.

Windhawk motioned for Gray Fox to bring her horse. He then walked beside Joanna and Tag to the river's edge. While he was speaking to Tag, Joanna allowed her eyes to roam across his handsome face and down his muscled chest. He was magnificent! Never had she seen a man such as he. She remembered the tales Crazy Farley had told them about Windhawk. Where she had doubted their validity before, she now believed they were true. This man, Windhawk, could be nothing less than a legend. His brilliant eyes spoke to her of things she couldn't understand.

Gray Fox handed Joanna Fosset's reins, presenting her with a problem. If she were to mount the horse, she would show a fair amount of her petticoat. If she chose to wade across the river, she would have to raise her gown to keep from soiling it. Windhawk seemed to sense her dilemma. She felt his hands about her waist, and she could feel their warmth through her clothing. With easy grace he lifted her onto Fosset's back. He then plopped Tag on behind her.

"Good-by, Windhawk," Tag said. "I'll never forget you."

Joanna was startled as Windhawk touched her hand, drawing her attention to his magnetic eyes. This time she saw sadness reflected in the dark depths, and it touched her heart.

"Napi will keep you from harm. It is a long journey from the white world to the Indian world. Will you make the journey, Jo-anna?"

Joanna could not understand what he was saying to her. What promise did his dark eyes ask of her? Fearing that which she could not understand, she urged Fosset forward and he plunged into the river. Once she was safely across the river, she propelled Fosset forward at a run. Her heart felt heavy, as if she had left a part of herself behind. No, she told herself, she had escaped from Windhawk's disturbing presence. She wouldn't ever see him again, and she was glad — wasn't she?

When Joanna and Tag reached the wagon train, they found all the men of the camp armed and mounted.

Captain Thatcher rode up to Joanna. "Have you been harmed in any way?" he asked, looking her over.

"No, I was not harmed."

Now that he saw Joanna was safe, Harland felt furious. "I am in charge of this wagon train, Miss James. I am angry that you would take it upon yourself to cross the river."

"I had to find Tag."

"I would have gotten your brother back. By your rash actions you endangered the whole wagon train. If you were one of my soldiers, I would have you court-martialed!"

Joanna raised her head, and her eyes gleamed with answering anger. "I am *not* one of your men. My brother did a very foolish thing by crossing the river, but I could do no less than go after him. My brother is *my* responsibility, not yours."

"Everyone who signed on this train is my responsibility. You and your brother are members of this train, and as such, you will obey all the rules from this day forward. Is that understood, Miss James?"

Joanna saw that everyone had gathered around and was witnessing her public humiliation. "I understand, Captain," she answered, nudging her horse forward and heading for her own wagon.

Franny was overcome with relief when she saw Joanna and Tag. "Lord deliver us," she said with tears sparkling in her eyes. "I thought I would never see either of you again."

Joanna slid from Fosset's back and hugged Franny tightly. "We are all right, Franny, don't cry."

"I don't know where Simon is. He rode across the river searching for you."

Joanna looked in the direction of the river and saw Simon riding across. "Look, Simon is safe," she told Franny.

Tag shuffled his feet and avoided Joanna's eyes. "I'm sorry I caused so much trouble, Joanna. The captain was angry with you, and it's all my fault."

He looked so forlorn that Joanna wanted to draw him into her arms, but she didn't. "What you did was wrong, Tag. I hope you have learned your lesson today. You were thoughtless and rash in your actions."

"Are you going to punish me?"

"Yes, I am afraid I must. Starting this afternoon, you will read three chapters a day in the primer."

"But, Joanna, that will take hours."

"Yes, it will, but it's small enough punishment for what you did."

Tag held the tomahawk that Windhawk had given him as if it were a fragile piece of glass. Joanna was angry with him, he thought, and with good reason. But he had gotten his tomahawk, and he had talked to Windhawk!

Joanna was weary. If one more person came by and asked her about her ordeal with the Indians, she thought she would scream. She just wanted the incident to be over and forgotten about. She felt bad that Captain Thatcher had been so angry with her. He had been right, of course, but that didn't make her feel any better.

She was lying on her pallet feeling sorry for herself, when Franny stuck her head in the wagon. "That nice Captain Thatcher is here to see you, Miss Joanna."

Joanna sat up, reaching for her hairbrush. "I suppose he wants to reprimand me as he would a child," she said, brushing the tangles from her hair.

"Like as not, he does, thus saving me the trouble," Franny told her.

Joanna felt she had stood about all she could for one day. She could not remember a time when she had been angry with Franny, but she was angry now. "You forget whom you are speaking to, Franny. You are not my mother; you work for me."

Franny bit her lip, feeling the sting of Joanna's words. Joanna had never spoken to her in anger before. "I don't forget for one moment that I held you in my arms when you was a baby, and nursed you when you was ill. If that don't give me some rights, what does?"

Joanna saw that she had hurt Franny, and she felt terrible about it. "Forgive me, Franny. I don't mean to take my anger out on you. It's just that everything seems to be going wrong."

Franny took Joanna's hand. "My poor little girl, you have had more dumped on you in a short time than most folks do in a lifetime, and you hardly more than a baby."

Joanna smiled. "It hasn't been too bad, with you and Simon looking after Tag and me."

Franny brightened. "Don't you think that you'd best go and find out what the captain wants to see you about?"

Harland paced back and forth with his hands clasped behind his back. He couldn't believe he had spoken to Miss James in such a high-handed manner. It was just that he had been so concerned for her safety.

"You wanted to see me, Captain?" Joanna asked.

Harland turned around to face her. She was wearing a soft violet-colored gown that brought out the color of her eyes. The campfire added sparkle to her glorious hair. She wore a guarded look, as if ready to do battle with him.

He cleared his throat. "I have come to apologize, Miss James. I was exceedingly rude to you this afternoon. I should never have reprimanded you in front of the whole train."

"If it's any consolation to you, I was humiliated," Joanna said, not yet ready to forgive him.

"Your humiliation would never be a consolation to me, Miss James. I have too much regard for you to want to belittle you."

There was such a sincere light in his blue eyes that Joanna knew that he was making an effort to gain her forgiveness.

"Many of the things you said were true, Captain. All I could think of this afternoon was my brother's safety. I didn't stop to weigh the consequences."

Harland smiled. "I doubt that an armed group of soldiers could have been as effective as you were."

"I was frightened," she admitted.

"With good reason," he told her. "I am informed by Crazy Farley that you were in the hands of Running Elk, chief of the Piegans, until one of Windhawk's warriors rescued you. Is that true?"

"Yes, that's true."

"Farley overheard some of the Indians saying that Running Elk intended to keep you as a captive. I believe we owe your freedom to the chief of the Bloods."

"Windhawk was very kind to Tag and me."

"I think it would be a very good idea if you stick close to your wagon until the Indians leave. I have cautioned all the other women and children to do the same."

Joanna smiled. "Yes, I will do that."

His eyes lingered on her face. My Lord, he thought, I am in love with her. I stand here making polite conversation and what I really want to do is take her in my arms and tell her how I feel.

"I wouldn't say no should you offer me a cup of that coffee you have brewing on the fire," he said instead.

Joanna laughed, and picking up the coffee pot, poured him a cup of coffee. "I'm afraid my manners are not what they should be. Had you come to my home I would have offered you some refreshments. It's hard to know what to do when one is traveling with a wagon train."

His eyes rested on her flaming hair. "Had I come to your home, would you have allowed me to call you by your first name?"

Joanna sat down on a camp stool. "I think, had I met you in Philadelphia, you would have been too busy with countless numbers of lovely young ladies to notice me."

He sat down on the only other available stool. "I would have noticed you in a room filled with beautiful ladies."

Joanna blushed in spite of herself. "I am not accustomed to receiving such compliments, Captain. I believe you are flattering me."

"One need not use flattery when he meets a young lady as lovely as you. I spoke only the truth."

Joanna laughed. "I suspect you say that to all the young ladies. I have noticed that you have spent a great deal of time with Claudia Maxwell. Should you not be saying these things to her?"

Harland ran his hand down the seam of his blue trousers. "I mean no disrespect to Miss Maxwell when I say I did not seek her out." He could have said that he tried to avoid her whenever possible, but he was too much of a gentleman to malign a lady's character.

As if talking about her made her appear, Claudia walked by.

"Captain Thatcher, I have been searching for you. You promised to take me for a walk. Have you forgotten?" Claudia gave Joanna a malicious glare before smiling sweetly at Harland.

Harland held his temper. Claudia's appearance made it seem as if he had been less than honest with Joanna. He could see the accusation in Joanna's eyes. He stood up, feeling trapped.

"Miss Maxwell, I do not remember saying that I would take you for a walk tonight."

"Well, it wasn't exactly a promise. You said that you didn't want any young ladies walking about alone."

Joanna stood up. "Good night, Captain, Claudia."

Claudia saw the admiration in the captain's eyes when he looked at Joanna, and her jealousy soared. "Wait, Joanna. I wanted to commend you for drawing the whole camp's attention to yourself once more. Lord, you do have a knack for dramatics. It's no wonder that the captain was so angry with you."

Harland looked uncomfortable. He had never cared much for Claudia, but now he was beginning to resent her. He had not been sure that Joanna had forgiven him for this afternoon, and Claudia was only making it worse.

"Come along, Miss Maxwell. I'll see you to your wagon," he said, knowing that he had lost ground with Joanna tonight.

Joanna watched Claudia and Captain Thatcher walk away. She had wanted to believe the things he had said to her. She liked him, and she thought he liked her as well. Was he the kind of man who needed to surround himself with many women?

Joanna thought of the darkly handsome Windhawk. She was afraid of the emotions he had awakened inside of her. Would it not be safer to think of someone like Captain Thatcher instead of the Indian, Windhawk, who seemed to tug at her heart?

Windhawk sat around the council fire waiting for Running Elk to finish speaking.

"I say that we could take the white train with very little effort. I know that you have no more love for the white man than I do. Let us drive them from these lands. Let us show them that they are not welcome."

Windhawk stood up and raised his hand. "Listen to me, my brothers. I have no more love for the white man than Running Elk does, but I will advise my braves not to raid the wagon train. I ask that you of the Piegans not commit this deed also. Where is the glory in raiding so small a train?"

Running Elk interrupted. "I think Windhawk is becoming soft. Did he not pick up the white woman's bonnet today. Perhaps he should have placed the bonnet on his head since he thinks as a woman," he taunted.

Before Running Elk could react, Windhawk had unsheathed his knife and held it to the chief's throat. "I could easily slay you, Running Elk, but I will not. I will say this: The Bloods will not raid the

103

wagon train."

Running Elk felt the point of the knife against his skin. He knew that Windhawk would not hesitate to drive the knife into his body. He felt relief when Windhawk released his hold on him and put his knife away.

"Let your warriors speak for themselves, Windhawk. If any one of you would stand with the Piegans in this matter, let him step forward."

The camp became silent as everyone waited to see what Windhawk's Bloods would do. Many of the Piegans did not like Running Elk, but he was their chief for now. One by one the Blood warriors walked over to stand beside Windhawk. Not a single one joined Running Elk.

"My warriors have given you their answer, Running Elk. Should you decide to raid the train, you would first have to meet me and my warriors."

"You would go against your own people for the sake of the white woman?" Running Elk asked angrily.

"I would go against you, Running Elk."

"I saw the way you looked at the white woman today. You want her for yourself," Running Elk accused.

Running Elk stared into Windhawk's eyes, and the fire in the piercing depths made him realize he had spoken foolishly. He watched Windhawk's hand tighten on the hilt of his knife, and he knew that his death was near.

"Let us put our differences aside," Running Elk said placatingly. He then quickly sat down cross-legged, picked up the peace pipe, and offered it to Windhawk. He knew that Windhawk and his Bloods would not allow him to attack the wagon train, but there would be other days, he thought, drawing on the peace pipe and exhaling the smoke slowly. Soon Windhawk would return to the Blackfoot Nation, and then Running Elk would take the white girl.


The people of the small wagon train slept peacefully, not knowing that their lives had been spared by Windhawk's intervention.

Crazy Farley watched the argument that had erupted between the two Indian chiefs. He had been alarmed that Running Elk might win, and he had been prepared to warn the people on the wagon train.

Farley's eyes rested on the young Blood Blackfoot chief. Windhawk was indeed a great man, and Farley could see why the Bloods were so devoted to him.

The old trapper crept away into the shadows and crossed the river as silently as any Indian could have. There would be no danger to the families on the wagon train tonight, he thought. Windhawk had destroyed any plans Running Elk might have in that direction. Running Elk was not worthy to be the leader of the proud Piegan Blackfoot. Tonight he had been humbled by Windhawk. Even so, Farley didn't trust Running Elk. He was as wily as a fox and would bear watching.

# Chapter Six

It was shortly past sunrise as Joanna sat on the wagon seat awaiting the orders to move out. Tag sat beside her, holding a book with bored indifference. Joanna had promised him if he would read a chapter to her now, he could forego his nightly lessons just this once.

Simon had ridden ahead with Captain Thatcher so Joanna was left to drive the team. She was becoming experienced at handling the horses by now; however, this morning she was having trouble with them. The lead horse had developed a sore ankle, so Fosset had been harnessed in his place. Fosset was acting up as usual, and it took all of Joanna's strength to control him. His misbehavior was making the other team horses nervous and jittery. Joanna was giving all her attention to the horses, so she didn't notice that Claudia had ridden alongside the wagon.

"What's the matter, Joanna, having trouble?" Claudia asked in a honey-sweet voice.

"Nothing I can't handle," Joanna said, pulling hard on the reins to prove she was capable of controlling the team.

"I'm surprised you aren't at the front of the train so you can make cow-eyes at Harland," Claudia said spitefully.

"I'll leave the batting of eyelashes to you, Claudia. You do it so well."

Claudia's face reddened, and she bit her lower lip. "I have a message to you from Harland; he says you will be taking the drag today," she said, hoping to goad Joanna into anger.

Joanna knew that Captain Thatcher had sent her no such message. Simon had told her earlier that she was to take the third position from the front. She smiled inwardly, knowing Claudia was trying to bait her. It was a well-known fact that anyone who had the end position was forced to eat the dust from the other wagons. Usually the positions were rotated so no one had to take the rear too often.

"I would prefer to take the drag today," Joanna said, knowing Claudia would get very little satisfaction if she acted complacent. "Fosset does not take well to the harness, so it will be best if we lag behind." Joanna gave Claudia her sweetest smile.

Claudia's face became distorted with unleashed fury. What was it about Joanna that made her so unsure of herself? She always seemed to come out looking like a spoiled child when she sparred with Joanna. Claudia whirled her horse around and rode off in a cloud of dust. The day would come when she would witness the proud Joanna James's downfall, she vowed.

Tag slammed his book down on the seat. "I don't like Claudia Maxwell. Why do you allow her to get the better of you?"

"She doesn't get the best of me, Tag. If you were older and wiser you would realize that she is the loser. I pity her because she is the most miserable, unhappy girl I have ever known."

"Well, I don't feel sorry for her. If she were a boy instead of a girl, I would punch her for treating you the way she does."

Joanna smiled at her brother fondly. "I can see that I have a champion in you. Perhaps if Claudia had a brother to care about her the way I do, she wouldn't be the way she is."

"I don't know how you can defend her. I don't know anyone on this wagon train who likes her."

"The only thing that needs concern you at the moment is finishing that chapter, Taggart James. Leave Claudia to me. I know how to handle her."

"It doesn't appear to me that you handled her very well," Tag said angrily. "It will be you and me that eats dust all day, not her."

"There are harder things to digest than dust, Tag."

"Such as?"

"Pride, Tag, pride."

"Sometimes I don't understand you, Joanna. You didn't always allow people to walk all over you. I remember how you stood up to Uncle Howard and Aunt Margaret."

Joanna ruffled his red-gold curls. "You talk too

much. If you don't read that chapter you will have to do it tonight," she reminded him.

The signal was given to move out, and Joanna had no more time to talk; she was too busy trying to control Fosset.

By early afternoon the wide prairies gave way to jagged cliffs and high plateaus. Joanna was exhausted from fighting with Fosset who seemed to grow worse as the day progressed. Her arms were aching, and she knew that by tonight her muscles would be sore.

She saw Claudia riding toward her, and she cautioned Tag with a warning glance not to voice his opinion.

"Eating dust, Joanna?" Claudia jabbed.

"Franny once told me that one must eat a bucketful of dirt before one reaches adulthood," Joanna said, smiling at her brother. "I was just saying to Tag this morning that there are far worse things to eat than a little dirt."

Tag returned his sister's smile.

Before Claudia could reply, a bloodcurdling yell pierced the air.

"Indians!" Claudia screamed. "We'll all be killed!"

Joanna watched in horror as a band of Indians rode toward the vulnerable wagon train. They were yelling and waving their weapons in the air. A few scattered shots rang out from the wagon train, and several of them hit their target, but the wagon train was badly outnumbered, and there was no time to form a circle to defend themselves.

"Tag, you and Franny get in the back of the

wagon and lie down flat!" Joanna cried out.

"No, I'm staying with you!" Tag objected loudly.

"Taggart, do as I say! I'm having a hard enough time controlling Fosset. I don't want to have to worry about you."

Franny lay down and pulled a coverlet over her head, praying loudly all the while, but Tag refused to budge.

"This time I won't mind you, Joanna," he said as he pulled the rifle out from under the seat and aimed it at an advancing Indian.

Joanna hardly had time to think as Fosset reared up and broke out of formation. The other team horses followed the fear-crazed Fosset's lead, and Joanna knew that they were out of control. She could see that the team was heading for a huge boulder, and she pulled on the reins with all her might, but the horses refused to obey her command. The wagon hit the rock with a force that sent Tag sailing through the air to land on the ground with a heavy thud.

Joanna pulled on the reins with renewed strength, but still the horses refused to yield. Her thoughts were more on Tag's safety than her own. Suddenly she saw the wagon heading toward a deep ravine. As the wagon neared the cliff, the horses made a sharp turn, and the wagon broke loose, careening down the steep ravine. Joanna screamed as the wagon turned end-over-end, throwing her onto the rocky ground. She landed hard against a huge boulder. The impact shot pain through her body, and Joanna knew that she had been injured. She tried to move and gasped from the intense pain.

"God, please help Tag," she prayed just before she lost consciousness.

Tag was too stunned to move for a moment. He could hear the sound of gunfire and yelling all about him. He shook his head to clear it, and then glanced about, trying to locate Joanna. Jumping to his feet, Tag saw the wagon teeter on the edge of the ravine. He held his breath as he watched it fall over the cliff.

Fear for his sister was the uppermost thought in his mind. He ran toward the cliff, praying silently that Joanna and Franny would be unharmed.

Tag heard a loud piercing scream, and turned just in time to see Amanda Phillips struggling with two Indians. He realized that he still clutched the rifle in his hand, so he quickly raised it and aimed at one of the Indians. He had never shot a man before, so he hesitated for a moment. Amanda screamed again as one of the Indians picked her up.

Tag pulled the trigger! Nothing happened; the gun was empty! He didn't pause to think, but ran to Amanda's aid. Lifting the rifle, he drew back and swung it at one of the Indians, hitting him hard across the back causing him to release Amanda.

"Run, Amanda, run," Tag cried. He had no time to run himself, for one of the Indians grabbed him roughly by the arm, raising his knife ready to plunge it into Tag's heart. Tag watched the knife as it descended, knowing he could do nothing to prevent his death. He was surprised when a third Indian grabbed the knife from the hand of his would-be slayer and spoke to the man. Tag remembered Running Elk, chief of the Piegans, and wondered why

111

he had spared his life.

Tag's arms were quickly bound with rawhide ropes, and he was tied to an old tree stump, unable to move. He was forced to watch as one of the Indians caught Amanda and bound and tied her to the same tree stump.

The horrible scene of death was all about them, and Tag shuddered when he saw an Indian run his spear through Amanda's father, Mr. Phillips. He quickly looked away rather than watch the savage ply his knife to Mr. Phillips's scalp. He was grateful that Amanda hadn't seen her father's death. She was crying hysterically, and Tag realized tears were washing down his face as well. His eyes moved to the spot where the wagon with Joanna and Franny had gone over the cliff. He was grateful that they had been spared the horror of what was happening to the families of the wagon train. Surely Joanna could not have survived such a fall. Tag's slight body began to tremble. He closed his eyes and tried to close his mind to the sounds of moaning and screaming.

Suddenly he was aware that the screaming had stopped. He opened his eyes and saw the Indians setting fire to the wagons.

"Tag, why do you suppose they didn't kill us?" Amanda asked between sobs.

"I don't know, Amanda. Close your eyes. I don't think you want to watch."

"They're all dead, Tag. All of them."

Tag wished he had the words of comfort to give Amanda; he somehow felt years older than she at the moment. His heart ached for Joanna. He remembered how painful it had been to lose his mother, but the pain was more intense now. He and Joanna had shared so many things . . . she had been his whole world.

Turning his head to where the wagon had gone over the cliff, he saw Running Elk. "I will kill him for this, Joanna," he said between clenched teeth. "One day I will avenge your death. I swear it."

Running Elk stood at the top of the gorge and looked down at the smashed wagon below. He could see the girl with the red hair. She was sprawled on the ground like a broken doll, and he judged her to be dead. Even in death she was beautiful, he thought. She was the reason he had raided the wagon train in the first place.

"Shall I climb down to see if she still lives?" one of his braves asked.

"No, if she isn't dead she soon will be. I have no use for a dying white girl." Running Elk turned away and ordered his warriors to mount up. He stepped over the body of a man and paused. Unsheathing his knife, he started to remove the dead man's scalp, then thought better of it. They must leave quickly because the fort of the long knives was nearby and they might spot the smoke from the burning wagons. He ordered the Blackfoot dead to be gathered up so they could have a proper burial. With one last glance toward the ravine where the girl with the flaming hair lay, he shook his head regretfully and rode away.

One of the Indians grabbed Tag up and placed him roughly on a horse, then mounted behind him. Tag was powerless to help Amanda as she suffered the same treatment. Her eyes sought his, and he saw terror in her glance. What would be their fate? he wondered. Surely if the Indians intended to kill them they would already have done so. Tag felt no joy in being alive since Joanna was dead. As they rode away he glanced once more at the smoldering wagons. It was hard to believe that so many had died.

Windhawk and his warriors had ridden hard all day. He purposefully pushed ahead, fearing he would weaken and ride back for Joanna. When they made camp that night, Windhawk walked away from the others, feeling such a heavy loneliness in his heart. Once more he questioned the great Napi for leading him to Joanna. Had he been mistaken in leaving her? Had Napi meant him to take her away with him?

"It is yet a long way home, my chief. I question your judgment to push so hard the first day," Gray Fox said, coming up beside Windhawk.

"I think I do not run home, but run away from something," Windhawk answered.

"You speak in riddles, my friend. Are you referring to the white girl with the flaming hair?"

"Sometimes I believe that you see too much, Gray Fox."

At that moment there was a great commotion in camp and Windhawk turned his attention to the white man who had come among them. He recognized the old trapper, Crazy Farley. The old man was talking loudly and waving his arms about.

. "Let us see why the crazy one has come to us," Windhawk said, walking toward the campfire.

When Farley saw Windhawk he ran to him. "They all been killed!" Farley raved. "I was on my way to Fort Leavenworth and I seed the smoke. I hid out in the bushes and seed Running Elk and his braves massacring the wagon train!"

Windhawk felt his muscles tense. "What are you talking about, old man? Why do you talk to me in the white man's tongue?"

Farley sat down on the ground, shaking his grizzly white head. He was too dazed to speak in Blackfoot. "I thought I'd seed 'bout everything, but I ain't never seed so much killing and carrying on."

Windhawk grabbed Farley by the shirt front and hauled him to his feet. "You make no sense, old man! Are you saying that Running Elk attacked the wagon train that was camped by the river?"

The old man nodded. "That's what I've been trying to say, ain't it?"

Windhawk felt anguished and enraged. He could not bear to think of Joanna being dead. "Were they all slain, old man?" he asked, fearing to hear the truth.

Farley shook his head. "I don't know. I was too far away to make out if there was anyone left alive."

Windhawk did not pause to consider, but ran toward the horses. "Mount up," he called to his warriors. "We ride at once."

"I'm going with you," Farley said, standing up.

"No, white man," Gray Fox said as he leaped onto his horse. "It would not be well for you to come with us. If you are wise, you will not be here

115

when we return."

Farley watched as the fierce Blackfoot warriors rode away, and a plan formed in his mind. He would follow the trail of Running Elk. Perhaps there had been some survivors, and the chief was taking them back to his village. He thought of Joanna and Tag James, and felt sorrow in his heart. He had liked them. He ambled over to his horse, mumbling to himself. It would be far better for them if they had been killed, rather than become captives of Running Elk, he thought.

The night was dark, and the horses and men were tired, but the band of Blood Blackfoot rode at a fast pace, following where their chief led without question. Not one of them voiced a complaint or asked where they were going. It was enough to know Windhawk wished it so.

Franny crawled out of the remains of the wagon. She knew she had been badly injured. She heard the distant sound of a howling wolf and shuddered. Somehow she had to get to Joanna. It was now dark and she was almost certain that the Indians had gone. She was tortured with the thought that Simon and Tag had probably been killed by the Indians. Simon had not been with them when the Indians struck; perhaps he had been spared. She prayed that he was still alive. Franny knew that she was dying, and she had very little regret. She didn't want to live if all the ones she loved were dead. She could see Joanna and it appeared she was dead because she hadn't moved at all. Finally, as the pale moon gave off its shallow light, Franny reached the boulder where Joanna was lying and touched her cheek. Thank God, her face was warm, so she wasn't dead.

"Joanna, Joanna," she whispered, shaking her roughly. "Wake up, they are all dead but you and me."

Joanna groaned but didn't show any signs of waking.

Franny closed her eyes. Her chest felt as if there were a heavy weight lying on it. She coughed and blood was running out of her mouth. Lying back, she knew that she had only a few moments to live.

"God," she prayed, "send down your angels to watch over my Joanna." Franny stiffened and she gasped for breath, her head fell sideways, and she was dead.

The first light of dawn lit the eastern sky as Joanna groaned and opened her eyes. At first she didn't remember where she was. She only knew that when she tried to move, severe pain shot through her body. Turning her head slowly, she felt dizzy. Why was she lying on the ground? she wondered.

Finally her eyes focused clearly, and she saw all that was left of the wagon was bits of canvas and splintered wood.

"Dear God, no!" she cried as she remembered what had happened.

She saw Franny lying beside her. Her eyes were blank and Joanna knew that she was dead. "Oh, Franny, have I brought this upon you?" Tears of grief blinded Joanna as she reached for Franny's cold hand. "Franny, what shall I do without you to boss and bully me?"

Her eyes went to the top of the cliff. There was such silence. Surely not everyone was dead! "Tag!" Joanna screamed. "Oh God, please no, not Tag!"

If she could only get up, she thought. She had to know what had happened to Tag. She gasped for breath, and her vision became fuzzy. Joanna closed her eyes, trying to think what to do. She had neither the will nor the inclination to live. Everyone Joanna loved had been taken from her, with the exception of her father, and he would never know what had happened to her and Tag.

Joanna sighed and closed her eyes. It hurt so much to move. Oh Tag, she thought. Have we come so far and been through so much only to have you die in this wilderness? A shuddered sob escaped her lips, and she lost consciousness again.

Windhawk dismounted with a heavy heart. The smell of burning flesh was all about him. He frantically searched through the burned wagons, looking for some sign of Joanna. She could not be dead! he thought wildly. He searched wagon after wagon, but it was impossible to tell if Joanna was among the dead since the bodies were all so badly burned. If she wasn't dead, then Running Elk must have taken her captive.

He walked slowly to the edge of the cliff and looked down at the broken wagon which had been smashed on the rocks below.

Joanna regained consciousness just as a dark shadow fell fleetingly across her face. She glanced up toward the high embankment to see two Indians peering down at her. They were no more than shadowy outlines since the sun was behind them. Wild, unbridled terror seized her. The Indians had returned! All Joanna could do was lie helpless as one of the Indians made his way down to her. She closed her eyes, fearing the worst. She only hoped he would be merciful and kill her quickly.

She felt one of them kneel down beside her, and opened her eyes. It was Windhawk! Her fear was joined by a burning hatred. She had trusted him and he had betrayed her!

"Kill me and make it quick," she whispered. Tears were streaming from her eyes. "You are nothing but a savage—harming people who have never done anything to you!"

Windhawk reached out his hand to touch her face. He felt pain in his heart when she flinched. Did she think that he was the one who had raided the wagon train? Did she not know that he would never do anything to harm her?

When he tried to move her, Joanna cried out in pain. "Leave me to die. You have killed all that I love in life. Allow me to die in peace."

Windhawk could see that she had been badly injured and must be moved carefully. His heart was glad that she was still alive. But she could yet die from her wounds.

Three of his braves joined him, and he sent two of them to search for any other survivors. Windhawk knew when he lifted Joanna into his arms that he was causing her pain, but he had to get her out of the ravine. Joanna closed her eyes refusing to look at Windhawk. What did it matter if he killed her — had he not already killed all she held dear in life?

She bit her lip trying not to cry out when he gently lifted her into his arms. No matter how much it hurt, she would not give him the satisfaction of witnessing her pain. Each step he took seemed to send a thousand knife blades through her body, but she didn't once voice her pain.

By the time Windhawk reached the top of the ravine, his two braves had joined him. He saw that Joanna's eyes were open, and he recognized the pain in the violet-blue depths.

"Don't hurt me," she pleaded in a weak voice. He nodded his head, knowing what it had cost her to plead for herself. He remembered her courage in coming to his camp to find her brother. She was a woman like no other, and he wished he could spare her any more pain. He used his body to shield her view of the death and destruction all about them.

He handed Joanna to Gray Fox while he mounted his horse, then Gray Fox lifted her up to him.

"Renew the search for her brother. If you find his body, lay him to rest. Then climb down below and search the wagon and bring all that might belong to Jo-anna."

Gray Fox nodded.

Joanna understood nothing the two men said, but she knew they were talking about her since Windhawk had spoken her name.

She was in such pain that she prayed for unconsciousness. She tried to turn her head to see if she could locate Tag's body, but Windhawk shielded her view.

He nudged his mount forward, knowing each step the horse took would cause her pain.

"I will camp beside the river. I dare not take her any farther in her condition — you will see the campfire," he told Gray Fox before he rode away.

Joanna turned her face against his soft buckskin shirt wishing she were dead, and thinking she might be before the day was over.

Windhawk dismounted, taking care not to cause Joanna undue pain. She groaned and opened her eyes when he laid her down upon the soft grass.

Joanna watched him return to his horse and remove a blanket through a pain-filled haze. What was he going to do to her? she wondered. When he returned, he placed the blanket down beside her and carefully moved her onto it. Joanna looked into his dark eyes and shivered at the unreadable depths. If she didn't know better, Joanna would have thought she saw sadness in his eyes.

Could he regret what he had done to the families of the wagon train? She hoped he was feeling remorse. One thing was certain, she would never forgive him. He turned away and she watched as he built a fire. His back was to her and she wished she had the strength to take his knife and drive it into his murderous body.

He seemed to sense her glare, and turned his head, looking deeply into her eyes. Joanna's heart fluttered at the dark eyes knowing they were filled with compassion for her. Was it possible for a man to have two sides? Could he murder and destroy human life one moment, and feel compassion and regret the next?

She cringed as he moved to her side and knelt down. His hand was gentle as he felt along both of her arms to see if they were broken. Joanna bit her lip, trying not to cry out when he touched her right forearm. Windhawk was grim-faced when he saw the beads of perspiration appear on her face. He feared her arm might be broken. Turning it over, he saw with a glance that it was not broken, but badly sprained.

An involuntary groan escaped Joanna's lips when he unsheathed his knife. Now was the moment of her death, she thought, praying for the strength to meet her death bravely. Instead of plunging the knife into her heart as she expected him to, Windhawk cut her gown along both sleeves. Joanna tried to protest when she realized he was going to remove her riding habit. Windhawk easily restrained her movements. Her eyes widened in fear. No, she wasn't going to die, not yet. What he had in mind for her was a fate worse than death. She had no intention of submitting to him willingly. He would have to kill her, she thought, renewing her struggle.

Windhawk knew what she was thinking. "Joanna," he said, shaking his head and laying the knife down to show her he only intended to help her.

"Don't touch me," she pleaded.

Windhawk gestured to her arm, then nodded his head. "I want only to help you," he said in broken English.

Joanna frowned, beginning to understand. He

was going to tend her injuries. She closed her eyes, knowing she was too weak to protest.

"Jo-anna," he touched her face softly and she opened her eyes. He had apparently torn a strip from her riding habit and wet it in the nearby river, for he began to wash the dried blood from the wound on her forehead.

Windhawk saw that the wound on her head was not too bad, so he carefully picked up her arm and began binding it tightly with a leather strap which he took from about his waist. He knew he was causing her pain, and was relieved when he felt her go limp, knowing she had lost consciousness. Her arm was the least of his worries. He feared she might have suffered internal injuries. He was glad she was unconscious so he could examine her thoroughly.

After Windhawk removed her riding habit and boots, he looked confused for a moment . . . he didn't know that white women wore so much clothing. He had never before seen a petticoat, nor the soft white garments she wore next to her skin. It took him several moments to remove her undergarments. When that was accomplished, he examined her entire body with the professionalism of a physician. He found no other injuries except for minor scratches and bruises, to which he applied some healing salve. He had done all he could for her . . . she was now in the hands of Napi.

Now that he had tended her as best he could, he allowed his eyes to wander over her body, starting with her long shapely legs, across her well-rounded hips that gently sloped to her tiny waist. He drew in his breath as his eyes traveled to her silky breasts with their rosebud tips. Her skin was so silky and white . . . his hands trembled as he lightly touched her creamy breasts. Never had he seen a woman of such beauty. Fearing where his thoughts were leading him, he decided it would be best to replace some of her garments. With considerable effort, he managed to pull her petticoat over her legs without causing her pain. Covering her with a blanket, he sat down to wait for his warriors to join them.

Windhawk knew Joanna was in no condition to travel, but he had to get her away from the area, fearing the long knives at the fort would soon be searching for the Indians who had raided the wagon train. He knew the soldiers would believe as Joanna had, that it was he and his Bloods who were responsible for the massacre. He had decided they would camp by the river tonight, and then tomorrow, they would ride for his village.

His eyes rested on Joanna's face. How was it possible for one to have such beauty? he wondered. Her long dark lashes rested against her pale cheeks, hiding her beautiful blue eyes. He reached out and took her limp hand in his, willing his strength to enter her body. He felt sorrow, knowing she thought he was responsible for the raid on the wagon train. Would he ever be able to convince her that he hadn't taken part in the deed? Somehow it was distasteful to him to think of defending himself to her. She should know in her heart that he would never harm her.

With his free hand he traced the outline of her face. Should she die, a part of him would die also. He softly touched her glorious hair. Would Napi be so cruel as to take her away from him when he had just found her?

Windhawk heard riders approaching, and stood up. He watched as his warriors dismounted. "Did you find Jo-anna's brother?" he asked Gray Fox.

"No, we searched among the burned wagons and around the countryside, but could not find the boy."

"You are sure you searched thoroughly for the little brother?"

"Yes, my chief."

Windhawk's heart felt heavy, knowing the pain Joanna would feel at the death of her brother. Windhawk had liked the flaming-haired boy. His eyes burned with hatred. Running Elk would pay for what he had done to Joanna. One day Windhawk knew that he and the chief of the Piegan would face each other, and one of them would die.

Joanna slept fretfully all night. Once she awoke to find Windhawk sitting beside her. When she felt his dark eyes scan her face, she closed her eyes and drifted back to sleep. She didn't want to dream, because her dreams were more like nightmares. She dreamed of Tag being tortured by the Indians.

The next morning Joanna was awakened by Windhawk touching her cheek. She shivered as the hands that had caused her brother's death touched her. Windhawk merely wanted to examine Joanna's arm to make sure the leather sling was still in place, but Joanna, not knowing his intentions, clutched the blanket tightly about her neck. Windhawk saw her cheeks take on a pink tinge, and he knew he was causing her embarrassment.

Joanna was relieved when he stood up and walked away from her. She had feared that he would ravish her before his warriors, and even though she had been spared this time, she couldn't stop her body from trembling. Her fear was renewed when Windhawk returned. Joanna was surprised when he laid her riding habit within her reach, then turned and walked away to give her privacy to dress herself.

It was a very slow and painful process putting on her riding habit, while trying to stay under the blanket so the Indians couldn't see her.

There were a great number of Indians in the camp, but not as many as there had been attending the games at the river. Joanna estimated there were somewhere around fifty savages.

She lay back on the grass, not knowing or caring what the Indians would do to her. For the most part, they seemed to ignore her, with the exception of a few curious glances.

At one point one of the Indians approached her with food and water. He avoided her eyes, while placing the food within her reach. She felt relieved when he left. Although Joanna was hungry, she refused the food since she couldn't identify its origin — however, her thirst caused her to drink deeply from the leather waterskin.

Joanna's eyes widened fearfully as Windhawk approached her. She groaned when he bent down to lift her gently into his arms then carried her to the horses.

He could feel her stiffen when he mounted his horse.

"Where are you taking me?" she asked.

His dark eyes searched her face, hating the fear he read there. "I am taking you to my home," he replied.

Joanna knew it would do no good to beg for her freedom. The man who had killed so many of her people would never listen to her plea, and she didn't want to lower herself by begging him.

As they rode away from the river, Joanna tried to close her mind to her future. Tag was dead, and she was a prisoner. She was lying across Windhawk's lap and she resented his nearness with every fiber of her being. She stared at the hands that held the reins. They were strong hands: hands that had murdered and burned. Those hands had also been gentle as he tended her wounds. She closed her eyes, wishing she were dead.

## Chapter Seven

In the days that followed, Joanna became slowly accustomed to the fact that she was a captive. The bruises and cuts were mending, the sling had been removed from her arm and she was no longer in pain. She had almost welcomed the pain, because in some way, she thought of it as her penance. It was her fault that Tag, Franny and Simon were dead. If she hadn't insisted on joining the wagon train, they would be alive today. Even if Tag had been sent to sea by her uncle, he would have been better off than he now was. If only she could turn back the clock, she would have done things much differently. What good did it do to bemoan the past — it wouldn't change anything.

With each passing day Joanna could feel the distance between her and the civilized world widening.

The Indians traveled at a swift pace, and Joanna was sore all over from the long hours on horseback.

She was glad that she had healed enough to ride by herself. She hated having to ride with Windhawk. He very seldom spoke to her, and approached her only when he wanted to examine her arm.

They were now camped in a heavily wooded area. So far, Joanna had not been harmed in any way. Each day Windhawk would clean and apply some kind of healing herbs to her head, and at those times, she would be terrified of him. At night she was forced to share a small tipi with Windhawk. She had been certain that he would ravish her, but so far he slept by the entrance while allowing her to sleep beside the fire.

None of the other Indians ever entered the tipi, but during the day Joanna would sometimes feel them watching her.

At first she had refused to eat the food that was offered to her, but hunger soon overruled her objections.

Joanna was offered very little privacy. Even when she went to the river to wash, someone was always nearby. She didn't know if it was to insure that she didn't attempt to escape, or if it was for her safety.

Joanna questioned the reason why Windhawk seemed to take such special care of her? Why had she been the only one he had allowed to live? She also wondered what he had in mind for her once they reached his village.

Windhawk and Gray Fox had just tethered the horses and the other warriors had gathered about for the evening meal. For the last two days they had been traveling through the territory of their old enemy, the Crow. There would be no campfire tonight. Windhawk wanted no signs that would reveal their position to the Crow.

Joanna had noticed that when Windhawk walked among his warriors, he would smile at one and speak to another. Although she couldn't understand what was being said, she could feel the camaraderie between the mighty chief and his braves.

Gray Fox pulled Windhawk off to the side so he could have a private word with him. "The white girl is healed, my friend. Would it not be better if you were to send her back to her own kind?"

"Why do you say this to me?" Windhawk wanted to know.

"I think it would be far better for you if you were to let her go. She is not of your world and can only bring you trouble."

Windhawk was thoughtful for a moment. "My heart is already in her keeping, yet I fear she will never give her heart to me. I know so little of her life, and yet I feel she is a part of me. I will never allow her to leave."

"I wonder if you have thought of how the flaming-haired one will be received by our people. They have no love for the white race. Already your warriors say that you are too soft on her."

Windhawk's eyes blazed. "Jo-anna is my woman! They must accept her."

"She is healed from her wounds," Gray Fox said again, looking at Windhawk knowingly.

"Yes." Windhawk took a deep breath. "She still fears me and believes that I led the raid on the wagon train. I have no words to tell her the truth. I do not wish to take her when she is unwilling."

"A woman must be taught from the first that a man is superior. You must show her this."

Windhawk smiled at Gray Fox. "Is that your practice with your wives?"

Gray Fox returned his smile. "No, but it is the way I would wish it to be sometimes."


Joanna sat on the bank of the river, trailing her hand in the water. There was evidence that autumn was in the air. The leaves on the trees had begun to change colors, and there was a crisp, clean aroma in the air. She heard the distant song of the whippoorwill, and was overcome with sadness. How Tag would have loved it here. With his strong sense of adventure, he would have been delighted with each new discovery. She remembered how he had admired Windhawk. It didn't make sense to her that Windhawk had once saved Tag's life only to end it later. She had to admit that Windhawk had been kind to her. It was hard to associate the man who had tended her wounds with the murdering savage who had killed all the people on the wagon train.

Joanna was so deep in thought she didn't hear the soft moccasin footsteps which came up soundlessly behind her. Windhawk could only see the back of Joanna's head, but he knew if he could see her face, he would see sadness there. He wanted more than anything to see her smile. He would do almost anything to bring her happiness.

As her injuries had begun to heal and she grew stronger, his desire for her had intensified. He dreamed of the day when he would take her in his arms and show her all the love that was in his heart.

Joanna sensed Windhawk's presence, and turned her head to stare at him for a moment. She stood up quickly with the intention of going back to camp, but he barred her way.

She raised her violet eyes to his dark ones and saw the soft light reflected there. The wind was blowing softly and the autumn leaves were drifting to the ground all about them.

"Jo-anna," he whispered, and his hand drifted up to lightly touch her face. "Jo-anna," he repeated, touching her hair.

Joanna blinked her eyes and tried to back away from him. Had the moment she dreaded come at last?

Seeing her fear, he dropped his hand to his side. "Does your arm still pain you?" he inquired.

Joanna shook her head. "Thanks to you, it is almost healed." Looking into his face, she saw such intense longing that it frightened her. She had to get away from him. She turned around so quickly that her foot became entangled in her gown and she lost her balance, falling into his arms. Tense moments passed before she could bring herself to look into his face. When she glanced up, he was watching her closely.

"Jo-anna, this feeling I have for you is such beauty . . . it fills my heart." His voice was deep and passionate, and the sound of it vibrated throughout her body.

She was now more frightened of him than ever. Surely he hadn't meant that he loved her. She would never allow him to touch her, never!

132

"Please, let me go," she whispered.

Windhawk drew Joanna closer to him fearing he had frightened her with the overwhelming love he felt for her. "I have not the words to say to you in English. If you could understand my language, I could tell how I feel. To love is to feel pain, yet . . . it is also beautiful."

Joanna felt his lips brush her forehead, and she felt a weakness wash over her. He lifted her chin and gazed deeply into her eyes. She saw that his throat was working convulsively.

"I want you for my woman, Jo-anna. I believe that it was meant for you and I to be lovers."

Joanna closed her eyes and felt his lips softly touch her eyelids. She could feel him take a shuddered breath. She wanted to leave, yet she wanted to stay. Joanna was experiencing a new feeling so consuming it pushed all other thoughts out of her mind. She could feel his warm breath on her lips and it sparked a deep pain of longing within her. His lips gently brushed hers, and she gasped. Her young body yearned for something from him, but she didn't know what it was. Opening her eyes, she saw his dark eyes asking her an unspoken question.

Suddenly she remembered that he was the enemy and she pushed him away from her. How could she have forgotten for one moment what he had done? Her heart was drumming like the rhythm of an Indian tom-tom. She backed away from him, fearing he would take her into his arms again. Joanna had fought for her honor against her Uncle Howard; she would do the same with Windhawk. He might overpower her in the end, but he would know that

133

he hadn't met with an easy conquest.

Her thoughts were troubled when she looked into his dark, velvet, soft eyes, and once again Joanna thought she saw sadness there. Windhawk had the most expressive eyes; they showed so clearly what he was thinking. His eyes could probably lie, she warned herself. It must be some kind of trick so he can do what he wants with you, the voice inside her head told her.

Joanna could not keep her eyes from moving across his face. His lashes were long and silky, framing those soft, melting brown eyes. His cheek bones were sharp and high-set. His chin showed a stubborn masculinity. She could not imagine any woman being unmoved by his beauty, when she, herself, was fighting to be free of the strong attraction she felt for him. Now his eyes were moving across her face as if he were lazily assessing her.

Joanna wanted to turn away, but his dark eyes were holding her prisoner. As his hand reached up to touch her cheek softly, her eyes drifted shut at his soft caress. She became aware that her breathing was coming out in short panting sounds, and her heartbeat was thundering in her ears. She could feel the bonds of civilization being stripped from her, as wild primitive feelings washed over her. There were no white and Indian world; there were no right and wrong—there were only she and Windhawk!

It was as if he were a magnet drawing her to him. Joanna felt herself sway and her hand came to rest against his bare, muscular chest. With a sudden lithe motion, he crushed her to his body. His thigh was warm and hard as it pressed against her soft body.

Joanna tried to speak, but the only sound that issued from her lips was a throaty sigh. His face was against hers and she felt him turn his head just a fraction to rest his lips at the corner of hers. Joanna could feel his breath enter her mouth. She felt as if a white-hot flash riveted throughout her body, leaving her breathless. Her knees went weak and she clung to his shoulders for support. A wild fire nipped at her most feminine core as his tongue traced the outline of her lips. Joanna's breath came out in a whimper of passion as her lips parted, inviting his kiss. All her resistance crumbled as his sensuous, hot mouth brushed hers. She knew she should pull away, but instead her body pressed tighter against his. His mouth was teasing and light as it brushed against hers. When he pulled away from her, she turned her head, seeking his kiss. The kiss she craved never came, and she opened her eyes to stare into passion-laced dark eyes.

Joanna's young virginal body cried out for a fulfillment that she couldn't fully understand. The feelings Windhawk now evoked in her were unexplored. Her body had never before been awakened . . . until now she had never been tested.

He knows, she thought wildly. He knows what I am thinking and feeling. Raising her face to him with her last bit of sanity, she tried to mask her confusion.

"Take your hands off me," she said in a throaty whisper.

Joanna was startled when he released her and she stumbled backwards. Now that her body was free of his, she longed to feel his closeness once more. Looking once more into his eyes, she knew that he could read the shameful truth in her eyes, and covered her face with trembling hands.

Windhawk, seeing the terror on Joanna's face, turned his back to her. "It would be wise if you would return to the tipi, Jo-anna. If you stay I will surely give you that which you know you desire."

Joanna turned around and ran back toward the camp as fast as her legs would take her. She fell once and jumped quickly to her feet, rushing into the tipi.

When she was inside, she glanced out to see if Windhawk had followed her, but to her relief he was nowhere in sight. She clasped her hands tightly over her mouth, trying to stifle the sobs that welled up deep inside her. What had she done? She knew that had he not pulled back she would now be giving herself to him, body and soul. Had she fallen so low that she would have allowed a man who was her enemy to rob her of her virtue?

She stumbled to the robe in the corner and huddled upon it, losing herself in total misery.

Joanna lay tensely upon the buffalo robe. The tipi was dark, and she dared not move, for fear she would awaken Windhawk. When he had come in a short time ago, he hadn't spoken to her, but had laid down on his buffalo robe near the entrance of the tipi. She hoped he might be asleep by now.

Every so often she would steal a glance in his direction, but it was too dark to see if he was asleep.

Since the afternoon, Joanna had begun to question many things about the mysterious Windhawk. Was he married? If he was, did he have more than one wife? Had he meant to make love to her today beside the river? What about the strange reaction she had had when he held her in his arms? Joanna had wanted him to hold her, she admitted, feeling a tightening in her throat. She closed her eyes, knowing she was being drawn to him against her will. She could not allow herself to forget who he was and what he had done.

Joanna drew in a shuddered breath. She had to think of something else. For some reason his presence in the tipi was so disturbing to her that she couldn't transfer her thoughts. Sitting up slowly she knew what she must do. She had to try to escape! It couldn't be more than a week's ride to the trading post. Joanna suddenly felt if she didn't get away she would cease to exist, and Windhawk would control her very soul.

Several moments passed, and she could hear Windhawk's steady breathing. Standing up cautiously and moving as quietly as possible, Joanna walked toward the tipi opening, hoping she wouldn't awaken Windhawk. If only she could make her way to the horses unobserved, then she might have a chance to get away. She didn't delude herself that it would be an easy task, but she just had to make a bid for freedom!

Windhawk had been aware that Joanna was restless, and he wanted to prove to her that she had nothing to fear from him. Pretending to be asleep, he hoped she would soon drift off herself. He knew he would have to earn her trust and then perhaps her heart. His keen hearing caught the sound of her movement—he knew without being told that she was trying to escape.

Joanna was trying to find the tipi opening when she bumped into a wall of human flesh, and knew that Windhawk barred her way. She felt his hand on her shoulder and tried to back away. She wanted to cry out as he lifted her into his arms and carried her to the buffalo robe and laid her down. Joanna's heart was pounding with fear as she tried to scramble to her feet, but Windhawk forced her back against the soft buffalo robe. She was making whimpering sounds as he lay down beside her and pulled her into his arms.

Windhawk wanted to tell Joanna that she had nothing to fear from him. Her slight body was trembling, so he ran a soothing hand down her back, while pulling her tighter against him.

For long moments he caressed her, until at last her trembling ceased. Suddenly the soft curves that were pressed against his body awoke the passion he had been trying so hard to control. Against his will, his hand slid up her back to her glorious hair.

Joanna could feel her fear being replaced by a feeling of contentment. For the first time in months she felt safe. This man who was not her kind and whom she had every reason to hate, had reached out to her and given her comfort as no one else ever had.

When he drew her head toward him, she did not resist, but rested her face against his smooth, bare chest. He was filling her whole being with his presence. She had always been led to believe that Indians were dirty, but that was not true of Windhawk. He smelled of leather and some unknown herb — manly, enticing.

Joanna could feel his breath stirring her hair, and suddenly she felt neither safe nor contented. She knew she must flee or she would be lost forever. She tried to remember all the reasons she had for hating him, but could only think of the strong, sensitive hand that traced the outline of her face.

"Windhawk, please, I don't want —"

His finger touched her mouth, silencing her plea. "Jo-anna," he whispered in a pain-filled voice. "Jo-anna, you spoke my name."

It was as if a thousand bright lights exploded in her head as his lips touched hers reverently.

Windhawk felt her lips tremble, and his body seemed to be on fire with yearning. He knew he would have to keep a tight control over his desire. Tonight Joanna would become his woman, but it would be because she wanted it as much as he did. He would show his love for her, and perhaps wipe away all her doubts and fears. Here was the woman who would walk beside him for the rest of his days. He would fill her body with sons, and perhaps a daughter with flaming hair.

Joanna felt a sensation like pain, and yet unlike pain, when his hand drifted down the front of her gown. Before she was aware of what he was doing, Windhawk had unfastened her gown. Slowly he pushed it off her shoulders, as his lips brushed the lobe of her ear, then moved down to nuzzle her neck.

"No, please, no," she moaned.

Windhawk covered her lips with his, closing off her protest. He had known many women, but he knew that what he was about to experience with Joanna would forever wipe out any desire he would have for any other but her. He kissed and caressed her, all the while pushing her clothing downward. He felt momentary uncertainty, not wanting to think that another man had been within her body—she belonged to him.

Joanna had never known that such a strong man could be so gentle. Her virgin body was ready to obey his slightest command. She could feel her heart drumming in her head, and she was unaware of anything but Windhawk and his gentle stroking hands, which caused new and unexplored feelings of delight to course through her body. When his hand slid down her throat to rest against her breast, she wanted to protest, but her body betrayed her. Joanna felt momentary relief when he withdrew his hand until she realized he was pushing her gown and undergarments downward.

It was totally dark inside the tipi, and the only sound that could be heard was Joanna's and Windhawk's heavy breathing.

Joanna gasped when she felt his lips on her stomach, tying her insides into tight knots.

"No," she cried, pushing against him with all her strength. Tag's face flashed through her mind, and she hit out at Windhawk, catching him with a loud slap across the face. She froze, thinking that he would strike her back. Seconds passed and she could feel his intense stare even through the dark-

140

ened tipi.

"Jo-anna, do not fight me. You know you want to feel the oneness with me. It will do no good to fight those feelings. Would it not be better if you would . . . submit?" he asked in his halting English.

He took her hand and raised it to his lips. "These hands were not meant to bring pain to a man . . . only joy." He then slid his body forward and drew her into his arms once more. She had not been aware that he had removed his breechcloth until he pressed his hot body against her.

Joanna closed her eyes at the unfamiliar feel of a man's body—which was hard and firm in all the places where she was soft. Her breasts were flattened against the wide wall of his chest, and she wanted to deny the pleasure that coursed through her veins. He slid his body against hers, and Joanna didn't even realize that she inched closer to him. She could feel his pulsing manhood pressed against her inner thigh and felt frightened again.

"Please, don't hurt me," she pleaded.

His lips nuzzled her ear. "I would sooner die than cause you pain, Jo-anna." His hot breath fanned her cheek, and suddenly Joanna had no more desire to fight him. He would win in the end, she vaguely reasoned, knowing that she was beyond resisting. She had no idea what he would do to her body, but his mouth sought hers, forcing her lips apart to receive his kiss. Where his kiss had been gentle before, he now plundered her mouth, and she groaned, surprised that Windhawk had so easily overcome her resistance. She might hate herself tomorrow, but tonight she would give him all he demanded of her.

Windhawk's kisses were hot and fierce, robbing Joanna of every ounce of strength and every thought of resistance. She was gasping for air when he raised his head at last. He moved his hand downward across her stomach, then lower to her thigh. With gentle pressure he moved her legs apart and caressed her inner thigh.

Joanna was in torment as she tossed her head from side to side. She wondered if this was some form of torture or punishment? Her body was aching and throbbing. Windhawk knew that Joanna was ready to receive his manhood. He could tell that she was inexperienced. He felt excitement thinking he would be the first man to be with her. He would teach her all the things that would bind her to him forever.

He parted her legs farther and knelt over her. His hand drifted down to her inner thigh, where he felt moistness, and knew she was ready to receive him.

"Jo-anna," he whispered in a passionate voice. "I want you to know before we can become as one, it must be because you want it as I do. If you do not want this, you must say so now."

Joanna felt confusion. What was he asking of her? The empty ache within her body cried out to be filled. She had not considered that he would ask her permission. He loomed above her, and she could feel his tension. If she asked him to leave her alone, would he comply with her wishes? Her stomach became tied in knots as her body quaked uncontrollably. She couldn't find her voice, so she reached out and laced her hands through his ebony hair, bringing his face down to hers.

She heard the primitive groan that issued from Windhawk's mouth, just before it covered hers. Lowering his body, he sought and found the core of her womanhood, introducing himself inside her carefully at first. Slowly he moved forward, and then stopped when he felt the barrier that proved no man had been where he now was. He leaned down and recaptured her lips, knowing that he would soon be causing her pain.

Joanna held her breath, not knowing what to expect. She felt Windhawk slip inside her and then stop before the ache was satisfied. She twisted her body, trying to find an end to her torment, but her movement only intensified her longing.

Slowly Windhawk slipped farther inside her and she felt a stinging pain, but it was quickly over. She felt as though Windhawk had filled her body, and in that moment, she knew no other man could have made her feel as if she were a part of him. She was flooded with sensuous feelings when his mouth covered her breast, rolling the rosebud tip on his tongue. A sob broke from her throat, and she closed her eyes as pleasure seemed to seep into every pore of her body. She didn't realize that there was a deeper pleasure yet to come.

Windhawk started moving slowly inside her, and Joanna turned her head from side to side, moaning. This was why man and woman were created, she thought. Her hands moved up the corded muscles of Windhawk's arms to rest against his back.

"Jo-anna, I will give to you what I have never

given another." His voice came out in a raspy whisper.

"I don't understand." She answered him through a haze of passion.

He cupped her face between his hands. "I have not the words to tell you. I . . . give you . . ." He paused, trying to think of the right words. "I give you my heart."

No, she thought, not wanting him to love her. She would have voiced her feelings, but suddenly she was incapable of speech when wave after wave of pleasure ran through her body like a wildfire out of control. When she felt at the brink of total exhaustion, Windhawk's body trembled and he eased himself down beside her, pulling her tightly against him.

Windhawk felt the invisible tie that now bound them together for all time. There were so many things that he wanted to say to her, but he knew she wasn't ready to hear them. Now would be the time to tell her that he had not raided the wagon train, but her next words silenced him.

Now that her mind was not controlled by passion, Joanna was hit in the face with stark reality. No matter how she tried to excuse her actions, she had allowed Tag's murderer to take her body. No, she thought, being honest with herself, she had willingly given her body to Windhawk. She was overcome with grief and remorse, knowing that she couldn't vindicate her actions, but she *would* voice her feelings.

"I detest you," she said between clenched teeth. "You have taken from me more than any person should have to give another."

"I do not know this word . . . detest. What does it mean?" he asked.

Joanna moved away from him and sat up. "It means that I hate you," she said, knowing he had brought out many other feelings in her—the least of which was hate.

Windhawk rose to his feet and jerked her upward until her body rested against his. "One hates his enemy, Jo-anna. I am not your enemy!"

"You killed my brother!" she cried, pounding her fists against his chest. "If I had the weapon, I would kill you!"

He shoved her away, and she landed hard on the bed of robes. It was too dark to see what he was doing so she lay silently, wondering if he would again take her body. She felt him beside her, and he took her hand and placed something into it.

"You wish me dead, Jo-anna? I place in your hand the knife to do the deed with," he told her.

Joanna's hand trembled as it closed around the hilt of the knife. She drew back her arm with every intention of plunging the knife into his chest. She would now avenge Tag's death!

"I wait, Jo-anna," his voice came to her from out of the darkness.

Suddenly Joanna knew that she would never be able to harm him. She wasn't a savage, she reasoned. Windhawk was the savage. She threw the weapon aside and fell on the robe. "Go away. I don't want you to ever touch me again!"

Joanna couldn't see the pain in his dark eyes. She was aware that he had moved away, but didn't realize he had dressed until he slipped silently out of the tipi.

When the tears dried on her face, she pulled on her discarded gown and curled up into a tight ball. Windhawk had not taken her by force, and that was almost worse than if he had ravished her against her will. I wish I had ended his life when I had the chance, she thought. Joanna knew she had been too much of a coward to carry out the deed. How could she take his life, when moments before he had held her in his arms and taken her to the heights of ecstasy. Joanna felt as if she had betrayed everyone who had ever loved her by allowing an Indian to make love to her.

Windhawk stood with his face turned up to the bright star-filled night. Joanna might as well have killed him; she had torn his heart into many pieces. How could she hate him when he loved her so much? How could she not know that what they had shared had been predestined. He knew he had given to her as much as he had taken away. She was too young and inexperienced to act a part. No, he had given her pleasure.

He made a decision; he would not take her again until she realized he had taken no part in the raid on the wagon train. Then, and only then, would he be able to stand before her and ask for her love. He knew the day would come when Joanna would realize that they were meant to be together.

The camp was quiet as Windhawk made his way down to the river bank. He stood silently, listening to the rushing river and the wind rustling the leaves in the branches. There were hundreds of stars twinkling in the ebony sky, and he felt as if he were a part of this land. Together he and Joanna would raise strong sons who would also belong to this land.

That night Windhawk didn't return to the tipi and Joanna was unable to sleep. She tried to plan some way to escape. After what had occurred between her and Windhawk, she knew that she must get away.

What kind of a person was she? Joanna agonized. Shouldn't she have fought Windhawk to the bitter end before allowing him to do as he wished with her body? There seemed to be no answer to her questions.

When the sunlight spread its rosy glow across the land, Joanna was still agonizing over her plight. How would she ever face Windhawk after last night? She didn't have very long to wonder, because at that moment the tipi flap was pushed aside and he entered.

She scrambled to her feet and faced him rebelliously, ready to do battle. "Don't you come near me," she said, feeling her knees go weak. She was frightened but there was nowhere to run; no one to turn to. Joanna took several steps backward as he advanced toward her. When she looked into his dark eyes, her face reddened, remembering what had transpired between them. She half expected to see a satisfied gleam in his eyes.

Windhawk stopped in front of Joanna, seeing the fear in her beautiful violet-blue eyes. He knew what she would be feeling this morning. Last night he had awakened her virgin body, but he had not touched her heart. He was confused, not knowing how to win her. She was different from the Indian maidens he had been with. He had never before faced a reluctant woman the day after taking her to his mat.

He extended his hand to her, but Joanna only raised her chin and gave him an insolent glare.

"I want no more than to take you for a walk, Joanna. I wish to talk to you."

"No! I will not go with you."

He smiled, and her heart quickened. Why did he have this strange effect on her? She was unaware that her violet-colored eyes dilated and she reminded Windhawk of a frightened little girl.

He picked her up in his arms, and when she began to struggle, he held her tightly against his body. How he loved her! He could not stand the thought that he had hurt her. It should not be that Joanna was frightened of him.

Windhawk carried her out of the tipi and down to the river. Joanna knew that it would be futile to struggle—he was stronger than she, and in the end his strength would win over her determination. She felt his hair brush against her cheek, and she remembered his gentleness the night before. He had shown her what it felt like to be a woman, and she could not deny that he had awakened her body. Even now, resenting him as she did, Joanna could remember vividly how it had felt when he made love to her.

Next time, she vowed, he would not have such an

148

easy conquest. If there were a next time she would fight him all the way.

When they reached the river, Windhawk set her on her feet. "If you would like to bathe I will turn my back," he said.

Joanna was sure she saw an amused twinkle in his eyes. She felt angry that he was referring to the fact that he already knew her body very well.

"How do I know I can trust you not to look?" she said, eyeing the water and knowing she would welcome a bath.

"I give you my word."

"I do not trust your word," she said raising her chin proudly.

Without further comment, Windhawk lifted her gown over her head and tossed it on the grass. She saw him smile as he turned his back and folded his arms across his chest.

Joanna stood undecided for a moment. If she didn't remove her undergarments they would be wet and uncomfortable, but she hesitated to go into the water naked. Even if Windhawk had given his word that he would not watch her, she didn't trust him.

With a stubborn determination, she waded into the river, still wearing her undergarments, and began scrubbing all over. She kept a watchful eye on Windhawk, but he didn't once turn in her direction.

Wading out of the water, Joanna quickly pulled her gown over her head and fastened it about her neck.

At last Windhawk turned to her and motioned that she should sit on the grass beside him. Joanna was reluctant to obey, but she decided against testing him, fearing a recurrence of the night before.

He didn't look at her, but stared instead across the river. Against her will, Joanna's eyes were drawn to him. He was beautiful, she thought. She could never remember seeing any man who could match him in handsomeness.

Windhawk felt her watching him and turned his head to look at her. Joanna drew back, fearing he would be able to read her thoughts.

"Jo-anna. I wish to say so many things to you, but I have not the words. I want you to know that I would never harm you."

"What would you call what you did to me last night?" she asked, looking away. "I have never been as harmed as I was by you!"

He took her chin and forced her to look at him. "What happened between us was meant to be. You will come to know this in time."

"Is that your way of justifying what you did to me?"

"I do not understand this—justify."

She pushed his hand away. "You think you were right in what you did to me? Are you trying to convince me also?"

"Joanna, had you ever been with a man before, you would know that what was between us was . . . good."

As his hand drifted down her cheek, Joanna looked into his eyes and found a soft light glowing there. She was unable to look away when he smiled.

"I once had a horse, Jo-anna. She was beautiful and untamed, allowing no one near her. I knew that there had never been such an animal, and I wanted to tame her. I knew that first I must win her trust. It is that way with you, Jo-anna."

"I don't think I like being compared to a horse," she said with a pretty pout on her lips.

Windhawk laughed softly. "The Indian treasures his horse, even as he loves his woman."

"I am not your woman!"

His dark eyes rested on her lips, and Joanna drew in her breath at the intense feelings that settled over her.

"You will be my woman, Jo-anna. One day you will come to me and take my hand willingly."

"Never!"

He gave her a look which made her doubt her own resolve, but he said nothing.

They both stared across the river without speaking, until Joanna broke the silence. "What became of the horse?"

Windhawk looked down at her with a smile on his lips. "When I call, she comes to me. She will eat from my hand and will allow no other man to ride her."

Once again color stained Joanna's cheeks. "I will never be like your horse, so you might as well allow me to return to my people right now."

Windhawk stood up and offered Joanna his hand. "One day, when I beckon, you will come. You will eat from my hand . . . and you will allow no other man to . . . to love you."

Before Joanna could protest, he bent and scooped her into his arms. "Come, it grows late," he said.

Joanna pondered his words. No, she would never

151

come at his bidding. She might be his prisoner, but her heart and her mind were still under her own control. One day she would find a way to escape. He couldn't watch her every day for the rest of her life. Sooner or later he would let his guard down, and that would be the day she would be free!

It would have surprised Joanna if she had known that Windhawk could read her thoughts. He was sad that Joanna should suffer so needlessly. In the end she would belong to him. Nothing on earth could stop the hand of fate from fulfilling its destiny.

## Chapter Eight

Joanna had lost track of the number of days they had been traveling. Each day they would continue to ride north, covering as much territory as they possibly could between sunrise and sunset. The civilized world as Joanna knew it had been left far behind.

Joanna was weary, and she wondered if they would ever reach the Blackfoot village. Some mornings she had to mentally force herself to climb on her horse. She had plenty of time to reflect on her plight, and at night she would think of Tag and Franny. She wondered if the pain of losing them would ever lessen. She tried not to think about what had happened between her and Windhawk, but each time he looked at her with those dark brooding eyes, her face would flush, and she would look quickly away.

Sometimes at night, she would dream about

when Windhawk had taken her body. In her dreams she could almost feel his stroking hands moving over her hips, then up to cup her aching breasts. Her young body had been introduced to sensuous feelings, and try as she might she couldn't seem to forget those feelings.

When Windhawk came near Joanna, she would feel her heartbeat accelerate, and she was honest enough with herself to admit that her body yearned for the touch of his hands. Many nights she would toss and turn feverishly, trying to put an end to her torment.

Once Windhawk had touched her hand when he handed her a drink of water, and Joanna had been horrified that she found herself wishing he would take her in his arms. It was becoming a daily battle, trying to appear aloof and unmoved by him.

Joanna pulled up her mount and gazed at the breathtaking countryside. They were now in a valley which was surrounded by huge mountains, and had stopped at a small stream to water their horses.

Her eyes wandered downstream where she saw a herd of deer grazing on the sweet green grass that grew beside the water's edge. Her eyes widened when she saw several huge shaggy brown beasts with humps on their backs grazing alongside the deer. She knew without being told that the strange looking animals were buffalo. She was so intent on watching them that she had not been aware that someone rode up beside her.

Windhawk was scouting ahead and he had told Gray Fox to stay near Joanna. Gray Fox and the other Blood braves had not approached Windhawk's woman before, and he hesitated to speak to her now. He saw the awe in her eyes as she watched the buffaloes, and he smiled at her.

"If you will look above the overhanging ledge," he said, drawing Joanna's attention, "you will see the stag keeping watch."

Joanna's eyes followed his direction and she saw the proud animal standing as a sentinel, guarding against trouble. Its great antlered horns gleamed in the afternoon sunlight.

"He is magnificent," Joanna said, unable to tear her eyes away. Somehow the stag's magnificent aloofness reminded her of Windhawk.

She turned to Gray Fox and smiled. "This land is beautiful. It almost seems as if we're intruding where we do not belong."

Gray Fox nodded. "I sometimes feel that way myself, Joanna. This is the land of the Blackfoot!" he said with pride.

Joanna was surprised that this man had spoken to her since he had not done so before. She recognized him as the Indian who had taken her away from Running Elk, the day she had crossed the river in search of Tag.

"You speak English very well. May I ask your name?"

"I am called Gray Fox. I learned to speak English when I was very young, as did Windhawk. He did not care for the white man's tongue, so at that time he learned only what he needed to know to be able to trade with them. Later he realized that if he did not learn the white man's language he would be unable to communicate with them. As you know, he speaks the English good. That's the kind of man Windhawk is. If he wants to do something, he does it well."

"Tell me some of the Blackfoot words," Joanna urged, not wanting to talk about Windhawk. "What is the Blackfoot name for white man?"

"That would be *napik wan,* which means, old man person."

She repeated the words hesitantly and Gray Fox smiled at her encouragingly. She would point out different things and he would tell her the Blackfoot word for them.

Joanna soon forgot that Gray Fox was the enemy, and began to talk and laugh with him. When they rode away from the stream, Gray Fox rode beside her. He is a kind man, she thought. Somehow she couldn't associate him with raiding and murdering. But then she reminded herself that he was an Indian, like Windhawk. His views on what was right and wrong would be different from hers.

Windhawk had been strangely distant and withdrawn for several days now. He still slept in the tipi with Joanna, but he never came near her. She began to feel hurt by his disinterest in her, and she chided herself for caring. She should be glad that he didn't want to come near her. Most of the time he was not with the group of Indians who rode beside Joanna and she wondered why he was avoiding her. Perhaps he didn't care for her any more after she had so easily given in to him, allowing him to make love to her.

Joanna's thoughts were troubled. What if he had a wife who awaited his return? Maybe he had more than one wife, she thought in horror.

They had slowed their pace to ford a shallow stream and she turned to Gray Fox. "I have heard it said that it is permissible for the Blackfoot to have more than one wife. Can this be true?"

Gray Fox nodded soberly. "I, myself, have two wives. Is it not the custom in the white man's world to have more than one wife?"

Joanna felt dejected for some strange reason. "No, it is not permitted. Do most of your men have more than one wife?" she dared to ask.

Gray Fox smiled to himself, knowing why she was so curious. She thought Windhawk might already have a wife, and she was feeling jealous. If Windhawk had not already told her he had no wife, it was not his place to interfere.

"If a man is wealthy, then more often than not he will have more than one wife," he answered.

He scanned Joanna's beautiful face. He could see why Windhawk had been drawn to her. She was very beautiful, and it was only right that a great chief such as Windhawk should have such a woman to walk beside him.

Tag lifted the heavy waterskin and hoisted it up to his shoulder. As he approached Running Elk's lodge, he paused outside the entrance. The Indians were holding a council meeting and he knew if he entered now he would be severely punished. His back was already streaked with red welts. Running Elk had given him a beating with a leather whip just two days ago when he had caught Tag talking to Amanda.

157

He hung the waterskin on a wooden peg, then sat down, feeling miserable. He ached all over, but he reminded himself that his suffering in no way compared to Amanda's. She had been forced to stay in Running Elk's lodge, and Tag knew that the chief had taken her to his bed.

Hatred burned in his heart for the man who had raided the wagon train and caused his sister's death.

One of Running Elk's numerous wives passed by, and when she saw Tag sitting down, she picked up a big stick and began hitting him across the face. He held up his hands, trying to protect himself, but the heavy blows found their target. He stood up when she motioned for him to follow her. Tag knew to refuse would mean his death, and he had developed a strong sense of survival since becoming a captive. He had many reasons to live, not the least of which was revenge.

The first thing he must do was to get Amanda away from Running Elk. She no longer resembled the happy, smiling girl she had once been. Until two days ago he had only seen her one time, and that had been at a distance.

Amanda had been standing in front of Running Elk's lodge and Tag had crept around the corner, hoping to speak to her.

Her eyes had filled with tears when she saw him. She had then begged Tag to try to escape, telling him there was no hope for her.

Tag knew he would never leave Amanda behind. When he left the village she would be with him.

His sense of value had changed over the past weeks. Before the raid, the uppermost thought in his mind had been to get to his father so they could deal with his aunt and uncle. Now the most important thing in his life was just trying to stay alive.

Running Elk's wife caught Tag by the ear and shoved him down on his knees, motioning for him to pick up the grinding-stone to grind the corn. He did not hesitate, knowing the woman would punish him should she think he was not obeying her.

Tag could understand why Running Elk had taken Amanda as his captive, but he had no notion why the chief had spared his life.

He began pounding the corn under the watchful eye of Running Elk's wife. Somehow, someway, he would find a way to escape—but not before he avenged Joanna's death by killing Running Elk.

Once again tears blinded Tag's eyes. He was glad that Joanna had not lived to be taken captive by Running Elk; for had she lived, she would now be suffering the same fate as Amanda. But, oh, he did miss her so badly.

The night was quiet, and the campfire had died down, leaving only smoldering ashes. While the days were quite warm and pleasant, the nights were often cold. Joanna snuggled down between two buffalo robes, glad for their warmth.

She rubbed her arms and shoulders thinking they were stiff and sore from riding so much. She tried to calculate what the date was, but she had lost all track of time. It must be late September, she thought.

Joanna looked at the empty buffalo robe where

159

Windhawk always slept. She had decided the reason he no longer showed an interest in her was because he had a wife waiting for him. If he did, his wife might be jealous of another woman. Had Windhawk merely used her? she wondered bitterly. Could that be why he no longer looked at her? Yes, that must be why he was ignoring her. She felt hurt and jealous thinking of some dark-eyed wife waiting for Windhawk's return.

She closed her eyes, wishing for sleep, but her thoughts wouldn't allow her the peace of mind she craved. When was it that she had begun to feel jealous at the thought of Windhawk having a wife? Why did she feel rejected because he paid so little attention to her now?

Windhawk entered the tipi, and Joanna closed her eyes, pretending to be asleep. After a time she opened them a crack to see if he was sleeping. He was lying on the buffalo robe, and his eyes were closed. Her eyes traveled the length of his long, lean body, which was visible in the soft glow from the burning embers of the campfire.

Windhawk was lying on his back with his head resting against his folded arms. Joanna could not keep her eyes from wandering over his chest, which was bare, with the exception of the bear-claws that he wore about his neck. His shoulders were wide and muscular. Her eyes traveled down his chest to his stomach, and she felt a tightening in her throat.

Ashamed of her daring thoughts, Joanna glanced at his ebony hair. He had removed the leather band, and his dark hair fell loosely across his shoulders. Had there ever before been a man such as he? His darkly bronzed skin took on a golden hue in the soft glow inside the tipi.

Joanna drew in her breath when she looked at his eyes and saw that he was staring at her. Even from across the tipi, she could feel the intensity of his dark gaze. Forcing herself to turn over, she faced the wall of the tipi. Her body began to tremble with some wild, pent-up emotion, and she placed her hand over her mouth, willing those feelings to go away. Joanna was aware that he still stared at her, and buried her face in her hands.

What did she want from him? Was she so brazen that she wanted him to make love to her as he had before? Moments passed, and she thought she would scream from the tension that knifed through the air.

Joanna heard movement and turned over quickly, fearing Windhawk was approaching her. She watched as he left the tipi, and instead of feeling relieved, she felt rejected again. What was happening to her? She was changing, and it was very unsettling. Her nerves were on edge, as if waiting for something to happen. Why did Windhawk no longer come near her? Did he not want her any more? Suppose she had displeased him when he had made love to her. She had been inexperienced.

Joanna turned over on her back and stared at the top of the tipi where she could see tiny stars twinkling through the opening. She tried to remember the girl she had once been, but could not associate herself with the girl who had worn silks and satins and was served tea in an exquisite drawing room. That girl was gone forever. She now wore a shabby blue riding habit and slept on a buffalo robe. Her life was not her own, but was dictated by the chief of the Blackfoot Indians. She tried to remember Captain Thatcher's face, but it was only a vague shadow. She was becoming resigned to her fate, she thought. She had lost the will to escape.

Joanna was amazed at the beautiful lands they were now traveling through. There were mountains, forests, lakes, and rivers. The wildlife was abundant. Joanna had seen huge herds of buffalo, elk, deer, antelope, and many different varieties of waterfowl and wild duck. She remembered the day they had sighted a large herd of buffalo. The shaggy beasts had passed in a valley below them, and the thundering of their hooves could be heard long after they had passed from sight.

She could feel this land closing in on her, separating her from her father. How would she ever be able to find her way to him?

She couldn't picture herself living out the rest of her life in some Indian village. What would become of her? Windhawk was still so distant and cold to her. Had it not been for Gray Fox, she knew she would be completely alone. Gray Fox would often ride beside her, explaining the many things that she questioned. Joanna was pleased that she was rapidly picking up the Blackfoot phrases he had taught her, and could even speak a few sentences.

When they rode to the top of a small hill Joanna saw a wide river which stretched on for miles. On the other side of that river was an Indian village.

Joanna could see the numerous tipis and her heart felt heavy. She didn't need to be told they had reached Windhawk's village.

How could she be expected to just forget about her old life? She wouldn't, and no one could make her stay where she didn't want to be. She would never allow herself to lose her identity. She would always remember that she was Joanna James, daughter of Russell and Althea James.

Joanna saw the Indians urge their horses forward to cross the river and she looked about for Windhawk, but he was nowhere in sight. When Joanna was halfway across the wide river, Windhawk appeared at her side. He did not look at her, but merely kept pace with her horse.

She could see the large number of people standing on the opposite shore, waving and shouting. She felt fear and uncertainty, wondering what would become of her once they reached the village. She glanced sideways at Windhawk, but he was staring straight ahead. She could almost feel his tension, and wondered what he could be thinking.

When they rode out of the water, they were met by many smiling faces. Windhawk's horse reared on its hind legs but he quickly brought it under control.

Joanna was receiving several curious stares, and she tried to act unconcerned, but her heart was drumming with fear.

Windhawk dismounted and was quickly surrounded by his people. It was apparent they were happy to see him. Joanna waited tensely, not knowing what to expect.

Suddenly the crowd began to move aside, and Joanna saw two women move toward Windhawk. The first woman was older and Joanna thought she might be his mother, but the second one seemed even younger than herself, and was very lovely. First the elder woman embraced Windhawk, and they talked for a moment before he turned to the younger one. Joanna could see his eyes sparkle as the young Indian maiden threw herself into his arms. He laughingly picked her up and hugged her tightly. There was little doubt in Joanna's mind that this was his wife.

All at once Joanna became the center of attention. Young children plucked at her clothing, and the older women poked at her body. One woman grabbed a handful of Joanna's hair and yanked so hard that she cried out in pain.

Strong arms moved the women aside, and Windhawk lifted Joanna from her horse.

"No one will touch this woman. She belongs to me," he commanded in a loud voice.

Although Joanna couldn't understand Windhawk's words, she was grateful that he had apparently made her tormentors move away from her.

Windhawk spoke to his mother. "You will take this maiden to my lodge, my mother."

Joanna's eyes met dark, hostile eyes. It was very clear that the older woman did not like her at all. She took Joanna by the arm and pushed her in front of her as the others moved aside to allow them to pass. They walked past many tipis until they came to the center of the village where a huge lodge stood.

The woman gave Joanna a shove, and she went flying through the opening to land face down on the floor. Joanna was grateful for the soft buffalo hide that cushioned her fall.

This was not what Joanna termed a rousing welcome. She could feel this woman's hatred and hostility which was directed at her. If Windhawk's mother felt dislike for her, how would his wife react to her, she wondered.

She stood up and flung her head back proudly, daring the woman to touch her again.

The Indian woman pointed to a corner of the lodge, indicating that Joanna should sit down. After a long silent moment Joanna thought it might be best if she did as the woman wanted.

Moments later the flap was thrown aside and the younger girl entered. "My brother has asked that you come to him," Morning Song said to her mother, while stealing a glance at the beautiful white woman.

"My son will hear angry words from me for bringing this white one into our lodge," Sun Woman said, pushing past her daughter.

When her mother had gone, Morning Song walked slowly over to Joanna. She had heard her brother say that this was to be his woman. She picked up a waterskin and approached Joanna cautiously. Morning Song did not have to be told that her brother loved this woman. She had seen the tender look in his eyes when he had looked at her. She stared in wonder at the red-gold hair that graced the girl's beautiful head.

Morning Song's eyes were shining and bright,

and a slight smile eased her face. She could tell that the white girl was frightened, and she wanted to tell her that no one would harm her.

Morning Song held the waterskin out to Joanna, who took it and raised it to her lips, taking a deep drink.

"Thank you," Joanna said, handing the waterskin back to the girl. Joanna looked into the soft brown eyes and saw compassion there; somehow, they reminded her of Windhawk's eyes.

Joanna could easily see why Windhawk had chosen this girl as his wife. She was small-boned and petite. Her dark hair was unbraided, and her face was lovely. On closer inspection, Joanna realized the girl was not as old as she had first thought. She could be no more than thirteen or fourteen. Surely she was too young to be a wife.

"You are welcome," Morning Song replied in very good English. "My name is Morning Song, what is yours?" The only white women Morning Song had ever seen had been teachers at the mission school she had attended. None of them had been either young or beautiful.

"My name is Joanna. I am so grateful that you speak English. It seems like so long since I have had another female to talk with."

"Your name is very beautiful," Morning Song said, sitting down cross-legged beside Joanna. "Does it have a meaning?"

"Yes, it means a gift from God."

Morning Song nodded. "I have been taught about your God at the mission school. He is very fearful, is he not?"

Joanna smiled and her eyes lit up. "He is also very compassionate."

"Are you hungry, Joanna?"

Joanna knew if she took a bite of anything at this point it would stick in her throat. "No, thank you. I am sorry to intrude on you, but as you can see, I had very little choice in the matter."

Morning Song took Joanna's hand. "You are welcome in the lodge of Windhawk."

The lodge was filled with the delicious aroma of roasting buffalo meat and wild onions, sizzling over the cook-fire. Joanna looked about the lodge with interest. To her surprise, she found it was neat and clean. A pile of buffalo robes was stacked in one corner, and there were shields, spears, and several quivers of arrows hanging from the lodgepole. She refused to look at what she knew to be human scalps.

There seemed to be no evidence of children about. Perhaps Windhawk and Morning Song were childless.

Joanna's eyes strayed to the blue sky that was visible through the opening at the top of the lodge. She must bide her time. Surely there would be an opportunity to escape.


Windhawk was tethering his horse when his mother approached. He secured the rawhide strap about the horse's forelegs, and then stood up, smiling at Sun Woman.

"It has been many moons since I have looked upon your face, my mother. It is good to be home."

Sun Woman's eyes softened as she looked at her tall, handsome son. Her pride in him was great, for he was a powerful chief and was well loved by all his people. But she was not happy that he had brought the white woman to the village, and she was angry that he said the flaming-haired one was his woman. There were many young maidens from wealthy, influential families who would gladly be wife to her son. She had waited many years for Windhawk to choose a wife, but not a white one — never a white one!

"The days have been many since you departed, my son. I thank the great Napi that you have safely returned."

"You have seen to the comfort of my woman?" he asked.

"I put her in your lodge as you said, but I do not like to look upon the white-face."

Windhawk frowned, knowing that his mother, like all his people, had no love for the white race. Until he had seen Joanna, he had felt the same. "Joanna is not like the others, my mother. You will see this for yourself when you come to know her. She is brave, yet kind. Strong, yet gentle. In time you will grow to love her as a daughter."

Sun Woman would have liked to say she would never love the white-faced woman, but Windhawk was not only her son, he was also her chief, and his words were law. "Is it your wish that your sister and myself follow the custom and move into another lodge?"

"Yes, but not for a while. I want you and Morning Song to help Jo-anna become accustomed to our ways."

Sun Woman was still a very beautiful woman, and her gray-streaked hair did not detract from her beauty. She stood straight and proud, but she felt no pride in her heart at that moment. Her son would shame her in front of the whole tribe by taking the white girl as his woman. No one would say anything, but they would think it. She feared there would be trouble ahead for them all.

"Shall I go and prepare your bridal bed, my son?"

He placed his hand on her arm. "No, there will be no bridal bed. Our ways are new to Jo-anna, and while you are teaching her about our customs, I will teach her to trust me."

Sun Woman's eyes narrowed. How dare the white woman keep her son, the chief, waiting! she thought angrily. "Would it not be better to sleep with the woman without making her your wife? She will never be one of us."

Windhawk knew what his mother was feeling. He knew she would not easily accept Joanna, but with time she would grow to love her, just as in time, Joanna would learn to trust him.

"I love her, my mother. You know I have not loved before, nor will I love again. For me there is only Jo-anna."

Joanna could tell by the paling light that it was nearing evening. She had not moved from the buffalo robe where she had been told to wait by the older Indian woman.

Morning Song had left the lodge, and the older

woman had returned. Every so often she would cast a furtive glance in Joanna's direction.

Joanna's legs were feeling cramped, so she stood up. The Indian woman detected her movements and started speaking rapidly and pointing back to the robe, indicating that Joanna should remain where she was.

"No, I will not," Joanna said, standing her ground. "I am weary of you Indians telling me what to do," she said defiantly.

Sun Woman could not understand Joanna's words. Her son and daughter could speak the white man's language, but she had never had any desire to learn it. She frowned at the flaming-haired girl who dared defy her. Her son might be taken in by the girl's beauty, but she wasn't as easily fooled as Windhawk.

Sun Woman arose and crossed to the girl. Taking her by the shoulders, she tried to force her to sit down once more. Her dark eyes collided with hostile violet eyes, and in that moment Joanna and Sun Woman both knew they were adversaries. Both were strong-willed and determined, and neither of them would yield to the other.

Joanna shrugged the woman's hands from her shoulders and placed her hands on her hips. "If only you Indians could learn to ask nicely! Must you always force your will on others? You would definitely benefit from some social graces."

"*Kyai-yi,*" Sun Woman said, showing surprise that the white girl displayed so much courage. Was this girl a fool that she did not know she was defying the mother of the chief?

170

Several moments passed while they both sized each other up. At last Sun Woman gave Joanna a shove which landed her none too gently on the buffalo robe.

When Joanna could catch her breath, she rolled over and scrambled to her knees. Her eyes flashed dangerously as she slowly stood up.

"I have never struck another human being in my life, but if you ever do that again, I won't hesitate to defend myself," Joanna said angrily.

Sun Woman motioned once more for Joanna to sit down, but Joanna shook her head. At that moment Morning Song entered the lodge, and she quickly assessed the situation.

"My brother is coming," she told her mother.

"Then he can deal with this white-faced one," Sun woman said, returning to the cook-fire to see to her son's food.

"I will not stand for that woman's high-handed treatment," Joanna said to Morning Song.

Morning Song placed her hand on Joanna's arm. "I wish that you could be patient with her. She is a good and loving woman, but she clings to the old ways. Give her time and she will love you."

"I don't ask her love! I don't even care if she likes me. I only want her to leave me alone."

Morning Song's eyes were wide with surprise. "Do you not want the regard of Windhawk's mother?"

Joanna sat down, too weary to argue. "I only want to go home."

All at once the air seemed charged with electricity as Windhawk swept into the lodge. His eyes went first to Joanna. From what he could see, the three women he loved most in life were adjusting well to each other. He leaned over his mother's shoulder.

"I see that you have prepared my favorite meal, my mother. I have not eaten so well since I left home."

Sun Woman was still angry, and it showed in her voice. She motioned at Joanna with a nod of her head. "I do not think you will ever train that one to prepare your meals, my son. I think she will be useless."

Windhawk smiled and touched him mother's head. "I have confidence that you will teach her all she needs to know."

"She is insolent and does not take orders."

Windhawk's eyes blazed with admiration as he looked at Joanna. "Yes, she is all that and more."

Joanna glared at Windhawk. Did he expect her to sleep in the lodge with him, his wife, and his mother? What would she do when he retired for the night with Morning Song? This was a big tipi, but there would be very little privacy.

Morning Song touched Joanna's hand. "I know what you are feeling. Our ways are new to you. I would be just as lost as you, should I be taken to your world."

Joanna could not help but be touched by the lovely Indian girl. Somehow she envied her for being the wife of Windhawk.

"Do you love Windhawk very much?" she asked.

Morning Song's eyes went to her brother, who had sat down while her mother served him the buffalo meat. "Yes, he is the most wonderful man I

172

know. I love him very much."

"Would it bother you should he take another wife?" Joanna wanted to know.

Morning Song looked at Joanna with a puzzled expression. "I do not think you should worry about that. Windhawk has never before loved another woman. I do not think he will take any other wife. There are many beautiful maidens from powerful families who would like to be his wife, but he has never looked at them."

Joanna closed her eyes. What would Morning Song think if she knew that Windhawk had made love to her while declaring his love for her? He was completely faithless.

She looked across the room and found Windhawk watching her. What were his plans for her? If he didn't want her for his wife, why had he brought her to his lodge?

# Chapter Nine

The night was cold, and Tag huddled against the outside of the tipi, trying to stay warm. His clothing was tattered and torn and gave him very little protection from the cold. Tears of self-pity made a trail down his dirty face. When he tried to move, pain caused him to cry out.

He gritted his teeth, feeling the cold ground beneath him. Running Elk's face flashed through his mind, and it gave him the strength to bear his pain. He began to plan how he would get even with the chief.

Today, when Tag had gone to the stream for water, he had seen Amanda with two of Running Elk's wives. He had dropped the waterskin and run over to her. Amanda had grabbed him and hugged him tightly before one of the women had torn her away from him.

Amanda had cried out for Tag to help her when

the other woman dragged her away. Later Running Elk had sent for Tag and had beaten him severely with a leather strap, and ordered him tied outside the tipi without food or water.

Tag was cold and hungry and his body ached from the beating he had received, but his proud spirit was not broken. If anything he was more determined than ever to get away from Running Elk.

Tag groaned in pain. His shirt had stuck to his back from the blood of his open wounds. The cold hard ground offered him no comfort.

"I remember the promise I made you, Joanna. I will make Running Elk pay for what he did to you." Fresh tears spilled down his face. "I'm scared, Joanna," he cried, as a frightened child might call out to his mother.

Joanna lay on the soft robe, staring into the darkness. She was both puzzled and relieved that Windhawk had not approached her since she had been brought to the village. She lay on a soft buffalo robe beside Morning Song and Sun Woman, while Windhawk slept on the other side of the lodge.

She was so tired, she closed her eyes and drifted off to sleep, wondering how she would ever gain her freedom.

The next morning when Joanna awoke, she was surprised to find she had slept soundly all night. There was no sign of Windhawk.

The older Indian woman was bent over the

cookfire, and when Sun Woman heard Joanna stirring, she gave her a noncommittal glance. Morning Song was hoisting a waterskin on her shoulder and motioned for Joanna to follow her outside.

The sun shone down warmly as she and Morning Song passed through the village. Joanna was met with many curious stares, but no one approached her.

Joanna observed the camp with interest. Windhawk's lodge was the largest, and it stood in the center of the camp. On the outside of Windhawk's lodge there were several brightly painted birds with their wings spread as if in flight. There were many different and colorful animals painted on other lodges.

Joanna noticed the healthy, active children who were running around playing games. It was a scene of tranquility. The Indians seemed to live such a serene and peaceful life. They were a part of the land, and still existed as they had for hundreds of years.

Joanna saw a baby strapped to a cradleboard, and couldn't resist pausing to speak to the infant. The child was securely strapped to the board, which was propped against a tipi. The mother was nearby, grinding dried berries into a fine powder. Joanna bent down and took the child's hand.

"This is Gray Fox's son, by his first wife," Morning Song told Joanna. "He has another son, and a daughter, by his second wife."

"The child is beautiful. Will you tell his mother that for me?"

Morning Song nodded and began talking to Gray Fox's wife. The Indian woman smiled, and then said something in return.

"White Dove wishes me to tell you that she is honored that Windhawk's woman should find her child pleasing. She hopes that you and Windhawk have many healthy sons."

Joanna stood up abruptly, knowing her face was flushed. "I am not Windhawk's woman! You are his wife; not me."

Morning Song giggled and took Joanna's arm, leading her toward the river. "I am not Windhawk's woman—I am his sister. Did he not tell you that?"

Joanna was thoughtful and silent until they reached the river. "If you are not Windhawk's wife, then who is?"

Morning Song dipped the skin in the water and then stood up, smiling widely. "You are Windhawk's woman. He has not before taken a wife."

"No! I do not belong to him. He raided the wagon train I was traveling in and killed my brother and my friends. I will never forgive him for that."

Morning Song looked very distressed. "You are mistaken, Joanna. My brother did not raid the wagon train. He found you injured and helped you. You would have died had he not cared for you."

Joanna stared across the river, feeling angry. "If you believe that, then you believe a lie. Your brother is a murderer of innocent families who never harmed him in any way."

"I want to like you, Joanna, but if you say these things about my brother, I will turn away from you. I do not see any scars on you where you have been beaten or mistreated. I see no rope to hold you captive. You do not appear to be starving. Windhawk has not harmed you."

Joanna looked into the soft brown eyes that were sparkling with anger. "Some scars do not show, Morning Song. I have lost my brother and others that I loved. Those scars cannot be seen with the naked eye."

Morning Song's eyes softened. "I am sad in my heart at your loss, but you place the blame falsely."

"It is to your credit that you defend your brother, but let me assure you that I know of the harm he has done. If he is blameless, as you say, why does he keep me as a captive? Why will he not allow me to return to my people?"

"I do not know the answer to this. I only know that you are my brother's woman. You will learn to cook and keep his lodge clean. It would be better for you if you would accept this."

"Never! He can force me to stay, but I will never accept him."

"I do not understand. Do you not think Windhawk handsome?"

"Yes, I cannot deny he is handsome, but there is more to a man than just a fair appearance."

Morning Song's eyes showed her hurt and confusion. "There are many maidens who look upon my brother, wishing he would notice them, but he does not. Many times my mother has said to him that he must take a wife, but he would not. I saw the way Windhawk looked at you with love in his eyes. I think you are most fortunate to have a man of honor and kindness look at you with love."

Joanna shook her head. "I do not belong here, Morning Song. I can no more fit into your brother's world than he would fit into mine. I can never love the man who has caused the death of my people."

"I could tell you of many times your people have caused the death of my people, Jo-anna," Windhawk spoke up from behind her.

Joanna whirled around to face him, but before she could speak, he continued.

"I do not hold your people's faults against you."

"You are responsible for the death of my brother," she accused bravely.

Windhawk's eyes became dark storm centers. He had no wish to defend himself to Joanna. If she did not believe in him, then she could not love him as he loved her. He had been very patient with her up until now—but now she had gone too far. He was angered by her accusations. He grabbed her arm and pulled her back in the direction of the village, while Morning Song stared after them in surprise.

"Stop, you are hurting me," Joanna protested, trying to pry his strong grasp from her wrist.

He picked her up in his arms and held her tightly as he continued through the village. Joanna could hear jeers and laughter from some of the men and women, and was grateful that she couldn't understand what was being said.

When they reached Windhawk's lodge, he carried her inside.

Sun Woman looked startled for a moment, until Windhawk spoke to her. She nodded her head and left the lodge hurriedly.

"W . . . What are you . . . going to do to me?" Joanna asked fearfully.

"I am going to do what I should have done from

the start," he answered, placing her on her feet, but retaining his hold on her.

"I don't want you to touch me!" she cried.

His hand slid up to her face. "Do you not, Jo-anna? I think you do."

"No, please don't. I'll never give in to you without a fight."

His lips brushed against her cheek. "You can fight me, Jo-anna, but I will win in the end."

She swallowed a lump of fear, making a quick decision. She wouldn't fight him; she would remain passive. Surely a man would not enjoy a woman who showed no emotions.

He picked her up and laid her on the buffalo robe. Joanna lay stiffly, as he removed his fringed shirt and tossed it aside. When he lay down beside her, she willed herself not to think or feel. He reached for her hand, and when he caressed her long sensitive fingers, she felt a flicker of something. No, don't think or feel, she cautioned herself, in a panic.

Her eyes flew open as he raised her hand to his lips and kissed each of her fingertips. She looked into his face, and his dark eyes burned so brightly they seemed to scorch her with their intensity.

"If you go through with this, I will hate you," Joanna told Windhawk, horrified that her voice came out in a throaty whisper.

"You already hate me. What will I lose?" he said, unfastening her gown.

She closed her eyes again as his lips settled on her neck. He pushed her gown aside to expose her breasts, and she gasped when his lips moved over the silken peaks.

"You are mine, Jo-anna. The time will come when you will know this."

She opened her eyes, not knowing that they were laced with passion. Windhawk knew he had the ability to arouse her body, but that wasn't all he wanted from Joanna—he wanted everything. He wanted to share all the things in life with her that a husband and wife shared. He wanted her violet-colored eyes to light up with happiness when he came to her.

"I will never submit to you again, Windhawk," she challenged.

His dark eyes blazed—he accepted the challenge. Windhawk pulled her into his arms, and his lips settled softly on hers.

At first Joanna struggled, trying to free herself, but she knew she was losing the battle as her love-starved body trembled when his hand moved caressingly across her breasts. She was no longer capable of objecting when he ran his hand over her back, pushing her gown downward. She ceased to struggle when she felt her naked flesh come in contact with his hard body. Joanna's body quaked with excitement when he dipped his head and covered her aching breast with his mouth. She groaned when his tongue circled the rosebud tip. Her hand slid up his back, and she gathered up a handful of ebony hair. Each move he made was designed to tease and torment her into submission. His hand moved to her parted thigh and he gently massaged her throbbing, aching, inner core.

Joanna buried her face against his neck, clamping her lips tightly together to keep from crying out as his expert hands brought her to the brink of surrender.

She tried to remind herself that she had sworn to be passive but his lips nibbled at her earlobes, then slid across her face to settle on her arched neck. His silky black hair brushed against her face, sending shivers down her spine. Miraculously, Joanna found herself completely undressed. She had no thought beyond the warm, hard body that pressed against her. Windhawk had only his breechcloth on and she wished he would remove that. Her arms went around his shoulders, and her parted lips invited his kiss.

Windhawk was poised above her and his head dipped to taste her soft mouth. In the back of Joanna's mind she knew she should be fighting him, but instead, her hands wandered across his shoulders, feeling the corded muscles underneath.

I love him, she thought with no surprise at all. He is my enemy, but I love him. It seemed the most natural thing in the world to have his lips pressed to hers. Again she had the feeling that she had known him in another time and place. It was an unsettling feeling, as if she had been loved by him many times before.

Windhawk raised his head and stared into her eyes. He could read total surrender in her violet-blue gaze. She was now his to do with as he wished. Her sweet body was issuing him an invitation, and he wanted her, but he must first show her that he was the master. Joanna must learn that she belonged to him, and he could arouse her desire any time he wanted.

Joanna was startled when he smiled and pulled away from her. She was crushed when he stood up and put his shirt on. Did he not want her? She felt totally humiliated when he handed her her gown.

"No one, not even you, Jo-anna, can say you are not the woman of Windhawk," he said. "Do not think I cannot take you any time I want."

Joanna was too filled with shame to answer, and she leaned forward so her long curtain of hair would hide her flaming face.

"Do you not think it would be wise for you to put your clothing on, Jo-anna? My mother and sister could return at any moment."

Raising her head, she saw Windhawk was standing in an arrogant stance, with his legs spread apart and his hands resting on his hips. Shame and anger brought a blush to Joanna's cheeks. She held her gown in front of her to hide her nakedness. Tears of frustration fell down her face as she watched him leave the lodge. She knew he had proved his point. How easily he had made her submissive to his touch.

When Windhawk was outside, he took a deep breath of air, knowing the last thing in the world he wanted to do was leave Joanna at that moment. Her creamy flesh had been so soft and inviting, and her eyes had registered total surrender. He had wanted to prove to her that he could awaken her body with very little effort, and he had done that—but what about the fire that still burned within his own body? No one could tame that fire but Joanna. He was a man experiencing love for the first time, and that

183

love was wild and uncontrollable. Windhawk knew he had been pushed to the limit, and tonight he would take Joanna, even if she fought him.

He thought of the long knife he had once seen her dancing with and wondered if she had loved that man. Windhawk felt jealousy burn within his heart. He could not bear to think of any man holding her in his arms.

He had the satisfaction of knowing he had been the first man to have her beautiful body, but did the other man hold her heart? Even if the long knife were now dead, he still troubled Windhawk's mind.

Throughout the long day there were many times when Joanna reproached herself for the reaction she'd had to Windhawk. He had humbled her into submission and then left her. Her heart felt heavy and bruised because she now knew that she was hopelessly in love with him.

Love wasn't something one invited, and in her case it had taken her unaware. Could the first flicker of love have come to her that first day when Windhawk had saved Tag's life?

Morning Song said that Windhawk loved her, but Joanna thought Windhawk's sister must have been mistaken. He could not love her if he had taken the life of her brother. At least not the true lasting love that she desired.

All day Sun Woman kept Joanna busy, and she welcomed the hard work, hoping it would distract her from thinking about Windhawk. But it didn't matter how hard Joanna worked, he still dominated her thinking.

She had been amazed at how easily she had followed Sun Woman's silent directions. She had helped grind chokeberries and chop buffalo meat. Morning Song had told her that they were making a food called *pemmican*. The meat would be pounded and mixed with berries and fat, then allowed to dry. It would then be stored for the long winter months when food was sometimes scarce.

Joanna sighed, feeling as if she had done something useful. She smiled when Morning Song handed her the waterskin to drink from. After her thirst had been eased, Joanna glanced at Sun Woman, hoping the older woman would show her approval at the work she had done, but Sun Woman showed no emotion whatsoever.


Windhawk rode away from the village at the head of his warriors. His plans for taking Joanna as his wife would have to wait until he returned. There had been a report that a group of Crow warriors had been seen near the mouth of the Milk River. The Crow were old enemies and must be driven from the Blackfoot lands.


Windhawk had been gone for several days. He had not told Joanna where he was going, and she had been too proud to ask when he would return.

The days Joanna spent with Sun Woman and Morning Song passed quickly because they were so busy. It was the nights which were long and lonely. Sometimes Joanna would lie awake listening to the sounds coming from the village: the barking of dogs and the sound of laughter that filtered into the lodge. She would listen to the singing and chanting which would often go on way into the night. At these times Joanna would realize that she was an outsider, because she was never included in any of the festivities.

Joanna was working beside Sun Woman and Morning Song. They were enjoying a quiet sort of companionship, as they dried the meat from a large buck which would provide them with food in the long winter months ahead.

Joanna had learned that Windhawk not only provided meat and skins for his mother's and sister's needs, but he often gave aid to the poor families of his tribe. She was amazed at how a Blackfoot man would take such good care of his family. The wealthy members of the tribe were expected to help the less fortunate. Windhawk would often give a whole deer or a buffalo to a needy family.

Since Windhawk had no sons to help him with his large herd of horses, he allowed several boys from poor families to tend his horses, thus giving them the experience and rewarding their families with meat and horses.

It was as if all the tribe belonged to a big family, with each member helping the other when the need arose. Joanna thought of the difference between the Indian world and the world she came from. The whites did not share the brotherhood that the Blackfoot took for granted.

She had often observed Gray Fox's two wives, surprised at how well they got along. Morning Song had told her the two wives were also sisters. It was a strange relationship, to say the least. They each watched over all the children, drawing no line between which child was their own. Joanna knew if she were married, she would never allow her husband to have another wife.

Joanna saw a woman pass by that she had often observed from a distance. The woman's nose had been cut off and she had been horribly disfigured. The other members of the tribe seemed to turn away from her when she walked by, as if they were shunning her. The woman's eyes were downcast, and she was little more than skin and bones.

Joanna felt pity in her heart for the poor, unfortunate woman. "Morning Song, who is that woman?" she asked, nodding to the disfigured woman.

"Do not look at her. Her name is Flying Bird, and she has disgraced her husband by being with another man. The society her husband belongs to had her nose cut off so all who saw her would know she was unworthy to look upon."

Joanna's eyes widened in horror. "What happened to the man?"

"Flying Bird's husband claimed his horses and then beat him," Morning Song replied.

"It does not seem fair that the woman was so severely punished and the man got off so easily," Joanna said, shivering at the injustice.

Sun Woman had been listening to the conversation, and she glanced at Joanna. "It is a bad thing for a wife to dishonor her husband."

Joanna found many things to admire about the Blackfoot people, but some things seemed harsh and unfair to her. She compared their laws with the laws which had allowed her uncle to come into her home and take over her and Tag's lives. Perhaps all societies had their bad laws, but the incident made her more aware than ever that she didn't belong to Windhawk's world.

It didn't matter how hard Joanna worked to prove herself to Sun Woman Windhawk's mother still looked at her sourly and very rarely talked to her unless it was to criticize her.

There was a great commotion; dogs started barking, and women and children started shouting and running toward the river.

Joanna's heart leaped in her throat when she saw Windhawk and several of his braves crossing the river. Everyone in the village had gone to meet the returning warriors except Joanna. She watched with misgivings as Windhawk approached. She fought against allowing him to see her joy at his return.

When Windhawk saw Joanna, he rode past the others until he reached her. She raised her eyes to give him a defiant look, but her mouth opened in surprise. His face was painted! There were black streaks across the bridge of his nose that fanned out over his cheeks.

"Are you not glad to see me, Jo-anna?" he asked as he dismounted.

She raised her head haughtily. "No! Why should I be?" Joanna tried not to stare at his face, but she had never seen him wear face paint before. It somehow made him appear menacing.

"Are you on the warpath?" she couldn't help

asking.

He smiled slightly. "No. Why should you think hat?"

"Your appearance is . . . your face is painted."

He laughed aloud. He had forgotten that his face was painted. "Going to war is not the only time the Blackfoot paint their faces, Jo-anna."

"I wasn't expecting you so soon," she said, hoping he wouldn't suspect she had missed him.

He smiled as if he knew what she was thinking. "I have a gift for you, Jo-anna."

"I don't want your gift," she said. In spite of her words, her curiosity was piqued.

His lips curled into a smile. "If you do not want the gift, I will just keep it," he told her, watching her face closely.

She lowered her eyes, studying the tip of her riding boot. After a moment of silence she raised her eyes to him. "What is it?"

"You will have to walk with me if you want me to show it to you."

He took her arm and led her to his lodge. Joanna saw a white horse tied out front, and she frowned, thinking it looked familiar.

Windhawk watched her footsteps lag and her face light up.

"Fosset!" She ran to the horse and moved her hand lovingly over his haunches. "Fosset, my poor baby! What has happened to you?"

The once proud animal was little more than skin and bones. His mane was matted with burrs, and his once sleek hair was caked with mud.

Fosset whinnied and shook his mane as if he recognized Joanna. "What has happened to him?" she asked Windhawk. "He appears to have been mistreated."

Windhawk reached out and patted Fosset's neck. "Tall Bear found him wandering freely but three days ago. I recognized him as your horse and gave Tall Bear three of my horses for him." Windhawk smiled slightly. "Tall Bear could not understand why I would pay so much for such a bag of bones. You and I know when Fosset has had the proper care, he will be worth twelve horses."

Joanna laid her head against Fosset's neck. He was her last link to her past life. "Thank you for bringing him to me, Windhawk. I am so glad to have him back. If the truth were known, Fosset probably saved my life."

"How can that be?"

"We had been forced to hitch Fosset to the wagon, and he did not take well to the halter. It was his fault that the wagon went over the cliff."

Windhawk nodded in understanding, guessing just what had happened. "We shall have to see that Fosset gets the best of care."

After Fosset had been washed down and the burrs removed from his mane, he was given hay and grain and put out to pasture. He would now be able to frolic and romp with Windhawk's horses until he grew stronger.

Windhawk held his hand out to Joanna, and she shyly placed her hand in his. His dark eyes drew her gaze, and Joanna felt a flicker of excitement.

She wondered if tonight he would take her in his arms and show her the warm loving world he had once introduced her to. Her face flamed, and she lowered her head, but not before Windhawk caught the wistful look in her eyes. He laughed softly, thinking it would not be too long before he would have Joanna where he wanted her. But he knew unless she was willing, he might frighten her away. Perhaps he would give her more time before he took her as his wife. He had already begun to construct a tipi for his mother and sister. It would be completed by tomorrow.

Windhawk was known for his patience, and he had exercised a great deal of tolerance where Joanna was concerned.

Joanna's disappointment deepened when Windhawk showed no more interest in her the rest of the day. When she went to sleep that night her thoughts were troubled. She lay restlessly beside Morning Song, wishing for sleep.

Every so often her eyes would stray to where Windhawk lay across the room from her. He was a puzzlement to her. He had been kind and considerate of her feelings today when he had given Fosset back to her. Tonight he acted as if she didn't even exist.

Joanna closed her eyes, remembering how his wonderful hands had felt caressing her body. Was she a fool, that she wanted that which would destroy her in the end? She should be counting her blessings that Windhawk was ignoring her. She should be . . . but she wasn't.

## Chapter Ten

Several weeks had passed since Windhawk first brought Joanna to the Blackfoot village. She had settled into a daily routine of hard work. There was no longer any resentment in her, because somewhere along the way she had become resigned to her new life. Deep inside she knew she was only biding her time until she would be able to return home. Until that time she would have to accept that which she could not change.

Sun Woman had sent Joanna into the forest to gather firewood. It was the first time Joanna had been allowed to be alone, and her heart felt light. As she made her way through the woods, she almost forgot her mission had been to gather wood.

She turned around in a wide circle and gazed at the beauty of the multi-colored leaves on the large cottonwood and birch trees.

It felt so good not to be under the watchful eye of

Sun Woman. Joanna gathered up several bright scarlet-colored leaves and tucked them into the pocket of her frayed riding habit. Hearing a soft chattering sound, she looked up to observe a furry gray squirrel leaping from branch to branch, then scampering into a hole in the tree.

Walking a little further into the woods Joanna stood beneath a huge pine tree. She loved the way its branches were spread wide and reached into the heavens, as if hoping to gather a piece of the sky. Her heart was attuned to nature in this wild and untamed land. Joanna knew that when she left she would always remember the beauty she had found here.

As she absentmindedly picked up several pieces of wood, her mind seemed to transfer to the tall chief of the Blackfoot. She very rarely saw him any more, and when she did, he seemed totally unaware of her.

What did he want with her? she wondered. Too often now she would remember the closeness they had shared, and found herself wanting him to notice her. She was changing against her will. She feared she had become complacent with her life, except where Windhawk was concerned. Sometimes at night she would dream of his hands touching her in the most intimate way. She would awaken, yearning for him to hold her in his strong arms.

Joanna dumped the wood she had gathered into a pile, and sat down, resting her head on her knees. Had Windhawk been dissatisfied with her the night they had made love? she wondered. Was that why he never came near her any more? Joanna didn't

193

like the way her mind was beginning to work, so she stood up and gathered up the discarded wood. She knew Sun Woman would not be pleased if she didn't hasten back to camp.

Windhawk stood in the shadows of a pine tree and observed Joanna. Her beauty was not marred by the shabby gown she wore. He had exercised forbearance where she was concerned, waiting for her to become accustomed to the Blackfoot ways. Many times he wanted to go to her and gather her into his arms while pouring out his love for her.

Windhawk noticed the glorious curtain of Joanna's hair hanging down her back like a flaming rivulet. Her slender body was so sweetly curved that he felt his body ache to hold her close to his.

He smiled at himself—tonight was the night he would take Joanna as his wife. He had finished the tipi for his mother and sister, and they were now moving some of their belongings into it. He felt wild excitement knowing that tonight he would caress that silky skin and taste those inviting lips.

Joanna heard a twig snap and turned around quickly to find Windhawk standing just behind her. Her face flamed because she had been thinking of him, and feared he would be able to tell.

He smiled and took the wood from her. "My sister tells me that you are learning to speak our language, Jo-anna. I want you to know this pleases me greatly," he said in the Blackfoot language.

"It is very . . . difficult to learn," she answered him, stumbling into the unfamiliar language.

"I am on my way to see how Fosset is doing. Would you like to ride along with me?"

194

Joanna looked into the black eyes that were as soft as velvet. "Oh, please, may I?"

He smiled. "Yes, but first we will take the wood to my mother."

Joanna had to run to keep up with his long strides. She was excited at the thought of getting away from the village, if only for a short time. Windhawk saw that she was having trouble keeping pace with him, so he slowed his steps to match hers. He smiled to himself, thinking he would have to learn to match his steps with those of a woman from now on . . . his woman — Joanna!

Joanna rode on a pinto pony and had no trouble keeping up with Windhawk's large stallion. It was wonderful to feel the sun on her face and the wind in her hair. Her eyes were bright with excitement, and Windhawk smiled at her childlike pleasure.

Soon they reached a secluded valley, and Joanna saw the large herd of horses that frolicked about playfully. It took her only a few seconds to locate Fosset. Nudging the pinto forward, she rode up to the white horse and dismounted. She walked around Fosset, examining him carefully, and seeing that he was completely recovered. Joanna blessed Windhawk with a smile.

"Thank you for taking such good care of my horse," Joanna said, smiling brightly.

Windhawk dismounted and ran his hand over Fosset's silky mane. Joanna was watching his hand as he stroked and caressed the horse. She felt a tightening in her throat, remembering what it felt like to have those hands caress her body. She glanced quickly into Windhawk's face and saw that he was watching her closely.

"Would you like to ride him, Jo-anna? He should not be ridden for any distance yet, but it will do Fosset no harm if you want to ride him here in the valley."

Joanna could not find her voice, so she merely nodded. Windhawk placed his hands about her tiny waist and lifted her upward. For a brief moment she was suspended above his head, and stared into burning black eyes. She felt her body tremble as his hands seemed to burn into her skin, even through her clothing.

Windhawk placed her on Fosset's back and smiled, knowing that the time was right to take Joanna unto himself. Her eager young body was ripe and willing. He knew she would fight him. It would be hard for her to accept being his wife at first, but not for very long, he thought confidently.

Joanna reached down and patted Fosset's neck and he whinnied. She was sure he recognized her and was glad to see her. Suddenly, she had the urge to ride the gelding swiftly, and she looked down at Windhawk.

"Will you accept a challenge?" she offered.

He raised a black eyebrow. "I have, and I will."

"I will race you to that far pine tree just beyond the valley."

Windhawk leaped on his stallion. "Jo-anna, there should be a reward to the winner of the race. Shall I name the terms?" he questioned.

"Yes, that will be fair," she agreed, feeling whatever the challenge, Fosset wouldn't let her down.

Windhawk looked serious for a moment. "If you

win, I will give *Puh Pom* to you."

Joanna nodded hesitantly, feeling he was much too confident. "If you win, will you expect me to give Fosset to you?"

He smiled and reached across to push a flaming curl away from her cheek. "No, should I win I will tell you what I expect from you."

This time Joanna agreed wholeheartedly. Fosset was prancing about and it was difficult to hold him in check without a rein.

"Done," Joanna said, nudging Fosset into a run. She laughed and looked over her shoulder as Windhawk raced about five paces behind her. She was confident that he would not be able to catch her. She laughed out loud as Fosset came to a clump of bushes and leaped over them with easy grace.

As they raced swiftly through the valley, Joanna was sure there had never been an animal to match Fosset. The other horses scattered when they approached them, and Joanna glanced back at Windhawk to find he was gaining on her. She began to feel uncertain of Fosset's ability and bent low over his neck, urging him faster.

When they neared the tree which was their destination, Fosset was at his top speed. Joanna glanced sideways to see that Windhawk had drawn even with her. Had she been foolish to issue a challenge to Windhawk? She watched in dismay as his horse shot out into the lead and he pulled up his mount when he reached the tree.

When Joanna reached his side she halted Fosset. "You won," she said, with very little enthusiasm.

"Perhaps it was an unfair race, Jo-anna. Fosset is

accustomed to taking orders with a bit in his mouth," Windhawk offered generously.

"What will you claim as your prize?" Joanna asked, raising her head and looking him full in the face.

Without speaking, Windhawk reached out to her and lifted her onto his horse. Joanna looked up into his face shyly, expecting to see a triumphant smile, but instead she was met with a searching glance from his dark eyes.

"My reward is to taste your lips," he whispered.

Joanna had no time to think as he dipped his head and his lips lightly caressed her mouth. Raising his head, he shifted her back so her head rested against his arm. Joanna was too stunned to react as his lips moved closer to hers. She heard a groan as his mouth covered hers, but she didn't know if the sound had come from her or Windhawk.

They had each hungered for the other's touch for so long that they were lost in the beauty of the kiss. Joanna's arms went around his neck and his hands slid down her back in a caressing movement.

Suddenly Windhawk broke off the kiss, much to Joanna's disappointment. She glanced up at him to see an amused smile on his face. Too confused to speak, she lowered her eyelashes as her face flamed. Windhawk laughed and raised her chin.

"Never have I received such a valuable reward after winning a race." He touched her cheek. "Would you care to have another race, Jo-anna?"

"No!" she answered hurriedly, trying to get down. "I want to go home."

Joanna had not realized that she had referred to

the Blackfoot village as her home, but Windhawk noticed.

"I will take you home," he said, laughing once more. Without hesitating he placed Joanna back on Fosset and they rode away from the valley.

Joanna's mind was troubled. After ignoring her for so long, why had Windhawk suddenly decided to pay attention to her today? she pondered.

She was further puzzled when they rode along silently as if nothing had happened between them. When they reached Windhawk's dwelling, Joanna slid off Fosset's back and entered the lodge without a backward glance.

She heard Windhawk ride away and she leaned against the lodgepole, trying to quiet her thundering heart. What a strange man Windhawk was! Joanna had ceased to fear him; she feared instead her own wayward heart.

It was now evening and the shadows of night had begun to fall. Sun Woman handed Joanna a doeskin gown, and motioned that she was to put it on.

"My mother says Windhawk wishes you to wear this gown, Joanna," Morning Sun told her.

Joanna held up the soft doeskin gown, noticing that it was embroidered with many different colored beads. "Why?" she asked, puzzled.

"Windhawk wishes you to put your old life behind you and look to your new life."

Joanna set her jaw stubbornly. Even though her blue riding habit was worn in places and faded from many washings, she had no intention of wearing the Indian gown, nor did she intend to forget who she was. How could Joanna forget that she had a father who would be worried sick about her by now.

"I will wear my own gown, Morning Song. I will not allow your brother to tell me how to dress."

Morning Song's eyes widened in admiration. She would never have the courage to defy her brother. She loved him and he had always been kind to her, but he was the chief, and no one had the right to refuse his commands.

"I would not want you to be punished, Joanna. It would be wise if you would do as Windhawk says."

Joanna folded her arms in a stance of defiance. "No, I will not wear this gown."

Sun Woman's eyes twinkled when she realized that the white girl was refusing the gown. Her son would show the flaming-haired one that his word was not to be disputed. She wished that she would be able to watch when he punished the girl for her disobedience.

Morning Song shook her head. "Please, Joanna. I do not think you understand that my brother said you were to wear the gown."

"I understand all right, but I am not of your tribe; therefore I am not subject to Windhawk's commands."

Morning Song's eyes were sad. "My mother and I must leave you now. When we are gone, Windhawk will come to you."

Joanna noticed that Sun Woman was gathering up clothing and blankets, which she wrapped into a bundle. "Where are you going? Can I not go with you?"

"My mother and I have been moved to a new tipi which my brother had erected for us. This is now your lodge."

Joanna grabbed Morning Song's hand. "You cannot leave me alone with him! Please ask your mother to allow me to accompany you."

"It is not my mother's decision. You will have to ask Windhawk."

Joanna watched helplessly as Morning Song and Sun Woman left. She wanted to beg them to take her with them. She had very little time to reflect on her fears, however, for at that moment Windhawk swept into the lodge.

He looked at her, and then at the gown she had thrown on the floor. He said nothing as he walked over to her and picked up the gown. Joanna gritted her teeth when he extended it to her.

"First, you can put this on and then I will have my meal," he said in a quiet voice that was laced with irony.

"You can eat or not, that is your privilege. But I will not put that gown on." She raised her head and clenched her fists tightly together.

"You will put on the gown; then *you* will serve the meal, Jo-anna."

"Not as long as you live," she said in a voice that trembled with anger.

He reached out and took her arm. Joanna flinched, fearing he would strike her, but he only laughed softly. "Jo-anna, do you remember the horse I once told you about?"

She blinked in astonishment. "Yes," she replied, wondering what point he was trying to make. She had expected him to be angry with her. She waited, not knowing what to expect because he had thrown her off balance for the moment.

"You will remember that I told you I trained her with patience and kindness?"

"Yes, I remember," she said, wondering where his reasoning was taking him.

He smiled as he began to unfasten her gown. "I have found that one can gain more with patience than with force where a woman is concerned."

Joanna bristled. "I just bet you have had plenty of experience with women." She did not know that her lips curved into an appealing pout.

He raised his eyebrows. "I would not be truthful with you if I said I had not."

She raised her chin. "I don't want to hear about your other women."

There was amusement in Windhawk's eyes. "I have no intention of telling you about my past. I was speaking of my horse, if you will remember." He took a step closer to her.

"What are you going to do?" she questioned fearfully.

"I have a desire to see you in the soft doeskin gown. My mother and sister made this gown for you. Do you not think it fine?"

Joanna had expected his anger and she could have dealt with that; however, she did not know how to handle this mood. She stood still while he lifted her frayed riding habit over her head. She was too amazed to even feel embarrassment. Windhawk seemed totally uninterested in her nakedness. He slipped the doeskin gown over her head, and then stood back to admire her.

"Something is missing," he said. He led her over

to the buffalo robe, sat her down, and picked up a pair of knee-high moccasins Morning Song had placed there for Joanna. Slipping off her boots, he pulled the moccasins up over her calves and laced them. When that was completed he took her hand and helped her to her feet. Windhawk's eyes roamed over her approvingly.

"You were beautiful before, Jo-anna, but now you are even more so."

Joanna beamed at his praise. Did he truly think her beautiful? she wondered. She had to admit that the doeskin gown felt soft next to her skin, and it allowed her greater freedom of movement than her frayed riding habit had. Besides being worn and faded her blue habit was torn in several places. Yes, she would wear the doeskin gown, she thought, since it seemed to pleased Windhawk.

She was not aware that the gown hugged and molded her beautiful body. Nor did she know that the tint in her cheeks was very appealing to Windhawk.

"Come," he said, taking her hand. "We will eat together."

Joanna allowed him to lead her to the cook-fire and sit her down on the soft buffalo robe. He knelt down, dished up some meat into a wooden bowl, and handed it to her. She took it reluctantly, still dazed by his gentle treatment. When he filled his bowl with the meat, he sat down beside her.

"I . . . I had always believed that Indian men ate before their women," Joanna said, looking into his eyes questioningly.

"That is the practice, but between you and me,

Jo-anna, we will each try to respect the other's feelings."

Joanna blinked, not knowing what to expect next.

Windhawk picked up a piece of meat from his bowl and held it out to her. Joanna hesitated for only a moment before taking it into her mouth. She found the meat tender and delicious.

"Jo-anna, do you remember me telling about the mare who ate from my hand?" Windhawk said with an amused smile.

Joanna stopped chewing, realizing the significance of his words. Oh yes, she remembered only too well. He was implying that he now had her eating out of his hand.

"What's that supposed to mean?" she asked arching an eyebrow daringly.

"Do you like the meat?" he asked ignoring her question, and smiling slightly.

"Yes but . . ."

"Let us get to know one another, Joanna," he said interrupting her. "You will tell me about yourself, and then I will tell you about me."

"I know that you are not married, Windhawk. Why is that?" Joanna asked without thinking. "Gray Fox has two wives."

He touched her hair softly. "I was waiting for you, Jo-anna." His eyes caught and held her gaze. She felt as if she were drowning in the dark depths. "When I first saw you, Jo-anna, I knew that we would one day be together."

"I don't belong in this world, Windhawk."

He drew in a deep breath, thinking now was not

204

the time to tell her she belonged wherever he was. "Tell me about your life, Jo-anna."

Joanna took a bite of the meat and chewed it while she thought where to begin. "I was born and raised in England. I came to this country with my mother, father, and Tag," her voice broke. "They are all dead except my father."

"Was your mother also on the wagon train?"

"No, she died of an illness before we joined the wagon train."

"Where is your father?"

"He is in Oregon waiting for Tag and me. He will not know what has happened to us."

"Where is this Oregon?"

"It is on the western shores of the Americas."

He tilted her chin up. "Jo-anna, I am grieved that your little brother is dead. I loved him because he was brave, but I loved him mostly because he belonged to you."

Joanna saw the sincerity in his eyes, and she knew in that moment that he had had nothing to do with the raid on the wagon train. "Why didn't you tell me?" she asked.

He didn't need to ask what she meant. He knew that she had now realized that he hadn't ordered the raid on the wagon train. "I waited for you to know in your heart that I could never harm you, or anyone you love."

Joanna felt tears in her eyes. How could she ever have thought that Windhawk had committed such an atrocity? Her heart swelled with love for him. He was so sensitive and kind. She had never known anyone like him before. She didn't want to love him, but she couldn't seem to help herself.

Windhawk saw the different emotions play across her beautiful face. He knew she was wrestling with her feelings, but he didn't know why.

"How did you find me when I was at the bottom of the gorge?"

"I heard that Running Elk had raided the wagon train. I came to look for you, fearing you had been killed, or that Running Elk had taken you as his captive."

"Why did Running Elk attack the wagon train? There was so much senseless killing."

"I do not mean to defend Running Elk to you, but his people and mine have been badly treated by your race. He did not consider it wrong to raid the wagon train."

"But why? I need to know, so I can justify my brother's death."

Windhawk picked up a shining red-gold curl and ran it through his fingers. "He wanted you, Joanna."

"What are you saying?"

"When he saw you at the river, he wanted you."

Many things became clear to Joanna at that moment. She remembered being held in Running Elk's tipi. He had meant to take her as a captive that day, but Gray Fox had prevented it by taking her to Windhawk.

"You saved me from Running Elk the day Tag crossed the river, didn't you?"

"No, Gray Fox was the one who saw you and brought you to me."

"But Running Elk would never have relinquished

me had Gray Fox not threatened to tell you I was being held against my will, would he?"

Windhawk laid his uneaten food aside and took Joanna's hand in his. "What does it matter? You are safe now. I will never allow anyone to harm you," he said in a deep, meaningful voice.

Joanna reached up and touched his face. "I have been blaming you for so many things when I should have been thanking you. Why did you put up with my little tantrums? I feel like such a fool."

He closed his eyes as her hand drifted across his face to touch his mouth. "Forgive me, Windhawk, for all the horrid things I said to you."

Opening his eyes he scanned her face, searching for any sign of love, but he saw nothing but gratitude in her eyes. "There is nothing to forgive. I lay no blame on you."

Joanna could feel him weaving a magic spell about her, so she decided to change the subject before she was lost forever. "Tell me about your childhood."

He smiled. "There isn't much to tell. I had a good boyhood. My father was a great warrior and chief. He taught me many things. My mother is a kind and loving woman and I also learned from her."

Joanna didn't agree with his assessment of his mother, but then perhaps she was being unfair. She had been stubborn and willful since being brought to Windhawk's lodge. Perhaps if she hadn't acted like such an ungracious guest, Sun Woman might have accepted her. If she had acted in such a rude manner in any white person's home, she would have been shown the door long ago.

"Tell me, Windhawk. Did you once find a white buffalo?"

Again he smiled. "Yes, that is so."

She looked into his darkly handsome face. "Are you a man or the god your people believe you to be?"

He pulled her head over to rest against his chest. "I am a man, Jo-anna. Feel how my heart is racing because I hold you in my arms."

Oh yes, she knew he was a man for she, as a woman, was reacting very strongly to him. She felt frightened as he lifted her in his arms and carried her to the buffalo robe. This man would take from her what she was so willing to give, and then she would lose sight of who she was.

He placed her down on the robe and then he lay down beside her.

"I am not of your world, Windhawk, and you are not of mine. We are all wrong for each other."

His dark eyes blazed. "To walk, Jo-anna, one must take one step at a time. It is but a short walk from your world to mine. If you will take my hand, I will lead you every step of the way."

Suddenly, Joanna felt like a child who needed to be led by the hand. Lately she had been forced to deal with so many tragedies. Even though she had met them head-on and with bravery, she needed Windhawk's strength. What he was offering her at the moment was a beacon of light at the end of a dark tunnel. If she took his hand, she would be accepting his way of life.

Windhawk's dark eyes stared at her questioningly. Joanna hesitated for only a moment before she placed her hand in his. His eyes softened and he drew her into his arms.

"I will be to you all things, Jo-anna. You have been hurt; I will help you heal. You have been lost; I will help you find your way."

Joanna laid her head against his shoulder, feeling a strong tide of love wash over her. Could their love possibly bridge the gap between their two cultures? Could she forget that she was Joanna James, and become Windhawk's woman instead? It was as if she were two people. One side of her was strong and rebellious, needing to right the wrong committed by her aunt and uncle. The other side of her wanted to bask in Windhawk's love, to be by his side no matter what hardships the future threw in her way.

Windhawk seemed to sense her dilemma. He lifted her chin and laid his face against hers. "Jo-anna, I can feel that you are troubled. I do not know what passed in your life before, but I can feel in you a great unrest. I want you to be my wife, but I cannot bind you to me if you are unwilling."

Joanna squeezed her eyes tightly together, trying to stop the flow of tears caused by his beautiful words. Had any girl ever had a man such as Windhawk professing such an unselfish love for her? Her lips brushed his smooth cheek, as her love for him filled her heart to overflowing.

What did anything matter to her in life if she couldn't be with Windhawk? This was where she belonged, warm and safe in his arms.

Once again he raised her chin, and seeing her tears, he kissed them lovingly away. "Stay with me, Jo-anna. I need you to walk beside me. Become a part of this land with me. Allow me to fill your body with strong sons who will also belong to this land." His eyes were beseeching, and his voice was deep and husky.

Joanna laced her fingers through his ebony hair, and held him tightly to her. "I love you, and tonight I want to be your woman, but I cannot say that tomorrow I will not feel differently."

He closed his eyes, loving the feel of her in his arms. She had said that she loved him. He had known from the beginning that they would love each other. It had just taken her longer to admit it than it had him.

Windhawk removed the bear-claw necklace which he wore about his neck and placed it around Joanna's neck. "From this moment forward, you are my wife. This necklace has powerful medicine and will keep you from harm. I have placed it around your neck, so that all who see it will know that you are Windhawk's woman. The only way you can return it to me, is if you no longer love me."

"What if one day you ask me to return it to you, Windhawk?" Joanna asked, running her fingers lovingly across the necklace.

His hand closed over hers. "The day I would take this from you would be the day I die. Each time you see this necklace it will speak to you of the love that burns in my heart."

Joanna raised the necklace to her lips, feeling in that moment she was indeed his wife. She felt bound to him stronger than if they had gone through a proper wedding ceremony. Again she had the feeling that she and Windhawk had loved one another in the far distant past.

"Joanna, I feel that there are two important times in a man's life. The time when he is born, and the time when he dies. For me there are two other times that are important."

"What are the other two, Windhawk?"

He touched the necklace which rested against her breast. "The moment you allowed me to make you my wife was the one."

"And the other?"

He swallowed a lump in his throat, before answering. "The other will come the day I have a son born of our love."

Joanna's eyes were blinded by tears. "I am honored to be the wife of Windhawk," she whispered. "I cannot explain my feelings very well, but I feel as if I have traveled a great distance to find you."

Windhawk looked at her in astonishment. "I did not know that you felt as I do. Do you feel that we have always known each other?"

"Yes, oh, yes," Joanna said, glad that he understood her feelings, and hadn't laughed at her.

Windhawk smiled and his whole face seemed to light up. "Come into my arms, Jo-anna. I want to show you my love."

Joanna went willingly into his arms. For a long moment he just held her tightly, allowing his heart to overflow with happiness.

When Joanna felt his hands slide sensuously over her hips, she drew in her breath. When he knelt down to lift her gown over her head, she felt hot and cold at the same time. Her body ached for his touch. The gown and moccasins that he had insisted on dressing her in earlier, now lay in a heap on the floor. They were quickly joined by Windhawk's clothing.

The firelight gave off a rosy glow, and the flames flickered playfully across Windhawk's naked body. Joanna's eyes widened in admiration. Although they had made love before, she hadn't seen his body. She had no idea that a man's body could be so beautiful. His ebony hair hung loosely about his broad shoulders. His face, which was half cast in shadows, was handsome, and the passionate look in his eyes sent tiny shivers of delight down her spine. Her eyes wandered down his smooth chest and across his taut stomach, skipping quickly across his pulsating manhood to return to his face.

Windhawk dropped to his knees in front of her and pulled her up beside him. "Jo-anna, do you not know you should never look at a man like that?" His lips pressed against her closed eyelids.

"Why?" she whispered.

"Because, it makes me want to . . ." He never finished whatever he was going to say, because Joanna moved forward and touched her mouth to his. Windhawk could only groan softly.

He raised his head and looked deeply into her eyes. She became lost in the burning depths of his eyes, which caressed her face lovingly, before they traveled down her silky body. He was making love to her with his eyes. Joanna's heart skipped a beat when his hand traced a pattern across her face, then slid across her shoulder and down her neck to cup her waiting breasts.

She raised her face to his, and Windhawk slowly

lowered his head to take her lips in a soft kiss.

She arched her neck back as his lips moved down her throat to settle on her breasts. She swayed toward him, and her body seemed to fit perfectly against his.

"I have never felt like this before, Jo-anna," he whispered. "Your love takes me to the highest peak of a mountain."

"Love me, Windhawk," she whispered in a throaty voice. "Make me truly your wife."

Windhawk drew in his breath and gently pushed her back against the buffalo robe. Joanna held her arms up to him and he came to her. His lips were like a raging fire as they plundered her mouth. Joanna slid her arms around him, trying to draw him closer to her. Her body craved the oneness she had felt with him before.

Windhawk slid her legs apart and thrust forward with an urgency. Joanna cried out as he entered her warm, throbbing body. She closed her eyes as wave after wave of pleasure carried her higher and higher. It flashed through her mind that she had been created to love, and to be loved, by Windhawk.

At first Windhawk began to move slowly inside her, but soon they were both consumed with a burning urgency, and Joanna's body came alive as if guided by some primitive instinct, and she began to move with him. Windhawk closed his eyes as feelings he had never before experienced rushed through his body. He felt as if his body had long hungered without truly being fed, until now.

"Jo-anna, my beloved," he whispered, taking her

tender lips in a burning kiss of passion.

Joanna gasped in pleasure when her body answered Windhawk's, and they both trembled in total fulfillment.

Windhawk rolled over and drew Joanna's body tightly against his. "This time and the one before are not the first time we have loved each other, Jo-anna." His lips brushed her red-gold hair. "Do you feel this also, beloved?"

Joanna slid her arms about his waist and looked up into his dark expressive eyes. "Yes, I feel as you do."

"Do you feel that the two of us have lived other lives, Jo-anna?"

"My reasoning tells me that it is not possible, however, I cannot deny the feeling of reliving a moment out of another time, Windhawk."

"Could it be possible that in another time we loved each other so much that Napi wanted us to be together again?" Windhawk asked.

She looked into his eyes. "I don't know, Windhawk. It is a little frightening to me."

His arms tightened around her protectively. "I will never allow anything to harm you, Jo-anna. You are my life."

Joanna turned her head away so he wouldn't see the tears that came to her eyes because of his beautiful words. Windhawk could feel her mood, however, and he raised her face to kiss the tears away.

The fire died down and the tipi became dark. Windhawk and Joanna lay in each other's arms. No words were necessary to communicate their feelings for one another.

Windhawk knew in his heart that the time would

come when their love would be challenged, but for tonight, Joanna belonged to him.

Joanna feared that something would happen to tear her and Windhawk apart. She wished that she could stay in his warm protective arms forever, but deep inside, she feared they would only have a short time together before something would rip her from his arms.

The night was spent with Windhawk introducing Joanna to the joys of the body. When she would become exhausted, he would hold her in his arms until she fell asleep.

Joanna never knew that one could feel so many different emotions. At times she would feel drained, and then, when Windhawk would touch her in a certain way, her body would come to life. At last she sighed contentedly and curled up against his warm body.

Windhawk felt his heart swell with love and pride. Joanna had delighted him with her sweet innocence. Her lovely soft body had taken him higher than he had ever flown before.

When the sun rose, Windhawk knew Joanna needed the sleep. He kissed her satiny cheek and stood up.

Gazing down at her lips which were swollen from his kisses, he was tempted to awaken her. No, he would let her sleep, he thought. There would be tonight, and many other nights to come, when he would hold her in his arms.

# Chapter Eleven

Joanna awoke when someone roughly shook her by the shoulders. Opening her eyes sleepily, she saw Sun Woman bending over her. Her face flushed red, and she grabbed the buffalo robe, pulling it over her nakedness. She remembered the night before when Windhawk had made her his wife. With a sweeping glance of the room, Joanna saw that Windhawk was not present. She was hurt that he had sent his mother to awaken her, instead of being there himself.

Sun Woman threw the doeskin gown at Joanna and motioned for her to put it on. Unlike the night before, Joanna quickly did as Sun Woman told her to. She slipped into the gown and then pulled on the soft knee-high moccasins and laced them securely about her knees.

When she was dressed, Sun Woman shoved the waterskin at her and nodded toward the river, indicating that Joanna should go for the water. Joanna met the hostile, dark eyes without flinching. Windhawk's mother still resented her, and she was making sure that Joanna realized it. Joanna wanted to ask Sun Woman where Windhawk was, but she doubted his mother would tell her.

She walked outside thinking it was a glorious day. The sun was shining warmly, and the birds were singing. For the first time in many weeks, Joanna felt at peace with herself. Last night she had truly become a woman . . . Windhawk's woman.

As Joanna progressed through the village, she noticed that many of the women would look the other way when she raised her hand in greeting. She sighed, thinking she would never be accepted by the people of the Blackfoot tribe. She knew instinctively that if Sun Woman would only accept her, the other women would also. It was critical to Joanna that she win Sun Woman's friendship, knowing how important it was to Windhawk.

"Joanna, wait," Morning Song called out, running to catch up with her. "I will walk with you to the river, my sister."

Joanna smiled brightly at Windhawk's lovely sister. "Is it not a glorious morning, Morning Song?"

"It is for me, my sister, for I can see the light of love shining in your eyes." Morning Song gave Joanna a mischievous smile. "Did I not tell you that my brother was wonderful?"

Joanna raised her eyebrow. "That you did, but I suppose I had to find out for myself."

Morning Song laughed delightedly. "I always wanted a sister, but I began to think my brother would never take a wife. I am glad he chose you."

Joanna paused and put her arms around Morning Song. "I am glad you feel that way, for like you, I myself never had a sister."

As the two girls continued to the river, Joanna was unaware that she was humming. Morning Song felt her heart would burst with happiness. Windhawk had at last taken a wife, and she was kind as well as beautiful.

"Joanna, my brother has asked my mother and me to teach you about our customs. I am to teach you to speak the language of my people. I know you can already speak many words. I do not think it will be difficult for you to learn the rest."

"Yes, I would like that. Could we start today?"

By now they had reached the river, and there were many women and children gathered there. The children were playing and laughing gleefully, while the woman went about their endless work.

"Yes, we will start now." Morning Song answered her. Many of the women came up to Joanna, and Morning Song would introduce them to her. Most of them were withdrawn, and many of the young maidens gave Joanna unfriendly glares. Joanna didn't have to be told that they were jealous because she was Windhawk's woman.

One of the women touched Joanna's red-gold hair and exclaimed in surprise at its glorious color. Others would touch her hand to show their approval. Joanna accepted their curious interest with good grace, and soon they went back to their tasks.

Joanna knelt down to wash her face and hands in the river. She then filled the waterskin, and she and

Morning Song walked back to the lodge together. Along the way Morning Song began to instruct Joanna in the Blackfoot language.

By mid-morning Windhawk had still not appeared. Sun Woman had worked Joanna mercilessly. She had swept out the lodge, cleaned the buffalo robes that were used to sleep upon, and helped butcher a deer.

Her back was aching and her knees were cramped, so she stood up, stretching her arms over her head. She smiled to herself, thinking how different she was from the girl who had always had her meals prepared for her, and had relied on servants to clean her home.

Sun Woman had deliberately been hard on Joanna, assigning her the hardest tasks, hoping she would complain. She saw the smile on Joanna's face, and knew she hadn't succeeded. This white-face girl was not what she seemed. One could not hide their true character for long. Windhawk would soon see the girl for what she was and drive her from their village, she thought.

By late afternoon the lodge was spotless. A delicious smelling venison stew, not unlike the ones Franny had often prepared, was bubbling over the cook-fire.

Morning Song motioned for Joanna to follow her, while Sun Woman returned to her own lodge. Windhawk's sister led Joanna to a secluded part of the river that was surrounded by trees. Joanna looked startled when Morning Song began stripping her clothing off, and dove into the water.

"Come on in, Joanna, the water is not cold once

you are in it."

"Won't someone see us?" Joanna asked, wanting to go for a swim, but reluctant because she didn't want anyone to come upon them.

"Come on, no one will come here," Morning Song called out before she dove beneath the water.

Joanna hesitantly removed her moccasins and gown and rushed into the river. She sank down in the water quickly to cover her nakedness. "I have never done anything so unconventional before," Joanna said, loving the way the water caressed her naked skin.

"Have you never been swimming before?" Morning Song asked.

"Of course, but not without my clothing on."

"How can one possibly swim with clothing on?" Morning Song questioned.

Joanna laughed out loud. "Not very well. This way is much better."

After a while, the girls reluctantly swam to shore and pulled their gowns on. As they leisurely made their way back to the village Morning Song continued to instruct Joanna in the Blackfoot language.

Joanna wanted to ask Morning Song where Windhawk had gone, but she had refrained from doing so all day. She supposed there would be many days when he would leave her without telling where he was going.

Joanna was discovering that the Indian way of life was hard, but she could tell that they enjoyed a peace and tranquility that was unknown to the white world. The Blackfoot were nature's children. The women were not bothered by what hat went with which gown. They were concerned only with the health and well-being of their families. Not that they didn't have fun. They played games, gossiped, and did many things to amuse their children. The uppermost thought in their minds seemed to be wanting to please their husbands.

In spite of the tedious work today Joanna felt exhilarated. She felt as if she had accomplished something important. She wanted Windhawk to be proud of her. She also wanted his mother to think well of her.

When the two girls entered the lodge Joanna was shocked to find her trunk and many other articles that had belonged to her stacked against the back of the tipi. She thought she had lost everything in the raid.

"Where . . . how did Windhawk get all my belongings?" Joanna asked, wondering if her mother's jewel case was in her trunk. She had grieved thinking she had lost her mother's jewels. Not only were they extremely valuable, her mother had treasured them. Joanna hated the fact that she had been forced to sell some of them to finance the ill-fated trip to Oregon. For some strange reason, she couldn't bring herself to look into the trunk. She supposed she associated it with Tag's and Franny's death.

"I was told by Gray Fox's wife, White Dove, that some of the braves were traveling many days behind you and my brother when he brought you to our village. Windhawk wanted to make sure he was not being followed. I suppose those braves also carried your belongings."

Morning Song lifted up a copper kettle and exclaimed over its beauty. "I must leave you now. My mother will expect me to help with the evening meal. Tomorrow will you show me the wondrous things that belong to you, Joanna?"

Joanna nodded. She was hardly aware that Morning Song was gone. Seeing the things that belonged to her reminded Joanna of her past. She covered her eyes with trembling hands, thinking about the raid on the wagon train. She remembered that she was Joanna James, and that she had a father waiting for her in Oregon.

. How could she have allowed herself to forget even for a moment that she didn't belong here. Had last night made her forget her obligations?

The aroma of the bubbling stew reminded Joanna of the present. She walked over to the cook-fire and absentmindedly picked up a long wooden spoon and stirred the contents in the pot.

As if in a daze, she glanced at her trunk. She had been deluding herself all day by thinking she could be a part of Windhawk's world. As much as she loved him, she could never remain with him. She knew she would never be content until she and her father had dealt with her aunt and uncle.

A slight breath of air touched the back of her neck, and Joanna knew before she turned around that Windhawk had come in.

His eyes sought hers, and she could see the love shining in those dark depths. She wanted to run to him and have him hold her, but she didn't. She could do no more than stare at him in confusion.

Windhawk walked to her and clasped her in his

arms. "It has been a long day, Jo-anna. I wanted many times to return to you."

She raised her head and brushed his cheek with her lips. "Why didn't you?"

He smiled and her heart seemed to melt. "I could not have my warriors say a woman kept me from my duties."

"What duties?" she asked.

"It is the autumn season, a time when game must be killed to sustain us through the long winter months."

"Is that what you were doing? I wish I could go with you on a buffalo hunt. Are women permitted to take part in the hunt?" Her eyes spoke of her enthusiasm, and Windhawk smiled to himself, thinking how child-like she appeared at the moment. She somehow reminded him of her brother the day he had wanted a tomahawk.

"It is not unusual for a wife to go on the hunt with her husband, but you are not experienced. It could be very dangerous for you."

"I would be very good, and do just what you told me to, if you would allow me to go along."

Windhawk picked her slight body up in his arms, and held her tightly to him. He couldn't find it within his heart to refuse her anything. "We shall see, little wife. Perhaps you can go tomorrow."

Joanna threw her arms around his neck and laughed delightedly. For the moment the trunk and the memories it had brought back were all but forgotten.

"Morning Song told me that when you go on a buffalo hunt, you have a special horse which is used for nothing but hunting the buffalo. Will I be allowed to ride one of your buffalo runners?"

Windhawk sat down and held her in his lap as he would a child. "The buffalo horse is trained to run among the buffalo. It would be too dangerous for you to ride among the buffalo until you learn how the horse moves."

"I am a good horsewoman. You have seen me ride Fosset, and he is a highly spirited animal."

"Yes, but do not forget that Fosset pulled your brother into the river." Windhawk had not been thinking or he would never have brought up the subject of the little brother. He knew that her brother's death was still too painful for Joanna to deal with.

"Yes, Fosset can be a handful," Joanna said with a faraway look in her eyes. "My father gave him to me on my sixteenth birthday."

Windhawk brushed a red-gold curl from her face. "What is your age now?"

"I am seventeen, almost eighteen I believe. I do not know what the date is."

He kissed the tip of her nose. "You are still so young; have I taken a baby for my wife?"

Joanna jerked her head up, but when she saw the twinkle in his eyes she knew he had been teasing her. "You didn't seem to think I was too young last night."

He smiled. "When one is young she is much easier to teach."

"Perhaps I can teach you a few things, Windhawk."

He laughed and pulled her tighter against him.

"You already have, Jo-anna, although I think I will be an old man before I learn all there is to know about you."

She smiled up at him. "You are the complicated one. I have overheard many of your people speak of you in awe. To me you are very wonderful."

Windhawk gazed at her for a moment. When he looked away he seemed to stiffen. He saw Joanna's belongings piled on the floor of the tipi. He hadn't meant for his braves to bring her trunk to his lodge. First, he wanted Joanna to accept his way of life with no reminders of her past.

Joanna's eyes followed his gaze. "They were here when I came back from swimming with Morning Song."

"I will have them taken away," Windhawk said, standing up and placing Joanna on her feet.

Joanna grabbed his arm. "It will do no good to have them hidden away, Windhawk. I shall always remember who I am. You must try to understand this. There is something I must do. I would love to stay with you for the rest of my days, but I must find my father."

His eyes flashed. "I will never allow you to leave me, Jo-anna."

"Do you intend to keep me tied up night and day to prevent me from leaving?"

"You are acting like a child, Jo-anna. Have I ever tied you up? Have you not been allowed to roam freely?" he asked, with a stubborn set to his chin.

"I am not a child, Windhawk. I don't think I ever have been. In the past there were too many people depending on me. I had to grow up fast."

Windhawk half closed his eyes and stared at her through lowered lashes. "I will never allow you to leave me," he repeated.

"Then I am not your wife, but your captive!" she said, raising her voice.

Windhawk started to answer her, but instead he turned away and walked from the lodge. Joanna dropped to her knees, and a sob broke from her throat. She had to get away! Somehow she had to reach her father.

It was very late when Windhawk returned. The stew had gone uneaten and the cookfire had died down when he lay beside Joanna. He knew she was awake and he wanted to take her in his arms.

"Jo-anna, tell me about this thing that pulls you back to the white world."

Joanna turned to face him. "I doubt that you would understand, so I will explain it this way to you. What if a stranger came to your lodge and moved in, taking it as his own. Suppose he threatened Morning Song's life, as my uncle threatened my brother's life?"

"There is no question that I would have slain the man," Windhawk said with conviction.

"Suppose the law said that this man had the right to do as he wished with your property and with your life?"

"That is not the Indian way. If it is the white man's way, then the law is wrong."

"You and I both know that our worlds are different. I don't know why I couldn't have been born into your world or you in mine. I only know that I must find my father."

226

"If you must go, then I will go with you," Wind-hawk said, pulling her into his arms. "You are my wife, and it is my duty to protect you."

Joanna laid her head against his shoulder. "No, you cannot go with me. This is one road I must walk alone. Please try to understand."

Windhawk could not understand. He knew he would never allow Joanna to leave him. "The things that happened to you before we met no longer have any meaning. One day we will send word to your father, and he will know you are safe."

Joanna knew that nothing she could say would change Windhawk's mind. She would just have to take what happiness she could for now. In the near future when the opportunity presented itself, she would leave. Would it be wrong of her to want to have this short time of happiness with the man she loved? she wondered.

Joanna's arms slid around Windhawk's shoulders, and she raised her face to receive his kiss. No, it was not wrong to steal a little happiness before the real world came crashing down around her.

Windhawk's lips settled on hers and Joanna was soft and yielding in his arms. As his hands moved over her body, she knew that when the time came to leave, she would leave her heart and her happiness behind.

## Chapter Twelve

Joanna was extremely happy as the golden days of autumn settled over the land. The giant ponderosa pines, the cedar, the fir, and spruce trees retained their greenery, while the oak and cottonwood trees dominated the countryside with their glorious autumn colors. The majestic mountains rose above the valley and their tallest peaks were awash with sparkling white snow.

Joanna's days were filled with hard work as Sun Woman continued to instruct her in the work of the Blackfoot woman. Her nights were filled with love as she lay in the arms of Windhawk.

At times Joanna would almost forget that there was another world outside the Blackfoot village; at other times she could feel that other world beckoning to her.

Windhawk often allowed Joanna to accompany him on a hunting expedition. Those times were the happiest of all for her. She loved to ride alongside her tall husband, feeling as if time had forgotten her when it had placed her in this land as an adopted daughter.

The men of the Blackfoot tribe seemed to have readily accepted her, but that was not true of the women. She was forced to feel like an outsider by Sun Woman and her friends. Windhawk's mother was still as disapproving and distant as she had always been. Joanna had begun to respect the older woman, and wished desperately for Sun Woman's approval and acceptance.

By now Joanna spoke the Blackfoot tongue, if not well, at least understandably. She never spoke in English unless she didn't know a certain word in Blackfoot. It was as if a whole new world had opened up to her. She loved to talk to the young children. They did not seem to share their mothers' distrust of her. When the young girls were playing ball, they would often ask Joanna to join them.

Joanna had ridden out with several of the women to a nearby valley where there was an abundance of chokeberries growing beside a small stream. The berries would later be dried and mixed with meat for added flavor.

The day was sultry and hot. Joanna could feel rivulets of perspiration running down her back. The berry-picking process was slow and tedious. She dropped a handful of berries into the leather pouch which she wore about her neck. Looking down at her hands, which were now brown and rough, she wondered if they would ever be soft and white again.

Sun Woman gave Joanna a disgruntled glance. "Your hands are no longer soft, white woman. Do you find the Indian ways hard?" she asked in her usual haughty tone.

"Yes, Sun Woman, the way is hard, but the rewards are great," Joanna answered, wishing she could find some way to reach the older woman's heart.

"You are not one of us, nor will you ever be," Sun Woman told her. "Nothing you can do will make your white skin darken, or your white heart beat as that of a Blackfoot."

Joanna felt the sting of Sun Woman's criticism. Windhawk's mother had a very powerful influence over the other women. Joanna knew she would never be accepted by any of them until she won Sun Woman over.

Joanna picked a wine-colored berry and popped it into her mouth. It was mostly seed with very little juice.

Her mind began to drift as she looked toward a small cove and spotted a lone elk with its great antlers pointed toward the sky. She watched as the animal moved its head as if to test the wind. The elk had either detected the women or the presence of something else.

Joanna glanced at the other women, but they seemed unconcerned by the animal's fright, so she returned to her berry picking.

Suddenly there was a rustling in the nearby bushes and a hideous sound which Joanna had never before heard split through the stillness. The other women heard it too, and Morning Song called out. "It is the wild boar, run for cover! Climb a tree if you can!"

Joanna looked about in total confusion. She saw Gray Fox's infant son propped against a tree in his cradleboard. The thrashing and grunting from the wild boar was getting closer. Joanna stared in fear as the animal came out of the bushes, charging straight ahead. Gray Fox's son was right in its path!

With no thought of the danger she was in, Joanna ran toward the baby. There was no time to pick the child up and carry him to safety for the crazed beast was too near.

The boar had long tusks and was using them to root up the dirt as he charged toward Joanna. She was surprised at how swiftly the animal could run on its short stubby legs. The boar was now near enough that she could see its beady little eyes and the dirt that clung to its snout.

What could she do? she wondered in a panic! She couldn't abandon the child, the boar would kill him for sure. Without thinking, Joanna placed her body in front of the child and reached for the spear that one of the women had leaned against the tree earlier.

With no time to consider, Joanna grabbed up the spear, and thrust it forward, bracing her back against the tree. The spear entered the animal's body between the shoulder blades, and pierced its heart. The impact slammed Joanna sideways and she dropped to her knees. Gasping for breath she fell to the ground. It all happened so quickly that the other women had no time to react.

Gray Fox's young wife ran to her baby and picked him up in her arms. Sun Woman knelt down beside Joanna and lifted her head onto her lap.

"Are you hurt?" Sun Woman inquired.

Joanna was still in a daze. "The child . . . ?" she asked.

"The child was unharmed because of your brave deed," Windhawk's mother assured her.

By now the other women had gathered around and were exclaiming their excitement.

"Look, Joanna has killed the boar!" Morning Song cried out.

Sun Woman helped Joanna to her feet and they all gazed at the dead animal. The boar was grayish-black and its hair was stiff and prickly. Blood ran from his mouth and from the wound that had pierced its heart.

Sun Woman looked at Joanna and smiled widely. "My daughter, Windhawk's wife, has done what only a brave warrior could have done. She had no fear when she put herself in danger to save Gray Fox's child."

Joanna caught the look of pride on Sun Woman's face. She had called her daughter! Sun Woman placed her arms about Joanna. "Everyone shall hear of my daughter's brave deed. She is truly a woman worthy of my son, Windhawk."

Now that the incident was over, Joanna felt her knees go weak. She had not set out to be brave, she had only followed her instincts. "I am feeling very weak, Sun Woman," she said, leaning on the older woman for support.

"You have done well, my daughter. It is only right that you should feel frightened now that the deed is done."

Gray Fox's wife hugged Joanna tightly. "You are very brave, and I can never show my gratitude to you for saving my baby."

All the other women came up to Joanna to either touch her or to praise her for her bravery. She caught the gleam in Morning Song's eyes and saw the joy reflected there. Morning Song was pleased that her mother and the others had accepted Joanna at last.

Windhawk would be pleased also, she thought.

Joanna was learning that no meat was ever wasted by the Indians. The boar was butchered and loaded onto one of the horses to take back to the village.

When the women reached the village, Sun Woman went from lodge to lodge proclaiming her daughter's bravery. By evening everyone knew of Joanna's daring deed.

Joanna sat beside the cookfire, feeling her body tremble. The others wouldn't think her so brave, she thought, if they could see how sick she felt inside. Her body was sore, and she couldn't still her hands, which shook in spite of the fact that she clutched them tightly together. She was glad that Sun Woman and the others had finally accepted her, but she didn't agree with them that she was brave. She had acted on instinct, nothing more.

Windhawk swept into the lodge. When he saw Joanna lying on the buffalo robe he rushed to her, and lifted her into his arms to cradle her gently against him. "Are you unhurt?" he inquired, looking her over carefully.

"I am but shaken up, nothing more."

"When I heard what had happened, I came at once. The whole village speaks of nothing but your bravery today."

"I'm not brave, Windhawk. I was very frightened when it was all over."

He smiled and touched her lips with his finger. "The most courageous man thinks not of his own safety while in battle, but will sometimes tremble when it is all over. There are many things that separate the valiant from all others."

Joanna basked in his praise. "I do not know what you mean, Windhawk?"

He laid his cheek to hers. "The coward will run in the face of danger. The courageous will stand and fight. A coward can very seldom become brave. The brave will never become the coward. It is something that one is born with, I believe."

"I am glad that the child was unharmed, Windhawk," she said, not knowing what else to reply.

He raised her face and his eyes roamed lovingly over every beautiful feature. "Do you know what they are now calling you, Jo-anna?"

"No, what?"

"They are calling you Flaming Hair. Your name will be sung around the campfires for many years to come."

Joanna felt tears in her eyes, and laid her head over on Windhawk's shoulder. Never had she felt so good about herself. Never had she cared so deeply about the opinion others had of her. It was wonderful to have the approval of Windhawk's people, but most important of all, she had won Sun Woman's respect.

"May we enter?" a familiar voice called from outside the lodge.

Windhawk stood up and helped Joanna to rise. "That will be Gray Fox wanting to reward you for saving his son," he told her.

Gray Fox entered with his two wives, and Windhawk solemnly motioned for them to sit beside the fire while he and Joanna joined them.

"I wish to speak with your wife, my chief," Gray Fox said.

Windhawk nodded.

"Joanna, I have no words to say that can show my heart's gladness that my son still lives. I think there are no earthly goods which I can give you that would reward you for saving my son."

"I do not wish a reward," Joanna said.

Gray Fox's youngest wife stood up and placed a beautiful white doeskin gown in Joanna's lap. It was elaborately embroidered with beads and porcupine quills. "White Dove wishes you to have her finest gown, while I give to you my best horse," Gray Fox said.

"No, I could never accept . . ."

Windhawk interrupted Joanna, knowing she was about to refuse the gifts, thus insulting Gray Fox. "My wife accepts with gratitude, my friend," Windhawk said.

"I thank you for the gifts," Joanna said, not knowing how to react to their kindness.

At that moment Sun Woman and Morning Song

entered carrying a big pot of food. They had cooked the boar and were bringing it to Windhawk's lodge to celebrate.

There was merriment and laughter inside the tipi as many people came in to join the festive occasion. Joanna smiled as she felt the strong bonds of love encircle her. At last she was being accepted by the Blackfoot tribe.

To everyone's surprise, no one sang Joanna's praises louder or longer than Sun Woman.

The hour was very late when the last guest departed. Joanna was so exhausted that she curled up in Windhawk's arms and fell asleep.

Windhawk gathered her close to him, thinking of the danger she had been in today. If anything had happened to her, he would have died as well. He stared into her sleeping face, feeling as if he held the greatest gift Napi had ever given a man. Today she had proved her worth to his people. No one would ever challenge her right to be a member of the Blackfoot tribe.

Joanna was his woman and nothing could change that. How was it possible to feel so much pride in such a small girl, he wondered, laying his face against her hair.

Picking her up carefully, he carried her to their robe and laid her down. He removed her clothing and covered her with a soft robe. Yes, she was but a small girl, but inside her beat the heart of a brave warrior.

Windhawk removed his clothing and lay down beside her. His mind wandered ahead to the time when he and Joanna would have children. What exceptional children they would grow to be, with a mother like Joanna to guide them. They would have the blood of chiefs in their veins, and the brave heart of their mother.

Joanna sighed in her sleep, and Windhawk gathered her closely to him. He watched as she slept, knowing she had earned the right to sleep deeply.

In her sleep Joanna moved closely against Windhawk and curled up to his body. His eyes flamed for a moment as he felt his desire fan to life, then he smiled.

"Sleep, little wife," he whispered as he kissed her eyelids.

## Chapter Thirteen

Joanna sat on the riverbank with several of the other women, watching Windhawk break one of his horses. Many of the women and children had gathered around to view the spectacle.

The Blackfoot often broke their horses in rivers and streams, because the animals would tire quicker and were much easier to break than when on land.

Windhawk rode into the water, leading the horse that was to be broken. Once the water was up to the horse's stomach, he leaped from his mount onto the wild mare. The animal bucked and snorted, trying without success to throw her rider off. Windhawk's strong leg muscles gripped the sides of the horse, and he hung on while the horse thrashed about, splashing water onto the riverbank.

Joanna thought how magnificent he looked with his dark hair flying about his handsome face, and his muscled body tense and alert. She heard some of the young maidens proclaiming Windhawk's handsomeness, and was amazed that she felt a prickle of jealousy.

"Do not mind them," Morning Song said to Joanna. "There have always been those who looked upon my brother with favor, but he never gave them a glance."

Joanna laid her head on her folded arms and watched her husband. One day she would have to leave. Would Windhawk grieve over her going, or would he replace her with one of the maidens who sought a smile from him?

The mare Windhawk was riding gave a last defiant leap into the air and then stood passive, with her sides heaving in exhaustion. Man had conquered the wild animal once more, Joanna thought.

Windhawk rode the now tame horse out of the water and upon the bank. He stopped in front of Joanna and dismounted, handing the reins to a young boy who stood nearby.

Joanna smiled up at him and he helped her to her feet. "Once again you tamed the mare as you tamed me," she told him teasingly.

He ruffled her red-gold curls and gave her a doubtful glance. "No one will ever tame you, my flaming-haired warrior; least of all me." He led her toward their tipi, and once inside, away from prying eyes, he drew her into his arms. "I believe you are the one who has tamed me, Jo-anna."

She placed her arms around his waist and looked up at him. "Have you no wish to take another wife as Gray Fox and many of your other

239

warriors have?"

"I am content with just you. I have no need for any other wife." He raised his eyebrow. "Perhaps you want me to take another wife to relieve you of my lovemaking?"

Joanna's eyes widened in defiance. "No, never. I would scratch another woman's eyes out if you looked at her."

Windhawk laughed. "I will never take another to my mat. Why should I when I have you."

Joanna laid her head against his chest. "Windhawk, if I were to go away, or if anything should happen to me, I would like to think that you would not be sad."

She felt him tense. "I will never be content without you by my side, Jo-anna."

His eyes moved to the corner where Joanna's belongings were still stacked neatly against the back wall of the tipi. "Have you been going through your trunk? Is that why you say this to me?"

"No, I have not touched them since they were first brought here."

Windhawk had hoped that Joanna would become content with their life together. He knew in his heart that she loved him, but at times he could feel her unrest, and it troubled him. He wished they would have a child, then perhaps Joanna would feel bound to him, forgetting her past life.

He picked her up in his arms and carried her to their bed. When he was making love to Joanna was the only time he felt she really belonged to him. At other times he could feel her troubled thoughts and knew that she was thinking about her past life.

He undressed her and allowed his eyes to wander over her silky body. He lay down beside her and clasped her tightly to him.

"Time will pass, Jo-anna. You will soon forget all that you left behind."

She looked up at him and could tell he was troubled. "Some things I will never forget, Windhawk. I would never forget you."

His dark eyes narrowed. "One does not forget the one he is with. You must be parted from someone to forget him. Tell me, do you ever think of the long knife whom I saw you dancing with?" He had often thought about the long knife and wondered if Joanna had cared about him. He had avoided asking about him, fearing he would hear that she had loved him in the past.

Joanna frowned trying to think who he meant. "By long knife, do you mean soldier?"

"Yes."

"No, I rarely think of Captain Thatcher. I knew him for such a short time, and I am grieved to think that he might be dead."

"Did you love him?"

Joanna smiled and shook her head. "I have never loved a man as I love you."

Windhawk cupped her face as if trying to memorize every detail. He laced his hands through her red-gold hair and drew her face up to his, while his lips hungrily devoured her mouth. He rolled her over and crushed her body beneath his. Joanna could feel his hard body pressing her into the soft buffalo robe and she wound her arms about his neck.

"I love you, Windhawk. I think that there has never been a love as deep as what I feel for you."

His dark eyes blazed triumphantly. She loved him, and had finally admitted it. With that love he would bind her to him. He spread her legs apart and poised above her. "I will fill your body with mine, and you will never want to leave me," he whispered.

Joanna gasped with pleasure as he plunged inside her. She closed her eyes and let the glorious feeling wash over her. She could feel him pulsate inside her, and ran her hand across his back. She wondered how would she ever be able to leave him when the time came. She felt tears in her eyes and turned her face away so he would not see her cry. She would give Windhawk all a woman could give the man she loved. When she had gone, she hoped he would remember only the love they had shared.

Windhawk felt his senses reeling as Joanna's silken body arched up to meet his forward thrusts. His body trembled and quaked as her soft mouth opened beneath his. He was a slave to the love she gave him. He would do anything for a smile from those soft lips.

Joanna rested her face against his as his hands circled beneath her, and he raised her up, thrusting her tighter against his hips. Her legs slid around his waist, and she watched his eyes burn into hers.

His hand tangled in her hair and he raised it to his lips. "Jo-anna," he whispered. "Your hair is soft . . . so soft." She gasped when he buried his face in the rivulet of red-gold. His breath was ragged as he nipped at her ear.

A wild tempo that was beating inside Joanna's

head seemed to match itself to her body movements, and her movements were timed perfectly with Windhawk's. They rolled on the buffalo robe locked in a fiery embrace. Joanna was panting softly, and Windhawk was breathing heavily. Their bodies were wet with perspiration, which only heightened their pleasure.

Windhawk tasted Joanna's lips and, she cried out as the world seemed to tilt upside-down with wild sensations she had never before felt.

Suddenly Windhawk thrust forward, reaching deeply within Joanna's body, and she shivered with pleasure as her body seemed to explode simultaneously with his.

For a long moment she lay beneath him, too exhausted to move. He had distributed his weight so he wouldn't be too heavy for her. Joanna was learning that with Windhawk the loving didn't stop with the climax. He would hold and caress her while he whispered words of love in her ear.

"Jo-anna, each time I enter your body it is a new adventure." His breath stirred her hair as he kissed her cheek. He rolled over on his side and pulled her tightly against him while his hands ran lovingly over her hip.

She tilted her face up to him. "Windhawk, can I ask you something?" she queried almost shyly.

His dark handsome face eased into an earth-shattering smile. "You can always ask me anything."

"Can one . . . is one woman the same as another?"

Again he smiled. "Is one horse the same as another?" he countered.

Joanna pushed against his shoulder. "You are forever comparing me to a horse," she said in an irritated voice.

He laughed as he traced the outline of her jaw. "I was but teasing you. To answer your question . . ." he paused as his eyes moved over every detail of her beautiful face. "I have never known a woman like you, Jo-anna. You know I have never loved before you. Does that answer your question."

"No. I want to know if when you make love to one woman it is the same as with any other."

He smiled to himself thinking how like a woman she was at the moment. Could he dare tell her that when he was intimate with her that he felt deeper than he had ever felt with another woman. Could he reveal to her that she was the reason why he lived. She was more important to him than the very air he breathed.

His hand drifted down to rest between her legs. "Jo-anna, when I am here, it is a bit like dying. You give me pleasure as no other ever could."

Suddenly the hand that rested against her thigh began a soft circular motion and she no longer had any unanswered questions. She moved her body closer to him and turned her face up to receive his kiss.

She wondered, how will I ever be able to walk away from such a perfect love? When the time came could she leave without regret?

Crazy Farley started across the river and was immediately surrounded by twenty Blood braves.

244

They were silent as they escorted him out of the river. When they reached the village he dismounted and one of them spoke to him.

"What do you want here, crazy one?" one of the warriors challenged him.

Farley spoke and understood the Blackfoot language as well as any Indian. He knew that Windhawk didn't welcome many white men in his village, and he knew he was taking a grave risk in coming here.

"Take me to your chief, Windhawk. I have something to say to him," Farley said, unafraid.

The Indian nodded. "Come with me, old man, I will take you to him."

Joanna and Windhawk were standing in front of Sun Woman's tipi talking to Morning Song when Joanna saw Farley. She could hardly believe her eyes. Windhawk had been watching her and he saw her face pale. His eyes followed hers and he stiffened when he saw the white man.

Joanna ran toward the old trapper and threw her arms around him. "I am so glad to see you, Farley."

Farley saw the murderous light in Windhawk's eyes, and loosened Joanna's arms from about his neck. He stepped back a pace, knowing he wouldn't live long if he didn't do some fast talking. He was glad to see that Joanna James was alive, but if Windhawk had taken her for his woman, he didn't want to appear too interested in her.

"I surely do recollect you, Miss Joanna. I am plumb tickled to see you alive."

Windhawk rushed forward and grabbed Joanna by the wrist, pushing her behind him. "Take her to my mother," he told Gray Fox, who was standing nearby.

Joanna wanted to protest, but the dark look in Windhawk's eyes silenced her. She allowed Gray Fox to lead her over to Windhawk's mother. Sun Woman took Joanna's hand and led her inside.

"It was most unwise of you to speak to the white man, my daughter."

"Why? I see no harm in talking to an old friend." By now Joanna had had time to think clearly, and she resented Windhawk's high-handed treatment. "I will not stay here like a child who has been sent to her room," Joanna said, walking purposefully toward the opening. When she reached the outside, she saw Gray Fox standing with his arms folded across his chest, barring her exit.

"Let me pass," she said, forgetting to speak in the Blackfoot tongue.

"I dare not, Joanna. Windhawk has ordered me to see that you remain with his mother," Gray Fox answered her in English.

Joanna's temper mounted, but she knew that Gray Fox would carry out Windhawk's orders and she would not be allowed to leave Sun Woman's tipi. She walked back inside and sat down. Sun Woman sat down beside her, offering her a cold drink of water.

"Do not worry, my daughter. Sometimes it is hard to understand a man. It is best not to try too hard."

"I do not understand Windhawk. He has never been so . . . domineering with me before."

"Why do you come among us, crazy one?" Wind-hawk asked.

Farley looked away from the chief's piercing gaze, wondering how much to reveal to him. "There were other survivors from the wagon train massacre," he finally replied in the Blackfoot language.

"That is not my concern, old man. If this is why you came to me, I will hear no more."

Farley shifted from one foot to the other, knowing he was treading on dangerous ground. "You might not care, but the girl will. One of them is her brother."

Windhawk grabbed Farley by the shirt front and jerked him forward. "What are you saying? Where is the little brother?" he demanded in a commanding voice.

Farley could feel the cold hand of fear move over his heart as he looked into dark blazing eyes. "If you let me go, I'll tell you," he said.

Windhawk released his hold on him and Farley fell backwards, barely able to keep his balance.

"Speak, white man," Windhawk ordered.

Farley straightened his buckskin shirt and tried to appear unafraid, when in truth his knees were knocking together. "You remember when I told you about the raid on the wagon train?"

"I remember."

"I went to Running Elk's village and I saw the little brother. I was told by one of the Piegans that there was also a white girl there."

Windhawk's eyes revealed nothing of what he was feeling. He was glad in his heart that Joanna's brother still lived. "Is the boy well?"

"I cannot say. I was not allowed to speak to him." Farley looked toward the tipi where Joanna had been taken and saw the brave who was on guard there. He knew he was again inviting danger, but he liked the girl and her brother. "Where did you find the James girl?"

Windhawk's dark eyes settled on Farley, and in that instant Farley held his breath, knowing how unwise he had been to speak of the girl again. "You will leave now, old man. Do not again come to my village."

The old trapper knew it would not be wise to say more. Glancing one last time at the tipi where the James girl was, he nodded. Almost immediately he was escorted to his horse by three Blackfoot braves. They watched him suspiciously until he crossed the river.

When Farley was out of sight of the Blackfoot village, he pulled up his horse and dismounted. He then tied his mount and pack horse to a tree. He hadn't survived among the Blackfoot for so many years without being crafty and cunning. He couldn't just ride away and leave the James girl. He decided he would hide out in the vicinity, hoping for a chance to catch Joanna alone.

Farley knew if he was discovered it would mean his life, but he had to try and get that pretty little lady away from Windhawk.

Windhawk called his warriors together. They watched him expectantly, wondering what was on his mind.

"I have been told by the white man that Jo-anna's

little brother is a captive of Running Elk. I will go to the Piegan village and see if I can take him. I know that the Piegan is our brother, and we do not wish to go against a brother. That is why I will not ask any of you to go with me."

"I will go with you, my chief," Gray Fox spoke up. Soon many of the others also volunteered to go.

Windhawk held his hand up for silence. "I do not know if there will be bloodshed. I have known for a long time that Running Elk and I would one day meet on the field of battle. Perhaps that time has now come. I do not think he will easily give up Joanna's little brother."

They all agreed that they would accompany Windhawk. Not one among them liked the chief of the Piegans. It was well known that many of Running Elk's own warriors did not think well of him.

"Do you tell Joanna that her brother still lives?" Gray Fox asked.

"No, let no one speak to her of this, for if I cannot free him, it will be as if she lost him a second time."

"When do we leave?" one of the warriors asked.

"We leave as soon as you tell your families where we are going. Tell no one that we go to bring Joanna's brother home," Windhawk cautioned.


Joanna stared into space. She was hurt and resentful of the way Windhawk had treated her. When he had come into his mother's tipi to explain to Joanna that he was going away for a few days, she had turned her back to him, not wanting to speak to him.

She now lay in the big empty lodge, feeling heartsick. Windhawk had been so overbearing, without considering her feelings at all. She wished that she had at least voiced her reasons for being angry with him before he rode away.

Joanna heard a scratching sound against the back of the tipi near where she was lying. She sat up, thinking it might be a wild animal. Easing herself off the buffalo robe she inched her way over to the lodgepole where one of Windhawk's weapons hung. Grabbing a knife, she held her breath as the back of the tipi was split open. Joanna now knew it wasn't a wild animal, and it couldn't be a friend for he would come in the front way.

Staring down in complete bewilderment, she saw Farley crawl through the opening. He raised his finger to his lips to silence her.

"Ifen you want to be free, you best hurry up and come with me now," he whispered.

Joanna was undecided. Hadn't she wanted to escape? This might be her one and only chance to get away! Why did she hesitate? She thought of Windhawk; what would he do when he returned and found her gone? No, she must not think of him or she would weaken.

"Tell me what you want me to do, Farley," she said, quickly making up her mind.

"Let's us go out the way I came in," he said, taking her arm and pulling her toward the slit he had cut in the back of the lodge.

The night was dark as Joanna and Farley made their way cautiously out of the Blackfoot village.

Several of the dogs barked, but fortunately no one came out to investigate. Joanna held her breath, fearing at any moment she and Farley would be discovered.

As they reached the river, Farley led her downstream where he had hidden the horses.

When Joanna rode away into the night, she had to fight the impulse to turn around and go back. Her heart was heavy, but she knew she must not weaken. Hadn't she always known in her heart that she and Windhawk would have only a short time together? Her worse regret was that she had been unable to tell him she was leaving. But had she done so, he would never have allowed her to go. She had taken the only recourse open to her by leaving with Farley. There could never have been a good-bye between them.

Hot tears scalded her eyes as they left the Blackfoot village behind.

Joanna and Farley rode hard and fast, long into the night. There was no joy in Joanna's heart that she was now free. She knew when Windhawk discovered she was missing, he would come after her. She knew they would have to put a great distance between them and the Blackfoot village before he returned and discovered she had escaped. She hoped he would be away from the village for a few more days. That would give her and Farley a good head start.

Tag huddled in the corner of Running Elk's lodge. The sores on his back where the chief had

251

beaten him had healed, but the hatred in his heart festered. He gazed across at Amanda, who was now only a shadow of her former self. She had lost weight and was little more than a walking skeleton. Her eyes were always downcast, and any time Running Elk approached her, she would cringe.

Tag stared at Running Elk with hatred in his eyes. He had learned enough about the Blackfoot by now to know that not all of them were like Running Elk. Sometimes Tag would see pity in the eyes of the women when they looked at him. Running Elk would be a scourge on any race he belonged to, just as Uncle Howard was, he thought bitterly.

Tag detected the sound of several horses being ridden into camp. He watched as Running Elk walked out of the tipi to see who the riders were. Tag heard Running Elk speaking to someone, and he hoped he would be gone long enough for him to sneak over to Amanda. The two of them had never been left alone before. Usually Running Elk's wives were present when he left the tipi.

He made his way cautiously across the lodge, keeping a wary eye on the opening in case Running Elk should suddenly return. Amanda's eyes went furtively to the doorway, fearful that she and Tag would be punished should they be seen talking to one another.

"Are you all right, Amanda?" he asked, taking her thin hand in his.

Her eyes were sorrowful. "I will never be all right again, Tag. I wish I could just die and get it over with."

"Don't say that, Amanda! Some way you and I

are going to find a way to escape. I don't know how just yet, but I'm waiting for the right moment."

Amanda smiled sadly. "I don't know what I would have done had you not been here; you give me cause to hope."

The tipi flap was thrown aside and Running Elk entered. His dark eyes bored into Tag. In three strides, Running Elk was across the room and grabbed Tag by the scruff of the neck, dangling him in the air.

Tag closed his eyes waiting for the blow to fall, but it never came. He opened his eyes and saw Windhawk!

Windhawk had grabbed Running Elk's arm, and the two men were staring into each other's eyes.

"You dare come into my lodge and stay my hand!" Running Elk hissed.

Windhawk's eyes traveled to Tag, and he frowned when he saw how thin Joanna's brother was. "I have come for the boy," he said in a deep voice.

Running Elk released his hold on Tag and faced Windhawk defiantly. Others had crowded into the chief's tipi to see what was taking place.

"I have come for the boy," Windhawk said again. "I am willing to pay for him, but if we cannot agree on a price, I shall take him anyway."

Running Elk remembered only too well the other time Windhawk had forced him to back down in front of his warriors. Today would be different. Windhawk had come to his village with only a handful of warriors.

Running Elk was aware that many of his braves had become dissatisfied with his leadership lately.

Perhaps if he were to slay the legendary Windhawk he would impress them with his power.

His eyes moved to the tall, powerful chief of the Bloods. No one had ever called Running Elk a coward; however, he knew there was no way he could ever beat Windhawk in a fair fight.

"You cannot come into a man's lodge and say to him: 'Give me what I want,' " Running Elk said.

Windhawk nodded in agreement. "This is true. I came prepared to give you twelve of my best horses for the boy."

Running Elk's eyes gleamed with greed. Twelve horses was a great price to pay for the scrawny boy, he thought. "I have become very attached to the boy and would not want to give him up."

Windhawk looked at the scars on Tag's back, and he knew that Running Elk merely wanted to haggle over the price; he could not care for the boy since he had beat him so severely. "Set your price for the boy, and I will meet it," he said in an angered voice.

Running Elk looked at Windhawk suspiciously. "What is this white boy to you, that you would offer to purchase him at such a high price?"

"That is not your concern."

Tag understood enough of the Blackfoot language by now to know that Windhawk was bargaining for him. He glanced at the tall chief of the Bloods and could read compassion in the eyes that looked back at him. He didn't know why Windhawk had come to save him, but he hoped and prayed that he would succeed.

"Let us smoke the peace pipe and decide what is to be done with the boy," Running Elk said smiling.

Windhawk nodded and sat down cross-legged while Running Elk removed his medicine pipe from the leather pouch where he kept it. Windhawk motioned for his braves to wait outside, but two of Running Elk's warriors remained behind.

Tag saw Running Elk nod to his braves, and he knew instinctively that the Piegan chief was signaling to them. Tag glanced quickly at Windhawk to see if he knew of the impending danger, but he seemed totally unaware that Running Elk was up to something.

The boy saw Running Elk's hunting spear leaning against the lodgepole. He backed up cautiously until the weapon was within his reach.

Windhawk took the peace pipe Running Elk handed him and took a long drag. Out of the corner of his eye, he could see the two Piegan warriors around behind him. He knew in a flash that the chief was up to treachery. He started to stand up, but in that instant Running Elk made a dive for him while his two braves grabbed Windhawk from behind.

Windhawk's muscles were straining from the effort he was making to free himself. Tag saw that Windhawk wouldn't stand a chance against the three Indians, and he knew he had to help his friend, so he reached for the spear.

Running Elk gave Windhawk a satisfied smile. "At last I have you where I want you, Windhawk. Your people say that you are not mortal like the rest of us. Let us see if you will bleed when my knife pierces your heart."

Windhawk struggled and almost gained his freedom, but one of the braves grabbed a leather strap and wound it around his neck. Windhawk fell back, turning red in the face. He tried to free himself, but each move he made, the man tightened the strap to cut off his breathing.

Windhawk watched as Running Elk drew his knife, feeling as helpless as a baby. "Today is the day you will walk with the spirits, Windhawk," Running Elk said with a malignant grin. "If you are one of them, the spirits will welcome you."

The hand that held the knife moved forward, and Windhawk heard a soft thud. He saw the look of surprise on Running Elk's face as he fell forward with his own spear protruding from his back.

After Tag had thrown the spear, he raced across the room and threw his slight body against one of the other Indians.

The two Piegans had been staring at their dead chief, and that gave Windhawk time to free himself. He drew his knife and plunged it into the heart of one of the braves. He then pulled Tag off the other man and plunged his knife into him as well.

Grabbing Tag by the arm, Windhawk picked him up and carried him out of the tipi. By now many of the Indians had gathered in front of the chief's lodge, wondering what had taken place inside.

Windhawk held up his hand to gain their attention. "People of the Piegans, your chief is dead along with two of your braves. If there is any among you that will challenge me, let him step forward now."

A hush moved over the crowd as the Piegans digested Windhawk's words. They looked at each other for direction. One man stepped out of the crowd and began to speak. "I am Yellow Wing, and I will not challenge my brother until I know why this thing was done."

"I was set upon by two of your braves while your chief offered me the pipe of peace."

There were loud murmurings among the crowd, and Yellow Wing spoke again. "Running Elk has brought dishonor to his people by offering the peace pipe under false pretenses. The Bloods are our brothers; we will not challenge their chief."

"I think it would be wise for you to hold a council meeting to select a new chief," Windhawk said. "I would caution that you look deeper into the heart of the man you choose to lead you. Running Elk was not worthy of the mighty Piegans."

"That is so," Yellow Wing spoke up and was soon joined by a chorus of voices that agreed.

Windhawk looked down at Tag and drew him to his side. "I am taking this boy with me. Are there any who would challenge me for him?"

There was silence. No one dared challenge the mighty chief of the Bloods, for had he not just slain three men?

Tag pulled at Windhawk's sleeve. "I can't go with you if you don't take Amanda. I won't leave without her."

"Who is this person you speak of?" Windhawk asked.

Tag dashed into the tipi. He found Amanda huddled against the wall staring at the three dead men. "Come on, Amanda! We are saved! Windhawk is taking us away with him."

257

Amanda stared blankly at Tag. He took her hand and led her out of the tipi. "This is Amanda," he told Windhawk, placing a protective arm about her waist.

Windhawk nodded. Gray Fox led the horses forward, and Windhawk placed Amanda and Tag on one of them. As they rode away from the Piegan village, Tag felt his heart lighten. Today he had taken a man's life, and he wasn't sorry. He had fulfilled a promise he had made to his dead sister. Tag had no notion where they were going, or even why Windhawk had rescued him and Amanda, but it didn't matter. He looked over at Windhawk and received an encouraging smile. Tag laughed out loud as he rode beside the man he admired most in the world.

After riding a few hours, Windhawk called a halt so the horses could rest. He leaned back against a rock and invited Tag to sit beside him.

"I bet you never expected to see me in Running Elk's lodge, did you?" Tag asked, scooting close to Windhawk.

Windhawk looked at the boy who had been so badly mistreated. He remembered a time when Tag's face was smiling and happy. Now he looked careworn, older and wiser.

"You are the reason I went to the Piegan camp, little brother. I was told by the crazy white man where to find you."

"You mean you came to get me?"

Windhawk's eyes gleamed. "Yes, I had a good reason for wanting you safe which I will tell you about later."

Tag felt the long weeks of tiredness slip away. It didn't matter why Windhawk had rescued him. He was free!

"Am I going to go to your village with you, Windhawk?" he asked happily.

Windhawk smiled kindly at the small boy, thinking one of the first things he would do would be to see that Tag had some proper clothes to wear. His heart gladdened, thinking how happy Joanna would be to see her brother.

"Yes, little brother, I am taking you to my village," he answered, knowing now was not the time to tell him Joanna was alive.

Tag became serious. "I'd better get back to Amanda. She needs me to look after her."

He stood up. "Thank you, Windhawk. I'd rather be with you than anyone I know of."

Windhawk watched the small boy walk away. His clothes were ragged and he probably hadn't had a proper meal in weeks, but he held his head proudly, reminding Windhawk so much of his sister.

## Chapter Fourteen

Tag stood over Amanda with a look of concern on his young face. She was sitting beside the campfire staring into space, and hadn't uttered a word since Windhawk had taken them away from the Piegan village. He had tried to talk to her and assure her that they were safe now, but she didn't seem to comprehend anything he said to her.

Windhawk came up beside Tag. "I have seen women like this before."

"Do you think she will be all right?"

"I cannot say, little brother. Perhaps with time . . ."

Tag looked up at Windhawk. "I'm real worried about her, Windhawk. She doesn't even answer me when I speak to her."

"As I said, Tag, give her time."

"I guess time is all we have now, Windhawk. Amanda hasn't got any family to go to . . . of course I have my father." His eyes brightened. "I'll bet if Amanda could talk, she would thank you for saving her from Running Elk."

Windhawk's hand rested on the red-gold hair which was so much like Joanna's. "I owe you my life, Tag. Had it not been for you I would now be dead."

Tag smiled. "You once saved my life; now we are even." Tag looked up at the tall Indian. "Windhawk, today I killed a man, and I don't feel bad about it. I'm glad Running Elk is dead. I made a promise to my dead sister that I would avenge her. I've kept that promise."

"Walk with me, Tag. I think there are some things you should know."

Tag fell into step beside Windhawk. The night was cold and he hadn't eaten all day, but he felt neither the cold nor the hunger. "I bet no one but you could have killed both of those men today, Windhawk."

Windhawk smiled down into the blue eyes that were filled with admiration. "I could not have done it without you, little brother."

They both lapsed into silence as they neared the side of a deep cliff. "I gotta find a way to get to my father," Tag said, looking out over the vast wilderness and wondering how he would ever find his way back to civilization.

"Why is it important that you leave, little brother?" Windhawk said, thinking he could feel the same restlessness in the boy that he had seen in Joanna.

Tag's eyes narrowed. "I have an old score

to settle."

Windhawk sat down and braced his back against a pine tree, motioning for Tag to join him. "Tell me about this thing that pulls at you."

Tag sat down and laid his head over on his bended knees and stared across the valley thoughtfully. He told Windhawk all that had happened to him and Joanna since their mother had died. Windhawk listened quietly, trying to envision what Tag was telling him.

When at last Tag lapsed into silence, Windhawk put his hand on the boy's slight shoulder. "I can see that you feel you must find your father, little brother. You must be patient in this. First you must have food and rest so you can grow strong again."

"Windhawk, have you ever lost someone that you really loved?" Tag questioned.

"Yes, I lost my father."

"I missed my mother a lot after she died, but she was sick for a long time. Joanna was taken from me so suddenly. One moment she was smiling and happy, and the next moment she was . . . dead."

"Little brother, put your grief for your sister aside. She is not dead, but is living in my village. In two days time you will see her."

Tag thought he couldn't have heard correctly. How could Joanna be alive? Surely Windhawk would never jest about anything so important. His eyes were wide and hopeful as he searched for the truth in Windhawk's eyes.

"Joanna . . . is . . . alive?" he asked hesitantly, fearing he had misunderstood.

Windhawk smiled kindly at the boy. "Yes, Joanna is alive, have I not said so." He watched as tears gathered in Tag's eyes and his face lit up with overwhelming happiness.

"Joanna is alive!" he shouted, propelling himself into Windhawk's arms.

Windhawk laughed as he held Tag close to him. His heart felt lighter than it had in days. He would give Joanna the one thing she wanted most in the world: Her brother, Tag. Perhaps now Joanna would be contented.

Joanna and Farley had ridden all night and well into the next day before the old man called a halt.

Farley led the horses up a steep incline where he would hide them behind a thicket. Joanna followed closely behind him, trying to keep her balance on the rocky hillside.

She was too tired to even think straight. All she wanted to do was lie down and sleep.

Farley knew that they were still deep in Blackfoot territory. If he wasn't careful to take every precaution, Joanna would again be prisoner and he would be dead. He knew that the rocky ground would hide their tracks and throw anyone who was following them off the trail for a time. They would stop only long enough to sleep a few hours and rest the horses, before starting out again.

Joanna sat quietly, watching Farley unload the pack horse. She felt numb inside. Her heart ached at what she had left behind. She leaned her head over, too weary to examine her feelings too deeply.

Farley watched her head slide sideways to rest

against a tree. He placed a warm blanket over her and then lay down nearby. His rifle was beside him, cocked, and ready to fire. Tonight he wouldn't have the luxury of sleeping.

Windhawk stood over Tag, watching him sleep. The little brother was brave and had a valiant heart like his sister. Windhawk was anxious to return to Joanna. She had been angry with him when he left, and he could still feel her anger in the depth of his heart. He wanted to see her eyes light up when she saw her brother.

He lay on his bedroll and gazed at the darkened sky. He would do anything to please Joanna. He was a strong-willed man, but she was his one weakness. She was his wife and she would be waiting for him to return. Did she regret being angry with him? The ground he lay upon was hard, and he began to think of Joanna's soft body lying next to him. He was impatient for the night to end so he could start the journey home. He wanted to hold Joanna in his arms and tell her how much he had missed her.

Farley gathered up the reins of Joanna's mount and led him to the stream to drink. Should he tell her about her brother being a captive of Running Elk? he wondered. No, he had best wait to tell her until he had her safely at the fort. Then she would have women about her to comfort her in her grief. To Farley's way of thinking, it was better to be dead than be in the hands of Running Elk.

He scanned the horizon, looking for any Indian signs. He knew that devil, Windhawk, would come after the girl, but they had a good head start on him. If they continued at the pace they were going, they would easily outdistance him.

Walking back to Joanna, he stared at her sleeping form. She surely was a pretty little thing. He wondered if Windhawk had left her untouched? It wasn't likely. Windhawk had been too possessive of her, and hadn't he found her in Windhawk's lodge?

He bent down and shook Joanna lightly. "Best be on our way, little lady. We don't dare light a fire to cook grub. You'll have to make do with jerky for a spell."

Joanna opened her eyes and stared blankly at the old man. It took her a few moments to gather her thoughts enough to remember where she was. Sitting up, she felt as if her body ached all over from sleeping on the hard ground.

"Do you think he will come after me, Farley?" she asked, standing up and folding the blanket that had been covering her.

Farley didn't have to ask who she meant. "He'll come. But ifen you do just like I tell you, he ain't 'bout to catch up with us."

Joanna handed Farley the blanket, and followed him over to the pack horse to watch him slip it into a leather saddlebag. "I will never be able to thank you for helping me get away. It was a very brave thing you did, Farley."

"Shoot, ma'am. I couldn't just ride away and leave you there. It weren't the Christian thing to do."

She placed a delicate hand on his arm. "I shall always be grateful to you."

"Save your thanks, we ain't out of this yet. Are you up to some more hard riding?"

"You lead and I promise I'll keep pace."

"All right, here's the way it is. We ain't got no time for lolly-gagging. We'll ride 'til you think we ain't never gonna stop. You ain't gonna get much sleep, and there is danger from not only Indians, but wild animals as well. You look kinda puny to me. Are you sure you're up to it?"

"I will do anything you say, Farley. I am strong for a girl, and I promise I can keep up."

He looked at her slight form thinking she didn't look very strong to him. "You had best eat now. I want to be away as soon as you've finished." He handed her a slice of dried meat and watched as she bit into it.

Hell, he wasn't about to let them Blackfoot take her again. He shivered, thinking how angry Windhawk would be when he discovered his captive had gotten away. Farley knew he was now a marked man, and Windhawk would never give up until he was dead. There wasn't a corner of this land that would be safe for him to hide in. He was an old man and had lived a full rich life. All that mattered now was that he save the little lady.

As Joanna mounted her horse, she could feel something tugging at her heart. She would never see Windhawk again. She would return to her own world, but she would never be happy, for she had left her heart behind. She wished in the deepest recesses of her heart that she didn't have this obligation to her father.

Joanna had changed from the person she had once been. She had been Windhawk's wife, and she knew wherever she went, and whatever the future held for her, she would always feel married to him.

As the distance separated her from Windhawk, her heart grew heavier, but she knew she must not weaken. Please understand that I loved you, Windhawk, she sent him a silent message. I love you, but I could not stay with you.

She thought that with the passing of time, Windhawk would turn to one of the lovely dark-eyed maidens who adored him. Would he find forgetfulness in the arms of another? That thought was so painful that Joanna pushed it out of her mind.

She nudged her horse in the flanks and rode ahead of Farley. I must not look back. I have to be strong, she told herself.

It was barely daylight and the Blackfoot warriors were preparing for the long day's journey. Tag had taken Amanda some food and had fed it to her. She still had not uttered one word. It was as if she no longer cared about anything. All she did was stare blankly into space.

Windhawk looked toward the sunrise and saw a cloud of dust on the horizon. There were several riders coming in his direction and he became alert. They were too far away for him to tell if they were friend or foe.

"Look to your weapons," Windhawk called out. His warriors gathered about him and stood tensely waiting to see who the riders were. As they rode into view Windhawk could see they were men from his village. He waited for them to reach him.

Long Bow halted his horse and looked down at his chief. "The crazy one has taken your woman," he blurted out.

Windhawk's eyes narrowed dangerously, "When did this take place?"

"It was but two nights ago, my chief. We found evidence that the crazy one was in the village, and your wife left with him."

"Did he take her away by force?" Windhawk had spoken hardly above a whisper, and his heart cried out to know the truth. Joanna would never leave him. The old man must have forced her to go with him.

"There was no sign of a struggle. A slit was cut in the back of your tipi where they escaped."

Windhawk's eyes swept the countryside as he calculated in which direction they would have gone. "Did anyone try to follow their trail?"

"Yes, my chief, but no sign was found of them. The crazy man is clever, I think."

Anger swept through Windhawk's body like a strong wind. He would see the old man dead. Joanna had told him many times that she could not stay with him, but he hadn't thought she would leave him. He was sure that she had come to love him. Joanna had betrayed their love and ripped his heart to pieces. He would not readily forgive her.

"I will track them alone," he said, looking at Gray Fox. "The rest of you take the boy and the white girl back to the village."

Tag could see the confusion about him. He watched as Windhawk mounted his horse and rode swiftly away. "What has happened?" he asked Gray Fox.

Gray Fox shrugged his shoulders. "Windhawk has something to do. We will go on to the village," he replied, thinking Windhawk would not want the boy to know about his sister's disappearance.

The breeze tossed Windhawk's ebony hair as he rode across the wide prairie. There was a look of hatred in the depths of his dark eyes. The woman who had taken his heart had played him false. She would pay for what she had done. He pushed the love he had felt for her to the back of his mind. His heart had been wounded and cried out for revenge.

Only Gray Fox knew the torment Windhawk was feeling. He had seen the anger in his chief's face and could almost find it in his heart to pity Joanna. Windhawk would find her, Gray Fox was certain of that. What would be her fate when Windhawk saw her? He had rarely seen his chief so angry. The few times Windhawk's anger had made itself known, he had been merciless.

Gray Fox had liked and admired Windhawk's woman. Had it not been for her bravery, his son would now be walking among the spirits.

He mounted his horse and motioned for the others to do the same. He wished Windhawk had allowed him to go with him. Windhawk wasn't thinking too clearly and Gray Fox wanted to be with him when he found Joanna. Perhaps had he gone, he could stop his friend from punishing her too severely when he caught up with her. He never doubted for a moment that Windhawk would find Joanna and the old trapper. No one could outsmart his chief. Windhawk had some kind of uncanny ability when it came to tracking.

Joanna and Farley had bedded down for the night. They had eaten dried jerky and washed it down with water from the waterskin. The weather had turned colder and Joanna could feel the chill through the heavy blanket which covered her. The tall pine trees they were lying under swayed with the wind, giving off a lonesome sound.

"Farley, have you any idea what month it is? I have lost all track of time."

"Surely I do. I always keep a calendar in my head. It would be November the twentieth. I don't recollect the weekday, though."

"It's still autumn, then."

"I reckon it is. But out here the weather can fool a man. You can wake up to a warm sun shining, and by noon, you can be facing a blizzard. We've been lucky so far. This autumn has been a mild one. The winters here are mighty fierce, I can tell you. I hope this fine weather holds 'til we make it to Fort Leavenworth."

"Is that where you're taking me?"

"Yep, it were the only safe place I knowed, where Windhawk won't dare attack. Leastwise, I'm hoping he won't. You can't never be sure 'bout him though."

Joanna closed her eyes tightly, but still the tears seeped through. Oh, Windhawk, she cried silently.

How painful it is knowing I will never again look upon your face. I will go through life wondering what you are doing. I will never forget that for the space of a few short weeks, I was your wife.

She turned over on her side, feeling misery in the depth of her soul. Many times today she had wanted to turn her horse around and ride back to Windhawk. She dared not give in to the weakness. She heard the distant call of a wolf and the answer of its mate. When she was an old woman she would still remember the dark handsome Indian who had touched her life so briefly.

Would the pain ever stop? she wondered. Was she to drift for eternity like a lost soul searching for her true home? She closed her eyes and willed her mind to be a blank. She had no time to look back and regret. She had made the right decision. Now she would live with the consequences.

## Chapter Fifteen

Farley had found a small abandoned cave where he and Joanna could spend the night.

Joanna sat on a blanket while Farley built a fire. "I'm using only willow branches 'cause they don't smoke," he informed her. She watched with interest while he struck a fire-steel against a piece of flint. The branches soon caught, and they had a cheerful fire to brighten the dark recesses of the cave.

"Aren't you afraid the fire can be seen by . . . Indians, Farley?

"Nah, that's why I stacked them branches at the mouth of the cave. You can sleep warm tonight, and there ain't no reason for you to be scairt."

Joanna was quiet for a long time, lost in thought. It would be so good to be able to sleep in a shelter tonight. "You know, Farley, it's funny how one's values can change in such a short space of time."

He eyed her speculatively. "In what way?"

She smiled brightly. "There was a time when I was concerned whether to have the cook serve roast duckling or baked ham. Now I just wish I had a warm meal and a good cup of coffee to go with it."

Farley's eyes sparkled and he grinned from ear to ear. "You are 'bout to get your wish, 'cause I'm gonna make you up some flapjacks that will just melt in your mouth. Course they would be better ifen I had me some sourdough."

"I can hardly wait. What can I do to help you?"

"You just sit there looking pretty. I'm fixing the vittles tonight."

When Joanna tasted the light, fluffy pancakes, she swore she had never tasted anything half so good. After she finished her third flapjack, she felt contented. The coffee was strong, and there were grounds in the bottom of her cup, but to Joanna it tasted heavenly.

After she had helped Farley clean and pack away the cooking utensils, she lay back on her blanket, staring at the walls of the cave.

Joanna had not allowed herself to dwell on Windhawk often, but when she closed her eyes, she could remember every detail of his face. In her mind she could picture him as he always looked, standing tall and proud. He had such a noble spirit. She could never envision him doing anything that was not honorable. Would he think her dishonorable because she left without telling him? She knew had she told him she was leaving, he would never have allowed her to go. She hoped Windhawk would remember that she had told him she would someday have to leave him.

Oh, Windhawk, I do miss you so much, she thought. I believe I shall miss you every day of my life.

Farley spread his blanket out and lay down. He could tell Joanna was having troubled thoughts, so he decided to distract her. "Joanna, did I ever tell you 'bout the winter of twenty-two?"

She turned to face him. "No, I don't believe you did, Farley."

He scratched his beard in thoughtfulness. "That were the winter the Indians called, *Ai-so-pwom-stan,* which means . . . the windmaker. That year the winds started blowing in mid-October and didn't let up nary a bit 'til long into December. What we had was three months of blizzard. The snow fell most every day and it weren't fit for man nor beast to be out. I was holed up in a cave, pretty much like thisun. I woke up one morning, and to my chagrin, found that I was plumb snowed in. The snow filled the whole front of the cave and there weren't no way I could dig myself out."

"That must have been awful, Farley." Joanna said wide-eyed. "What did you do?"

"Well . . . I tried to dig out with the butt of my rifle, but it weren't no good. I was 'bout to give up, when I seed something furry and black in the back of the cave. Now mind you, it had been dark when I entered the cave the night before. Being half froze, I didn't search the cave none too good. That's one mistake I don't make no more."

"What was in the cave with you, Farley?" Joanna asked, holding her breath.

"It were the biggest grizzly you ever seed. I

reckon I woke him up from his sleep. That bear must have stood seven feet tall."

Joanna sat up. "What did you do, Farley?"

"Well, sir, I found strength I never knowed I had. I grabbed up that rifle and dug out of that cave so fast it would make your head spin. I run out of that cave and buried up in at least ten foot of snow. I couldn't get out of that snow, but that bear couldn't get to me neither. Never thought I'd want to be buried alive in snow, but I prayed the snow wouldn't melt 'til that griz lost interest in me."

"Why do you like to live in this wilderness, Farley? Don't you ever yearn to be with your own people?"

"Nope, I ain't lost nothing in the white world. You ain't never lived 'til you stand atop a mountain and know you're the only human being fer as far as you can see."

"Will you ever be able to return to this land, or did you forfeit that right when you helped me escape from the Blackfoot village?"

"I don't reckon Windhawk is gonna be too forgiving. I don't expect he would welcome me back with open arms."

"I'm sorry, Farley. You made a great sacrifice when you helped me. I can only tell you how grateful I am. It's a pity that by helping me, it has cost you so much. I wish it didn't have to be so. I'm fearful at what Windhawk might do to you, should he catch up with us."

"I was glad to help you, Joanna. Don't you go fretting none 'bout me. I have been in tighter places afore, and I always managed to keep my scalp. I ain't figuring on cashing in just yet."

"He's out there somewhere in the dark, Farley . . . I can feel it."

"Yep."

"You don't think he will catch up with us, do you?"

"Not ifen I can help it. Course, he's not one to give up easy. I don't dare let my guard down."

Joanna sighed and lay down. She was too tired to think. She would be so glad when they reached the fort so she could rest. She thought she could easily sleep for a week without ever waking.

"It's gonna snow afore morning, Joanna. I can feel it in my bones."

"Will that be a handicap for us?"

"It could be a blessing ifen it keeps on snowing; that way it would cover our tracks. Ifen it just snows a bit and then quits, we'll be in a heap of trouble, cause Windhawk won't have to look for our tracks. They'll show up as plain as the nose on your face."

Joanna prayed silently for the snow to fall. "How long will it take until we reach the fort, Farley?"

"Barring trouble, we should be there in 'bout three more weeks."

Joanna's eyes felt heavy. Three more weeks to freedom, and then what? She would still have to wait out the winter before she could go on to Oregon. What if by the time she reached Oregon, her father had returned to Philadelphia? Face one problem at a time, Joanna, she chided herself. First you make it safely to the fort, and then you worry about what comes next. Her eyes drifted shut, and she could feel herself falling asleep.

She couldn't help thinking how heartbreaking it would be to return home without Tag. Perhaps if it weren't for the fact that she felt obligated to find her father, she would turn around and ride back to Windhawk.

It no longer seemed important to her that her aunt and uncle had stolen Tag's heritage since he was not alive to claim it. Her father wouldn't need her. He was capable of throwing her aunt and uncle out of his home.

Why had she begun to question herself? She had done the right thing in leaving. She would not allow herself to have any regrets. What she and Windhawk shared had been beautiful, but it was over. She would not allow herself to look back, for it would serve no purpose. She had an obligation to her father, didn't she? Why then did the future look so dark and dreary? she wondered. Why did she feel so empty inside? She brushed a hand over her face, angrily wiping away the tears.


Windhawk dismounted and bent down to examine the ground with an expert eye. The snow had begun to fall heavily, making it nearly impossible to find any signs that might have been left by Joanna and the old man.

That morning he had discovered a cave where they had stopped one night before. He was closing in on them. The old man was sly and wily, and at times Windhawk would lose the trail altogether.

Windhawk had ridden day and night, switching

from one horse to the other. He didn't feel the fatigue: All he could think about was the fact that Joanna had betrayed him. He hadn't allowed himself to dwell on what he would do to Joanna once he caught up with her . . . he was too angry. He only knew that the old man would die.

They were no more than a day ahead of him now. He had one slight advantage they couldn't know about . . . he knew where they were going. The old man was taking Joanna to the fort of the long knives. If the snow would stop falling, they would be unable to hide their tracks, and he would catch up with them by tomorrow night.

Windhawk remounted and nudged his horse forward. The old man had cleverly taken the rocky trail, but Farley had outsmarted himself. He had not known that Windhawk knew a shortcut across the valley.

The next day the snow continued to fall. By late afternoon the wind had blown it into high snowdrifts, making it hard for the horses to plod through. Farley could see that the horses had been pushed to the limit. He didn't fancy walking to Fort Leavenworth, so he called for Joanna to dismount.

"Like as not, we won't get no farther today, Joanna. We might as well set up camp for the night. The weather don't seem to want to let up, and them horses are just plumb tuckered out."

Joanna slipped off her mount, grateful for her tall moccasins which protected her legs from the deep snow. She doubted that Windhawk would allow the snow to slow him down. She feared that if they stopped now, he would gain on them.

"What of Windhawk? Shouldn't we push on, Farley? I don't think he will allow this storm to deter him."

"That may be, but he ain't 'bout to pick up our trail in this snow."

In no time at all, Farley had stretched a heavy bearskin across four poles he had hammered into the frozen ground. He motioned for Joanna to crawl underneath the shelter. Farley had given her one of his heavy beaver jackets and she was more than grateful for its warmth.

She watched as the seemingly never-ending snowflakes drifted downward. The strong wind whirled the white flakes around, pelting them into her face and making visibility impossible.

Windhawk was out there somewhere, she thought. Perhaps he was a day, or even a week behind them, but he would come.

Joanna shivered and huddled beneath a warm buffalo robe. It was as if she could feel Windhawk's nearness. She closed her eyes, not knowing if she wanted him to find her or not. At first she had been so sure she was doing the right thing by leaving him. Now she wasn't so confident.

Farley tromped out of the woods and stood over Joanna's sleeping form. She had been a mighty brave little lady, not once complaining when the going got rough. She was such a beautiful girl, too delicate and frail to be exposed to all the hardships she had been forced to endure. She seemed to bring out the best in him. He wanted nothing more than to see her back safely where she belonged. He knew very little about her life, or just where she had come from.

Joanna felt Farley watching her. Her eyes opened and she favored him with a smile. Sitting up, she made room for him to join her under the shelter.

They both stared out into the swirling world of whiteness. "Have you ever seed any snowstorm like thisun?" he inquired.

"No, but I was told by my father that in the Oregon Territory the winters are often severe."

Now was his chance to find out more about her, he thought. "Was you on your way to your pa in Oregon when the wagon train was raided?" he asked .

"Yes, my father's name is Russell James. Because of circumstances that I don't want to go into, my brother, Tag, and I were on our way to join him."

Farley saw the tears gather in her blue eyes, and he thought if he was going to tell her about her brother still being alive, now would be the time.

"It has been very difficult for me to accept Tag's . . . death. He . . . he was such a wonderful boy. He was always so full of life and curiosity."

Farley felt choked up and cleared his throat. "Have you come to terms with him being dead?"

"Yes, I had no choice."

No, he thought, he would not tell her just yet that her brother was still alive. If she had already begun to accept the boy's death, it would be a double blow to her if she found out he was a prisoner.

The gale force winds whistled and howled. The reins of the horses had been tied to a tree so they wouldn't wander off to be lost in the snowstorm. Every so often Farley would check on them to make sure they didn't freeze to death.

Farley looked speculatively skyward. These storms could sometimes last for days, or even weeks. Tomorrow they would have to push on, regardless of the weather. Farley knew Windhawk wouldn't allow the storm to slow him down. If he had to make his choice about which danger he would rather face — being lost in the storm, or facing an angry Windhawk — he would rather choose the storm.

Windhawk pushed onward through the blinding snow. He had some built-in primitive instinct that kept him from losing his way. This was his land and he knew every mountain and stream. He couldn't underestimate the old trapper; however, he also knew the land well. Windhawk was trusting Joanna to slow the old man down.

The next morning the snowstorm still raged on. Joanna and Farley made very little progress since the horses were having such a difficult time plodding through the high snowdrifts. They were forced to stop every so often to rest the exhausted animals.

Joanna was beginning to think she would never feel warm again. Her hands felt numb and frozen. Her cheeks were red and stung painfully from the sharp particles of frozen snow the wind hurled against her.

They had scarcely gone any distance when Farley decided that they could go no farther until the storm let up. He had unloaded the horses and tethered them near the camp site.

Joanna watched Farley driving stakes into the frozen ground, so he could stretch a buffalo hide to make a shelter for them to escape from the storm. She was puzzled when she heard a loud clinking sound. She watched in confusion as Farley's face paled, and he fell forward into the snow, gasping in pain. She ran to him and knelt down beside him.

"Farley, what's the matter? Are you hurt?"

"I think I blundered into a trap, Joanna. I've done some damned fool things in my life, but I didn't never think I'd get caught in another man's trap."

Joanna started digging frantically while pushing the snow away from his legs. She gasped when she discovered his right leg was caught just above the ankle in a big-toothed trap. The clinking sound she'd heard had been the trap springing shut. The snow near the trap was becoming bloodstained and Joanna was frantic, fearing she would be unable to free Farley. If she couldn't free him and stop the flow of blood, she knew he would bleed to death. With furious determination, Joanna began digging deeper into the snow. She discovered that the trap was securely chained to a tree, and no amount of pulling and tugging would make it give way.

Farley groaned as he sat up. "That there's a wolf trap . . . I 'spect I'm lucky my ankle ain't broken. Hurts like hell, though. You're gonna have to help me pry them teeth apart. I feel weak as a newborn baby."

"Just tell me what to do and I'll do it, Farley." She

282

could see that he was in a great deal of pain. At the moment his face was drained of color and she feared he would soon lose consciousness.

Farley leaned forward trying to help Joanna, but feeling dizzy, he lay back gasping in pain. "What you have to do is push them two levers on either side of the trap down at the same time. I don't seem to have the strength to help you none."

Joanna examined the trap and found the two levers Farley had told her about. She armed herself mentally, knowing she was going to need all of her strength. When she touched the metal it was so cold her hands stuck to it. She braced her back against the tree and with all of her strength, she pushed down on the levers. She felt them move a little, but not enough to free Farley.

"I think I'm a gonna slip away, Joanna," he said in a whisper. Joanna watched helplessly as the old man lost consciousness. She was determined to free him.

She set her chin stubbornly and grasped the trap with renewed strength. She strained with all her might, and after what seemed forever, the hinges began to move apart. Joanna pushed them down by throwing all her weight into it. Then she heard the click that told her the trap was wedged open. With considerable effort, she managed to pull Farley's leg free. She was careful not to spring the trap shut again.

It was some time later before she was able to stretch the shelter over Farley. Joanna pulled a warm blanket over him to ensure he wouldn't freeze to death. She found a bottle of liquor among his belongings and poured it over his wound. She then bound his ankle with a clean piece of cloth, which she had soaked with the liquor.

Laying her head against his chest, she could hear his steady heartbeat and hoped he would be all right. Perhaps it would be best for him to remain unconscious for a time. Joanna couldn't tell if his ankle had been crushed by the trap. She had done everything she could to make Farley comfortable. Now it was a matter of waiting. She felt lost and alone without Farley to guide her.

As night began to fall, the cold became even more intense. Joanna wished that Farley would awaken so he could tell her what to do. Joanna managed to build a fire and then lay down beside Farley, exhausted. She was too tired to think. Closing her eyes, she drifted off to sleep.

Joanna had no idea how long she had slept, but something disturbed her and she sat up suddenly. It was dark and the fire had died down. She had an uneasy feeling that was hard to define. It had stopped snowing and the clouds had moved away, revealing a pale moon.

Joanna checked Farley to see if he had awakened and found him watching her.

"Where's my rifle, Joanna?" he said in a quiet voice.

She felt around in the half-light until she found it. "I have it, Farley."

"Get both the rifles, Joanna. Check to make sure they's loaded."

Joanna did as he asked. "Yes, they are loaded," she told him, wondering at the urgency in his voice.

Farley rose up on his elbow. "Build up the fire, but don't move out of the firelight. Hurry!"

"Why, Farley?" she asked, beginning to feel frightened for the first time.

" 'Cause we are 'bout to have company."

Joanna's eyes probed the darkened shadows, but she could see nothing.

"Do as I say, Joanna! We got troubles and I ain't got time to explain."

The urgency in his voice spurred her into action. If it was Windhawk, Farley wouldn't want her to build up the fire, she reasoned. She gathered up several sticks of wood she had piled nearby and threw them on the fire. All the while her eyes were searching the darkness. The wood caught, and soon the campfire was ablaze.

Joanna backed up slowly and sat down beside Farley. "What's out there, Farley? I don't see anything."

"You may not see it, but it sees you. We got us a panther prowling 'bout."

Joanna slowly picked up the rifle. "W . . . what will it do to us?"

"Joanna, heed me. I ain't feeling none too good. I don't know how long I can keep from passing out on you. You gotta keep the fire lit and keep them rifles handy."

"I'm frightened, Farley," Joanna said as she held onto one of the guns as if it were a lifeline.

"I ain't gonna tell you there's not nothing to be scairt 'bout. Ifen that devil comes at you, aim fer between its eyes."

Joanna nodded. "I will, Farley. I'll try."

Farley leaned back and closed his eyes. "I wish I could help you, but . . ." his voice trailed off and Joanna knew he had lost consciousness again.

Never had she felt so alone. Her thoughts went to Windhawk. If she were to die, he would never know how hard it had been for her to leave him. She wished she could see him just one more time.

Hours passed — Joanna had used up all the wood and remembered that Farley had told her not to leave the ring of light. She strained her eyes trying to see past the dense trees. If there was a panther out there lurking in the darkness, she couldn't see it.

Suddenly, she heard snow falling from the tree branches overhead and it landed on top of the shelter. Oh, God, no, she thought. The panther was just above them.

Joanna crawled out of the shelter and gazed up into the tree branches. She caught her breath as she saw the huge panther which was poised, waiting to spring down on her. The animal made a hideous sound and Joanna froze. She had foolishly left the gun behind.

"Windhawk!" she screamed, and her voice was carried away by the wind.

# Chapter Sixteen

Windhawk heard Joanna calling out to him. He vaulted off his horse, taking in the situation with one glance. He could see the huge cat poised above Joanna, ready to spring. Without pausing to consider, he ran toward her while unsheathing his knife. He leaped across the campfire, grabbed Joanna by the shoulders, and shoved her behind him.

It was as if the panther became aware that he was now faced with a stronger adversary. The animal snarled and paced back and forth on the tree branch. All the while its eyes never left Windhawk.

Joanna realized that Windhawk had placed himself in danger to protect her. She was trembling, knowing that he faced certain death because of her.

Joanna wanted to tell Windhawk that she was glad he had come for her. She now knew she had been secretly hoping he would catch up with her and

Farley. If he were to be killed by the panther, it would be her fault. She wanted to tell him so many things as she watched his body tense and his hand grip the knife tightly.

This was the man she loved. He was her husband; she couldn't just cringe behind him, waiting to see him torn apart by the cat. Joanna saw Farley's rifle lying not three feet away. If she went for the gun, would the panther spring? She decided it was worth the chance. Without hesitating, she leaped forward and in one smooth motion grabbed the gun, swinging it up toward the cat.

At that moment the panther sprang into the air. Joanna knew she had no time to take careful aim, so she merely pulled the trigger.

The cat caught Windhawk with a force that knocked him to the ground. Joanna could see that she had only wounded the animal. She watched as Windhawk's muscles were strained to the limit as he tried to hold the panther's sharp teeth away from his throat. He raised his knife and plunged it into the animal's heart.

Moments passed and Joanna held her breath. She heard Windhawk groan. He pushed the dead panther off him and rolled over, staggering to his feet.

Joanna noticed he was covered with blood, but she didn't know if it was his blood or the cat's.

Windhawk's eyes swept Joanna's face, and she saw unbridled anger in the dark depths. She wanted to run to him and throw herself into his arms, but she hesitated. There was no softening in his dark eyes that glinted with anger. He showed no sign that he was happy to see her.

"You are hurt! Let me help you," she said, taking a step toward him.

She saw him tense and knew that he would not want any help from her. "The time will come when you may wish I had allowed the beast to kill you, Jo-anna," he told her in English.

"Windhawk, I . . ." She saw him stumble and fall, clutching his shoulder. Running to him, Joanna knelt down and reached out her hand to help him. "Please allow me to help you, Windhawk."

He pushed her away and stood up. If he was in pain, it didn't show on his face. Was he too proud to accept help from her? she wondered.

"Windhawk, please, I . . ."

He silenced her with a dark gaze, then looked at the makeshift shelter, searching for Farley. "Where is the old man?" he asked, retrieving his knife from the dead cat and cleaning the blood from it by plunging it into the snow.

Before Joanna could answer him, Farley raised up on his elbow and poked his head out of the shelter. "What's happened?" he asked, looking at the dead panther which was sprawled out on the snow-covered ground.

Windhawk walked slowly toward Farley. "Tonight you die, white man."

Joanna was stunned as she looked from one man's face to the other. Surely Windhawk hadn't meant that he was going to kill Farley!

"I figured as much, Windhawk," Farley said, lying back already resigned to his fate.

Joanna realized that it was Windhawk's intention to slay Farley and she wasn't about to stand helplessly by while he killed the old trapper. Without thinking, she ran to the second rifle and picked it up, aiming it at Windhawk. "If you go near Farley, I will shoot, Windhawk; I swear I will," she challenged.

Windhawk turned to face her, feeling she had chosen the old man over him. He saw the determined look on her face and knew she wouldn't hesitate to pull the trigger if he were to harm the old man. Had she no feeling for what had passed between them?

His eyes narrowed and he felt wild unleashed fury. In his heart he had once believed Joanna had loved him but he now knew she had only been pretending. He did not feel the cold that seeped into his body, nor could he feel the pain from the deep gash where the cat had mauled him. He felt only betrayal, and a strong need for revenge.

Joanna prayed that Windhawk wouldn't force her to shoot. How could she destroy that which she loved most in the world? She watched as he raised his proud head. His eyes were cold as he stared at her.

"Don't make me do it," she pleaded. "Just go away and leave us alone."

Windhawk had no thought for his safety. If Joanna shot him it would end the torment he was feeling. He took one step toward her, then another.

The rifle swung wide and then the barrel leveled at his chest. "Don't test me, Windhawk," she said, feeling as if she were being forced into a corner.

He advanced on her, never taking his eyes from her face. Those dark eyes challenged her to pull the trigger.

Joanna closed her eyes, her hand trembled and her heart cried out at what she was being forced to do. A loud sob escaped her lips and she knew in that moment that she would never be able to shoot Windhawk.

He suddenly lunged at Joanna and knocked her off balance. She fell backwards and Windhawk fell on top of her. The impact made the rifle discharge and the shot fired harmlessly into the air.

Windhawk sat up, straddling her. He wrenched the gun from her hand and threw it aside. "You should never have hesitated, Jo-anna. There will be many times for you to regret that you did not kill me when you had the chance," he said in a harsh whisper.

His eyes were so cold and unfeeling that it sent a shiver down the back of Joanna's neck. She had once seen those dark eyes softened by love, but there was no evidence of tenderness in the ebony depths at the moment.

Joanna closed her eyes when she saw him draw back his hand. Windhawk struck her hard, catching her firmly on the jaw. Pain exploded in her head and darkness engulfed her.

Windhawk picked her up in his arms and carried her to the shelter where he laid her down beside the old man. As he bound her arms and legs with leather ropes, tears blinded his vision. His anger had caused him to hurt her. He touched her face where he had struck her and saw that it had already started turning blue in color. He had never before struck a woman. This woman was white, he thought, trying to vindicate himself. She had taken the love he had offered her, replacing it with treachery and deceit.

Never again would he allow her to touch his heart. He would take her back to his village, and she would be treated as any captive who had been taken in battle.

Windhawk glanced at the old man and noticed that blood had seeped through the cloth which was wrapped about his ankle. With a sweeping glance he saw the white man's trap and knew immediately what had happened. He smiled, thinking the old man had been caught in a trap which had been set by his own kind. Windhawk had not yet decided the old man's fate. The sleepless nights and long days he had endured trying to catch up with Joanna had taken their toll. He was much too weary to think.

He stood up, feeling the pain of his wounds. Removing his shredded buckskin shirt, he took a handful of snow and rubbed it over the wound. The gash was deep and ran across his shoulder and down his arm. He gritted his teeth in agony when he pulled a clean buckskin shirt on and it rubbed against his wound. The pain from his injury did not hurt him as much as the anguish that Joanna had caused him.

Piling a stack of wood on the fire, he watched the hungry flames lick at the wood and burst into a warm blaze.

Tomorrow they would start for his home, he thought, and he pitied Joanna if she caused him the least bit of trouble. His expression was grim as he pulled a warm blanket over her.

He lay down beside her, hoping he would find forgetfulness in sleep. He watched the firelight flicker across Joanna's face, and fell asleep.

Joanna opened her eyes. The bright sunlight reflected off the snow, blinding her for the moment. She tried to sit up, but found to her dismay that Windhawk had bound her arms and legs with ropes and she couldn't move.

She glanced around, trying to locate Windhawk and Farley, but neither of them were about. Her jaw felt sore and she remembered Windhawk striking her the night before. She was Windhawk's captive now. Her bid for freedom had ended in disaster.

Joanna realized that it had stopped snowing, but the cold wind prevented the snow from melting. She was acutely aware of the heaviness in her heart. It had been apparent to her last night that Windhawk detested her. Where had his love gone? She still loved him, in fact, her love seemed deeper than it had before.

She thought about him standing between her and the panther last night. He had risked his life to save her. She remembered he had been injured, and wondered how badly.

Where was Farley? Had Windhawk harmed him? She struggled against the ropes trying to get loose. The more she struggled, the tighter the bonds became, cutting off her circulation. She had been so intent on trying to remove the ropes that she hadn't heard Farley come up beside her.

"It won't do no good trying to get loose, Joanna. Windhawk ain't never gonna let neither one of us go."

She quickly looked at his ankle and saw that it had been freshly bound. "Is your ankle very painful, Farley?"

"It don't feel none too good, but I'm glad there ain't no broken bones. Windhawk put a fresh dressing on it. I didn't figure on him helping me none, but you can't never tell 'bout him."

Joanna's eyes moved toward the woods searchingly. "Where is Windhawk?"

"He's getting the horses ready." Farley looked at Joanna. "I reckon you saved my life last night."

"I couldn't allow him to harm you, Farley."

He saw the pain in her eyes. "I don't know if you did me a favor or not. That'll depend on what his plans are for me."

Joanna sighed. Her life hadn't been hers to control for a long time. Once again the future looked bleak and uncertain. She had no idea what Windhawk had in mind for either her or Farley. Last night she had tested him to the limit. She knew he would never believe that she could not have pulled that trigger. She knew there wasn't any point in discussing it with him. He was in no mood to listen to anything she had to say.

Windhawk walked toward Joanna, leading the horses. His eyes were cold as he tossed a piece of pemmican at her and it landed in her lap. He spoke no words to her as he stood over her waiting for her to eat.

294

Joanna swallowed a lump of fear as his dark eyes narrowed. She didn't want the food and knew it would stick in her throat, but the look Windhawk gave her told her that if she didn't eat, he would cram the food down her. Her teeth tore into the meat, and she chewed, then swallowed without tasting.

When Windhawk was satisfied that she had eaten enough, he handed her the reins of her horse. Joanna noticed he had exchanged the buckskin shirt which the panther had shredded for another one. She wanted to ask if he was hurt, but his dark gaze did not encourage conversation.

Farley limped around, packing the blankets and cooking utensils. Joanna would have helped him but Windhawk stalled her. She stood motionless as he unbound her legs and swung her onto her horse.

When Windhawk mounted, Joanna and Farley looked at each other in surprise. Was he allowing Farley to go free? Joanna wondered. Her relief was overwhelming as she realized that was exactly what he was doing.

Windhawk paused beside the old trapper and looked down at him. "Colder weather is coming on, old man," he said, speaking in the Blackfoot language. "I do not think you will last past the first few days."

"I reckon it's a fer piece to walk to the first white outpost," Farley agreed in English.

Joanna watched as Windhawk swung his mount away. "I will kill you the next time I see you, old man," he said, grabbing hold of Joanna's horse's reins.

"You can't just leave him here to die," Joanna pleaded when she saw it was Windhawk's intention to take Farley's horses, leaving him afoot.

Windhawk paid no heed to Joanna's pleading. He jerked on her horse's reins, pulling her forward, and she had to grab on to the horse's mane to keep from falling off. When they rode away Joanna turned to look back at Farley. He looked so forlorn standing there alone. She wanted to protest, but she knew her pleas would fall on deaf ears.

The leather rope cut into her wrists and she squeezed her eyes tightly together, trying not to cry. She had tested fate by trying to escape, but fate had accepted her challenge and she was now the loser.

Her eyes rested on Windhawk's broad back. He held his head so straight and proud, and her heart went out to him.

This was a Windhawk she didn't know. He was hard, cold and unforgiving. He would not bend. Emotions would never rule this man: He would always be in control.

Had she killed his love for her? She knew instinctively that he would not be a forgiving man.

The vast wilderness stretched before them. The snow was beginning to melt, causing a slushing sound beneath their horses' hooves. Joanna turned to look back where they had left Farley, but he had already been swallowed up by the thick pine forest.

Where was her spirit? she wondered. She should insist that Windhawk turn around and go back for Farley. Why did she not fight him? Because, she answered herself, you love him and want to be with him under any circumstances.

Joanna now knew that had she reached civilization, she would never have been free. Her heart would always have been the prisoner of the tall proud chief of the Blood Blackfoot tribe.

By nightfall Windhawk halted his horse and dismounted. He reached for Joanna and pulled her roughly from her horse. Picking her up in his arms, he carried her to the river and tied her to a nearby tree. He hadn't spoken to her all day and even now, he refused to look at her.

Joanna watched him while he tended the horses and felt tears of misery in her eyes. When would he break this wall of silence which existed between them? She crawled to the edge of the river and cupped her hands, drinking deeply from the icy water.

What had happened to the girl who had defied her aunt and uncle? What had happened to the Joanna James who had escaped from the Blackfoot village? Was her spirit completely broken? Had Windhawk sapped all her strength? Yes, she answered herself. She had no more fight left in her. She was too weary to think past a good night's sleep.

Joanna's eyes widened in fright as Windhawk approached her. He untied her and pulled her toward the campfire. He then pushed her down upon a blanket and tied her once more to a nearby tree.

Joanna lay back, closing her eyes. She loved him so much it was painful. He would never understand why she had tried to escape. Apparently he still hadn't forgiven her for pulling the rifle on him.

She curled up in a tight ball and felt him drape a

blanket over her. She needed sleep. She had been totally drained, physically as well as mentally. Tomorrow would be soon enough to reflect on her future, she thought sleepily.

Windhawk stood over her watching her deep intake of breath. She had become almost docile, as if she were resigned to her fate. He didn't want her to be beaten. At least not yet. He wanted to see her suffer before he finally broke her spirit. He wanted to see her grovel at his feet, begging him for mercy. The tender feelings he had once had for her had been replaced with a strong resentment. She would feel his wrath and displeasure many times before he was finished with her.

He lay down beside her, thinking what he would do to make her feel pain as he had. Turning his head, he stared into her hauntingly beautiful face. Her pale cheeks looked soft and smooth in the firelight. He looked at her jaw where he had struck her the night before. Reaching out, he gently touched the bruise.

He fought against the tender feelings that crept into his heart. How he had loved her! Had she returned his love he would have done anything to please her. Now, she would feel his anger every day for the rest of her life.

Joanna sighed in her sleep and Windhawk glanced at the gap at the top of her doeskin gown. He could see the swell of her breasts and remembered how soft her body was. He turned his back, angry with himself for wanting her, and angry with Joanna for making him want her. He might hate her now, but he still wanted her as much as he ever had.

Windhawk stared into the night. He would push his desire for her out of his mind. Was he not Windhawk, chief of the Blackfoot? He would never again allow a woman to rule his heart, least of all the flaming-haired Joanna.

The next day Windhawk was still silent and brooding. Joanna could feel his coldness like a knife in her heart. The eyes that had once looked at her lovingly, now stared at her with icy contempt.

In the past Joanna would have fought anyone who had attempted to tie her up as Windhawk had, but his attitude toward her seemed to have sealed her lips.

It was long after sunset when they stopped to make camp for the night. As usual Windhawk had tied Joanna's ankles while he tended the horses and built a campfire. The night was cold and a strong wind was blowing down the valley. Joanna huddled closely to the fire and held her hands out to the flames to warm them.

Farley had been on her mind all day. She couldn't bear to think that he might be freezing to death or suffering from his wound. Glancing at Windhawk, she wanted to ask him if he thought Farley would be all right. He must have felt her eyes on him because he looked straight at her.

Joanna took a shuddered breath at the coldness in his dark eyes. She bit her trembling lip, knowing she would only anger him further if she voiced her concern for Farley. In spite of her fear she gathered up her courage.

"I have been wondering about Farley. Don't you think it was a bit severe to leave him to die in the wilderness? Could you not have left him at least one horse?" she asked in English.

Windhawk was adding more wood to the fire and he paused to give Joanna his full attention. "The old man is no concern of mine. Had I done as I should have, he would already be dead," he answered her in Blackfoot.

"I . . . Farley was merely trying to help me . . . he . . ."

Windhawk's eyes narrowed. "Did you need help then? Did I beat you, or treat you in any way but with the greatest respect?"

Joanna moved to her knees. "I told you many times that I had to . . ."

"I will listen no more to you," he said, standing up.

Joanna's eyes followed him, knowing she could not back down now. "If you are angry with me, then take it out on me, but you had no reason to harm Farley."

Windhawk walked over to Joanna and stood staring down at her. "Did I not, Joanna?" She flinched as he knelt down in front of her and studied her face closely. "I will now use your own words against you, Jo-anna. Did you not tell me about a man who came into your home and took that which belonged to you?"

Her mouth opened to deny his charge until she realized that he was speaking of her Uncle Howard. "Yes, but . . ."

His hand went out to touch her face, but he gave

her no gentle caress. His fingers bit into her chin as he tilted her face up to his.

"You cannot have it both ways, Jo-anna. Did you or did you not tell me it was wrong for a man to come into another's home and take what belonged to him?" his dark eyes were grilling as he used her own words against her.

"My circumstances were quite different from yours," she said, pulling away from him.

Windhawk stood up, towering above her. "Yes, what belonged to me was not stolen. You left with the old man of your own free will."

Joanna had to look away from his dark accusing eyes. "I never belonged to you, Windhawk," she said, feeling the weight of her lie in the very depth of her being. "You knew that you and I could never have a lasting life together."

Joanna did not see his dark eyebrows meet in a frown. "What are you going to do with me?" she found the courage to ask.

Windhawk tossed a buffalo robe at her and the impact knocked her backwards. Joanna tried to scramble to her feet but the leather ropes confined her movements.

"Let me go, Windhawk. I implore you to have mercy," she pleaded.

He jerked the ropes tight, bringing her up toward him. "There was a time when I would have denied you nothing, Jo-anna. I trusted you, but now I will keep you bound like I would my worst enemy."

She saw his eyes dilate with anger and knew that he was having trouble controlling his temper. Joanna wanted to reach out and smooth the frown

301

from his face. She wanted to lay her head against his shoulder and pour out her love for him, but pride and uncertainty kept her lips sealed.

Windhawk's eyes moved to her parted lips, and he became angry at the weakness in him that cried out to touch her. He wanted to take her in his arms and make her retract her cruel words.

A lock of his ebony hair blew across her face and Joanna blinked her eyes. She met his gaze, showing more courage then she actually felt. "You can't always keep me tied. One day you will have to set me free."

"You will never know freedom, Jo-anna. You will live every day of your life craving that which you cannot have."

She wanted to tell him that all she craved at the moment was his kiss. His lips were so near that if she moved forward the least bit, her lips would touch his. She tried to concentrate on the pain of the ropes that were cutting into her tender skin.

Suddenly Windhawk gave her a shove that sent her sprawling backwards. "Pray that you are strong, Jo-anna. Tonight is the last restful night you will have until we reach my village. It is a four day journey to my home—we shall make it in three days."

Joanna watched him move to the other side of the campfire and roll up in a buffalo robe. With sheer strength of will she held the tears at bay. She wished she had never tried to leave him. She wanted only to see the love shining in his eyes once more. Her body was a traitor to her. She craved the touch of his hand against her throbbing breasts. Her body was hungry for the closeness they had once shared.

Joanna turned over on her side and buried her face in the soft robe. She knew that tomorrow he would push them both beyond endurance. She was stubbornly determined that she would not beg him for mercy.

*Chapter Seventeen*

Joanna could not help but dwell on the fact that for a short space of time, she had known freedom. She became angry thinking that no one, not even Windhawk, had the right to control her life. Why did she allow him to treat her with such contempt? Suddenly Joanna's anger overruled her common sense. Sitting up, she tossed the buffalo robe aside.

"I want to talk to you, Windhawk," she said, feeling good about herself because her courage had returned.

He was gazing skyward and gave no sign that he had even heard her. She tugged and yanked at the ropes that held her captive and to her surprise, the one that was bound about her ankles came untied.

Joanna looked quickly at Windhawk to see if he had noticed, but he appeared to be asleep. She must not do anything rash, she cautioned herself. She would give Windhawk plenty of time to fall into a deep sleep. Then she would make her bid for freedom.

Time passed slowly. Joanna noticed that Windhawk hadn't moved in a long time. The campfire had died down to smoldering ashes, and his face was cast in shadows. She was glad that he slept on the other side of the fire. That would give her a better chance to get away.

Joanna passed the time by planning what she would do when she escaped. First she would have to make it to the horses which were picketed some fifty feet away. She would take Windhawk's horse since it was the fastest. It would be safer if she were to turn the other horses loose, then Windhawk would be unable to follow her.

Joanna smiled to herself. It would be left-handed justice if Windhawk was forced to walk back to his village. After all, hadn't he left Farley with no horse?

Joanna glanced at Windhawk as she stood up slowly. He seemed to be sleeping soundly now. She realized her greatest disadvantage was that her hands were still tied. She knew the time to act had come. With one last look in Windhawk's direction, Joanna walked quietly away from the camp.

Her heart was drumming so loudly she was sure Windhawk would hear. When she thought she was a safe enough distance away, Joanna broke into a run. She knew she had never run so fast in her life. She leaped over fallen logs and dodged around trees.

Joanna was horrified when she heard Windhawk chasing her. Gasping for breath, she renewed her effort. With a feeling of dread, she realized he was gaining on her. She could hear him just behind her. When she had almost reached her goal, she felt Windhawk's hand on her shoulder.

"No!" she cried, as he spun her around and lifted her in his arms. Joanna started kicking and squirming, but with very little results. His arms tightened about her and she knew it would be futile to continue to fight him.

Lifting her head, Joanna expected to see anger on Windhawk's face, but instead he was staring at her heaving breasts.

"Put me down, Windhawk," she said in a small voice. She looked into his eyes and knew that she had pushed him too far this time. "What are you going to do?" she asked, although she already knew the answer.

He was silent as he carried her back to her blanket and laid her down. Joanna waited tensely as he hovered over her. She closed her eyes when she realized he was removing the leather strap he wore about his waist.

He was going to beat her! she thought wildly.

Raising her head, she gave him a scalding glance to prove that she had no fear of him.

"I will not let you touch me, Windhawk, I swear it. I will fight you."

There was amusement on his face. "Just what do you think I am going to do to you, Jo-anna?"

Her face flamed red and she lowered her eyes. "I will not allow you to . . . I don't want you to . . ."

He laughed out loud. "What makes you think I want to touch you, Jo-anna? An unwilling woman never did tempt me," he said in English.

Joanna felt the sting of his words. Why didn't he want her? she wondered. "Are you going to beat me?"

"It is not my habit to beat women," he said in an irritated voice.

"You hit me last night," she reminded him.

"I was angry."

"You may as well tie me up again, because if I get the chance, I will run away."

He knelt down beside her. "I had already thought of that. This time you won't get loose." He took his leather belt and began wrapping it about her ankles, tying it into a tight knot.

"Did you really think you could get away from me so easily?" He tested the ropes about her wrists to make sure they were secure. When he was sure she would be unable to free herself, he lay down. "I am a very light sleeper, as you know. If I were you, I would not again attempt anything so foolish, Joanna."

"What will you do, hit me again?"

He raised his eyebrow, but didn't answer. Joanna felt frustrated when he turned his back to her.

She was determined that she would just sit up all night rather than lie beside him. But after a long while of silence she became sleepy and lay down. She told herself she would only rest for a few moments, but soon her eyes closed and she fell asleep.

The heavy snows continued and a strong wind blowing out of the north made visibility impossible. Joanna thought of Farley and hoped he had found some kind of shelter to keep him warm. She tried to remind herself that he was accustomed to this country and would know how to take care of himself. She worried about his ankle and whether it was healing properly.

After plodding through the storm all day, Joanna was relieved when Windhawk halted his horse and dismounted.

Without looking at her, he took the reins of her horse and led it up a steep incline. Joanna could hardly see the mouth of the cave through the blanket of falling snow. She was almost sure it was the cave where she and Farley had stayed just a few nights earlier. Once she was inside the cave, she knew it was the same one; there were the cold ashes from their abandoned campfire.

Windhawk tended the horses and ordered Joanna to build the campfire while he was gone. She used the wood that she and Farley had stacked in the cave. Soon a warm fire was burning, casting a friendly glow on the walls of the cave.

It was a long time before Windhawk joined Joanna. Her hands were numb and she held them out to the fire to warm them. She was wrapped in a buffalo robe and huddled close to the fire, basking in its warmth.

Windhawk removed his warm fur wrapping and threw down his pack. He turned to face the mouth of the cave with a troubled frown on his face.

"Will the storm delay us for very long?" Joanna asked.

Windhawk swiveled around and pinned her with a dark gaze. "Am I Napi that I can predict the weather?" he asked in an angry voice.

Joanna did not bother to answer him. If he was going to act so high-handed she just wouldn't talk to him at all, she thought, trying to hide her hurt.

Windhawk picked up his pack and removed a slice of dried meat. Without even looking at Joanna, he tossed it onto her lap.

"I don't want this," she said, picking it up and handing it back to him.

He shrugged his shoulders and took the meat, biting into it.

Joanna watched as he sat down on the other side of the fire. Her spirits had never been lower. It was becoming clear to her that Windhawk was not a man to be crossed.

As the moments passed, she could feel the tension rising. She and Windhawk were cut off from the rest of the world. Both of them prisoners of the raging storm which seemed to intensify with the passing of time. Joanna still worried about Farley. While she and Windhawk were warm and secure inside the cave, he was exposed to the elements.

The wind swirled snow into the mouth of the cave—the fire flickered and almost went out.

Windhawk arose and took one of the buffalo robes. Joanna watched as he used two huge boulders to secure it to the mouth of the cave. He then placed rocks across the bottom, anchoring the robe so the wind wouldn't seep through the cracks.

Her mind raced ahead to the time they would bed down. They were now one robe short. Would she and Windhawk be forced to share the same blanket to keep warm?

She was determined that she would not share a bed with Windhawk again tonight. Placing more wood on the fire, she huddled miserably near the flames, hoping to absorb some of its warmth.

Joanna was unaware that Windhawk was standing over her until he touched her on the shoulder. "You must remove your wet clothing. I do not want a sick woman on my hands, Jo-anna." The words were spoken without warmth.

Joanna gave him a bitter glance. "I most certainly will not remove my clothing, I would rather freeze to death first. And as for taking care of me, who asked you to?"

She read anger in his eyes, but she was angry too, and it caused her to throw caution to the wind. Standing up, she faced him bravely.

"I have remained passive while you left Farley to die. I didn't complain when you pushed me beyond endurance. I have suffered your bad temper in silence . . . but I will not remain silent any longer!" she said, stomping her foot.

Windhawk raised his head and glared at her. Joanna realized it had been unwise to challenge him. When would she learn that he was not like other men. He was a rule unto himself, and she had seen many different sides of him. The side he had shown her since taking her as his prisoner was one she had never seen before. He was hard and cold — not at all like the man she loved.

"I will not listen to you when you speak in the white man's tongue. Remove your wet clothing or I will remove them for you."

"No, I will not," she said, defiantly.

310

Windhawk's face clouded over with anger. He grabbed her roughly by the shoulders, then held her against his body.

Proudly raising her violet-colored eyes to his, she dared him to try to force his will on her. She had reached the end of her endurance, and she would no longer allow him to assert his authority over her.

His hand slid down her arm. When Joanna saw it was his intention to forcibly remove her gown, she started to struggle. Windhawk lifted her into his arms and threw her over his shoulder while he reached for a robe. Joanna kicked and struggled, trying to get free, but it was impossible. She knew he was too strong for her to win in any kind of physical contest.

When Windhawk placed her on her feet, she stumbled backward and fell. "Has it become your habit to abuse women?" she said, gaining her feet hurriedly. She wasn't feeling quite so brave now.

He didn't answer, but lifted her easily, then turned her around and with very little trouble lifted her gown over her head. Joanna covered herself as best she could and was relieved when he dropped the robe over her nakedness.

He had gotten his way, she thought bitterly. She hoped he would be satisfied and leave her alone.

She gave in without a struggle when he picked her up and sat her beside the fire. She was almost passive when he removed her moccasins.

Joanna turned her head away, trying to hide the pout on her face. His coldness was hard to deal with and she was too tired to even try. After a long moment she turned back around, and saw he had hung her gown and moccasins beside the fire to dry. She shuddered, knowing they would be stiff and uncomfortable when she put them on tomorrow.

Windhawk moved away from her and she breathed a sigh of relief. At least he wasn't going to tie her hands tonight, she thought gratefully.

Joanna stared into the fire, almost hypnotized by the brightness of the flames. Her eyes drifted shut and her head began to nod. Pulling herself up straight, she met Windhawk's glance. He stood up slowly and circled the fire until he stood over her.

What a proud woman she was, he thought. He expected her to beg him for mercy, but so far she hadn't. "Do you intend to see if you can outlast me, Jo-anna?"

"I don't know what you are talking about," she said, covering a yawn with her delicate hand.

He bent down and scooped her into his arms. By now she was so sleepy that all the fight had gone out of her. She leaned her head against his shoulder.

Windhawk stared into her face as her eyes drifted shut. The woman who had taken his love and then tossed it aside still held him prisoner, he thought bitterly. He carried her over to the buffalo robe and laid her down on it. She didn't move as he pulled the robe up around her neck.

Windhawk's eyes never left her face as he undressed and hung his wet clothing beside hers to dry. He hesitated before he lay down beside her and pulled the robe over them both.

In her sleep Joanna rolled over to seek the warmth of his body and Windhawk stiffened. He was a man, and it didn't matter how deeply Joanna had wounded him, his body was on fire as her soft curves settled against his naked form.

His hand trembled as he slipped it about her tiny waist. Against his will, he began to caress her satiny stomach. His breathing intensified and he knew he would take her tonight, whether she was willing or not. For some reason, he felt a moment of apprehension knowing the hold Joanna seemed to have over him.

Joanna opened her eyes as his hand brushed against her breast. Staring into his eyes she saw no softness there and no answer to the love that she felt for him. She tried to pull away, but his grip tightened on her shoulder.

"Don't, please, not like this . . ." she pleaded.

His mouth crushed hers in a savage kiss which almost cut off her breathing. She tried to get free of him, but he pulled her tighter against him. She could feel his arousal and she knew if he took her now it wouldn't be with love, but instead in anger.

Turning her head away, Joanna pushed against him with all her strength, but she knew it was a losing battle. Already her body was yielding to his touch. She tried to remind herself that what was happening between them was wrong, but soon his hands began stroking, and he was no longer causing her pain.

Joanna whimpered as he raised her chin and his lips fastened on hers. His lips slipped to her eyelids and then began a long journey down her neck to nibble at her breasts, first one and then the other. She could feel her body quiver as his lips encircled her stomach, while his hands massaged between her thighs.

No longer able to think or reason sanely, she parted her lips to welcome his kiss. He was making smooth stroking motions and Joanna's body began moving against his hand. Soon the caresses were not enough. Her body craved more; she arched her hips in a silent invitation.

Windhawk ignored her need and continued the stroking motion. He would torture her in this way, he thought. It had been easy to make her want him. Now all he had to do was turn his back on her. That was his plan, but when her hand slid over his smooth stomach to touch his pulsating manhood, he groaned.

Pushing Joanna backward, he moved on top of her and nudged her legs open to receive him. When he entered her they both trembled, feeling the oneness that always accompanied their lovemaking.

"Jo-anna," he breathed in her ear. "I need you, Jo-anna."

He was unaware that he had voiced his need for her, but Joanna heard him in a fog of passion. She would give him all he asked of her, she thought. Her hips moved against his and soon they were locked in fiery lovemaking.

This time there were no words of love spoken between them, and still they obtained the fevered height that they always found together.

Joanna stared into Windhawk's eyes, waiting for him to say something—anything, but he merely stared darkly at her. Her eyes shied away from his and slid down to his chest. She gasped when she saw the gash where the panther had mauled him.

"Windhawk, you are hurt," she said, turning misty eyes to him.

He tried to push her away, but she grabbed his arm. "You must allow me to tend this wound. It is very bad. If you don't receive attention, it could become infected."

"I want nothing from you, Jo-anna," he said roughly pushing her away. Windhawk realized that she had caught him in her tender trap once more. If he would allow it, she had the power to destroy him.

Joanna felt an ache deep inside thinking how he must be suffering from his wound. There was nothing she could do for him, if he was too proud to accept her help.

Standing up, he looked down at her. In his hurt and anger he wanted to wound her and he knew the way.

"The white man call a woman like you a whore. I have had some Indian maidens who would fit that name, but you are my first white woman."

Hot tears of humiliation scalded Joanna's face. She didn't know how to answer his charges. He was right, she had acted wantonly and forward, but she loved him so much. Turning over on her side, she pulled the covers over her head, fearing he would see her cry.

She didn't see Windhawk kneel down beside her and reach out to her. In striking out at Joanna, he had also hurt himself. His hand dropped to his side. When would the pain stop? When would he be able to forget that Joanna had betrayed him? Never again would he show her mercy. He had to get her to the village, then he could put some distance between them. He would go away by himself for a while so he could think.

Windhawk pulled on his clothing and went out into the storm. He knew that tomorrow they would journey on to his village regardless of the weather. He would push them both beyond endurance if he had to.

Joanna buried her face in her hands, feeling miserable. Would Windhawk never forgive her? Would she be forced to live with his coldness for the rest of her life? If only she didn't love him so desperately, it wouldn't matter what he did to her. Before the tears were dry on her face, Joanna had fallen asleep.

The next morning when Joanna opened her eyes she found Windhawk was lying beside her staring into her face. Her heart skipped a beat when she saw the way his eyes moved over her body. She felt no satisfaction in the fact that she read desire in his dark eyes. After all, you could desire someone without loving her.

For a long moment his dark eyes locked with her blue ones, and neither one of them spoke. Joanna had no idea that her eyes were soft and pleading, and Windhawk felt himself being drawn to her.

Against his will his hand reached out to touch her cheek, and she flinched. His heart was wounded and bleeding because she had betrayed him and still he wanted her.

Joanna almost cried out when he pulled her slowly into his arms. She knew she should resist, yet she just didn't have the will power. She made a whimpering sound when his finger outlined her lips.

Windhawk crushed her in his arms feeling the agony of heartbreak. Suddenly he became angry that she still retained so much power over his life. Jerking her head around he tilted her head back and ground his lips against hers.

Joanna tried to struggle out of his arms, but he pulled on the leather strap holding her immobile. She twisted and turned but still his mouth continued to punish her. He wasn't kissing her out of love or even lust, she thought. It was more like hate and revenge. His hand was brutal as it clamped her jaw painfully. Joanna couldn't breathe and she renewed her struggle to free herself.

Suddenly Windhawk raised his head and stared at her. He saw a trickle of blood that ran down her lip, and felt remorse. Never before had he felt such a need to punish. He gave Joanna a shove that sent her rolling off the robe onto the ground. Standing up he looked away from her.

"I will not allow you to slow me down, Jo-anna. You will pace yourself to keep up with me. Should you lag behind . . ." His voice trailed off and he walked away from her.

Joanna stared after him dry eyed. She would show him that she could take anything he would throw her way. She was determined that she wouldn't ask him for mercy. He would find out that she was as strong as he was. Glancing at the snow-shrouded countryside she felt a chill wash over her.

Joanna's spirits might be low, but she wouldn't give Windhawk the satisfaction of seeing her weakness, she vowed silently.

# Chapter Eighteen

Joanna was awakened when Windhawk pulled her to her feet. She was still in a sleep-drugged state when he led her to the river. He roughly pushed her down to her knees, and indicated that she should drink.

She looked up into his face hoping to see some softening in his attitude toward her, but his darkly handsome features revealed nothing. Joanna cupped her hands in the icy water and bathed her face.

Windhawk knelt down beside her and removed his knife. Joanna drew back in fear, not knowing what he had in mind. He saw her fright and looked at her grimly.

"You were unwise to get the rawhide rope wet, Joanna," he told her, slicing through the rope with his knife. "When the rawhide dried it would have cut into your skin."

"Do I have to be tied up? It's not very comfortable," she ventured to ask.

Windhawk avoided her eyes as he pulled another rope from his pouch. "I would trust you no more than I trusted the panther." He bound her wrists tightly together and pulled her to her feet.

Joanna jerked her head back, and Windhawk drew in his breath at the hurt he saw in her eyes. Why did she have to be so beautiful? he wondered. He had to force himself not to reach out and touch her flaming hair which seemed to be on fire in the early morning sunlight.

The place where he had struck her had turned blue-black and he knew it must be causing her pain. When his eyes swept her face to settle on her violet-colored eyes, he wanted to look away but couldn't. Her eyes were soft and shining, as if pleading for mercy, and he felt himself weakening. How could he have hurt the one he loved most in the world?

Windhawk became angry with himself because he was having such tender feelings toward the woman whom he felt had betrayed him. He hardened his heart when he saw tears glistening in her eyes.

Joanna knew the moment she saw Windhawk's dark eyes narrow that she could expect no mercy from him. She raised her head proudly and gave him a look of disdain. She would never beg him for anything. Let him do his worst; she would endure it silently.

Windhawk met the challenge in her eyes and knew that she was preparing to do battle with him. He wanted to see her crawl. He needed to see her proud spirit defeated. Jerking on the rope he pulled Joanna forward and led her away from the river. He felt satisfaction in knowing the time would come when she would beg him for his forgiveness.

The weather had turned colder. A bright sun shone down on the white wonderland, but it lent no warmth to the frigid land. Joanna closed her eyes against the glare of the sun reflecting off the snow. Her face felt as if it were on fire as the sun's rays penetrated her delicate white skin.

She felt so thirsty and wished Windhawk would stop so she could have a cool drink of water and rest for a while. But he pushed on relentlessly, sparing neither himself, Joanna, or the horses. Joanna began to wish that they would reach his village. Anything would be better than the blinding rays of the sun that beat down on her.

How was it possible for one to feel the blistering rays of the sun on such a cold day? she wondered.

She wanted to ask Windhawk to stop, but her pride wouldn't allow her to. Glancing at his rigid back she knew he would not listen to her pleas, even if she did voice them. She got the impression he took some kind of pleasure in her discomfort.

By late afternoon Joanna felt as if her face were burning. Her eyes felt as if they had needles sticking in them. She squeezed them tightly together, trying to shut out the painful glare of the sun.

On they plodded until Joanna slumped forward on the horse to lay her face against its neck. She was feeling so dizzy she gripped the side of the horse, fearing she would fall off.

Would Windhawk never stop? She was in torment and wanted to cry out to him, but she clamped her lips tightly together, too stubborn and proud to ask him for mercy.

That night when they made camp, Joanna stumbled over to her robe and lay down. She buried her head in her hands, feeling ill. She felt her body tremble uncontrollably.

At times she felt hot and would kick the cover off. Other times she would shiver with cold, thinking she would never be warm again.

Windhawk paid little attention to Joanna. He had been aware that she was overly quiet, but that suited his mood. He was still too angry to talk to her.

He sat by the campfire brooding. Every so often his eyes would stray to Joanna. Her back was turned to him and he thought she might be asleep. He dared not lie down beside her, remembering what had happened between them last night. Many times today he had fought the urge to look back at her.

He placed more wood on the fire and rolled up in his robe, hoping he would fall asleep.

The next morning Joanna was still overly quiet. Windhawk noticed she pulled the blanket over her head, hiding her face from him. If she wanted to pout, that suited him just fine, he thought. He had no intentions of engaging her in conversation.

He lifted her onto the horse thinking they would reach the village by early afternoon. What would he do with Joanna then?

He hastened their pace, anxious to be home. Glancing back at Joanna, he noticed she was slumped over her horse. He knew she was tired, and she hadn't eaten since the morning before. If she was trying to evoke pity in him, she had failed.

When they reached the Milk River, Windhawk halted his mount and looked across at his village. Joanna would now know the full extent of his displeasure. He glanced back at her just in time to see her slide off her horse, falling beneath its prancing hooves. He dismounted, thinking how frail she was. A Blackfoot maiden would not have tired so easily. They were much stronger than the puny white women.

He lifted her into his arms and the blanket fell away from her face. He frowned, feeling distressed when he saw that her face had been burned by the sun. It was as if someone had set fire to her face; the skin was all red and covered with tiny blisters.

Windhawk felt great anguish for Joanna. Not only was she very ill, but he also feared that her beauty had been marred. He had not known that one could burn so easily by being exposed to the sun. Why hadn't she told him that she was in pain? Her eyes fluttered and she opened them, staring blankly into space.

He saw her lips were cracked and dry and she wet them with her tongue. "Is it . . . day or . . . night?" she asked weakly.

322

Windhawk's eyes were wild with grief as he cradled her to him. Great Father, what had he done to her? She was blind! The sun had robbed her of her sight. Napi would not be so cruel as to take the sight from those beautiful violet-colored eyes.

He had meant to punish her, but never this severely! Not once had she cried out or asked for his help. Why hadn't she told him she was suffering?

Windhawk raised his face to the wind, feeling hot tears in his eyes. He, not Napi, was responsible for the damage to Joanna's eyes. He had been hurt and had wanted to strike out at her, but in doing so, he had wounded his own heart.

He gathered Joanna close to him and waded across the icy river. He would take her to the medicine woman. She Who Heals would know how to help her.

When the people of the village heard that Joanna had returned and was very ill, a large crowd of them had gathered outside the medicine woman's tipi. They waited quietly to hear about her condition.

Windhawk was surprised to see how well the people of his tribe loved Joanna. His mother and sister stood beside him with troubled expressions on their faces.

"Is Joanna in danger of losing her life, my brother?" Morning Song asked.

"I do not know. She is gravely ill. We can do no more than wait for She Who Heals to tell us her condition."

"Joanna's brother should be told," Sun Woman said. "It will bring comfort to her, having him with her."

"Where is he?" Windhawk asked.

"He and the other white woman have been staying in our lodge," Morning Song answered, as her troubled glance went to the tipi where Joanna lay. "He rode out with Gray Fox this morning; they have not yet returned."

Joanna stared into darkness. Her body seemed to ache all over, and she was so thirsty. She felt as if the skin on her face was on fire.

"Where am I . . . why can I not see?" she asked in a weak voice.

"Do not talk," a woman's voice answered her in the Blackfoot language. Joanna felt the woman apply a wet cloth to her eyes, and she cried out in pain.

"The herbs and salve will bring you comfort," the unknown voice said.

Joanna tried to push the woman's hand away from her face when she applied the salve to her tortured skin. "Do not fight me. If I do not put the medicine on your face, you will be scarred."

As day passed into night Joanna could no longer stand the pain. She couldn't see who this strange woman was who was hurting her. Her fever was high and she no longer remembered where she was. When the woman touched Joanna's arm, she thought it was Franny; her body relaxed and she slept.

Tag had just ridden into camp, and when he saw Windhawk, he dismounted and ran to him. "Where is Joanna? I want to see her!"

By now, most of the people had gone to their

lodges and only Windhawk, his mother, and sister waited outside the medicine woman's tipi. Windhawk was tortured by what had happened to Joanna. It was his fault that she might die. Seeing Tag's eager eyes, he nodded toward the tipi.

"She is very ill, little brother. You cannot see her until the medicine woman says it is time." The hardest thing Windhawk had ever been called upon to do was wait patiently while Joanna lay so near death. He had to keep reminding himself that he was chief, and should not let his emotions show where others could see.

Tag pushed Windhawk's hand from his shoulder and bolted into the tipi. When he saw Joanna, he hardly recognized her. Her face was blistered and peeling, and her breathing was so shallow he could barely detect it. He fell down on his knees beside her and carefully picked up her hand, laying it against his face.

For so long he had been forced to live with the thought that Joanna was dead. It was very hard to find she still lived, but was gravely ill.

Tears fell from his eyes onto her hand. "Joanna, it's me, Tag. You just gotta get well, Joanna. You gotta!"

She Who Heals placed her hand on Tag's shoulder and motioned for him to leave.

"No," he said stubbornly. "You can't make me leave my sister." Seeing she did not understand his words, he repeated them in the language of the Blackfoot.

Joanna heard Tag's voice. It seemed to come from a long way off. She was dying, she thought,

325

and Tag was waiting for her.

She Who Heals left the tipi thinking, it might give Joanna comfort to have her brother with her, should she awaken.

Windhawk stood up as the medicine woman approached, fearing that she had come to tell him Joanna was dead. He took a deep breath and waited for her to speak.

"It does not go well for your woman, my chief. She has the light skin and was badly burned from the sun. We are dark skinned and do not suffer so from the sun-sickness."

"What about her vision?" Windhawk asked.

She Who Heals made a hopeless gesture. "As her skin is light in color, so are her eyes. She suffers from snow-blindness. I have used very powerful medicine, and I have asked Napi to save your woman. I do not know if she will ever recover her sight. Her face was very badly burned, and she may have lasting scars."

Morning Song gasped, and placed her hand on her brother's arm. She could feel his body tremble, and knew that he was hurting on the inside. If one didn't know Windhawk, he would never suspect how the medicine woman's words had affected him. But Morning Song knew him and could tell that he was grief-stricken at She Who Heals's work.

Sun Woman also knew what her son was feeling. "Come with me and I will prepare your food," she told him.

Windhawk acted as if he hadn't heard his mother's voice. He walked past her and entered the tipi where Joanna lay.

Tag raised tear-bright eyes to Windhawk. "Is she going to die, Windhawk?" he asked in a choked voice.

Windhawk knelt down and looked into the face he loved so well. It was swollen and red, bearing no resemblance to his lovely Joanna. He had wanted revenge, but not this way. His heart cried out to her, wishing he could take her in his arms and beg for her forgiveness.

"I do not know, little brother," he answered at last. "All rests with Napi."

Windhawk sat down beside Tag and they both became silent. When She Who Heals returned, she also sat down and the long night's vigil began. No one spoke as all eyes watched Joanna's shallow breathing.

Windhawk reached out and touched Joanna's bright hair. He wanted to tell her that he had not really meant to harm her. He had taken a fragile flower that should have been cared for with tenderness, allowing harm to come to her from his neglect.

He saw Tag slump over and knew the boy had fallen asleep. He pulled his red-gold head to rest upon his lap while he reached for Joanna's hand. He felt great love for both the brother and sister.

Windhawk remembered Joanna had once told him that she couldn't remain with him forever. At the time he had pushed her words out of his mind, not wanting to think that she could ever leave him. He now realized that he had used her harshly. He knew if she recovered, he would see that she was returned to her own people.

327

Though he would always carry the love in his heart for the flaming-haired one, Joanna had never really belonged to him. He had been allowed to hold her for a time, but now he must let her go free.

After a while, She Who Heals got up and began applying the healing ointment to Joanna's face again. Joanna groaned but did not awaken.

Windhawk stood up and lifted Tag in his arms. With one last glance at Joanna, he carried her little brother to his mother's lodge. He knew there would be no sleep for him tonight. He would return to sit beside Joanna. He felt the need to be near her, on the small chance that she might call out to him.

# Chapter Nineteen

Joanna awoke and stared into darkness. She felt like a hot poker had pierced her eyes. Reaching her hand up, she felt someone grab her wrist.

"Do not touch the pads which I have placed over your eyes," the old woman said.

"Where am I?" Joanna asked.

"You are in the village of the Bloods. I am She Who Heals, the medicine woman. You are very ill."

"What is wrong with me?" Joanna asked in the Blackfoot language.

"You are suffering from the snow-blindness, and you have burns on your face."

Joanna's hand trembled as she reached up to her face, but as before the old woman grabbed her wrist. "No, do not touch your eyes or your face."

"I am thirsty," Joanna told her.

She heard the woman move away, and when she returned, she lifted Joanna's head for her to drink.

The water felt cool and soothing as it went down Joanna's parched throat. She wondered who the old woman was and what she was doing to her.

It was not yet daylight when Windhawk made his way to She Who Heals's tipi. Windhawk had not been able to sleep. Several times during the night he had gone to the medicine woman's tipi to see Joanna. Each time he found her to be sleeping fretfully.

When he entered the tipi, he found Tag sitting beside Joanna. The young boy's face was careworn and he lifted troubled eyes to Windhawk.

"How could this have happened to my sister?" Tag wanted to know.

Windhawk peered down at the boy. "It was my fault. I was angry with her, and I did not take proper care of her."

"You were angry because she ran away, weren't you?"

"Yes. I think you should know that Jo-anna is my wife."

Tag smiled. "I know that; your sister told me."

"I could not understand why she wanted to leave me. It was a bad thing I did, little brother. If it were possible I would wish myself in her place."

"She is going to be well," Tag said with confidence. "I know she did not survive the raid on the wagon train to die now." His brow furrowed. "I am worried about her eyesight, though. I would hate for Joanna to be blind. She always saw such beauty in everything, and she taught me to look for that

330

beauty as well."

"I would give up my sight if it would bring hers back, Tag." Windhawk looked into the boy's eyes. "I am to blame for this."

"You don't know my sister very well, if you think she will hold you responsible. She has a kind and forgiving nature. She Who Heals said it was not your fault."

At the moment Windhawk was not ready to face Tag's forgiveness. His guilt was like an arrow in his heart. "Come, little brother, I think you should have something to eat," Windhawk said.

"I want to be here in case she wakes up," Tag replied.

Windhawk took Tag's hand. "First you will eat, and then you will return to your sister," he insisted.

Windhawk delivered Tag to his mother's tipi, and then went to search for Gray Fox. Often when he was deeply troubled about something, he would seek his best friend's advice.

Gray Fox was sitting in front of his tipi sharpening his hunting knife when Windhawk approached him. He had known his chief would soon come to him. Had they not always turned to each other in times of trouble?

"How is Joanna this morning, Windhawk?"

"I do not think she is much better," Windhawk replied, sitting down and absent-mindedly testing Gray Fox's knife for sharpness.

"I am saddened for her, my friend." Gray Fox looked at Windhawk closely. "Was she in this condition when you found her?"

Windhawk avoided his eyes. "No."

"I see."

Windhawk took a deep breath. "I have decided when Joanna is healed, I will take her back to her own people."

Gray Fox nodded, knowing how much it would cost Windhawk to send the woman he loved away. "Have you thought this through?"

Windhawk stood up. "Yes. I have thought of little else. It was a mistake for me to think Joanna would be happy with me."

Gray Fox watched as his friend walked away. In the past they had helped each other, but this time Windhawk had to do what he thought was best. His heart was sad that Joanna and Windhawk would be parted. He knew that they loved one another, but sometimes love was not enough.

Tag and Windhawk entered She Who Heals's tipi. They could tell Joanna was awake because her head turned in their direction.

Tag stood silently for a moment. Joanna's face was smeared with some kind of white salve, and there was a white cloth tied about her head to protect her eyes.

"Is that you, She Who Heals?" she inquired.

Tag ran to her and dropped to his knees. "Joanna, it's me!" Tag cried, taking her hand in his.

Joanna turned her head and bit her trembling lips. "Tag?" she said in a disbelieving voice.

Tears were streaming down Tag's face as he clutched Joanna's hand, fearing if he hugged her as he wanted to it would hurt her. "It's me,

Joanna. It's me."

Joanna reached out a trembling hand and lightly explored his face. Her hand moved up to feel his red-gold curls. "It can't be. My God, Tag, you are alive!" She sobbed and pulled him to her, cradling his head against her.

Windhawk could see her throat working convulsively and knew she was having a hard time believing her brother was alive. He felt a prickling sensation in his own eyes and slipped quietly out of the tipi.

"I don't understand, Tag. How can you be alive?" Joanna asked, running her hand up and down his back.

"I was taken prisoner by Running Elk, and Windhawk rescued me. He saved Amanda too."

"Oh, Tag, I feel as if . . . I want to . . . Oh Tag!" she cried, as loud sobs racked her body. For long moments they were locked in each other's arms, until She Who Heals came in and made Joanna lie down.

Tag sat beside his sister, telling her all that had happened to him since he had been taken captive. He told Joanna about how badly Amanda had been treated by Running Elk, and finally about Windhawk's daring rescue of them both.

"How did Windhawk know that you had been taken captive by Running Elk?" Joanna wanted to know.

"Gray Fox told me that he found out about it from Farley."

"But how . . . Farley never told me that you were still alive."

"I don't know why he kept it from you. He might have thought me the same as dead."

Joanna lapsed into silence. Windhawk had gone to save her brother, and while he was away, she had left with Farley. No wonder he hated her now. He had risked his life to save Tag, then he had placed himself in danger to save her from the panther. How ungrateful he must think her. She clasped Tag's hand tightly.

"Stay with me, Tag. Don't leave me," she said, closing her eyes.

"I'll stay right here, Joanna. Sleep now, and when you awake, I'll still be here."

Amanda walked beside Morning Song, who was taking her to see Joanna. She was anxious to see Joanna and know she was all right. She thought how differently she was treated now compared to the way Running Elk had abused her. Everyone here in the Blood village had been so kind. Today she was almost happy because she would see Joanna again.

As they neared She Who Heals's tipi, Amanda saw a handsome young Indian brave whom she had seen watching her on several occasions. He had never spoken to her, but she could tell that he wanted to.

"Who is that, Morning Song?" she asked.

"That is Tall Bear. He is the brother of Gray Fox."

"He makes me feel uncomfortable."

Morning Song laughed. "I think he likes you but is afraid to say so."

Amanda remembered the abuse and degradation she had suffered at Running Elk's hand, and she wanted nothing to do with another Indian man.

They entered the tipi, and Amanda couldn't help but gasp when she saw Joanna. Once Joanna had been blessed with extraordinary beauty, but no one would recognize her now as the beautiful, carefree girl she had once been.

Amanda walked slowly, hesitatingly toward her. Tears blinded her eyes when she dropped to her knees beside Joanna.

"Oh, Joanna, what have they done to you?" she cried, touching her arm.

"Amanda, how glad I am to see you," Joanna told her, clasping her hand. "Although to say I see you is a badly chosen word."

"Joanna, I am just glad you are alive. Tag and I thought you had been killed."

"Are you really well, Amanda?"

"I am growing stronger every day. Now that you are here we can all be happy."

Joanna's head was aching and she was frightened of the darkness that enclosed her. Could she be happy now? Her face had been hideously damaged, and she was blind. She loved Windhawk so desperately and he despised her. He had not even come to see her. No, she saw no happiness in her future.

As the days passed, Joanna had found that without her sight, her hearing had become more acute. She was now able to tell who had entered the tipi just by the sound of their footsteps. Tag's footsteps were springy and lively. Sun Woman's footsteps were slow and careful, and she could tell Amanda's as well. Sometimes she would hear a silence and would know that someone whose footsteps she had not detected had entered. She didn't hear him but felt his presence, and she knew it was Windhawk. On these occasions he never spoke to her. He would stand silently for a moment, and then leave. Joanna would want to cover her face, knowing how dreadful she must look, but she never did.

She Who Heals had told Joanna that she was now well enough to sit up, but the medicine woman would not allow her to get up yet. Joanna was beginning to love the old woman who tended her so faithfully. The love she had once given Franny, was now transferred to She Who Heals.

She Who Heals was sought after by all the tribe for her healing powers. At night when she and Joanna were alone, Joanna would hear her grinding her berries and herbs to make healing potions.

The old woman had never married and lived a solitary life. She had wealth in horses, and plenty of food, for she was well-paid for her healing services. She had told Joanna that Windhawk had given her twenty horses for tending his woman while she was ill.

While Joanna was recuperating, she became better versed in the Blackfoot language. She Who Heals would sit with her for hours, telling her what different words meant.

One night when the camp was quiet, She Who Heals came to Joanna and sat down beside her. She gave Joanna some foul-tasting medicine to take, and then handed her the water to wash it down with.

"What do you look like?" Joanna inquired.

The old woman laughed. "I look like I am old and tired, and have lived too long upon this land."

"I am very grateful to you for tending me."

"I was paid to give you the cure," She Who Heals said in a gruff voice.

Joanna smiled. "That may be, but I thank you all the same."

She Who Heals gazed at Joanna, whose eyes were bound with a soft doeskin blindfold to keep the sunlight from penetrating them. The skin on her face looked red and angry beneath the pasty white powder the old woman had put on it.

She Who Heals had not once heard the young girl complain, although she knew her to be in pain most of the time. The medicine woman had grown to admire the flaming-haired one, and to look on her as the daughter she had never had.

"She Who Heals . . . do you think I will ever regain my . . . eyesight?" Joanna asked hesitantly.

"I cannot yet tell. You must keep the blindfold in place for many moons."

"Is my face going to be scarred?"

"This I do not know either. Your fate rests with Napi."

Joanna felt panic rise up from deep inside her. She couldn't bear to think that she would never again see the bright blue skies or a field of spring flowers. She would not be able to watch Tag grow to manhood, and she would never look upon Windhawk's face again.

Perhaps it was best, for she wouldn't be able to stand the look of horror in his eyes when he looked at her scarred face.

She Who Heals could tell that Joanna was troubled so she tried to distract her. "Tomorrow I will allow you to get up and walk outside for a little while. The *chinook* wind has caused the weather to turn warm."

"What is the *chinook* wind?" Joanna asked with interest.

"It is a warm wind that sometimes blows down from the mountains to melt the snow. It is a gift from Napi, so the buffalo can graze near the village and our hunters can slay them to replenish the winter meat."

"I am afraid to go outside and have everyone stare at me. It is unsettling to know that people can see me and I cannot see them."

"One cannot hide from life, Joanna. It is time that you faced the world again," She Who Heals said, knowing what Joanna was feeling.

"I am not sure I am quite ready to face the world, She Who Heals."

"Yes, it is time. You will face what you must."

Joanna shivered, thinking how everyone would stare at her. Tomorrow would be an ordeal for her to overcome.


Windhawk and Tag raced down the valley. Windhawk's horse pulled easily into the lead, and he drew back on the reins so Tag could catch him. Tag grinned up at him and Windhawk could see the admiration in the boy's eyes. He loved this boy and wished that he could have a son just like him. If Joanna had loved him enough to stay with him, he might one day have realized his dream.

"You allowed me to catch you, Windhawk! I bet if I had been riding Fosset, I would have been able to stay even with you."

"Fosset is Jo-anna's horse." Windhawk stated.

"Why can you not say Joanna's name right, Windhawk?"

Windhawk halted his horse and dismounted before he answered the boy. "You will teach me to say her name correctly."

Tag slid from his horse and leaped onto a boulder, grinning down at Windhawk. "That's easy. Say Joanna."

"Jo-anna," Windhawk said.

"No, you are saying it as two words. You have to run it together. Joanna."

"Joann-a." Windhawk repeated.

Tag laughed so hard he almost fell off the boulder. Windhawk smiled and tried once again. "Jo-anna, Joann-a, Joanna!"

"You did it! You said it correctly," Tag beamed.

Suddenly Windhawk became serious. "Little brother, do you want to return to the white world?"

Tag was thoughtful for a time. "I would not want to leave you, but as I told you, there is something I must do."

"When Joanna is well enough . . . I will take you both to the fort."

Tag looked into Windhawk's eyes and saw pain. "I will miss you, Windhawk, and some day I shall come back. I promise."

Windhawk mounted and waited for Tag to do the same. "You will not come back, little brother."

Tag leaped onto his horse. "I will, you'll see. Joanna said that one should not make a promise unless he intends to keep it. I said I would come back, and I shall."

"Joanna will never return," Windhawk said, more to himself than to Tag.

"I can't see why you are sending her away. You said she is your wife. If you love Joanna, shouldn't you keep her with you?"

"Sometimes you have to love someone enough to let her go, Tag."

"I don't understand."

"You will understand when you grow to manhood. I will race you to the river," Windhawk said, quickly changing the subject.

When they entered the village, Tag rode directly to She Who Heals's tipi. He wanted to tell Joanna that Windhawk was taking them to the fort as soon as she was healed enough to travel.

As he neared the tipi, he saw Joanna holding on to the arm of the old medicine woman. He leaped to the ground and watched her take a hesitant step. She was going to be all right, he thought happily. Joanna was going to recover!

He walked over to her and took her hand, and she drew him to her, ruffling his red-gold curls.

"I feel like walking farther, She Who Heals. I am not as weak as I thought I would be."

"No, you must not do too much the first day. Each day you will walk more. Soon you will be able

340

to walk as far as the river."

Windhawk watched from a distance. His heart was lighter than it had been in many days. He was happy that Joanna was recovering her strength, but sad that she still wore the blindfold about her eyes. It was not a fair trade, he thought; she had stolen his heart, and he had robbed her of her eyesight. Turning away, he entered his lodge, thinking how empty it seemed without Joanna.

Joanna could hear the sound of childrens' laughter and the occasional barking of a dog. She had never known how precious her eyesight was until she had lost it.

She wished she could talk to Windhawk. Why did he never speak to her? She wished that she could tell him that she was sorry about running away from him. She wanted and needed his comforting arms more than ever. He didn't love her anymore; she would have to live with his coldness from now on. She knew she must appear ugly, and when her skin began to heal, it would leave horrible scars. Windhawk would never look upon her with favor again.

Tag led her back into the tipi and helped her lie down. He sat down beside her, telling her how he and Windhawk had spent the day. "I'm going to hate to leave Windhawk when the time comes, Joanna. Won't you miss him, too?"

"What are you talking about, Tag?" she asked, feeling pain in her heart.

"Windhawk told me today that when you were well, he would take us to the fort."

Joanna felt tears soak into the leather blindfold. He was going to send her away: He no longer wanted to be near her. She turned over on her side and felt the misery of heartbreak. She had tried to run away from him and he had brought her back. Now she wanted to stay with him and he was sending her away. Why was life always so unfair? Why was she always forced to do what she didn't want to do?

"You're tired now, Joanna, I'll leave you alone to rest," Tag said, standing up.

Joanna nodded her head, too miserable to answer him.

Amanda stumbled and dropped the armload of wood she had been carrying. When she bent down to pick it up, a strong hand went about her waist, moving her aside. She looked fearfully at Tall Bear as he knelt down and picked up the wood. She wanted to flee, remembering the cruel way Running Elk had treated her. Did this Indian have the same thing in mind for her? Amanda wondered.

"This is much too heavy for you since you have been ill," Tall Bear said in Blackfoot, which Amanda understood very well. "I will carry the wood for you."

Amanda felt her legs tremble as his dark eyes swept her face. No, he was not like Running Elk. He was kind; she could see it in his eyes.

As he walked along beside her, she slowly began to relax. He had been watching her for a long time, but this was the first time he had approached her.

"My name is Tall Bear," he told her.

"I know, Morning Song told me."

342

"I think you have great beauty," he said, without looking at her.

Amanda had never had a man tell her she was beautiful, and her face flushed with pleasure. When they reached Sun Woman's lodge, he placed the wood on the ground and smiled at her.

"I would like to come and talk to you again sometime, if you would allow it."

"Yes, I would like that," she answered him shyly.

When Tall Bear walked away, Amanda felt her heart beating wildly. She had never felt this way about a man before and it frightened her.

Joanna had told her that Windhawk would be taking them to the fort as soon as she was able to travel. Amanda had dreaded facing anyone after what Running Elk had done to her. She was happier now than she had been since the raid on the wagon train. She wasn't so sure she wanted to go with Joanna and Tag when they departed.

# Chapter Twenty

The *chinook* wind continued to blow across the land, warming the days and holding winter at bay.

With each passing day Joanna grew stronger. Every afternoon Tag would take her for a walk down to the river. At these times, many of the Indians would come up to talk to Joanna. They were always kind and inquired about her health. She had grown to love this strong, fierce race who had taken her in and treated her with such kindness.

Joanna could not bear to think she would soon be leaving them all behind. There was Windhawk's mother, Sun Woman, who still lovingly called her daughter. Morning Song was sweet and loving and Joanna would miss her terribly. Then there was the tall chief, whom she had at one time laughed and loved with. She would miss him most of all.

Joanna had no idea how her face looked. She was afraid to ask for fear it was horribly scarred. She

Who Heals continued to put the salve on it each day, and it was no longer painful. Joanna would often run her hand over her face; it felt smooth to the touch. She hoped that she didn't look hideous any longer.

The worst part of the whole ordeal was not being able to see. There had been many times when Joanna had wanted to rip the blindfold from her eyes. She Who Heals had cautioned her against removing the bandage, fearing it would cause further damage to her eyes.

Joanna held on to Tag's arm and raised her head to the sky, listening to the sound of the wind rustling in the tall pine trees. She thought how her senses were becoming so attuned to sounds. She could hear the river rushing over a small dam, and the sounds of some unknown birds, singing in the nearby forest. But she didn't hear Windhawk's soft footsteps as he walked up behind her, nor did her brother Tag.

"Tag, sometimes I think when one loses something, God gives him something else to replace it."

"What do you mean, Joanna?"

"It's just that now that I can no longer see, I can hear and smell things that I never paid attention to before. I can smell the sweet scent of the pine trees. I can tell what an object looks like when I hold it in my hand. The other day She Who Heals let me feel her face, and I think I know exactly what she looks like."

"You will see again, Joanna. I just know you will."

"I don't think so, Tag. I think we should prepare

ourselves for the inevitable."

"You once told me that only weak people gave up, Joanna. I never knew you to be a quitter," Tag said, feeling anguish at her admission.

She laughed aloud. "How could I ever give up with you badgering me."

Windhawk watched the brother and sister, wishing he were a part of their lives. His eyes lovingly caressed Joanna's slight form. He loved to see her in the soft buckskin she now wore. When he took her to the fort she would return to the white woman's way of dressing. She was thinner now, but she seemed to be enjoying good health. When he looked at her face he saw it was no longer red, but a deep golden tanned color. He could not see if there was any scarring, because the leather blindfold covered much of her face.

Tag turned around just in time to catch a wistful look on Windhawk's face, and in that moment he realized that Windhawk loved his sister.

"Look at Joanna, she is so well that She Who Heals said she could stay here by the river for a while, if I would keep her in the shade."

Joanna turned, wondering who Tag had spoken to.

"I can see she is doing well," she heard the deep voice she loved so well reply.

She felt Windhawk move closer to her and raised her face to him.

"It is good to see you looking so well, Joanna," he told her softly.

She smiled. "You spoke my name differently."

His eyes moved over her upturned face caressingly. "Little brother taught me to say it the white man's way."

"I think I prefer the way you spoke it before," she answered him, wondering why he should take the trouble to learn to say her name correctly.

"Has Tag told you that Fosset is completely recovered? You will be able to ride him any time you want."

"Yes," she answered, turning away.

Tag sat down and folded his arms around his knees, watching the two people he loved most in the world. It had just occurred to him that Joanna didn't want to leave Windhawk, and it took only one look into Windhawk's eyes to know he didn't want her to go. Why was he sending her away, and why was she not putting up a fight to stay?

Windhawk came up behind her and the breeze whipped her hair, blowing it across his face. He closed his eyes as the silky strands brushed against his cheek. "I am told by She Who Heals that she is going to remove the protection from your eyes in two days' time."

"Yes, she said we should know then if I will be able to see."

Tag stood up, thinking he would leave the two of them alone. He hoped they would straighten out whatever was wrong between them. Joanna never discussed Windhawk with him, and he hadn't asked any questions, knowing she would tell him what she wanted him to know.

"I think I'll go see if Sun Woman has any more of those berry cakes," he said casually. "Joanna, will you be all right here with Windhawk?"

"Yes, but . . ."

"I will return you to She Who Heals's tipi, when you are ready," Windhawk told her.

Joanna heard Tag leaving and wanted to call out to him. She was frightened of being alone with Windhawk. What if she were to weaken and beg him not to send her away?

Windhawk could feel Joanna's unrest, and he thought she was remembering his cruelty to her. It hurt him to think he had brought her to this state.

"Joanna, I have many things to be sorry for. I cannot tell you how I hurt that you have lost your sight because of me. I will always remember that I was the one who robbed you of your vision. If, by putting out my eyes, I could bring sight back to yours, I would do so."

"No, it's not your fault. I feel only gratitude to you. You saved my life when the panther would have killed me. You gave my brother back to me, and you spared Farley's life. How could I not be grateful to you?"

Windhawk raised his face to the heavens and took a deep breath. He didn't want her gratitude . . . he wanted her love.

"Come, I will walk you back. I think you have been out long enough." He reached for her hand and felt it tremble. She was frightened of him, he thought bitterly.

"Windhawk, I asked She Who Heals about your wound and she told me she applied healing salve to it, and it had healed very nicely."

"It was not as bad as it appeared."

"Did it leave a scar?"

"No," he said abruptly, not wanting to discuss himself.

"I saw . . . there was so much blood. How could there not be scarring?"

"She Who Heals is known for her healing powers. This was not the first time I have depended on her to treat a wound for me. Your brother has told you that I am taking you to the fort?" he asked, changing the subject.

"Yes. When do you think we will leave?"

"As soon as the medicine woman says you can travel. I do not think it will be very long."

Joanna felt his hand tighten on hers and she knew he was staring at her. She felt her heart race. Now was the time to tell him that she no longer wanted to leave. The silence between them was almost deafening as he turned her around, leading her back to camp. The moment had passed; she could never tell him she loved him so deeply that it filled her whole heart and body.

When they reached the tipi, Windhawk helped her inside, then left without a word. Joanna felt around in her darkened world until she found the buffalo robe and she lay down, becoming totally lost in misery.

She didn't hear She Who Heals until the medicine woman spoke to her. "I was told that you are leaving Windhawk. It is not good for a woman to leave her husband."

"I am not leaving him; he is sending me away."

"You left him before," She Who Heals said accusingly. "Will you not be glad to return to your people?"

Joanna propped her head up on her hand. "No, this is where I belong, beside the man I love. I know that now, but it's too late."

"Have you said this to Windhawk?"

"No! And I don't want you to tell him either. He no longer loves me, and I don't want his pity."

"I will say nothing. This is between you and your husband. Only you can choose the road you will walk."

"I have not been able to choose for myself in a long time. Someone else has taken the decisions out of my hands."

"One can always choose the road he will travel, if he has the courage."

"I'm tired and I don't want one of your lectures," Joanna said, wishing she had the courage to go to Windhawk and . . . and what?

Amanda walked beside Tall Bear. Every so often she would steal a shy glance in his direction. For over a week now, he had come every day to Sun Woman's tipi, asking permission for Amanda to walk with him. While they were walking he would talk to her of the Blackfoot customs and ask her about her life before she had been captured by Running Elk.

Today he seemed strangely silent and Amanda wondered what he might be thinking. She had begun to have such deep, tender feelings for him. He was so kind and when he looked at her with his dark eyes, she felt all funny inside.

"I will not be seeing you for a while, Amanda," he told her.

"Why?" she asked, before she could stop herself.

"I am building a new lodge. I am thinking about taking a wife," he answered with deep searching eyes.

"Oh," Amanda said, feeling crestfallen. How would she bear it if she could never talk to him again? "I wish you happiness," she told him, knowing she meant it with all her heart.

They were walking through the woods and the thick undergrowth cushioned their footsteps. Tall Bear turned to her and took her hand. "I do not yet know if I will be happy."

"Why is that?" Amanda asked, shyly raising her eyes to him.

"I do not know if the one I love returns my love. I have not yet asked her to become my woman."

Amanda began to think he might mean her and her eyes lit up with joy, only to turn to disillusionment a moment later. No, he would not want her after what Running Elk had done to her. No man would ever want her.

He tilted her chin up and smiled. "You are the one I want to be my wife, Amanda. I have spoken to Windhawk and he told me it would be your decision."

"I . . . you want me!" She felt tears in her eyes and blinked to clear them away. "No, I can never marry you or any other man. I am not fit to be anyone's wife."

His eyes showed tenderness and compassion. "I know about Running Elk; that was not your fault. It makes no difference to me what happened to you before I met you. I know only that I love you and if

351

you will not have me, I will be unhappy."

"Yes! Oh yes, I will be your wife," Amanda cried as he pulled her into his arms.

He lowered his head, tasting her sweet lips for the first time. His heart was filled with happiness, as was Amanda's.

The time had come to remove Joanna's blindfold. She Who Heals's tipi was crowded. Tag, Amanda, Sun Woman, and Morning Song were waiting to see if Joanna would be able to see. Windhawk had not entered the tipi, but stood just outside, waiting to hear if Joanna had regained her eyesight. He raised his head and sent a silent prayer to Napi asking that he return Joanna's sight to her.

Everyone was silent as She Who Heals bent over Joanna and untied the soft doeskin band. "I want you to keep your eyes shut, Joanna. Do not open them until I say."

Joanna nodded, while clenching her hands tightly together. She wanted to see the sun and the flowers; she wanted to see Tag's dear face and most of all, she wanted to see Windhawk.

She felt someone kneel down beside her, and Tag slipped his hand into hers. "You are going to see, Joanna. I know you are," he said encouragingly.

She Who Heals removed the covering and everyone held their breath. All Joanna could see was the deep void of darkness, and she began to panic. She had waited so long for this day and now that the time had come, she was afraid to open her eyes.

"I can see no light. It is still dark," she whispered.

"It is dark because I have shut out the light in the tipi," She Who Heals said, motioning for Sun Woman to go outside and bring her a burning piece of wood. "Keep your eyes closed, Joanna," she warned.

Sun Woman returned and handed the torch to She Who Heals, who waved it before Joanna's face.

Joanna could feel the heat from the fire but she could see nothing beyond the deep, dark, shadowy world that enclosed her.

"What do you see?" She Who Heals asked.

"I . . . I see nothing," Joanna whispered.

"Open your eyes, Joanna," She Who Heals said.

Joanna's eyelids fluttered and she opened her eyes. She Who Heals saw the blank stare in the beautiful violet-colored eyes and knew that Joanna was still blind. The others waited tensely.

"I can see nothing . . . nothing. I am blind!" Joanna screamed, clasping her hands over her eyes.

Joanna could hear Amanda crying softly as everyone but Tag filed out of the tipi. Tag put his arms around Joanna and laid his head on her shoulder. He tried to brush the tears away, not wanting her to know he was crying. When she clasped him to her, their tears blended together.

"Don't worry, Joanna. I will never leave you. I will be your eyes," he cried.

Windhawk moved silently away. He mounted his horse and rode out of camp where he could be alone. The beautiful eyes that he loved so well would never again see the light of day. He would never again see his own image reflected in her eyes. It was his fault; he had done this thing to Joanna.

How she must hate him now. He wished he could go to her and hold her in his arms, giving her comfort, but she would not welcome him.

Windhawk crossed the river, looking about the land, knowing that Joanna would never see the beauty of it again. Urging his horse forward, he rode like the wind, not knowing or caring where he was going.

It was later that night and Amanda sat beside Joanna, talking softly to her. She had no words of comfort to give Joanna, but she wanted to be with her friend in her hour of grief.

Joanna turned her face to Amanda. "Tell me what you see. Do I look hideous? Is my face scarred?"

Amanda looked carefully at Joanna's face. It was as lovely as ever, perhaps even more so. Her delicate features were enhanced by a deep golden tan, but her beautiful eyes stared blankly into nothingness.

"I don't see even one scar, Joanna. She Who Heals has performed a miracle. Your face hasn't changed except that you now have a deep tan."

"You aren't just saying that, Amanda? I want to know the truth."

"I promise you I would not speak falsely. Your face is beautiful."

"Is it dark outside now?"

"Yes."

Joanna sighed. "It will no longer matter if it is day or night. It will all be the same to me."

Oh, Joanna . . . I wish . . ."

"Do not pity me, Amanda. I, myself, am wallowing in self-pity. Be strong for me so I can draw courage from you."

Amanda was glad Joanna couldn't see the tears in her eyes. She had never known anyone with the kind of courage Joanna possessed. Joanna would be returning to the civilized world and she would be able to face whatever awaited her.

"Joanna, I don't quite know how to tell you what I have decided to do. I wanted to wait until you were better, but I suppose now is the time."

"Is something wrong, Amanda?"

"No, in fact I am deliriously happy. I have decided not to go with you and Tag when you leave. Tall Bear has asked me to become his wife, and I have accepted."

"Tall Bear, he is Gray Fox's brother, is he not?" Joanna asked in a surprised voice.

"Yes, and I love him. I want nothing more than to spend the rest of my life with him."

"I am happy for you, Amanda. If you had said this to me a few weeks ago I would have doubted your sanity, but I now know one can love a man enough to want to give up everything to be with him."

"Are you talking about yourself and Wind-hawk?"

"Yes, I love him, but he is sending me away. I regret having ever tried to leave him, because now he detests me."

Amanda put a comforting arm about her friend's shoulder. "Maybe he thinks you want to leave, and he is taking you back because he loves you so much."

"No, he no longer loves me. There was a time

when he did, but I killed his love. I didn't tell you this, but when I thought he was going to harm Farley, I aimed a rifle at him. I could never have pulled the trigger, but he doesn't know that."

"Oh, Joanna, I am so sorry. When you and Tag leave, I am going to miss you both so much. I don't suppose we'll ever see each other again."

Joanna squared her shoulders. She had never been one to complain about her lot in life and she wasn't about to start now. "Is there anyone you want me to get in touch with when we get to the fort, Amanda?"

"No. All the ones I cared about were killed in the raid. I have a few distant kinfolk, but we were never close. Let them think I was killed along with my folks."

Joanna almost envied Amanda. She was able to stay with the man she loved, or did she love him? Perhaps she was only staying because she didn't want to face her own people. Could Amanda be so ashamed of what Running Elk had done to her that she wanted to hide away in the Blackfoot village?

"Amanda, are you positive that you love Tall Bear enough to stay with him forever? Suppose you were to change your mind later on?"

"I will never change my mind, Joanna. This is where I want to be."

"The life of an Indian is a hard one, and you will seldom have a permanent home," Joanna said, stating some of the hard truths to her friend.

"I will love making a home for Tall Bear, wherever it may be."

Joanna smiled. "I can see that your mind is made

up. I just hope you find all the happiness in the world."

"I wish you could be happy, Joanna. Perhaps when you find your father again, he can take you to a doctor who will be able to restore your eyesight."

"I wonder if I shall ever be truly happy again, Amanda. Do you think there is such a thing as total happiness?"

"I don't know. I doubt it, but when I am with Tall Bear it's as near to perfect happiness as I have ever come."

"That's all that counts then. I will take comfort in knowing that you are with someone you love and who loves you in return."

"When do you leave?" Amanda asked.

"I'm not sure. Windhawk will decide that."

"Joanna, Tall Bear has told me enough about Windhawk to make me see he is an extraordinary man. If you love him you should tell him so."

"I feel very tired now, Amanda," Joanna said, not wanting to talk about Windhawk.

Amanda stood up and stared at her friend. Unhappiness was etched on Joanna's lovely face. Joanna would be leaving the man she loved without putting up a fight for him. Perhaps it was best. Joanna came from a different kind of world than Amanda had. Maybe she would never be happy living the nomadic life of an Indian.

Amanda left, feeling sadness for the only real friend she had ever had.

Joanna now felt totally alone. Suddenly she felt panic and stood up, groping in the dark. She bumped into the lodgepole and hung on to it for support. She felt as if the whole world had come crashing down upon her shoulders.

How would she stand it if she could never hear Windhawk's voice again. How could she live if she never felt the touch of his hand?

A sob issued from deep within her throat and Joanna buried her face in her hands. Why had life become so unbearable? She wanted to be able to see! She couldn't stand the thought of being locked into a darkened world forever. How would she watch time passing? She wouldn't be able to see the seasons change. She would never know the joy of having Windhawk's baby, and looking upon their child's face.

She knew that she was feeling sorry for herself, but she couldn't seem to stop. Today she had been forced to face the fact that she would never see again, and that the man she loved didn't want her anymore.

Joanna felt comforting arms go about her shoulders and she was held against Sun Woman's shoulder. "Cry, cry, my daughter, for no one has a better reason than you do. There is no shame in tears of grief."

Joanna felt the tears on Sun Woman's face and knew Windhawk's mother shared her grief. "I . . . hurt so badly, my mother," she cried.

"I also hurt badly for you, my daughter. Only time can heal when the heart is hurt."

Joanna allowed Sun Woman to lead her back to her bed. Windhawk's mother sat beside her, holding her hand until Joanna fell asleep.

## Chapter Twenty-one

Joanna stood outside She Who Heals's tipi, feeling the cold wind penetrate her buckskin gown, while the snow crunched beneath her moccasins. She felt completely recovered now. If it weren't for the fact that she couldn't see, she would be enjoying the crisp, cold morning.

She had become so accustomed to the sounds of the village that she could identify many of the people's voices. Hearing light moccasin steps, she turned her head.

"Hello, Gray Fox. It's a lovely day, isn't it?"

Gray Fox looked at her in surprise. "How did you know it was me, Joanna?" He saw that her eyes were still bound with the soft doeskin cloth.

She laughed. "I am becoming very good at detecting sounds. You wear two metal stars on your moccasins. When you walk, they jingle together."

Joanna reached her hand out to Gray Fox and he

took it. He had watched her courage from a distance, and against his will, had begun to feel more for his best friend's wife than friendship.

"I just left Sun Woman and she asked if I would bring you to her. She says you are well enough to move in with her and Morning Song."

"Yes, I am completely recovered . . . almost. Gray Fox, I have a desire to walk in the woods. Would you take me?"

He removed the blanket from about his shoulders and placed it around Joanna's shoulders. "I will be happy to be your guide, Joanna."

Gray Fox reached out his hand and took Joanna's small delicate hand in his. He thought Windhawk was a fool to send his woman away. If she were his woman he would never allow her to leave him.

As they walked along, he would describe many of the sights to her. She listened quietly as he described the icicles that were hanging off the branches of a pine tree.

After they had walked deep into the forest, Gray Fox found a fallen log and dusted the snow from it. Taking Joanna's hand, he sat her down. He had wanted to talk to her, and now might be his only chance. It was hard for him to watch the pain Windhawk was going through. He wanted to help his friend, even though he knew it was unwise to interfere.

"Joanna, are you sure that you want to leave us?"

She was quiet for a moment pondering his words. Gray Fox was Windhawk's best friend. She could never tell him that she loved Windhawk and dreaded the time of their parting. "I will miss many things here in this village. The Blackfoot have been so kind to me, but I feel that I have overstayed my welcome," she said, lapsing into English.

"What does this . . . overstayed your welcome mean?" he asked in the same language.

"It means a guest who has stayed longer than his host intended him to."

"I do not believe that is true. I know my wives love you. She Who Heals looks on you as a daughter. Somehow you have won the formidable Sun Woman over. I have heard that she is sad because you are leaving."

"I think that your chief does not share his mother's views," Joanna said sadly.

Gray Fox was quiet for a long time. He wished he had the courage to ask her if she loved Windhawk. "Will you not miss Windhawk?" he asked instead.

Joanna stood up. "It has turned rather cold. I think I would like to go back now," she said, ending the conversation.

Gray Fox took her arm and led her back toward the village. When they emerged from the trees, Windhawk saw them. His eyes narrowed with jealousy and he walked toward them with anger in his heart.

Gray Fox saw him approach and recognized the danger signal. Never had Windhawk given him such a murderous look.

"Should you not be tending to your own wives, Gray Fox?" Windhawk said in a deadly calm voice.

Joanna was so engrossed in her thoughts that she had been unaware of Windhawk's presence and stumbled against a protruding root. Gray Fox reached out to steady her and she fell forward into his arms.

Windhawk sprang forward and tore Joanna away from Gray Fox. He lifted her into his arms, and sent his friend a heated glance. "We will talk of this later," he told him, turning his back and walking away.

Joanna was surprised at the anger in Windhawk's voice. She had done nothing to make him angry. It felt so right to be in his arms, she thought, laying her head on his shoulder. She would stay in his arms for the rest of her life if he would allow it.

"Where are you taking me?" she asked.

"I do not want to speak to you, Joanna. Remain silent."

"Why are you angry?"

"I said do not speak," he said, trying to gain control over his jealousy.

When Windhawk had seen Joanna coming out of the forest with Gray Fox, his anger had soared. She was his woman, and no other man had the right to touch her. Windhawk would always feel in his heart that she belonged to him. He could not bear to think that one day another man would hold her soft body the way he had once held her. He held her tightly in his arms, thinking how precious she was to him. If only he had not treated her so cruelly. If he had guarded her more carefully she would not have lost her eyesight. Joanna had never said that she blamed him for her blindness, but he knew that she must hold him responsible.

He was so guilt-ridden that he was haunted day

and night by Joanna's blindness. He knew that he must take her back where she belonged. She had once told him that they were from different worlds, and neither would fit into the other's life. He should have listened to her.

"Where are we?" Joanna asked, when he set her on her feet.

"We are in my lodge," he told her, taking her arm.

"Am I going to stay with you?" she asked as her heart beat wildly.

"No, I merely wanted to speak to you alone."

Joanna felt her hopes dashed. If she were to ask him to take her in his arms, would he reject her? What if she should tell him that she loved him and never wanted to leave him?

"I can't think what we have to say to each other, Windhawk."

His eyes glazed. "What I have to say to you is not of a personal nature. You need have no fear that I am going to ask anything of you." His voice sounded cold to Joanna, and she sighed when he helped her sit down.

"I think it is time we discussed your leaving." His words seemed to hang in the air, and Joanna knew that the time she had been dreading had come at last.

She raised her head to him and he caught his breath. How would he ever be able to let her go. Her bright red-gold hair was shimmering in the firelight and he wanted to take her in his arms and bury his face in its softness.

"When . . . will we leave?" she asked, feeling as if her whole world had just come tumbling down around her.

"I thought we would start in the morning before severe weather sets in."

"I had not thought . . . I did not think we would be leaving so soon."

He watched her face closely. It was hard to tell what she was thinking when he couldn't see her eyes. "Can you think of any reason we should not leave tomorrow?"

"No, of course not," she said hurriedly. Joanna stood up and unfastened the bear-claw necklace he had given her on their wedding night. Holding it out to him, she felt tears in her eyes. "I do not know the procedure of divorce in your tribe," she said, lapsing into English. "If I give you back this token will that suffice?"

"I do not understand what this word . . . divorce means," he said, lapsing into English and staring at the necklace.

"It means when a marriage is ended," she said, relieved that her heartbreak didn't show up in her voice.

Windhawk's hand closed over hers. "You keep the necklace. It was a gift from me to you."

Joanna remembered the night he had given her the necklace. That night he had said it was a symbol of their love. She also remembered he said he would never take it back. She would test him now to see if he would take the necklace back, thus showing her that he no longer loved her.

"It belongs to you, Windhawk, please take it," she said, holding her breath. If he didn't take it back, it would mean he still loved her. Oh she hoped and prayed he would refuse the necklace.

Joanna felt Windhawk's hand brush hers as he took the necklace from her. Dear God, she prayed silently, don't let me cry in front of him! Don't let him know how badly I am hurting, she cried silently.

"I am tired, Windhawk. Would you take me to your mother now?" She was glad her voice hadn't betrayed her feelings.

Windhawk stared at the necklace. Joanna did not want anything to remind her of him, he thought. Taking her hand, he led her out of his lodge.

Tomorrow would be the beginning of the end for him. How empty his days would be when he could no longer see Joanna's face or hear the sound of her voice. He would be dead on the inside. Never again would he allow a woman to touch his heart as deeply as Joanna had. He would never feel love again.

Joanna was going to a world that he could never reach. When she was gone, she would leave his world as devoid of sunlight as her blindness shut out the light from her eyes.

Glancing down at her buckskin-clad form, Windhawk tried to remember a time he had ever seen her completely happy. There had always been a shadow hanging over her, some urgency about her, as if there was something she had to do.

Windhawk had reached his mother's tipi and when Sun Woman came forward, he handed Joanna over to her and left without a word.

"Come, my daughter," Sun Woman said, leading Joanna to the warm fire and helping her sit down.

"There are many things that I would say to you."

Joanna waited silently for Sun Woman to continue.

"As you know, Joanna, there was a time when I did not accept you. I thought you were other than what you seemed, but I was to learn that you were not false. I have come to love you, my daughter; I grieved with you when you lost your sight. I grieve now because you are going away. Will you not stay with us?"

Joanna reached out her hand and Sun Woman placed hers in it. Raising the older woman's hand to her cheek, Joanna spoke. "I have come to love you also, my mother. Although my heart is heavy at leaving, I know it is for the best."

"My son needs you, Joanna. I see this every day. If you love him, you would not go away."

"I am not going of my own free will. Windhawk is taking me."

"He thinks it is what you want."

"No, you are wrong. I think that for a time Windhawk loved me, but he no longer feels that way. I believe he does not want a wife who is sightless. I also believe he will never forgive me for trying to run away."

Sun Woman sighed. "It is not my place to interfere. I only want you to know that when you leave you will leave behind many who will not soon forget you."

"I will never forget you, my mother, nor will I forget Morning Song who is so dear to me."

It was a dark night when Tall Bear made his way to Sun Woman's tipi to claim Amanda as his wife. He paused at the door, asking if he could enter. Amanda waited anxiously, not knowing what to expect when Sun Woman bid him enter.

His dark eyes were sparkling as he reached for Amanda's hand and she looked shyly up at him. Her heart was drumming as he led her out of the tipi and to the lodge he had built for them.

This was their wedding night. Amanda wore a white doeskin gown that Sun Woman had helped her make. Her rich, brown-colored hair hung loosely about her shoulders.

A light snow had begun to fall, and Amanda could hear the laughter coming from the other tipis they passed. This was where she belonged, she thought. She had found her happiness at long last.

When they reached their tipi, Tall Bear led Amanda inside and pulled her into his arms. Her lips invited his kiss, and she sighed when his lips covered hers. When he led her to their wedding bed, she went willingly. Her only regret was that Tall Bear wasn't the first man to be with her. As his hands roamed lovingly over her body, Amanda forgot the cruelty with which Running Elk had treated her. She surrendered herself totally to her husband.

That night Joanna fought against falling asleep. This would be the last night she would spend with the Blackfoot people she had come to love so dearly. Their life was a hard one compared to what she was accustomed to, but they enjoyed a peace of mind and satisfaction in their day-to-day life that no white man would be able to understand.

Joanna lay beside Morning Song knowing that she was not sleeping, because she tossed restlessly.

"Can you not sleep, my sister?" Joanna asked.

"I do not want to sleep. I will never see you again," Morning Song cried, slipping her hand into Joanna's.

"I will miss you also, but I will think of you growing into a beautiful woman and one day marrying a man whom you will love."

"The way you love my brother?" she asked.

"Morning Song, I do love Windhawk, but you know it is right that I return to my people."

"You are leaving because you blame my brother for your blindness?"

"No, you are wrong, my sister. I do not blame anyone for the fact that I can no longer see."

Morning Song threw her arms around Joanna and hugged her tightly. "My heart will be so empty after you are gone. I will never have another sister," she cried.

Joanna pushed the tumbled hair out of Morning Song's face. "One day Windhawk will marry, and you will . . ." Joanna's voice became choked and she tried not to cry as she continued, "you . . . will love her."

"No, I will never have another sister. Windhawk will never love again."

"You are wrong, little sister. Windhawk . . . is a very loving man. He will . . . he will." Joanna couldn't finish. Hot tears scalded her eyes. Dear God, she prayed silently, give me the strength to walk away without looking back. Help me have the courage not to beg him to allow me to stay.

The next morning Sun Woman silently helped Joanna dress. Joanna knew how much Windhawk's mother had admired the copper pots and pans which had once belonged to Franny. She had given them to Sun Woman the night before, hoping it would cheer her.

Her personal belongings had been packed in the trunk and loaded onto a pack horse. Once more Joanna was dressed in a riding habit. She carried her mother's jewelry case in a leather pouch, knowing she and Tag would need to sell more of the jewels to finance their trip to Oregon.

When she walked out of the tipi, there were many people lined up waiting to say good-bye to her. First, She Who Heals stepped forward and embraced her.

"Take my heart and flee, Joanna. You care not that you break an old woman's heart."

Joanna kissed the wrinkled face that was wet with tears. "Not so. I will always remember you gave me back my life."

Gray Fox and his two wives wished her happiness, and Joanna kissed the cheek of the baby boy whose life she had once saved.

Amanda was crying so hard that after she hugged Joanna, she ran to her tipi and threw herself down on her bed, sobbing uncontrollably. Tall Bear knelt down beside her, giving her comfort.

Joanna had said her good-byes to Sun Woman

and Morning Song before she left the tipi. She was glad she wore the blindfold, because it hid her tears from everyone. She held her head up proudly as Tag took her hand and led her to her horse. No one would know, she thought, that her heart was breaking into a thousand pieces.

Windhawk did not speak to her as he lifted her onto her horse. When they rode out of the village, Joanna could tell they had been joined by many other riders. Evidently Windhawk was taking a small army with him.

When their horses entered the river, Joanna could hear the sounds of the village fading into the distance. She felt as if she were leaving her true home behind and riding into the unknown.

Joanna had changed. She no longer wanted to be Joanna James. She only wanted to be Windhawk's woman!

## Chapter Twenty-two

At any other time, Joanna would have enjoyed riding Fosset. The animal was his old self again. Joanna had to pull back on the reins several times to slow Fosset's swift pace.

Tag rode beside Joanna. He was ever-watchful in case she should need him. They had been riding all day and she had been strangely silent. Windhawk rode just ahead, and Tag would see him glance back at Joanna every so often to make sure she was all right.

Tag found himself torn between two loyalties. He wanted to see his father, yet he hated the thought of leaving Windhawk. He wondered if Joanna was feeling much the same. He could tell by the set of her chin she was not very happy. Sometimes he just didn't understand grown-ups. He knew that Joanna loved Windhawk, and Windhawk loved Joanna. Why couldn't they just tell each other how they felt and have it done with? he wondered, puzzled.

The snow was falling heavily when they stopped that evening to make camp. A tipi was quickly erected to accommodate Joanna. Later the others would raise their own shelters, but Windhawk had ordered Joanna to be out of the biting cold weather as soon as possible.

Tag led her into the tipi, and Joanna felt around until she found the buffalo robe. Easing herself down she could feel the tiredness creep into her body.

"Did Windhawk tell you where he was taking us, Tag?" Joanna inquired. "All I know is he is taking us to a fort."

He sat down beside her, noticing how pale and wan she appeared. "Yes, he is taking us to Fort Union, which is about a week's journey from here. It's not an army post. Windhawk told me it had been established by the American Fur Company, so they could organize trade with the Indians."

"A week," she whispered. She would have only seven days to be with Windhawk. She had the strongest urge to go to him now and beg him to hold her in his arms. How would she ever be able to go on without him?

In her world of darkness, Joanna cried out for the only ray of light in her torment. She would be able to bear her darkened existence, if only she had Windhawk to share it with her.

"I'm going to get you something to eat, Joanna. You just lie down and rest until I get back," Tag said, standing up and leaving quietly.

When he was outside he saw Windhawk and

walked over to him. "I think my sister is very tired. She doesn't seem quite herself."

"Do you think she is ill?"

"No, it's nothing like that. It's as if she is just deep-down tired and doesn't want to go on. I've never seen Joanna like this before."

"I will talk to her," Windhawk said, walking toward the tipi.

Joanna knew Windhawk had entered the tipi, even though she hadn't heard him. Turning her head in his direction she waited for him to speak.

"Little brother has told me that you are not feeling well, Joanna," he said, dropping down beside her.

She sat up and folded her legs back behind her. "I am fine, just a little tired, that's all."

"If you think the trip will be too hard on you at this time, I will take you back to the village until you are more rested."

If she told him yes, perhaps she would get to be with him for a few weeks longer. No, she thought, it would be better to get the painful ordeal over as soon as possible. It would be just as hard to leave him later on.

She could not see the hopefulness in his dark eyes when she answered him. "No, I want to go on. You probably have many things you need to do without chasing after the whims of a woman." She was not aware of the bitterness that had crept into her voice, nor did she realize that she had spoken to him in English.

Windhawk stood up and quietly walked away. He had felt like taking her into his arms and making her want him. He knew that in the past he had easily awakened her desire. But Joanna was different now. Too many things had gone wrong between them. He had once thought that their love could overcome any difficulty, but it had not.

Windhawk gazed across the prairie to Fort Union in the distance. It was situated on the bank of the Missouri River. Just behind the fort was a chain of small mountains that were now snow-covered. Across the wide river was a heavily wooded area. The fort itself had been constructed of heavy logs around the outer stockade walls. Windhawk saw a number of Indian tipis scattered near the fort, and knew that they belonged to the Assiniboin tribe, who had been long-time enemies of the Blackfoot.

One of Windhawk's warriors rode up beside him staring down at their enemies with a look of distaste. "I did not know the Assiniboin would be here, my chief. Will we ride down and surprise them?"

Windhawk glanced at Joanna thinking how strange she looked in her blue wool riding habit and high-top black boots. "No, I will take Joanna and Tag alone. I do not want any of you to show yourselves unless there is trouble. We have not come to war on our enemies."

Windhawk motioned to Tag and the boy moved his mount forward, leading Joanna's horse. As they descended onto the flat prairie, Windhawk's senses became alert. When they drew near the Assiniboin his eyes swept past them as if they didn't even exist.

Several of the warriors stared at the Blackfoot

chief in disbelief, thinking he was either the bravest man they had ever seen, or the most foolish. Not one of them raised his hand to stop him as he made his way to the fort entrance.

When they neared the fort the gates were standing open, so Windhawk boldly entered. Since it was not an army post, he was surprised to see several of the long knives eyeing him suspiciously.

Joanna heard voices speaking in English and she knew they had entered the fort. Was Windhawk still with her and Tag? she wondered. Since she couldn't hear him, she feared he had left her without saying good-bye.

"Windhawk!" she cried reaching out her hand. "Where are you!"

Windhawk heard the unbridled panic in her voice, and knew it was because of her unfamiliar surroundings. "I am here, Joanna," he said, dismounting and reaching up to help her from her horse.

Captain Harland Thatcher descended the steps from the wooden walk that ran the length of the stockade wall, two steps at a time. He could hardly believe his eyes when he saw Joanna and Taggart James. Running across the compound, he grabbed Joanna by the shoulders and spun her around." Miss James . . . I" He saw the blindfold on her eyes and lapsed into silence.

"Is that you, Captain Thatcher?" she asked joyfully, hardly believing he was still alive.

Windhawk's eyes blazed when he recognized the man whom he had once seen Joanna dancing with. He did not like the familiar way the long knife touched her. He wanted to slam the man against the gate and plunge his knife into his heart.

Windhawk saw Old Farley limping forward and that didn't improve his temper any.

"Yes, it's me, Miss James. This is a strange coincidence. Farley came to Fort Leavenworth and informed the commander you were alive and living in the Blackfoot village. I volunteered to take a company of men and try and res . . ." His eyes moved to Windhawk's and he saw the murderous glare that chilled him to the bone. "We were sent to . . . rescue you," he said hesitantly, pulling his eyes away from the chief of the Bloods.

"Joanna, you are surely a sight for sore eyes," Farley said, coming forward and grasping her hand. "And I'll declare ifen it ain't Taggart, too."

Windhawk stepped back a pace. He could see several long knives closing in on him with their hands resting threateningly on their sabers. Tag saw this too, and he moved to stand beside Windhawk. He could see that the soldiers were only waiting for the signal from Captain Thatcher to overtake Windhawk.

"Call off your men, Captain Thatcher," Tag yelled. "Windhawk is our friend. If you lay one hand on him, my sister and I will . . ."

"Captain Thatcher," Joanna intervened. "Windhawk saved my and my brother's life. Let him go free." She felt confusion, not being able to see what was happening.

Harland looked at the tall chief. Farley had informed him that Windhawk had forcibly taken Joanna back to the Blackfoot village after the old

376

man had rescued her.

"Stand easy, men. Allow him to pass," Harland ordered.

Windhawk looked at Joanna one last time. He turned slowly away, mounted his horse, and rode out the gate.

Joanna held up her hand in a beseeching manner. "Windhawk, do not leave me!" she cried in the tongue of the Blackfoot. But Windhawk did not hear her plea; he had already ridden away.

Joanna stumbled forward and fell to the ground. Tag knelt down beside her and hugged her tightly. "He's gone, Joanna," he said.

Joanna shook her head, crying softly. "He didn't even say good-bye, Tag. He left without a word."

"Miss Joanna, Master Taggart, I thought it was your voices I heard, but I couldn't be sure." Simon took Joanna's hand and helped her to her feet.

By now Joanna was in total confusion. Windhawk had left her, and she had heard the voices of three men she feared were dead.

She grabbed Simon and hugged him tightly. "Oh, Simon, I thought you had been killed. Thank God, you're still alive."

Joanna's happiness at knowing Simon wasn't dead was short lived. She felt such pain and emptiness in her heart. How could Windhawk have left her? He had ridden away as if he couldn't wait to get away from her.

"Watcha wearing that thing on your eyes fer, Joanna?" Farley asked.

"Farley, I am so glad you are safe. How is your ankle?" she asked.

"I'm doing right nicely. Right after you and Windhawk left, Nate Boscow, the trapper whose trap I stuck my leg in came by to check his line. He took me to Fort Leavenworth. You never did say why you have your eyes covered," he added.

Joanna knew there would be many questions to answer before she could be alone with her broken heart.

Harland Thatcher looked at Joanna. He had grieved when he thought she had been killed by the Blackfoot. When Farley had told him she was still alive, he knew he wouldn't rest until he had freed her or died trying.

"Take my arm, Miss James. I think you need to rest now," Harland said. "After you are refreshed will be time enough to answer questions."

Windhawk stared at the fort below. Joanna was back where she belonged. He had hated the way the long knife had touched her, but she was no longer his woman. Let her return to her meaningless white world.

Windhawk turned his horse and headed westward. The snow had begun to fall again and he felt the chill of the cold wind. His dark eyes stared straight ahead and his hands gripped the reins tightly. He felt as if his heart had turned to ice.

# Chapter Twenty-three

The common room was a huge structure with rough log walls and ceilings. There were several wooden benches and chairs, and a crude table. Many different kinds of animal furs were stacked against the wall, almost to the ceiling.

Joanna and Tag sat before a big roaring fire while Captain Thatcher and several other men were gathered about a table asking them questions. They wanted to know if there were any other captives in the Blackfoot village. They also wanted to know if Joanna and Tag could give them any details about the raid on the wagon train.

Joanna was strangely quiet, leaving Tag to answer most of the questions that were put to them. In truth, she paid very little attention to the proceedings. Her mind was on the tall Indian who had taken her to the gates of paradise only to cast her adrift. Joanna placed no blame on Windhawk. She was the one who had left him first. Of course if he had truly loved her, wouldn't he have forgiven her and taken her back as his wife? she questioned.

Tag nudged Joanna and she was brought back to the present. "What? . . . I'm sorry, I didn't . . . Did you ask me something?" she asked in confusion.

"Captain Thatcher said he has something important to tell us, Joanna," Tag said, leaning close to her and lowering his voice.

Joanna heard the jingle of Harland's spurs and knew he was standing next to her.

"I have sent the others out, Miss James, with the exception of your man Simon, and Farley. Simon is the one who has something to say to you."

Simon knelt down beside Joanna, dreading what he had to relate to her and Tag. He cleared his throat nervously. "Miss Joanna, Master Taggart, after I thought you had perished with the others on the wagon train, I hired a guide to take me to Oregon. It was rough going at times. After several weeks I reached my destination."

"Did you see Papa?" Tag asked excitedly.

"I . . ." Simon paused. "No, that's what I want to tell you. I don't know any other way to say it except to just say it right out. Master Russell is . . . dead."

The room became strangely silent. The only sound that could be heard was the crackling of the fire in the fireplace. Tag placed his hand in Joanna's and she hugged him to her. She could feel his shoulders shaking and tears choked off her breathing.

Farley shook his head sadly, thinking the two of them had been through so much lately and this was just one more final blow.

Tag stood up and took Joanna by the hand. "If you will excuse us," he said, pulling his sister to her feet, "Joanna and I would like to be alone."

"Miss James, is there anything I can do?" Harland offered, feeling sorrow for her and her young brother.

"No, thank you, Captain. Tag and I will be fine. Thank you for your kindness."

"When you feel up to it, Miss James, we will talk about what you should do next."

"Yes . . . later, Captain," she said, before Tag led her from the room.

Farley glanced at Simon, and then at Captain Thatcher. "Them there are mighty fine young people. Guess I admire them 'bout as well as anyone."

"Yes," Harland said, turning to Farley. "You did say that Miss James had been mistreated by Windhawk?"

"I said maybe he had taken her as his woman. I don't know that for sure. I can't think why he set her free after fighting to get her back when she run away. There's something mighty fishy going on here," the old man said. "It just don't fit with what I knowed about him."

"What do you think Miss James' plans will be?" Harland asked, turning to Simon. "Do you think she will want to return to Philadelphia?"

"At this point we haven't made any plans. Let's give them a few more days to adjust to their grief." Simon had no idea what Joanna would decide to do. She couldn't return to Philadelphia now that her father was dead, because that would mean that

Howard Landon was still her and Tag's guardian.

What Simon hadn't told Joanna and Tag was what he had been told about their father's death. Richard Land, who had been Russell James' friend had told Simon that there had been a strange man hanging around their father the day he died. He had still been bedridden with a broken back and it appeared someone had placed a pillow over his face, smothering him to death. Simon had his suspicions that Joanna's Uncle Howard had something to do with their father's death, but he hadn't been able to prove anything.

"I would like to have a physician examine Miss James' eyes," Harland said. "I think we should convince them to go to Fort Leavenworth where they have a fine doctor who can treat her."

"They 'bout as well go to Fort Leavenworth," Farley said. "With winter coming on, they can't go nowhere else."

"That will be up to Miss Joanna," Simon stated stiffly. He had always been close-mouthed about the James' affairs. He would never discuss their personal matters with anyone.

Farley crinkled his face up and looked at Harland. "You wouldn't be sweet on our little lady would you? I seed the way you looked at her. Ifen I were to guess, I'd say you wanted her at Fort Leavenworth so you could be near her."

Harland smiled. "Perhaps, Farley. It never hurts a man to hope."

Farley turned his attention to Simon. "I don't know why you come back here after you seed that Joanna and Tag's pa was kilt. Did you have a hunch you would find them alive?"

"No, not at all. I came back because I wanted to see that my wife, Miss Joanna, and Master Taggart received a proper burial. That's when I ran into you at Fort Leavenworth and you told me that Miss Joanna and Master Tag were still alive."


Joanna and Tag sat in the middle of the bed, talking quietly. They had cried out their grief for their father. Once again they had been called on to withstand heartache. The two of them had faced still another tragedy. Anyone with less fortitude would have given up long ago. Joanna and Tag seemed to have an inner strength that carried them through one disaster after another. They seemed to draw strength from each other. It was now time to put their grief aside and decide what was to be done about their future.

"We cannot go back to Philadelphia, Tag. You know what we would face with Uncle Howard and Aunt Margaret. What do you think we should do?"

"I've been thinking about that. What would you say if we went to Oregon as we originally planned?"

"I don't know, Tag. We don't know anyone in Oregon. We still have Mother's jewels. They will bring a great deal of money if we need to sell them."

"As I see it, we have to avoid Uncle Howard until I come of age. Then we can return to Philadelphia and claim what by rights, belongs to us."

Joanna smiled to herself. Tag was becoming quite grown-up. It was a little sad that he had not been allowed to have a childhood like other boys did.

Now he would miss growing up with a father to guide him. She remembered how he had admired Windhawk, making him the missing father-figure in his life. She didn't know where the future would lead them, but she was grateful that she and Tag still had each other. The fact that they were now together was due to Windhawk.

Windhawk . . . he had touched their lives so briefly, yet both Tag and Joanna knew that they would never forget him. In Joanna's world of darkness she would still see his face so clearly. She knew his image would haunt her for the rest of her life.


The two-week journey to Fort Leavenworth had passed in comfort for Joanna. Captain Thatcher had procured a dog sled for her to ride on. She was not only able to stay snug and warm, but was also able to rest from her long ordeal as well.

Thirty-five cavalry men, Simon, and Farley also made the journey with them. At night a tent was pitched so Joanna and Tag were able to sleep in comfort with warm blankets to keep them snug.

Captain Thatcher went out of his way to see that Joanna wanted for nothing. She was beginning to think he was one of the kindest men she had ever known.

Joanna had very little hope that she would ever regain her sight. She had become resigned to her world of darkness.

In some ways it seemed as if Tag had assumed the role of head of the family. He was never very far away from Joanna in case she needed him.

It seemed that Joanna had many who were interested in her well-being. Farley had attached himself to her and Tag, and of course, there was the ever-faithful Simon.

Fort Leavenworth was in view when Captain Thatcher halted his troops. He dismounted and walked over to Joanna while the others looked on.

"Miss James, we are now ready to enter the fort and the terrain is too rugged for the dog sled. If you will allow me, I will take you upon my horse and carry you to the fort."

Joanna offered him her hand. "That would be kind of you, Captain."

He mounted his horse and Simon handed Joanna up to him. Harland carefully placed her across his lap.

Being in such close contact with a man brought back memories of Windhawk to haunt Joanna.

Harland looked down at the beautiful face and felt an ache deep inside. Would her beautiful eyes never be able to see the light of day? He wanted to hold her and protect her from anyone who would ever try to harm her.

"Miss James, I don't know if I told you or not, but Claudia Maxwell is at the fort."

"How did she manage to survive? I feared she had been killed."

"As you know, Simon and I were scouting on ahead when the Indians struck the wagon train. I blame myself for not being prepared for the attack."

"It was not your fault, Captain. No one could have foreseen that the attack would take place."

"I think I will always feel responsible for what happened. After all, I was in charge."

"Had you been there, Captain, you would have been killed. I am glad you and Simon were spared. I am also happy about Claudia."

"When Simon and I saw the smoke from the burning wagons, we rode back as quickly as we could. When we got near enough, he and I hid in some bushes. It appeared that everyone had been killed. We were outnumbered, fifty to one. It did not seem wise to make our presence known."

Harland did not tell Joanna how he had returned later, searching for her body. Nor did he tell her how he had grieved thinking she was dead.

"I can see that you did the wise thing, Captain."

"Simon and I decided the best course for us to take was to ride to the fort for reinforcements. On the way we came across Miss Maxwell. Her horse had thrown her and she was half out of her mind with fright."

"Has she recovered?"

Harland thought of Claudia and how she was now the belle of the fort. She flirted outrageously with all the officers, including Harland himself. "Yes, I think you could say she is completely recovered. I don't know what her plans are for the future, but like you, she is forced to stay at the fort until winter passes."

Joanna was thoughtful. Even though she had never cared for Claudia, she was happy that her life had been spared.

Joanna could tell the moment they entered the fort by the sounds of activity. She detected the sound of the flag being lowered on the flagpole, and a group of soldiers marching in unison. She felt momentary fear, knowing she was back in the so-called civilization. It seemed a whole lifetime ago since she had been Joanna James. Would she be shunned by the wives of the soldiers because she had been Windhawk's woman?

Harland seemed to know what she was feeling. "Don't worry, Miss James, there is nothing to fear. There are many here who will be your friend."

Claudia was standing outside the post exchange, talking to Lieutenant Bryant, when she saw Captain Thatcher's unit ride into the post. She searched the faces of the soldiers, looking for him. Claudia had decided that before the winter was out, Harland Thatcher would ask her to marry him. She flirted with all the other officers hoping to make him jealous. So far he had kept his distance from her. She knew he was from a very wealthy family and she could see herself as his wife, wearing silks and satins.

Claudia had not been told why Harland had left the fort but she was happy that he had returned.

Her eyes brightened when she saw his golden hair shining in the bright sunlight. Her eyes narrowed at the woman he held in his arms. Dear Lord, there had to be a mistake, that couldn't be Joanna James. She was dead! Claudia saw Taggart James ride up beside Harland and knew that Joanna and her brother had somehow survived the Indian raid.

Once more jealousy burned in Claudia's heart. The one female she despised most in the world had returned to stand between her and Harland.

Claudia ground her teeth together when she saw how carefully Harland lifted Joanna to the ground. It didn't help her temper when Lieutenant Bryant stared in open admiration at Joanna.

"Who is that angel?" he asked. "It's hard to tell from this distance, but I would venture to guess she is the most beautiful girl I have seen in a long time."

Claudia gave Lieutenant Bryant a malicious glare. "Do you think she is prettier than me?"

Lieutenant Bryant's face became flushed. "Present company notwithstanding," he said hurriedly, trying to make amends for his *faux pas*.

Joanna and Tag had each been given a small bedroom in Colonel Jackson's, the commanding officers' living quarters. His wife Katharine Jackson, was a kind, motherly woman. She felt pity for Joanna and Tag and had taken them to her heart.

Katharine entered her husband's office and set a tray containing his dinner down before him. "Why must you keep these late hours, Richard? It appears to me that you could use the daylight hours to do the paperwork. I don't know how many times I have had to bring your supper to you on a tray."

He smiled fondly at his wife of forty years. "Kate, you have been an army wife long enough to know that when you're in charge you don't go by the clock."

"I know, but you aren't as young as you once were, Richard. I worry about you overworking."

He caught her hand, "I may be getting older, but you are just getting prettier, Kate." Kate's hair was completely white and she wore it pulled away from her face in a bun. Her gray eyes held a twinkle as she jerked her hand away.

"That's not true and you know it. I look exactly like what I am, an old woman."

Richard laughed. "Not so, Kate, you are what keeps me young. How are our two young guests?" he asked, changing the subject.

"Oh, Richard, my heart just goes out to them. They have suffered so much, and I took a liking to them right away. Joanna seems such a lady with her soft-spoken ways, and she is so pretty. It's a crying shame that one so young has lost her sight."

"What about the boy?"

"You should see him, Richard. He's such a little gentleman, and to see the way he takes care of Joanna. I declare it just about melts my heart."

"Everything melts your heart, Kate."

"I don't have time to stand here talking to you. I need to get back to our guests. It is going to be such fun having young people around the place."

## Chapter Twenty-four

The atmosphere in Kate's kitchen was festive. Tag and Joanna sat at the table helping Kate make candy and sweetmeats.

Tag smeared butter over Joanna's palms and handed her some taffy which Kate had just poured from a pan.

"Have a care, Joanna. It's hot," Kate warned her.

Joanna nimbly shifted the candy from one hand to the other. "This is such fun, Kate. I was never allowed to help in the kitchen at home," Joanna said, smiling.

Kate dried her hands on her apron. "How can that be? Didn't your mother prepare you for one day looking after your own home?"

"No . . . I . . . she didn't."

Tag laughed aloud. "I think my sister is embarrassed, Kate. What she is hesitating to tell you is that we always had servants to look after the house and kitchen."

Kate clicked her tongue. "Nevertheless, you should at least have been allowed to cook."

"Kate, although I cannot see, I can imagine what your kitchen looks like," Joanna said, pulling at the taffy now that it had cooled.

Kate had been stirring the batter of a cake and she paused. "Tell me how you picture this room. I'd be interested to know."

"Well, I think that the floors are of polished wood, because they are slick after you have just mopped them."

"What color wood?" Tag asked.

"Dark. Let's see . . . Kate, you have a sunshiny personality so I would associate you with bright cheerful colors. The curtains at the window are yellow. The tablecloth is white trimmed in yellow. Am I right so far?"

"Not too bad," Kate said, pouring the cake batter into a pan and placing it into the oven. "The curtains are yellow and white checked; the floor is dark wood, but you were wrong about the tablecloth; it's yellow with white trim."

"Joanna, how did you figure all that out?" Tag asked in amazement.

"I don't know. It's like I once told you. Being blind has sharpened all my other senses."

By now the taffy had hardened and Tag cut it into small pieces and placed them in a jar which Kate handed him.

"Why are we making all these desserts, Kate?" Tag asked, popping a piece of taffy into his mouth.

"Didn't I tell you? The young officers and a few

young ladies are going on a sleigh ride. All the women are contributing to the food."

"That sounds like such fun," Joanna said wistfully.

"Of course it will be," Kate said, looking down at Joanna's bandaged eyes. "You can tell me if you had a good time after you return."

"What . . . I can't go. How could I?"

"I don't want to hear any excuses, Joanna. Harland came by late yesterday morning to ask if you would go with him, and I accepted for you."

"I had no idea. Why didn't you tell me?"

Kate winked at Tag. "Because, I didn't want to give you time to think about it, so you could come up with some excuse to say no."

Joanna stood up. "Should I not be getting dressed?"

Kate could hear the enthusiasm in Joanna's voice. She thought the sleigh ride would do her good, and Harland was such a nice young man.

"Come along, dear," Kate said, taking Joanna's arm. "I'll help you select what you should wear."


Joanna placed her hands into the warm fur muff Kate had loaned her. She could hear the tinkling of the bells as the sleigh glided over the snowpacked roads. Joanna, Captain Thatcher, and another couple were riding in the lead sleigh, while three other couples occupied a second one.

Harland stared at Joanna and felt a warmth spread throughout his body. He knew his feelings for her were becoming deeper. Since the first day he had seen her, he had been overwhelmed by her beauty. Now that he had come to know Joanna, he admired her courage.

She was so fragile and delicate looking and yet she had endured more hardships than any other girl he had ever known. He wished it were within his power to wipe out all the hurt she had been through.

He had been aware since the wagon train that Claudia didn't like Joanna. That was the reason he had excluded Claudia from today's activities. He wanted Joanna to be happy with nothing and no one to mar her joy.

Seeing a soft white snowflake float down to land on Joanna's lip, he reached over and touched it.

She smiled. "Has it started to snow again, Captain?"

"Yes, but not hard. Just a few scattered flakes here and there."

"Tell me what the countryside looks like."

He gazed across the flat desolate prairie which had no trees or foliage. "Well, picture if you will, a world of whiteness that stretches as far as the eye can see. Add to that a gray overcast day and you have summed it all up."

"You have no romance in your soul, Captain," Joanna said laughingly.

His eyes rested on her lips and when he realized Lieutenant Carson was watching him, he looked quickly away.

Lieutenant Carson laughed. "I don't think you would say that about our good Captain here, Miss James, if you could see the look on his face."

Becky Miller stifled a giggle as Captain Thatcher

gave her and Lieutenant Carson a scalding glance which quickly silenced them.

Joanna was totally unaware that the other three were watching her so closely. The group was silent until they turned off the road. They reached the designated place where they were to build a huge bonfire.

Harland carefully helped Joanna out of the sleigh and led her over to a fallen log. Dusting the powdery snow off, he placed a blanket over the rough bark and helped Joanna to sit down.

"You stay right here, Joanna, while I will help get the fire going. I will return shortly," he told her. "Will you be all right?"

"Of course," she replied.

Joanna could hear the others talking and laughing, and she began to withdraw into herself. Even when she was with a crowd, she felt lonely. She didn't really belong here. Would she ever get over this lost feeling? Where do I belong? she asked herself. You know where you belong,' the voice inside her head answered.

She wondered what Windhawk was doing now. Did he ever think of her? Had he forgotten her and taken one of the many maidens, who adored him, as his wife?

"What were you thinking just now, Miss James?" Captain Thatcher asked, sitting down beside her.

Joanna had been so deep in thought she had not heard him return. "I was just remembering someone in my past, Captain."

"Were you perchance thinking about some young man you once knew?"

"Yes . . . yes I was," she answered, not bothering to elaborate. "The fire feels nice," she said, changing the subject.

"They are now laying out the food. It looks like we are to have a feast," Harland said. "Are you hungry?"

"Yes, I'm starved. The one thing I missed when I was . . . in the Blackfoot village was a variety in my diet."

"Are you saying that their diet is very much the same each day?"

"Yes, but it's not as bad as it sounds. The women are very good cooks and make some very delicious meals."

"I haven't asked before, and you can tell me to mind my own business if you want to, but were you mistreated by the Indians?"

"No, quite the contrary. At first some of the women didn't accept me, but later on I became very close to them. I miss . . . some of them dreadfully."

"You never did say how you lost your vision."

"It was because of snow-blindness. You see, the Indians have dark eyes and are not as susceptible to the sun's rays as you and I would be; therefore, Windhawk didn't realize that I was being affected by the sun."

Harland could tell she didn't want to talk about her experience with the Indians. Even though he wanted to know more about Joanna's ordeal, and especially about the Blackfoot chief, Windhawk, he decided to change the subject.

"Simon tells me that he and his wife came to this country with your family from England. Had he been in your family's service very long?"

"Yes, he was with my mother and father long before I was born."

"He seems a good man. I have been talking to him about seeking out my family if he should need employment. He seems to think he needs to stay with you and your brother though."

"I wouldn't like him to feel bound to me and Tag. I will speak to him and see if he would like to return to Philadelphia."

"Farley is a real character, isn't he?" Harland asked. "It seems he has adopted you and your brother."

"I am very fond of him. I suppose he has become the grandfather Tag and I never had," Joanna said, laughing.

It was hard to think of the crusty old trapper being close to someone with Joanna's breeding, but she had a way of making everyone feel they were important to her. She seemed much older than her young years indicated. Harland could feel there was a sadness about her. He could attribute much of her unhappiness to the fact that she had lost both her mother and father in such a short space of time. He felt, however, it went much deeper than that.

Soon the food was served and all the young people gathered around in a circle. Joanna was enjoying the stories they told and the songs they sang. She joined in and soon began to feel happiness for the first time in many weeks. She raised her voice in song. Perhaps it wouldn't be such a difficult transition from Windhawk's world back to hers. With friends like Captain Thatcher and Kate, perhaps she could find her way back. For Tag's sake, she had to look to the future. For her own sake, she had to bury the past.

On the ride back to the fort, the happy group continued to raise their voices in song. The snow was now falling heavily and everyone was in a festive mood. Joanna was glad Kate had insisted on her going on the sleigh ride; she had enjoyed herself immensely.

When the sleigh pulled up in front of Colonel Jackson's house, Harland leaped down and swung Joanna to the ground.

"I had such a wonderful time, Captain Thatcher. Thank you for inviting me."

He was tempted to raise her hand to his lips, but he knew the others were watching. "It was my pleasure, Miss James. I hope you will allow me to call on you in the near future. There are many gaieties here at the fort and I would like to be the one to introduce them to you."

She smiled but said nothing. He helped her up the steps and opened the door for her. "Until next time, Miss James," he said.

Joanna smiled again and Harland watched her until she disappeared through the door. He had hope in his heart that one day soon, she would be willing to listen to the plans he had for their future together.

When he got back in the sleigh, Lieutenant Carson grinned at him. "Now there's a girl that I could learn to like in a hurry. I believe she is the prettiest girl I have seen in a long time. It's not hard to see that you are smitten with her, Harland."

Harland leaned back and studied his friend's face. "She is off-limits to you, soldier. That's the girl I'm going to marry!"

Joanna sat beside Kate on the sofa telling her all about the sleigh ride. Kate watched her as she talked, knowing she was not as happy as she pretended to be. When Joanna began to trust her more, Kate wanted to talk to her. She felt that Joanna was keeping something very disturbing to herself and Kate thought it might help if she could confide in someone. She feared Joanna had been badly mistreated by the Indians, and she wanted to convince her to put that part of her life behind her.

Kate had never been one to pry, and she very rarely interfered in other people's affairs. She was a rare person, who really cared about others and wanted to help them.

Kate was beginning to love Joanna and Tag and wanted to see them happy. She knew the time would come when they would have to leave her. When that time came, she wanted them to be armed with strength and self-confidence.

That night Joanna went to bed early. In her darkened world, there was neither peace nor serenity. Today, for a short space of time, she had allowed herself to forget about Windhawk. As each day passed, would she think about him less and less? she wondered.

There was a knock on the door and Tag entered her room. "Are you asleep, Joanna?" he asked.

She patted the bed beside her. "No, I'm not

sleepy. Sit with me for a while, Tag."

He plopped down on the bed beside her. "Kate said that you had fun today."

"Yes, it was nice."

"I'm glad," he said in a quiet voice. Joanna could tell that something was bothering him. She knew him too well not to recognize when he was troubled.

"Would you care to tell me what is on your mind, little brother?"

He stretched out on the foot of her bed and she could almost feel the frown on his face. "I was just wondering if you are fond of Captain Thatcher?"

Joanna smiled to herself. She knew exactly what was bothering him now. "I like him very much. He has been very kind to you and me, and we both need kindness in our lives at the moment."

"Kate and Colonel Jackson are kind," he reminded her.

"Yes, they are, Tag. I believe you and I have been very fortunate. It seems everywhere we go we find a friend."

"I overheard Captain Thatcher ask if he could call on you again."

"Yes, he did."

There was silence for a moment and Joanna waited for the question she knew would be forthcoming.

"Do you like Captain Thatcher better than Windhawk?"

She sat up and reached out her hand and he placed his hand in hers. "Tag, the way I feel about Captain Thatcher and the way I feel about Windhawk are entirely different."

"Windhawk is your husband," he reminded her. "A wife shouldn't forget about her husband."

"Yes, that's true. I love Windhawk and I like Captain Thatcher. Does that answer your question?"

"You wouldn't up and marry the Captain, would you?"

She laughed and pulled him to her. "No, silly, you don't marry a friend."

"Are you sure?"

She ruffled his hair. "What's the matter, don't you like Captain Thatcher?"

"I like him all right. He's nice. I think he makes a very good officer."

Joanna could hear the question in his voice. "But?" she asked.

"He isn't Windhawk. After you, I love Windhawk better than anyone in the world."

Joanna became serious for a moment. Tag had lost so many people he cared about in his short life. She didn't want him to think Windhawk didn't care for him.

"Tag, what occurred between Windhawk and me had nothing to do with you. I happen to know that Windhawk thought a great deal of you."

"Why did he send us away then, Joanna?"

She heard Tag's voice break and knew he had been affected more deeply than she thought by Windhawk's rejection of her.

"Tag, sometimes things happen that you have no control over. What happened between Windhawk and me was one of those times. I think you should remember only that he loved you and forget about the rest."

"He loved you too, Joanna . . . I know he did!"

"Taggart James," she said, trying to turn the conversation to a lighter note. "All the men love me, haven't you noticed, or are you as blind as I am?"

He grinned and kissed her on the cheek. "That's because they know you are the prettiest, and sweetest girl around."

Joanna grabbed him and pushed him down on the bed, ruffling his hair. "You old flatterer. No girl is going to be safe from your charms when you grow to manhood."

"I'm not going to have time for girls when I get grown. I gotta go back to Philadelphia."

Joanna leaned back against her pillow. "So you shall, Tag . . . so you shall."

Windhawk had not ridden back to his village after he had taken Joanna and Tag to the fort. He sent his warriors home, but he rode away to be by himself. he couldn't bear to return to his lodge which he knew would be cold and empty without Joanna.

Sun Woman had watched each day for the return of her son. She would walk to the river and gaze across, hoping for some sign of him. Every night she had trouble falling asleep, listening for the sound of his arrival. She knew what was going on in her son's mind; he was tortured with guilt, thinking he had caused Joanna's blindness. He loved the white girl who had touched all their hearts.

She remembered Windhawk once telling her that he would never love another woman, and she now feared that was the truth. Sun Woman knew when her son finally did return home, she would have to speak to him. He was the chief and there were many who needed his guidance. It was not like him to run away from his troubles, but that was what he was doing now. Her heart ached for what he was living through. There was nothing she could do to help ease his pain, but she could help him face some truths.

Everyone knew about Sun Woman's concern for her son, and each of them would also wait and watch for the return of their chief.

The light was waning and Sun Woman was sewing a new buckskin shirt for Windhawk. She had only the dim light from the cookfire to see by, and she squinted as she tried to take tiny neat stitches.

The flap of her tipi was thrown open and Gray Fox's wife, White Dove, stuck her head in. "He has returned, Sun Woman! The chief is here!"

Morning Song, who had been tending to the evening meal, ran to the opening. Her mother's words stopped her before she could leave.

"Do not go to your brother. I will see him alone."

Morning Song nodded and watched as her mother left the tipi.

Sun Woman entered her son's lodge, and found it to be cold and dark. When her eyes adjusted to the darkness, she saw Windhawk lying on his robe with his eyes closed. Dropping down on her knees beside him, she saw the fatigue in his face and wanted to reach out and comfort him.

Without opening his eyes, he took her hand. "I hope you have not been worried, my mother."

"Why should I be? Are you not now a man?"

He opened his eyes and she gasped at the pain in his dark eyes. "Yes, my mother, I am a man," he whispered.

Sun Woman knew she could not tell him that she was hurting for him. She must not show that weakness. "I kept your lodge clean and lit the fire each day thinking you would return. Today, I did not light the fire and you came home."

They were both quiet for a long time and finally Windhawk spoke. "I know that you have something to say to me, my mother. Why do you hesitate?"

"I do not know how to say what must be said."

He smiled slightly. "I have never known you to be at a loss for words."

"It is not a mother's place to give advice to her son."

"That has never stopped you before now," he said, squeezing her hand.

Sun Woman sat down and looked him straight in the face. "I think it is time you quit feeling pity for yourself."

"Is that what you think I have been doing?"

"Is it not?"

He sat up and removed his leather headband and tossed it aside. "You do not know what I have been feeling! No one does?"

"I know. I loved her, also."

His dark eyes narrowed. "I will not talk of this with you."

403

"Would you lie on your mat and lose yourself in pity, or would you act as the chief that you are?"

"What do you mean?" he questioned, knowing he had not tended to his responsibilities, but had run away.

"I have never known you to run from anything, my son. Why do you do so now?"

"What do you think I have run from?"

"One very small little girl who now needs you more than you need her."

"You think I should not have taken Joanna back to her people?" Windhawk asked in amazement.

"You abandoned your wife when she needed you most."

Windhawk felt his anger spark to life. "Would you defend her when she was the first to leave me?"

"Yes, I defend her because she acted with bravery. I think you thought to punish her for having the courage you first admired in her."

He was quiet for a long moment pondering his mother's words. "What would you have me do?" His words were more a plea than a question.

"I would have you go to Joanna and ask her if she loves you and wants to come home with you. Did you once ask her if she wanted to be sent away?"

Windhawk stood up abruptly. "Do you think me a fool? Did she not leave me? Was I not the cause of her blindness? Joanna will never forgive me for what I did to her."

Sun Woman stood. "If you were still the son that you once were, you would go to Joanna. I did not know that I had a coward for a son." Without a backward glance, she left the lodge.

Windhawk was silently staring into space. Could his mother be right? Had he acted the coward when he sent Joanna away? No, he had done what was best for her. It would have been easier to end his own life than give Joanna her freedom. He had loved her enough to let her go.

Sun Woman was blinded by tears. She had hurt Windhawk, but it had been necessary. "My son, my son," she cried, leaning her head against the outside of his lodge. "I feel your pain so deeply."

## Chapter Twenty-five

Tag and Joanna had been living with the Jacksons for three weeks. Kate was very protective of her young charges and would not allow any curious visitors to pester them. She had already turned away several curiosity seekers by telling them that Joanna and Tag had only recently learned of their father's death.

Joanna felt as if the walls were closing in on her. What she needed was a breath of fresh air, she thought.

She was alone since Tag had gone riding with Farley, and the Jacksons were attending one of the many functions in which they were expected to participate.

Joanna felt around until she found her fur-lined cape which was draped across a chair at the foot of her bed. Placing it about her shoulders, she made her way into the sitting room. Holding her hands out in front of her Joanna felt along the wall until she came to the door.

She stepped out into the cold night air and shivered, pulling her cape tightly about her. The wind was biting and stung her cheeks.

How she hated the world of darkness she was forced to live in! She resented the fact that she had to be dependent on others for help. Turning her face upward, she allowed the snowflakes to fall onto her face. How sweet it would be to watch a snowflake drift softly earthward, she thought.


Windhawk clung to the darkened shadows. It had been too easy to enter the fort under the guise of darkness. The gate had been left partially open and he had merely slipped through while the sentry was looking the other way. Gaining access to the fort had been easy; finding Joanna would be more difficult. He knew if he was discovered the long knives would not deal kindly with him.

Windhawk had gone to the fort where he had left Joanna and Tag, only to find out from an old trapper that they had been moved to another location. It hadn't taken him long to discover they had been transferred to the fort which was to have been their destination before the wagon train had been attacked.

Captain Thatcher was crossing the compound on the way to his quarters when he saw Joanna standing on Colonel Jackson's front porch. He had wanted to see her for days but had been out on patrol and hadn't gotten back until late last night. Now was his opportunity to see her alone, he thought, as he walked toward her.

"Good evening, Miss James. It's rotten weather to be out in, is it not? Aren't you afraid you will catch your death?"

Joanna smiled when she recognized Captain Thatcher's voice. "I have never had any objections to cold weather, Captain."

He walked up the steps and rested his hand on the porch railing, while gazing down into her lovely face.

"Have the Jacksons made you feel welcome in their home, Miss James?"

"Indeed, they have. No one could be kinder than Kate and the colonel has been most solicitous."

Joanna suddenly had the strangest sensation that someone was watching her, and the feeling had nothing to do with Captain Thatcher. The feeling was so strong that she turned her head in the direction from which the feeling came. Someone was definitely staring at her!

"Are we alone, Captain?" she questioned.

"Not entirely. There are two sentries pacing the stockade ramp. Other than that we are quite alone. Why do you ask, Miss James?"

Joanna pushed the hood of her cape back and shook her head. "No reason, it was just a feeling I had. It has passed now."

"Would you like to go for a stroll? I can guarantee you a firsthand guided tour, and this time you won't be able to accuse me of having no romance in my soul."

Joanna's laughter bubbled out. She stretched out her hand and Captain Thatcher took it. "I can think of nothing I would like better. I will expect you to describe everything you see in great detail. Are you game?"

Harland placed her hand on his arm. "I will start with you. Has anyone ever told you that your hair is of a color unmatched by any other?" he asked lightly.

"Not so, Captain. I am told that my brother's hair is the same as mine."

"Yes, that may be true, but I believe you will forgive me if I think he is nowhere as pretty as you."

Joanna smiled delightedly. "Would you turn the head of this poor blind girl, Captain?"

Windhawk could see Joanna and the long knife clearly from the light that came through the window. He wanted to tear her away from the white man. His anger caused him to act rashly and he stepped from the shadows just as an armed patrol entered the post. He leaped back into the shadows until they passed. Their appearance had given him time to control his rage.

Windhawk watched as Joanna and the long knife walked away talking quietly. He had discovered what he had come to find out. Joanna was not grieving for him as his mother had thought. She seemed to be happy with the long knife. He wanted to leave, but he couldn't. Unmindful of the danger he was facing, Windhawk waited for a chance to find Joanna alone.

Harland felt Joanna's hand and found it to be cold. "I think it would be wise if I took you back now, Miss James. It is much too cold for a young lady to be out this time of night."

Joanna nodded in agreement. "It is rather cold, but I have always found the cold invigorating, haven't you?"

"No, as a matter of fact, it can be quite a nuisance when one is out on patrol."

"Were you in Philadelphia last December, Captain?"

"As a matter of fact, I was."

"Do you remember the ice storm we had Christmas Eve?"

"Yes, but I can't say I enjoyed it, did you?"

She laughed. "As a matter of fact, I did. I remember Tag and me riding through the grounds and there were icicles hanging from the trees. It was like a winter wonderland. Later, my family gathered about the fire and we burned the yule log and sang Christmas songs . . ." her voice trailed off. "So much has happened since then," she said wistfully.

They had reached the front porch of the Jacksons' home and Harland helped Joanna up the steps. "I have found if one replaces old memories with new experiences, they will soon heal the old wounds," Harland said. He stared down into her face wondering how many wounds she had that needed healing.

"I suppose so. I will say good-night to you now, Captain. Thank you for the walk."

"It was my pleasure, I can assure you. Would you like me to see you inside?" he asked hopefully.

"No, I can manage alone."

Harland watched Joanna disappear inside. He then walked away, glad he had had the chance to spend some time alone with her.

Joanna made her way cautiously across the room, feeling fortunate that she had no misfortune other than bumping into a chair. She thought how pleasant Captain Thatcher had been to talk to. She liked him a great deal.

Fumbling with the door knob, she finally reached her bedroom where she sat down on the bed.

Windhawk stood in the darkened corner of the room watching Joanna. There was very little light in the room since the only source of light came from the open door leading from the sitting room. He heard her sigh and watched as she lay back and placed her hands over the bandages which covered her eyes.

Suddenly, she sat up listening. She felt a presence in the room. "Tag, is that you?" She waited, but there was no answer.

"I must be seeing things," she said aloud. "I mean, I must be hearing things," she corrected.

Joanna began to hear the silence which was almost deafening. She felt a prickle of uneasiness because she was alone and it was so quiet. She wished Tag would come home. Surely he and Farley wouldn't be gone much longer, since it was past the dinner hour. Lying back on the bed, she sighed. It was as if she could feel . . . Windhawk's presence. She chided herself for her overactive imagination. Windhawk wouldn't come to her. He no longer loved her, if indeed, he ever had.

Windhawk stood silently as his hungry eyes moved over Joanna. It had been a mistake to come here. Would it not have been better if he had never seen Joanna with the long knife? He watched as she relaxed and her hand fell off the side of the bed. He knew she had fallen asleep, but still he waited until he was sure she was in a deep sleep. He crossed the room and lifted the lid to her trunk. Removing the bear-claw necklace from around his neck, he placed it in a small wooden chest and then carefully closed the lid on the trunk so it wouldn't awaken Joanna.

Moving to the bed, he stood over her for a moment. He couldn't resist the impulse to touch a flaming curl that was nestled against her cheek. His heart filled with love as he gazed one last time upon the face he knew would haunt him until his death. She had been his wife for such a short period of time. Her laughter had filled his days, and her goodness had touched his heart. He moved to the window and opened it, slipping silently outside. He made no noise when he closed the window and slipped away from the fort undetected.

Joanna was dreaming. She tossed and turned restlessly on her bed. Her dream was so vivid that she could the crisp autumn wind blowing against her face. She was reliving a time when she and Windhawk had been so blissfully happy. The brilliant colored red and golden leaves were drifting down all about her and she turned her head when Windhawk called out to her. Her heart was racing wildly when he took her hand and pulled her down beside him on a bed of soft leaves. She could feel his hand brush against her cheek, and then he traced the outline of her lips with his finger. She closed her eyes as his hand then moved down her slender neck to brush across her breasts.

The dream was so real now, Joanna could feel

Windhawk's dark gaze, and see the special smile that he had reserved for her alone. She smiled back at him when he lifted her gown over her head and tossed it aside.

"Surely not here," she protested. "Someone will see us."

His only answer was the shake of his head. Her body trembled when his dark eyes moved over her naked body with approval. Joanna rolled away from him and tried to reach her discarded gown, but he merely laughed and pulled her into his arms. For a moment she lay tensely, until his magnificent hands began to move in a circle across her smooth stomach. She closed her eyes allowing the sensual feelings to take over her being.

"Look at me, Jo-anna," Windhawk said in a deep voice.

Opening her eyes she stared into dark eyes that were such a deep brown that it was almost impossible to see the pupil. The passion and fire she saw there made her draw in her breath.

Oh, yes, she remembered that day so well. He had gathered up several bright red leaves and had placed them across her breasts and along her thighs, while remarking in a teasing voice, that she would look beautiful dressed in a gown made of autumn leaves.

Looking above her, Joanna had watched the brightly-colored leaves drift softly to the ground.

Windhawk raised up and smiled at her. "Perhaps in the beginning of time, you and I loved each other in a place very much like this. It is possible that on a day much like today you gave yourself to me."

Joanna could feel tears on her face. She was aware that it was only a dream of remembrance, and that was all she would ever have of Windhawk now. She could feel herself waking up and tried to hold on to the dream.

"No, no," she moaned. "I want to stay with you, Windhawk."

"Say that you will always love me, Joanna," Windhawk said, touching his lips to hers.

"I will always love you," she cried feeling his hands becoming more intimate. Each time he would remove one of the red leaves from her body, he would kiss the place where it had been.

When he lay his face against her stomach, Joanna laced her hands through his ebony hair. The dream was so life-like she could feel his lips brush her stomach and move higher to nibble at her breasts, first one and then the other.

She felt her heart skip a beat when he slid his body against hers. With gentle pressure he drew her beneath him and her legs opened to invite his touch. Joanna couldn't stand the torture any longer. She felt him move away from her and felt momentary confusion. That wasn't the way it happened that day. He had made love to her lingeringly on that beautiful autumn day.

Looking into his face, she saw him scowl.

"Windhawk, please," she pleaded holding her arms out to him.

"What do you want of me, Joanna?" His eyes were cold and unloving.

"Love me, Windhawk. Don't ever stop loving me," she whispered.

He frowned down at her. "Was it not you who stopped loving me, Joanna? Did you not give me back the necklace that symbolized our love?" His voice was deep and accusing.

"I wanted to be with you, Windhawk, but you sent me away."

He stood up and looked at her with bored indifference on his handsome face. "It does not matter, Joanna. What would I want with a woman who cannot see. You are no longer Windhawk's woman."

Joanna held her hand out to him. "I will always be your woman. I am your wife."

She could feel her heart break when he turned and walked away from her. Burying her face in her hands, she cried out her misery. The dream wasn't supposed to end like this. That day in the woods he had held her and spoken words of eternal love.

"Windhawk, Windhawk," she cried, knowing she could no longer hold onto the dream. She awoke and sat up in bed, feeling her tear-wet face. It wasn't the autumn when she and Windhawk had been so happy together, but the middle of winter and she was alone many miles from the Blackfoot village, and the man she loved.

Joanna stumbled out of bed and moved to the window. Laying her head against the window pane, she shivered. It seemed that she could still feel Windhawk's presence so clearly. Dear Lord in heaven, she thought, was she going to feel tortured for the rest of her life? Would the memory of Windhawk be the only thing she had to keep her company in her darkened world?

Kate was glad she had convinced Joanna to go to the officers' dance. Doctor Morehead had come by that morning and examined Joanna's eyes, and she had been downcast ever since. Being with young people would cheer her up, Kate thought.

Kate buttoned the back of Joanna's soft blue wool gown. "Joanna, you musn't be upset because Doctor Morehead couldn't tell you if you will ever be able to see. Just remember he said that it *could* happen."

"I suppose I had hoped he would work a miracle, Kate."

"You must do exactly as he told you and keep the bandages in place for a while longer."

"Yes, I will, although I am very tired of wearing them."

"I know, dear, just be patient a little longer."

Kate picked up a brush with an ivory handle and began brushing Joanna's lovely hair.

"I had all your things laundered this morning, Joanna. You have some very lovely gowns."

"I forgot, what color did you say I was wearing tonight, Kate?"

"It's blue, dear."

"Oh, yes, I remember the gown. It has dark blue piping around the sleeve and the hem of the skirt."

"That's right—you look lovely."

"Kate, I can't thank you and Colonel Jackson enough for taking Tag and me into your home. I don't know what we would have done without you."

"Hush, you know I love having you here. Now,

turn around and let me look at you."

Joanna smiled as she turned around in a wide circle, causing the full skirt of her gown to billow out. Kate watched as the smile left Joanna's face.

"I'm nervous, Kate. I have never been to a formal dance."

"Nonsense! You will be the prettiest girl there tonight. I can't tell you how many young officers have inquired about you. They are all anxious to get to know you better."

"Oh," was all Joanna could manage to say. She had been at the army post for over a month, and in that time Kate had guarded her privacy, turning away many visitors.

"Are you ready to go, Joanna?" Tag asked, sticking his head around the door.

"I suppose so," she replied apprehensively.

"Kate, what has everyone been told about me?"

"As far as I know, very little. They know, of course, that you were a captive of the Indians."

Tag took Joanna's hand and the three of them went into the sitting room. Colonel Jackson was waiting to escort them to the entertainment hall where the officers' dance was being held.

The dance was already in progress when they arrived. Joanna held tightly to Tag's hand, hearing the sound of laughter and music. Now that she was here, she wished she had never consented to attend the dance.

Harland had been waiting by the door, and when he saw Joanna, he rushed toward her.

"Miss James, how lovely you look. Would you do me the honor of allowing me to lead you in a quadrille?"

"I don't know, Captain. Perhaps with my sight problem, it would be best if I were to sit out the dances."

"Nonsense! You and I have danced together before, have you forgotten?"

Joanna smiled. "No, I remember quite well, but that was when I could see what I was doing."

"I will be your eyes this evening," he said, taking her hand persuasively.

Joanna had very little choice but to allow him to lead her away from Tag.

"There are three steps leading down to the dance floor, Miss James," Harland coached her.

When they reached the dance floor, the music began and soon Joanna was dancing, changing partners, and weaving in and out with very little trouble. Once when she stumbled, Harland caught her and she laughed up at him. For the moment Joanna forgot her miseries and had put her troubles aside. She was young, and she was dancing on the arm of a handsome officer.

Claudia stared daggers at Joanna. She could see how all the men were watching her with admiration written on their faces. Was her life always going to be overshadowed by Joanna James? she wondered. What was it about Joanna that drew the men to her like bees to the honeypot?

Her eyes wandered jealously over Joanna's lovely blue ball gown. Claudia had been forced to wear cast-offs of the women at the army post. She gritted her teeth when Lieutenant Simms, whom she had been dancing with, asked to be introduced to Miss James.

By the time Claudia reached her, Joanna was surrounded by several young officers and Claudia had to move them aside to get to her.

"Well, Joanna, it seems once again you are the center attraction. I heard that you have lost your sight or is it another ploy of yours to gain sympathy?"

Joanna gasped at Claudia's hateful words, too stunned to even reply.

Harland's temper flared as he stepped between the two girls. "I am appalled at your insensitivity, Miss Maxwell! Miss James has been through a harrowing experience and you are being unduly harsh."

Claudia tossed her honey-colored hair and her hazel eyes flamed. "Poor Joanna! We musn't upset Joanna! Joanna this! Joanna that! I am sick to death of hearing about her!" Claudia said, turning on her heels and walking away.

"That is the most unpleasant girl I have ever encountered," someone remarked.

Joanna was still feeling the sting of Claudia's words. The fun had gone out of the evening for her. Moving forward, Joanna stumbled and several of the officers reached out to steady her.

"I think . . . I am tired. If you gentlemen will excuse me, I wish to retire."

Harland took her arm. "Miss James, I wish you wouldn't let what Miss Maxwell said upset you. No one pays the slightest attention to her spitefulness."

"It isn't Claudia, Captain. I just want to leave now," Joanna said.

"I wish you would reconsider—the evening is young yet. I would like to have at least one more dance with you."

Joanna had just been hit full-force with the feeling that she was out of place among people who live their day-to-day lives in a tight little world. She no longer felt right in her fashionable gowns, and she didn't know how to deal with unwarranted pettiness such as Claudia had demonstrated tonight.

"No, I want to leave now, but I don't want to disturb Colonel and Mrs. Jackson, Captain. Would you mind walking me to their quarters?"

Harland tucked Joanna's hand about his arm. "It would be my pleasure, Miss James."

As they walked into the night air, Joanna felt cold and pulled her fur-lined cape tightly about her. "Has it stopped snowing, Captain?"

"Yes. There are no clouds in the sky and a bright moon is lighting up the countryside."

She smiled, "You are becoming more descriptive. Tell me, is this a large fort?"

"Yes, considering that it's in the middle of nowhere. There are about one hundred and seventy-five men stationed here, not to mention a good number of women and children." He looked down at her delicate features and felt his heart swell with love. Tonight, he knew Claudia had hurt her deeply and he had been hurt for her. He had the strongest impulse to take her in his arms and hold her close to him.

"Miss James, do you remember I once asked you if I could call you by your first name?"

She smiled. "I remember."

"You never did give me permission, so I will dare to ask you again."

Again she smiled. "If my memory serves me correctly, Claudia also interrupted us that night."

"Indeed, she did, but you still have not answered my question Miss James."

"I feel you are a good friend, Captain. I would like for you to call me Joanna."

Harland drew in his breath. "My given name is Harland. I would deem it an honor if you would consider calling me that, Joanna."

By now, they had reached the Jacksons' residence and Harland helped her up the porch steps.

"All right, Harland. Friends should call each other by their first names."

"Would you like me to see you safely inside, Joanna?"

She shook her head. "I'm afraid there has already been too much gossip about me. I think if I invited you in, it would be most unconventional."

He squeezed her hand, wishing he dared bring it up to his lips. "In a day or so when you are feeling rested, perhaps you would like to go for a ride with me?"

"I would like that very much." Joanna felt for the doorknob and opened the door. "Good night, Harland."

He watched her until she was inside, then he turned and walked toward his quarters. He had no desire to return to the dance. Tonight he hoped he had taken the first step in winning Joanna's affection. His mind was on her flaming hair and velvety soft skin when he entered his room.

Lying down on his cot fully clothed, he wondered what it would feel like to kiss Joanna's soft lips.

# Chapter Twenty-six

Joanna felt her way around in the darkness, fearing she would bump into one of the low tables where Kate's what-nots were displayed.

When she reached what she knew to be her bedroom, she heard a loud rapping on the front door. She dared not try to make her was back across the room, fearing she would break something.

"Please come in," she called out.

The door opened and a cold blast of air hit her in the face. "Who's there?" she asked.

"You know very well who it is, Joanna," Claudia's voice spoke up.

"I have nothing to say to you, Claudia. Let us just say you drew blood tonight and let it go at that."

"Oh, no, Joanna! I haven't even begun to draw blood yet. I want to know what makes you think you can come here and bat your eyelashes and every eligible man on the post will fall at your feet?"

"In case you haven't noticed, Claudia, my eyelashes are covered. I believe I once told you I leave the batting of eyelashes to you."

"You think Captain Thatcher likes you, but he is going to marry me. I'll never stand idly by while you take him away from me."

Joanna could tell that Claudia was standing right beside her. "Claudia, I have no wish to take Harland or anyone else from you. All I want is to be left alone."

Joanna could not see the glazed look in Claudia's eyes. "You dare to call him Harland! Just what went on between the two of you on your way to the fort! Did you perhaps dally in the bushes?"

Joanna had remained calm up until now, but Claudia had just overstepped her bounds. Joanna's head jerked up and her cheeks flamed. "You dare to say this to me! I can assure you that Harland is too much of gentleman to act as you suggest, Claudia."

"I'm not suggesting that Captain Thatcher is not a gentleman. I was going more on the assumption that you are no lady," Claudia said sarcastically. "I have heard it said that you were living freely with an Indian savage. Do you deny that?"

"The only savages I know are white, Claudia. You come closer to being a savage than any Indian I know."

Claudia's hand shot out and she struck Joanna hard across the face. The blow was so hard it caused Joanna to slam into the wall with such force that it knocked her to the floor. Her head struck against a wooden table and she cried out in pain. She was too dazed to hear Claudia cry out in surprise.

423

Claudia was not aware that Tag had entered the room until he grabbed her by the arm and jerked her forward with a strength that startled her.

"I wish you were a man, Claudia! I would give you the licking you deserve," he said, through clenched teeth. Never had he wanted to strike a woman so badly. "If you ever touch my sister again, I will not stop just because you are a girl."

Claudia backed away at the anger she saw in Tag's eyes.

Kate bent down and helped Joanna to her feet. She and Tag had witnessed most of the scene between Joanna and Claudia, and Kate was fighting mad.

"Taggart, you take your sister to the bedroom. Since I am a woman, I believe that gives me the right to deal with Claudia."

Kate was a gentle woman who never raised her voice. She grabbed Claudia's arm and pushed her across the room. "I will just show you the door and invite you to never darken my doorstep again."

"Joanna called me a savage," Claudia cried out in her own defense.

"And so you are! It's too bad it's winter or I would have my husband show you the gate."

Claudia braced herself against the doorframe when Kate tried to push her through. "I don't see how you can have a harlot staying under your roof. Especially an Indian's harlot!"

Kate's eyes sparkled with anger. "Leave my house at once!" she demanded, too angry to say anything more.

"What's going on here?" Colonel Jackson demanded to know as he entered the room.

Claudia cringed when she saw the commander of the fort. Gathering up her gown, she dashed past him and darted down the steps. Joanna had won again, she thought bitterly. One day she would have the last say, Claudia promised herself.

Kate looked at her husband. "Richard, you must go for the doctor. Joanna may have been injured."

"I don't understand anything that was going on when I came up. Why were you ordering Miss Maxwell out of our house?"

"I don't have time to talk to you now, Richard — I have to see about Joanna. Just get the doctor!" Kate said, rushing into Joanna's bedroom.

When Kate entered the room, Joanna was lying on the bed and Tag was washing her face with a cloth. "My dear, are you hurt?" she asked, moving Tag aside and gathering Joanna into her arms.

"I am not really hurt, Kate," Joanna said. "It's strange, but I just feel a little dizzy. You wouldn't think that someone blind could feel dizzy, would you?"

"Just lie back and rest. Richard has gone for the doctor."

"I don't think there was any need . . ."

"Nevertheless, the doctor will examine you," Kate interrupted. "I will feel better when he tells me you have not been injured."

Kate turned to Tag. "You run on out and wait for Richard and the doctor. I'm going to help Joanna get into her nightgown."

Joanna stood up slowly, and Kate helped her remove her gown.

"I never did like Claudia, and I like her even less now. Whatever set off the argument between the two of you?"

"I'm not quite sure. I think she fears I am trying to take Captain Thatcher away from her."

"That's not likely. Harland never gave her the time of day. He has never been interested in her." Kate pulled the white nightgown over Joanna's head and helped her into bed.

"I believe Harland cares for you, Joanna. You should have seen him when Farley told him you were still alive. He lost little time riding out to rescue you."

"I like Harland a great deal, Kate, but I assure you, there is nothing but friendship between us."

Kate would have debated the point, but she saw no reason to continue. If Harland liked Joanna, he should be the one to tell her so. Kate fluffed up Joanna's pillow and noticed that her face seemed overly pale. Touching Joanna's forehead, Kate found it to be cool and was glad she had no fever. She was grateful when she heard the doctor's voice in the other room.

Doctor Morehead removed the bandages from Joanna's eyes, cautioning her to keep her eyes closed. Kate stood at the foot of the bed with a worried frown on her face. Joanna still appeared pale and shaken.

"I can't see anything other than a knot on the side of your forehead, Miss James," the doctor said. "How did you say you received your injury?"

"I didn't say," Joanna answered, not wanting the doctor to know about the argument between her and Claudia.

"I want to caution you against being left alone until you learn your way around," he said, going on the assumption that Joanna had fallen on her own. "I'm going to examine your eyes now, Miss James. You can open your eyes slowly. Kate, bring that lamp closer, will you?"

Joanna held her breath as she saw a flicker of light. It wasn't bright and she seemed to be viewing it through a dense fog.

"Doctor! Kate! I can see a light!" Joanna cried.

Doctor Morehead motioned for Kate to hand him the lamp, and he waved it in front of Joanna's face. "Can you see it now?" he asked.

"Yes, it seems a little brighter!" Joanna said excitedly.

Doctor Morehead moved the lamp slowly and he watched as Joanna turned her head to follow its brightness.

"Saints be praised!" Kate cried, "It's a miracle!"

"Don't celebrate too early, Kate," the doctor cautioned her. "Tell me, Miss James, can you see anything other than the light?"

"No, nothing but the light."

"I'm not sure what this means, Miss James, but I'm going to rebandage your eyes, and I want you to rest in bed tomorrow. I'll be by to check on you in the morning and then tomorrow night we will remove the bandages and see what's happened. It could be that the blow to your head in some way returned some of your vision. I just don't know."

"Do you think she will regain all her sight?" Kate asked.

"It's too soon to tell. Let's just take this one day at a time," the doctor cautioned.

"Doctor, don't tell anyone about this. I wouldn't want it to get back to my brother, Tag, until we are sure one way or another. I wouldn't want him to get his hopes up, only to have them dashed."

"I think it would be a good idea to keep it between ourselves," the doctor agreed. He patted Joanna's hand. "Don't you get your hopes up either. Just rest and we will see what develops in the next few days."

In spite of the doctor's warning, Joanna did allow her hopes to rise. She had definitely seen light where before there had only been darkness. She pushed all the ugliness that had occurred between her and Claudia out of her mind.

Without her wanting it to, her mind drifted back to Windhawk. If she got her sight back, would she dare try to find him? No, he had made it very plain that he didn't want her anymore.

"Joanna, are you asleep?" Tag asked, cautiously opening the bedroom door.

"No, I'm not asleep."

"I'm real mad at Claudia, Joanna. I may yet punch her!"

"Don't let her worry you, Tag, although I confess she got to me tonight."

"I know. I heard what she said about you. Why didn't you tell her you were Windhawk's wife?"

"Because she wouldn't understand, Tag."

"I miss Windhawk, don't you?"

428

"Yes."

"I promised him I would someday go back to see him, Joanna. That's one promise I intend to keep."

"Perhaps one day you will, Tag."

"Since Papa is . . . dead, and we can't go back to Philadelphia, couldn't we go back to Windhawk's village?"

"That's not possible, Tag. You really admired Windhawk, didn't you?"

"He's the best, Joanna. I want to grow up and be just like him."

"You could do worse."

"Are you sleepy, Joanna?"

"Uh huh."

They were both silent for a long time, until at last Joanna spoke. "Tag, thank you for caring about me. I don't know what I would do without you."

"I love you, Joanna."

"I love you, too, Tag."

Tag kissed her on the cheek and left quietly.

Soon Joanna fell asleep and the bright moonlight shone its light into the bedroom, kissing the darkness where Joanna dwelled. She sighed in her sleep, dreaming of the happy times she had spent as Windhawk's woman.

## Chapter Twenty-seven

The next morning a light snow began to fall. Tag was excited when he was invited to go sledding with several young boys from the fort.

Kate came bustling into Joanna's bedroom carrying a tray. She placed it across Joanna's lap and then fluffed up her pillows.

"Kate, I feel so bad because you have to wait on me. I am not the ideal guest, am I?"

Kate brushed a long lock of Joanna's hair from her face, and then handed her a fork. "Nonsense. I love having you and Tag here. An army post can become a lonely place when you don't have any family. You and Tag have become our family."

"You said that you had a daughter. Do you not get to see her often?" Joanna asked.

"No, Mary lives in Virginia, and I haven't been to see her in three years. I just don't like to leave Richard alone."

Joanna took a bite of ham, which was seasoned with raisin sauce, and declared how delicious it was. "You are going to spoil me, Kate. I wish you would allow me to get up so I can help you with the housework."

"When the doctor says you can get up then you can help me if you like, but until then, you will just have to be content with me waiting on you." Kate smiled at Joanna, whom she had come to love dearly in such a short time.

Joanna sighed, knowing Kate wouldn't give in. She intended to get up the next day with or without the doctor's permission. She felt wonderful and didn't want to stay in bed, forcing Kate to wait on her.

Kate drew a chair alongside Joanna's bed. She had known that Joanna was troubled about more than her sight. She thought perhaps the young girl was dwelling on something that had happened to her while she had been with the Indians. Kate was so kind-hearted she wanted to help, but it was not in her nature to meddle. This time, however, she thought if Joanna talked about what was bothering her it would help.

"Joanna, I'm not one to interfere, but would you like to talk to me about anything? I am a good listener and never repeat what is told to me in confidence."

Kate had a way of drawing people out, and Joanna thought it would be good to have a woman to talk to. "You may be shocked by some of the things I will tell you, Kate."

"No, Joanna. I already suspect that you were

badly treated by the Indians. But don't tell me anything you don't wish to."

"I wasn't badly treated. I know everyone believes that I was attacked, but it just isn't so."

"The Indians left you untouched?" Kate asked in surprise.

"Perhaps I should start from the beginning so you will understand, Kate. Have you ever heard about a Blackfoot chief called Windhawk?"

Kate was thoughtful for a moment. "Yes, they say he doesn't really exist but is some kind of Indian legend."

"He is not a legend, Kate. I can assure you he is a real person."

Joanna began telling Kate about her and Windhawk. She started with when they first met, and ended with when he left her at Fort Union.

Joanna was not aware that Kate was crying as she listened to her speak of her love for the chief of the Bloods.

"You and many others will not understand my feelings for Windhawk, Kate. But I love him and I always will."

"Joanna, I can see that you do, but perhaps things ended for the best. Do you think a young lady with your upbringing would have been happy living in some Indian village for the rest of her life?"

"Yes. I was extremely happy with Windhawk. He was kind and gentle, and possibly the most intelligent man I have ever known. He is nothing like the stories you hear about Indians. I grew to love the people of the Blackfoot tribe. They are warm and loving, and live by a code of honor that we could all

432

benefit from. If Windhawk would come for me right now, I would go with him without hesitation."

Joanna felt Kate's hand on hers and she squeezed it tightly.

"I feel like I am lost and adrift, Kate. I will never forget Windhawk, and no one can make me feel ashamed of loving him. I will always feel that I am his wife, even if he no longer wishes it so."

Kate could feel the pain in Joanna's voice. The love she had described between her and Windhawk was beautiful, but she was glad for Joanna's sake that he had brought her back. Perhaps he was intelligent enough to know Joanna needed to be with her own people.

"It will take time, Joanna, but someday you will realize it was for the best."

"No, you don't understand, Kate. He brought me back because he no longer cared for me. I would have been happy to remain with him for the rest of my life."

Kate doubted that was the case. She had never heard of an Indian returning his captives. "Perhaps there will always be a part of your heart that will belong to Windhawk, Joanna. That doesn't mean that you won't find love again."

"I don't want to love anyone else."

"Then you won't until you let Windhawk go in your mind. You are a lovely young girl; it would be a waste if you didn't allow yourself to feel love for a man again. I would hate to see you live such a lonely life."

"I doubt that anyone would want a woman who was blind. Windhawk didn't."

"You are wrong, Joanna. I can already tell that Harland likes you a great deal. If you were to give him the least bit of encouragement, you would know that for yourself."

"I don't want Harland to be interested in me other than as a friend." Joanna put her hand to her mouth. "Oh, no, I forgot! Harland and I were planning to go riding today."

Kate stood up and took the tray. "He came by this morning and I told him that the doctor ordered you to stay in bed. He seemed very concerned and asked me to tell you he hoped you were up and about very soon."

Harland entered his quarters and removed his greatcoat, then hung it over a chair. Someone moved out of the shadows, and he recognized Claudia.

"What are you doing here, Miss Maxwell?" he asked, removing his gloves and tucking them into his belt.

"I had to see you, Captain. I know it is not considered lady-like to come to a gentleman's quarters, but I must talk to you."

Harland's eyes narrowed. "You could have left word and I would have gotten in touch with you."

"I did that, but you ignored my request," she said with a pout on her mouth.

"All right, since you are here, I suppose the harm has been done. What can I do for you?"

"It's just that I care for you so much and you

always seem to ignore me," she said, moving closer to him.

"I am very busy, Miss Maxwell. As you know, I have very little time for socializing."

Claudia frowned. "You had time to be with Joanna last night at the dance, but you didn't pay the slightest attention to me."

Harland looked at Claudia's face which was pretty enough. She was petite and had a nice form, but there was something about her that had repelled him right from the start. She somehow reminded him of a leech who would grab onto a man and never let him go. She was jealous and petty, and he found it was distasteful to him when she touched him.

"Miss Maxwell, I am surprised that you would even seek me out after the cruel way you behaved toward Joanna last night."

Claudia's face became distorted and there was nothing pretty about her bulging eyes nor her lips that curled into a snarl. "It's always Joanna! Since the first day you saw her, you have been lusting after her. Well, I'll tell you something about her that you may not know."

"I will not stand here while you malign Joanna's character!" Harland said, becoming angry.

"Oh, I think you will want to hear what I have to say. I overheard Farley and Tag talking about Joanna and some Indian. Do you know what they said?"

Harland was of half a mind to shove Claudia out the door, but he paused, undecided. He had been wondering what had happened to Joanna while she was a captive. The night at Fort Union when he had questioned Joanna and Tag, they had only answered his direct questions. Of course, he hadn't inquired into anything of a personal nature.

Claudia's eyes gleamed, seeing that she had caught Harland's interest. "Farley and Tag didn't know I was listening, and let me tell you, you won't think dear little Joanna is so pure anymore."

"What are you implying?" Harland asked, hating the fact that he was listening to malicious gossip.

"I overheard them saying that one of the Indians had taken Joanna as his wife. She allowed a savage to take what she probably denied you."

Harland's hands tightened into a fist. "If what you say is true, I doubt that Joanna gave her consent."

"That's where you're wrong. I heard Tag saying that she loved this Indian . . . Windhawk is what he called him," Claudia said with a satisfied smile on her lips. "You remember him, he's the one who rescued Tag from the river."

Harland raised his eyebrow. "I don't believe you, Miss Maxwell. If you came here to smear Joanna's name, you have failed."

Claudia pulled her shawl about her shoulders. "Oh, don't take my word for it. Ask her brother or the old man. Ask Joanna herself."

"Get out of here, Miss Maxwell," Harland said in a quiet voice.

Again she smiled and walked leisurely across the room. When she reached the door she paused and turned back. "Good day, Captain."

Harland nodded without looking at her. He had

been sure that Joanna had been attacked by the Indians, but she couldn't love one of them: She was white! He knew Claudia for the trouble-maker she was. But suppose there was some truth to her accusations?

Claudia pulled her shawl over her head, feeling that, at last she had struck Joanna a blow that she would never recover from. She had no doubt that Harland would find out she was speaking the truth. Joanna would be shunned by everyone.

Claudia now knew that she would never have Captain Thatcher, but neither would Joanna. Harland was from a very prominent family. They would never accept a woman into their family who had been an Indian squaw! Her eyes gleamed with delight. At last her need for revenge had been satisfied. Before she was through, no one would even speak to Joanna.


Joanna was tense as Doctor Morehead removed the outer bandages from her eyes. The room was dark and as before, he cautioned her to keep her eyes closed.

All day Joanna had tried not to think about the doctor's visit tonight. When he had come by this morning he had merely checked the bump on her forehead, telling her he would examine her eyes tonight.

She heard the doctor in the outer room and waited tensely for him to enter her bedroom.

When Doctor Morehead had removed the bandages from Joanna's eyes, she thought she detected a far-off light but she couldn't be sure. Kate held the lamp waiting for the doctor's signal to turn up the wick.

"Do you see anything, Miss James?" the doctor asked.

"I'm not sure."

He motioned for Kate to hand him the lamp. "Open your eyes slowly, Miss James," he cautioned.

When the doctor moved the lamp in front of Joanna's face, it was as if an explosion of colors flashed before her eyes.

Joanna gasped and raised a trembling hand to her face. Slowly, the colors diminished and she saw Kate and Doctor Morehead clearly.

"Kate, I . . . I can see!" Joanna cried. "I can see!"

The doctor smiled and Kate rushed forward to hug Joanna, while crying tears of joy.

"It would seem that you are completely recovered from your blindness, Miss James," the doctor told her.

"How can I ever thank you, Doctor Morehead? It's so wonderful!"

"It's not me you should thank. You had the proper care when this first happened to you. The retina of your eye was damaged by the sun reflecting on the snow. The medicine woman you told me about did the right thing when she had you wear the protective covering on your eyes so they would heal. I would be interested to know what kind of salve she put on your eyes."

"I don't know, Doctor, I have no idea. All I can tell you is that it smelled awful."

"Be that as it may, it helped return your

438

sight to you. I would like to exchange ideas with this woman."

Joanna laughed. "She Who Heals would never talk to you. She has no love for the white race."

"Apparently she liked you well enough, Miss James."

"Yes," Joanna said, remembering the woman who had tended her so tenderly. "I loved her, too."

The doctor picked up his black bag. "You have no more use for me. I would caution you to take it easy when you go out in the bright sunlight for a few weeks. We don't want to take a chance on damaging your eyes again."

Joanna sat up on her knees. "Doctor, may I have a strip of bandage?"

"Yes, I was going to leave you some anyway. I would like you to wear it for a while when you are in the bright sunlight."

"I would like to put a thin strip on now so I can surprise my brother, Tag."

Kate laughed. "That young man has been so wonderful. He is going to be overjoyed to know you can see again, Joanna."

The doctor smiled and left the room.

Kate tied a thin strip of gauze about Joanna's eyes which still enabled her to see.

Joanna took her hand. "It's wonderful to see the face of the woman who has been so kind to me and my brother."

"I'm afraid it's an old face that has seen younger days," Kate replied.

Joanna touched Kate's face. "It is a lovely face, etched with kindness."

Kate looked for a moment as if her eyes misted with tears. "I'll just go out and tell Tag that you want to see him," she said softly.

Joanna sat back against the pillow looking about the room. She admired the whitewashed walls, the pretty checked curtains at the window, and the braided rug on the floor. How wonderful it was to be able to see the world she lived in!

Tag entered the room, and Joanna saw his eyes searching her face. "Kate said you wanted to see me, Joanna. What did the doctor say?"

She saw his dear face crease into a worried frown. "He said I am fine. Sit and talk to me for a moment." Joanna noticed that Tag had grown taller and he was not as thin as he had once been. It was surprising how much he had changed in such a short time.

Tag sat down on the edge of the bed and took her hand. "Will you be allowed to get out of bed tomorrow?"

"Yes, I could get up now except Kate would never allow it."

Joanna smiled to herself. "You have grown taller, Tag."

"Do you think so?"

"Yes, and where did you ever get that awful yellow print shirt?"

"I had outgrown all my other clothing so I . . . how did you know my shirt has yellow in it?"

Joanna picked up Tag's hand. "I see that your fingernails are clean. I remember Papa telling you that a gentleman never has dirty fingernails."

Tag's mouth flew open and his eyes lit up. Joanna

saw doubt dance fleetingly across his face. "Joanna
. . . can . . . you see?"

She slowly removed the gauze from her eyes and
tossed it into the air. Their eyes locked and Joanna
saw tears swimming in her brother's eyes.

"Oh, God, Joanna, you can see!" He touched her
face with a trembling hand and then hugged her
tightly while they both cried tears of joy.

## Chapter Twenty-eight

The long days of winter seemed to stretch end-lessly before Joanna. She was finding out of what it felt like to be living in limbo. There seemed to be no future to look forward to and the past was too pain-ful to dwell on. One day followed another to mark the passing of time. One way for her to pass the time was to ride Fosset when she was allowed out the gates of the fort.

It was a moderately warm morning. The wind had died down and the sun was shining brightly through a break in the clouds. Joanna and Tag were riding outside the fort with Simon and Farley in attendance. Fosset was prancing about and tossing his mane, enjoying the exercise.

Joanna's eyes would often turn northward and she fervently wished she could point Fosset in that direction and ride back to Windhawk.

Farley pulled up beside Joanna and let out a long

spew of tobacco juice. "It 'pears to me that winter is passing. I seed some green grass down by the creek yesterday."

"Yes, it is not nearly as cold as it has been," Joanna agreed.

"I figure you are thinking 'bout him, ain't you?"

Joanna didn't have to ask whom Farley meant. "Yes, I rarely think about anything else."

"I 'spect there be worse ways to live than the one them Blackfoot lead."

Joanna looked at the dear old man. "You miss that life don't you, Farley?"

"Yep, I ain't denying it. This here life's got me feeling boxed in. It gets so a fellow can't breathe with so many people hemming him in."

"You can never go back, Farley. You know what Windhawk would do to you."

"I've been studying on that. He didn't kill me afore; I doubt he would now."

"Windhawk left you, thinking you would never make your way back to civilization."

"Is that what you think?"

"Yes, of course. I remember thinking how grateful I was at the time because he let you live. But he left you for dead when he took your horses."

"Now that ain't zackly true. He left me with blankets and food. He knowed I would make it out all right, he just wasn't thinking to make it too easy on me. He kinda like paid me back for helping you get away from him."

"How do you explain the fact that he threatened to kill you that night?"

"Oh, he'd a dunit all right if you hadn't of

changed his mind. That man wasn't 'bout to do me in when he seed how you was agin it."

"I could never have shot him, Farley. He never forgave me for pointing that rifle at him."

"He knowed you weren't gonna shoot him. Hell, Joanna, me and him both knowed you couldn't pull down on a man."

Joanna shook her head. "I wish I'd never left him in the first place. If I had known then what I know now . . ."

Joanna's voice trailed off and Farley studied her face. He saw regret and heartbreak in the depths of her eyes. "I 'spect there's been a many of us who have leaped into the frying pan without thinking. You're mighty young to be living with a mistake. Ifen you want to go back to Windhawk, I'll take you."

Joanna smiled. "There is no going back, Farley; there is only forward."

"Seems to me the good Lord made our legs for walking backwards as well as forward. It's just a mite harder in reverse, that's all."

Joanna couldn't help but chuckle. Farley was a dear, loveable character, and he seemed to have a wise saying for any given situation.

She saw Tag racing toward them, and gave Farley a signal to drop the conversation.

"Joanna, guess what?" Tag asked excitedly. "Simon and I saw a robin, and he says, spring can't be far away."

Joanna smiled at her brother. "Yes, Tag, I believe spring is in the air, but unless I miss my guess those are rain clouds on the horizon and I don't plan on getting soaked. I think it would be wise if we returned to the fort."

The four of them rode swiftly back toward the fort in silent companionship.

Kate and Colonel Jackson were attending one of the officers' wedding, leaving Joanna and Tag alone for the evening. Tag had been restless ever since they had returned from their ride that morning.

"What should we do, Joanna? Can't we leave here now that spring has come? I don't like it here at the fort any more," Tag said, slumping down in the chair and staring at the ceiling.

"I don't know, Tag. I just don't seem able to decide on anything about our future."

"I wish we could go back to Windhawk's village, Joanna. I was happy living with the Blackfoot."

"Didn't you miss the life we had in Philadelphia, Tag? Or perhaps you would like to return to England? England would probably be the safest place for us to go right now," Joanna said thoughtfully.

"No, not England. Someday when I'm older I'll have to go back to Philadelphia, but until then, I wish we could stay with Windhawk."

Joanna shook her head, not knowing what to say to Tag. She wished more than anything that they could return to Windhawk, but it just wasn't possible. She was relieved when there was a rap on the door and she didn't have to answer him. Standing up, she crossed the room and opened the door, and to her surprise, saw Harland standing outside with his hat in hand looking very uncomfortable.

"Good evening, Captain. I didn't expect to see you tonight."

Harland cleared his throat nervously. "I wonder if you would allow me to come in and talk to you, Joanna?"

"Yes, of course," she said, moving aside so he could enter.

Tag nodded his head at Harland and then quickly asked to be excused. He didn't like Captain Thatcher coming to see his sister. He could tell that Harland was interested in Joanna and in Tag's mind, Joanna was still married to Windhawk.

"Won't you be seated, Harland?" she offered.

Harland nodded and then sat down. "I was elated to learn that you have your sight back, Joanna. I can only imagine how wonderful it must be for you to be able to see after living in darkness for so long."

Joanna looked at him, puzzled. "Yes, it's wonderful." She sat down in a chair, wondering why Harland had come to see her.

Harland noticed the way the violet-colored dress brought out the color of Joanna's beautiful eyes. Now that he was here, he felt nervous and uncertain. He had rehearsed over and over what he would say to her tonight, but now the words seemed to stick in his throat.

"I heard about what happened between you and Miss Maxwell, Joanna. It must have been a terrible ordeal for you to go through."

She lowered her lashes. "I . . . was not prepared for Claudia . . . It's over now. I would rather forget all about it."

"If it is any consolation for you, I understand

446

many of the ladies berated Miss Maxwell for her conduct and they stand ready to defend you."

"I find it really doesn't matter what Claudia says about me."

"I'm glad you feel that way. It's best not to put too much importance on anything Miss Maxwell says." Harland looked uncomfortable for a moment. "There is something I would like to ask you and I hope you won't think I am prying."

"If I think you are, I will tell you," she said smiling.

Harland leaned forward. "Joanna, is it true that you were married to this Windhawk?"

Joanna was taken off guard by his question, and it took her a moment to recover. "I was . . . and still am, Windhawk's wife."

"That answers my second question then. I was going to ask if you love him."

Joanna raised her head proudly. "Oh, yes, I love him. Do you intend to condemn me for that?"

Harland saw the defiance in her eyes. "No, Joanna, you completely misunderstand me. I have an entirely different reason for asking."

Joanna was ready to do battle if need be. "What could be your reason?"

"I find that I feel more for you than just friendship. I have for a long time. I came here tonight to ask you to be my wife," he blurted out.

Joanna looked astounded. She hadn't expected this turn in events. "Harland, I don't know how to answer you. I don't know why you would make such an offer unless you pity me."

He stood up, then moved to her side and knelt

down. "Pity . . . Joanna. The only one I pity is myself, because I am hopelessly in love with you. Haven't you guessed that by now?"

Her face lost its color as she read the truth in his eyes. "Harland, I like you very much, but I could never marry you!"

"Why, Joanna?" He reached out and took her hand. "Tell me why?"

"In the first place, I'm already married," she reminded him.

"That marriage was dissolved when Windhawk left you at Fort Union. Give me another reason," he persisted.

"I love Windhawk, Harland. I have nothing to give you but my undying friendship."

"I would marry you, knowing you don't love me, Joanna. Perhaps in time you would grow to love me." Harland pulled her into his arms and was relieved when she didn't resist. Nor did she resist when he lowered his head to kiss her.

Joanna wanted to feel something for Harland, because if he could stir her emotions, perhaps she could forget about Windhawk. Harland's lips covered Joanna's in a kiss that was tender and sweet. She willed herself to love him but the feeling didn't come.

Harland raised his head and stared at her, but he read only sorrow in her eyes, and knew that she had been totally unmoved by his kiss. He also knew in that moment, that she would never belong to him.

"What will you do, Joanna?"

"I have not yet decided."

"If you ever change your mind . . ." His hand

drifted up to touch her glorious red-gold hair.

"No, I'll never change my mind, Harland, but please try to understand, I love Windhawk."

He touched her face softly. "Windhawk must be someone special if he has won the heart of someone like you."

"He is special, Harland. I wish you could come to know him as I do."

He smiled slightly. "I doubt that he and I would ever be friends, Joanna." Harland stood up and smiled down at her. "I saw you before he did. Pity I didn't press my suit earlier."

Joanna stood on her tiptoes and kissed his cheek. "Thank you for the proposal. I think I needed to feel that a man still thought me attractive."

"Joanna, I don't know why Windhawk brought you to Fort Union, but you can bet it wasn't because he didn't love you." Harland gave her a wink and walked to the door. "You are letting a prize catch get away by not accepting my marriage proposal," he said lightly.

"I know that, Harland. But my guess is you won't dwell too long on my refusal." She laughed. "There are too many lovely women who pay a marked attention to you."

Harland stepped out into the night air and pulled the collar of his coat about his neck. He had an ache deep inside that would take time to heal. He knew he would not soon forget the hauntingly beautiful Joanna James.

Joanna stood silently for a long time. Had she been a fool not to accept Harland's proposal? No, it would not have been fair to either of them if she had consented to marry him. She loved Windhawk, and Harland deserved a woman who adored him.

She went into her bedroom and lifted the lid to her trunk thinking she would sort out her clothing. It was time to gather her belongings together. The day would soon come when she and Tag would have to leave the fort. Many of her gowns were in need of repair since she had been unable to see to mend them.

Seeing her mother's jewel chest, Joanna picked it up and lifted the lid. There were many valuable diamonds, rubies and emeralds inside. Someday Tag would be able to sell the remaining jewels to fight Uncle Howard for his inheritance, she thought absentmindedly.

Suddenly Joanna caught her breath. With trembling hands, she reached into the jewel case and removed what to her was more precious than any of her mother's jewels. It was Windhawk's bear-claw necklace! The one he had given her to seal their marriage. No one but Windhawk could have placed the necklace in the jewel chest! Joanna remembered giving it back to him, and she knew that until a few weeks ago, the necklace had not been in her mother's case! There was no way it could have gotten there unless Windhawk himself had placed it there. But how? And when?

Windhawk had been in this room! There was no other way the necklace could have gotten into her mother's jewel case. She remembered what he had said to her the night he had given her the necklace. She remembered Windhawk's exact words as if they had been etched on her heart.

"Each time you see this necklace, Joanna, it will speak to you of the love that burns in my heart."

Could this mean he still loved her? She held the necklace lovingly to her face. Was this proof that Windhawk had never stopped loving her? Tears of happiness blinded her as she ran out of the room, searching for Tag.

Joanna found her brother sitting at the kitchen table, sampling some of Kate's gingersnap cookies.

"Tag, go and find Simon and Farley! Tell them I want to see them right away!"

"What for?" Tag asked, cramming the last bit of cookie into his mouth.

"I'll tell you when we're all together. Hurry, Tag, we don't have any time to spare!"

Tag saw the excitement in his sister's eyes and wondered if Captain Thatcher had anything to do with her happiness. Before he could ask, Joanna shoved him toward the back door. "Hurry, Tag, this is important!"


Farley had always felt uncomfortable when he was inside a house. He had grown too used to the open spaces and was beginning to feel confined. He twirled his coonskin cap around in his hand, nervously, refusing to sit down on the fancy couch beside Simon.

Three pair of eyes watched Joanna expectantly, wondering why she had called them together.

She faced them, smiling. "I have made an important decision and I want each of you to know about it. I have decided to return to Windhawk!"

451

Simon looked at Joanna as if she had lost her senses. Tag jumped up and shouted. "We're going back, Simon! Did you hear Joanna, we're going back to the Blackfoot village!"

"Have you thought this through, Miss Joanna? Do you fully realize what you are going back to?" Simon asked in bewilderment.

Joanna beamed at Simon. "I do. I am going home to my husband."

Farley's laughter crackled. "I was wondering how long it would be afore you came around to that. What took you so long?"

"I had to have a gentle nudge," she said, holding up the bear claw necklace.

"I reckon you'll be asking me to take you?" the wily old trapper asked.

"Would you, Farley? I feel sure Windhawk will do you no harm."

"I been waiting around fer days for you to know what I already knowed. When do we leave?"

"The sooner the better!" Tag said excitedly.

"It's colder than a raccoon's tail caught in a froze creek out there," Farley warned.

"It doesn't matter, Farley. You and I have braved much worse weather than this," Joanna said, wishing they could leave right that moment.

"What am I to do, Miss Joanna? I have no wish to live in an Indian village but I don't want to leave you and Master Taggart either," Simon said, thinking they had all lost their reasoning.

Joanna handed Simon her mother's jewel case. "I have thought of that, Simon. I want you to take care of my mother's jewels and someday Tag will come to claim them from you," Joanna said, knowing the loyal Simon would guard the jewels with his life.

Simon nodded. "I have a mind to return to Philadelphia and just keep my eye on things for a while. I already talked to Captain Thatcher and he says he will write a letter for me to take to his parents. He thinks they will employ me."

"That would be wonderful, Simon. Are you sure that's what you want to do?" Joanna asked.

"That's exactly what I want to do. I will keep in touch with you through Fort Union, and I will wait for the day when Master Taggart comes knocking at the door. Don't you worry, the day will come when you will set your aunt and uncle straight."

"Now, that's settled, I wonder if we could leave tomorrow, Farley? I have money to buy horses and supplies."

"Slow down there, little lady. I know you be anxious to get back to that man of yourn, but you just don't go rushing out headlong without figgering ahead."

"How much time?" Joanna inquired.

He grinned broadly. "Give me 'bout two days."


That night, when Joanna went to bed, she was too excited to sleep. All she could think of was seeing Windhawk again. There was very little doubt in her mind that he still loved her.

She had a way to test his love, she thought, remembering how she had fooled Tag when he hadn't known she had regained her eyesight. She would allow Windhawk to think she was blind until she could read his eyes and know if he still loved her. His eyes were so expressive. He would never be able to disguise what he was feeling from her.

Two more days and she would be on her way back to her love!

## Chapter Twenty-nine

"Hold up there, Joanna. That horse of yourn is 'bout to run off and leave me and Tag," Farley said, riding alongside Joanna.

She laughed and patted Fosset's long sleek neck. "I think Fosset can tell that I'm happy, Farley. He wants to go home as much as I do."

Joanna slowed her pace so she could ride between Tag and Farley. Sometimes she had to draw rein on her horse to hold him back so Farley and Tag could keep up with her.

It had been difficult for Joanna to convince Colonel Jackson and Kate that she was doing the right thing by returning to the Blackfoot village. It had been hard to say good-bye to Simon, knowing it would be many years before they would see him again.

Harland had walked Joanna to the gate of the fort and kissed her soundly on the cheek, telling her that he would see her again someday. Joanna had been glad Claudia had not been around when she left.

As the days passed and the distance between her and Windhawk narrowed, Joanna's heart grew lighter. Farley had told her that by tomorrow afternoon they would reach the Blackfoot village.

Joanna looked around her, thinking she was now a part of this land. This was her home as nowhere else had ever been.

It was a cloudless day and the warm sun reflected off the snow. Doctor Morehead had given Joanna some gauze and told her to wear it over her eyes, should the sun be too bright. She now wore a thin strip to protect her eyes from the bright glare. The gauze was not thick enough to hamper her vision, so she could easily see where she was going.

How good it felt to be dressed in her doeskin gown again.

"Huh oh!" Farley said, pulling his rifle out of his saddle holster. "We got us some company. Can't tell who they are from here, but they be Blackfoot."

"What do we do?" Tag asked.

"Just stay close to me and let me do the talking," Farley said, slowing his horse.

Joanna saw the riders as they topped a small hill. They were moving swiftly and she knew it wouldn't be any time at all before the Indians reached them.

When the Indians were within fifty yards, Joanna recognized Windhawk's horse, *Puh Pom*. She began to doubt that she had done the right thing in coming back. Suppose Windhawk didn't want to see her? What if she loved him so much she had de-

456

luded herself into thinking he loved her?

"Don't tell him I have regained my eyesight," she said to Tag and Farley.

Farley reined in his horse and Tag and Joanna followed suit.

When the warriors were close enough for Joanna to recognize them, she noticed that they all had their faces painted! She felt a prickle of uneasiness when Windhawk drew even with them, while the others fell back.

Windhawk looked straight at Joanna for a moment and then his eyes moved to Tag. "Why have you returned, little brother?" he asked in a commanding voice.

His face was painted with wide black stripes that crossed his high cheekbones and spread across the bridge of his nose, giving him an ominous appearance.

"I told you I would come back, Windhawk. I have kept my promise!"

"You, old man, why have you returned?" Windhawk asked with his dark eyes boring into Farley.

Joanna noticed the proud carriage of his head as his eyes swept past her as if she wasn't even there. She wondered if he was purposely ignoring her?

"I am merely the guide, Windhawk," Farley answered in the language of the Blackfoot.

At last, Windhawk's eyes rested on Joanna. She could tell nothing he was feeling from his expression. He seemed to look at her with the eyes of a stranger. "Joanna, why do you come among us? Did I not take you to the white man's fort?" His eyes were as cold as his voice.

Joanna wanted to blurt out that she had returned because she didn't want to live without him. But her pride came to her rescue. "Our father is dead and we are no longer going to Oregon. Tag wanted to see you again. I miss Sun Woman and Morning Song. I hope you will allow me to see them."

His eyes narrowed and he was quiet for a moment. At last he spoke. "I will allow it." He turned his horse and rode back to his warriors.

Joanna's heart was pounding loudly. She had been afraid he was going to refuse her. What would she have done had he said no? She urged her horse forward to join Tag and Farley.

As they joined with the Blackfoot, Joanna could feel Windhawk's coldness like a sharp pain in her heart.

Did he feel she was intruding? she wondered. Perhaps it would be better if she were to visit with Sun Woman and Morning Song and then leave.

Joanna had never been one to give up easily when she wanted something. Now she wanted something so precious and rare she would fight to the bitter end to obtain it. She wanted Windhawk's love!

The Blackfoot warriors closed rank about them and Joanna saw a familiar face beneath the hideous yellow and black face paint.

"I am pleased to see you again, Joanna," Gray Fox said soberly.

"It is good to see you also, my friend," she answered, slipping easily back into the Blackfoot language.

Windhawk rode at the head of the fierce-looking warriors, and didn't once look back at Joanna.

Why had she returned? he wondered. Had she come back to torture him? The days since she had been gone had been nothing more than the passing of time to him. Each morning he had awakened, feeling as if a heavy weight was sitting on his heart. Windhawk had thought he would never see Joanna again, and here she was. Why had she chosen to come back now? There was a never-ending world beyond the Blackfoot Nation and he thought she had been swallowed up in that world.

For two days Tall Bear and several other braves had been tracking the movements of three whites. Yesterday he had sent word to Windhawk that one of the whites was a woman, and he thought it was Joanna.

Windhawk had lost no time in riding to intercept them. When he had seen Joanna he had been confused. Even though she couldn't see, he still hid his feelings behind a mask—a mask every bit as concealing as the paint he wore on his face.

Could she have come back because she loved him? She said that her father was dead. Did that mean she wanted to stay with him? Did she return simply because she had nowhere else to go? He had no answers to his questions, but he knew whatever her reason, he would never allow her to leave again. If he must keep her as an unwilling captive then he would do so.

The countryside was now very familiar to Joanna. She could see the winding Milk River in the distance and felt as if she had come home at last. Her heart was flooded with thankfulness. She had traveled so far to find out where she really belonged.

Joanna could only see the back of Windhawk's head, but she sent him a silent message of love. He was her husband, and as Sun Woman once told her, a woman's place was with her husband. He looked so proud and distant as he turned his head to issue an order to one of his braves.

Joanna smiled to herself. He had loved her once — she would make him love her again.

They rode swiftly the rest of the day. Just before sundown, Windhawk stopped to make camp.

Tag and Farley pitched the tent while Joanna built the campfire. Windhawk and his warriors were camped some twenty feet away. Every so often Joanna would glance in their direction to see if she could locate Windhawk. He had been very cold and distant but Joanna still had reason to hope that she could win him back. He had not threatened to harm them in any way, nor was he treating them as his prisoners. Surely that was an encouraging sign . . . and did she not wear his necklace about her neck, hidden beneath her gown?

When Joanna reached for the heavy iron skillet, the bandage slipped from her eyes and she readjusted it. She wasn't yet ready for Windhawk to know she had regained her sight. As she placed several slices of thick bacon in the skillet, Farley came up to her.

"You best let me do that, Joanna, you're overplaying your hand."

"In what way?" she asked as he moved her aside.

He gave her a crooked grin. "You move about mighty good for somebody who's 'sposed to be blind."

"Do you think I'm taking unfair advantage of Windhawk by not letting him know I can see, Farley?"

Farley placed another slab of bacon in the hot skillet and watched it sizzle for a moment. "I never was one to give ad-vice in matters of the heart. I 'spect a female has built-in learning on how to trap a man."

Joanna couldn't help but laugh. "Farley, you make us females sound mercenary."

"I found that to be the truth, and I thank my maker every day that that's the way it works," he said, giving her a toothy grin.

Joanna smiled, thinking how dear the old trapper had become to her. He seemed to have attached himself to her as her guardian angel, and she thought his role fit him perfectly. "Farley, what will you do now?"

"Well, I been studying on that. This here last trip to civil-i-zation plumb tuckered me out. I thought as how I'd ask Windhawk ifen he'd sorta let me hang around, lest he'd rather see my scalp hanging from his lodgepole."

Joanna saw the gleam in Farley's eyes and she knew he would be staying so he could be near her and Tag. She bent over and kissed him soundly on the cheek. Farley looked taken aback for a moment. He touched his cheek where she had kissed him, and his eyes glowed. He loved the flaming-haired girl and boy. They had somehow become his family. It warmed his heart to just be near them.

"Why'd you do that fer?" he asked.

"Because, you loveable old character, I love you."

Suddenly his eyes misted over and he turned quickly away with the pretense of dishing up the now overdone bacon. He cleared his throat. "You best call Tag, ifen he wants to eat while it's hot," he said in a gruff voice.

Joanna stood up and smiled down at Farley. His table manners were atrocious and he seldom ever bathed, but to her he was one of the dearest men she had ever known.

After they had eaten, Tag walked over to Windhawk's camp. Joanna and Farley sat talking quietly beside the warm fire.

"What if Windhawk doesn't want me back, Farley?" Joanna asked wistfully. "I mustn't forget that he was the one who sent me away."

"You can't forget that he's the one who brung you back when you run away."

"Perhaps it was his pride that made him come after me."

"Well, I 'spect you can ask him, yourself. He's coming," Farley said, standing up abruptly. "I 'spect I'll just mosey down and check on the horses."

The expected moment had come, as Joanna knew it would sooner or later. Now was the time she must face Windhawk. Suddenly, she felt nervous and undecided. Her whole future happiness rested on whether Windhawk loved her. She must find out one way or the other.

Windhawk towered above her. Joanna raised her head and stared up at his unreadable expression, noticing he had removed the paint from his face.

"It's a very cold night," she said, not knowing what else to say.

He knelt down and placed more wood on the fire. "I do not feel the cold as you do."

Joanna watched the firelight dance across his handsome features as he turned to face her. Her heart stopped beating when she saw his dark eyes move lovingly across her face. She saw him reach out his hand to touch her hair and then drop it to his side. His eyes then traveled to her lips and he closed his eyes.

Dear God, he did love her! Joanna could see it so clearly written on his face. She could tell he was hurting because the pain was reflected in his eyes.

"I would like to know why you have come back, Joanna?" Windhawk asked softly in the Blackfoot tongue.

She saw the anxious look on his face as he awaited her answer. She felt guilty for taking unfair advantage of him. He thought she was still blind. He didn't know she could read his face, which clearly defined his every thought.

"I came back because you and I left many things unsettled between us," she answered him in the same language.

Windhawk sat down beside her and stared into the fire. "I thought we parted with a perfect understanding of one another."

"No. When you left me, you neglected to say good-bye."

She saw his head snap up and his eyes searched her face. "I thought there was no more to say between us at the time. You had given me back the necklace, saying we were no longer as one."

Joanna reached inside the neck of her gown and drew out the necklace she wore about her neck. "I found this. I don't know how it got in my belongings. Did you mean for me to have it?"

She watched as he closed his eyes and then gazed skyward. When he looked back to her, Joanna bit her lip to keep from crying out. There were tears shining in his beautiful ebony eyes. His throat was working convulsively and it took him a moment to be able to reply.

"The necklace belongs to you," he said at last.

"Windhawk, why did you send me away?" she asked in a broken voice.

She saw his eyes narrow. "You ask me this when you are the one who left me first?"

"Yes, I ask you because I need to know. Did you want to be rid of me because I was blind?"

He looked disconcerted, and Joanna watched as he reached out to her again, but as before, let his hand drop. "I was the cause of your blindness. If I had taken better care of you, you would now be able to see."

Joanna felt tears in her eyes. She had not realized he felt responsible for her blindness.

"I never felt it was your fault that I lost my sight, Windhawk. I thought you no longer wanted me because I had become a burden to you."

He stood up and gazed down at her. "None of this is important, Joanna."

Joanna stood up to face him. "Suppose I told you I have come home to stay?" Joanna asked in English. She knew that the next few moments would be the most important in her life and she didn't want to take the chance of being misunderstood.

She watched closely as he took a hesitant step toward her. His eyes glowed with the softness of love and she knew without a doubt that he still loved her. She watched, fascinated, as a tear rolled down his bronzed cheek and he quickly brushed it away.

"Jo-anna," he whispered, slipping back into the old way he had spoken her name when they had been so much in love. It sounded so right to her ears.

"I have not been truthful with you, Windhawk," she said, removing the bandage and tossing it aside. "My sight has been restored and I can see perfectly. Forgive me for the deception but I had to know if you still loved me as I love you."

His eyes moved quickly to hers and he saw his reflection in the violet-colored depths. Her eyes were shining with the love she professed to have for him. He reached out and crushed her in his arms as he had wanted to do when he first saw her today. Closing his eyes, he let her sweet smell and soft skin fill his senses.

Napi had sent him and Joanna on the long road to happiness, but he had also thrown stumbling blocks in their path. But their love had overcome all the obstacles. Joanna had returned to him of her own free will. There would never again be any doubt in his mind that she loved him.

"Joanna, later I will have many questions to ask you. For now, nothing matters but that you are here and you love me," he whispered passionately.

Joanna raised her head and laid her face against

his. "I just couldn't go on without you, Windhawk. I have been so unhappy."

He allowed his lips to brush her cheek. "I, too, have been unhappy, Joanna," he said, lapsing into the Blackfoot language. "My eyes have missed your beauty. My lips have missed your kiss. My body has hungered for yours."

Joanna slid her arms around his broad shoulders, feeling his love reach out to her. This was where she belonged. She had come home at last.

Windhawk lifted her face up to him. "Who sleeps in the tent tonight?" he asked, nodding to the tent which Farley and Tag had erected.

She smiled up at him. "I do, with my husband."

Joy spread over his face as he lifted her in his arms and carried her into the darkened tent.

Joanna wound her arms about his neck. Windhawk found her eager lips and covered them with a hungry kiss.

"Joanna, this morning when I awoke it was a day like any other—a day filled with loneliness. I did not know that tonight I would hold you in my arms again," he said in a deeply moving voice.

Joanna felt his strong hands move down to her hips and she laid her head against his broad chest, listening to his erratic heartbeat. "I did not know if you would want to hold me tonight, although I hoped you would. I love you, my husband."

Windhawk felt the silkiness of her skin as she brushed his cheek with a soft kiss.

"Think well before you give yourself to me tonight, Joanna," he said in a passionate voice. "I will never again allow you to leave me."

For her answer, Joanna pulled his dark head down and parted her lips to receive his kiss.

All the past hurts they had caused one another seemed to fade into nothingness. The long days of being separated had come to an end.

Joanna knew she had found a man who was strong and yet sensitive to others' feelings. He was the leader of his fierce warriors and yet, he had the ability to feel so deeply that she had seen him cry tonight. There was no weakness in this man who was her husband, but a gentle understanding of a woman's heart. She doubted there had ever been a man to equal him.

Joanna felt his arms tighten about her and she knew that soon, oh so soon, she would be able to communicate her love to him with her body.

## Chapter Thirty

Windhawk set Joanna on her feet and she stood on her tiptoes, throwing her arms about his neck. She trembled with excitement when she felt his hands unhook the front of her gown. Turning her around, he easily slipped her gown over her head and dropped it to the floor.

It was dark inside the tent, but Joanna could imagine the glow that would be in Windhawk's dark eyes. She reached out to him and found that he had dropped to his knees to unfasten her moccasins and remove them. A gasp escaped her lips when she felt his hands travel up her legs. When they reached her waist, he gently pulled her down into his arms.

Her flesh seemed to melt into his as he clasped her tightly against him. She could hear his heavy breathing as his hands roamed across the hills and valleys of her body, becoming reacquainted with her shape.

"You have lost weight," he whispered against her ear.

"Do you want me to be fat?" she asked, as he pushed her hair aside and kissed the back of her neck.

"I want you just the way you are." He covered her lips with a gentle kiss, then pushed Joanna off his lap, and knelt down bringing her close to him. They were both now in a kneeling position and Joanna felt the heat of his body warm her. For long moments he caressed and stroked her, while bringing her even closer to him.

Joanna could feel the swirling heat of desire run like quicksilver through her veins, and she moaned softly. "Windhawk, my dearest, dearest, love," she cried out, sprinkling kisses over his face.

Windhawk was drawing her under his spell. Tonight they would have their second wedding night, but it would be different. This time Joanna had come home to stay. There was no voice calling to her from out of her past. His hands moved slowly over her body and a groan tore from his lips when her hand moved down his back and across his hips.

They were straining together, trying to find the closeness they both craved. Windhawk pushed Joanna gently backwards against the warm blanket and lay down beside her. Joanna felt him pull her into his arms as he kissed her eyelids, her ears, and then his mouth settled on hers in a deep, dragging kiss.

"Joanna, I have not been with another woman since I first had you," he whispered raggedly in her ear. "I want you to know this."

Joanna whimpered when his lips traveled along her neck and between the valley of her breasts.

A cold wind was blowing outside the tent and snow had begun to fall earthward, but the two lovers were unaware of anything but each other.

Windhawk caressed Joanna's silky skin while inhaling the sweet scent of her glorious hair. He wished it were not so dark so he could see her beautiful body.

Joanna pressed her face against Windhawk's chest; he was filling her whole being with his touch. His sensuous, manly smell heightened her sense of awareness.

She was startled when he rolled over on his back and lifted her above him. He lowered her slowly down to his body and his lips settled on her breasts.

"Windhawk," she breathed, as her body trembled with anticipation. He was loving her leisurely, lingeringly, and Joanna thought she would die from the ache that throbbed deep inside her.

He moved her hips until she fit firmly against him. Joanna could feel his swollen manhood pressing against her inner thigh and she began to squirm. Windhawk was trying to hold his desire under control, but when Joanna began moving on top of him, he could feel his restraint slipping.

His warm breath stirred her hair when he lifted her up and Windhawk plunged his pulsating manhood deep into her warm moist body.

His hips moved upward until he came to rest fully inside her.

"You have never done this before," she whispered with pleasure.

He laughed roguishly. "There are many things I will teach you, Joanna."

Yes, she thought, as he thrust forward again and again. He had taught her to be a woman. Since the first time he had made love to her he had stamped his ownership on her heart. She must have known that first night that she belonged to him body and soul.

Windhawk groaned as she threw back her head, slipping her legs on either side of him and sitting up. "Jo-anna, Jo-anna," he whispered, through a haze of unleashed pleasure.

She instinctively seemed to know how to move to please him. Her slight body was made to bring a man pleasure, he thought passionately.

Windhawk wished he could see her beautiful eyes. He knew if he could, they would be passion-laced and wild at the moment.

It seemed to Joanna that her sense of touch had been heightened as never before. She knew no matter how many times they would love each other in the future, she would always remember this night.

Windhawk arched his hips and Joanna rolled her head from side to side as beautiful feelings shot through her body and seemed to lift her higher and higher.

"Jo-anna," Windhawk whispered lovingly, as her body and his shuddered and trembled simultaneously.

Joanna went limp and lay forward to rest her head on Windhawk's chest. She closed her eyes and listened to his heartbeat slow while his hand moved caressingly across her hips. There were no words that could describe what had just happened between them so they just lay quietly—holding, feeling, touching.

Yes, Joanna thought, it had been a long way home but at last the journey was over. Since the day she had been born, fate had been moving her in the direction it had mapped out for her. She felt with Windhawk beside her there was nothing which could stand in the way of total happiness.

Windhawk kissed her closed eyelids. With this slight little girl at his side there was no mountain he could not climb and no feat he couldn't perform. She was courageous and loyal, and there were many things she could teach him. His love for her seemed to spill over when he heard her sigh contentedly.

"Joanna, I never thought I would say to any woman . . . teach me to be the man you want me to be . . . show me the way to walk so our footsteps will meet."

She raised her head and placed her cheek to his. "Oh, my dearest love, I would not want you to change. Stay the man you are."

"Do you regret that I am of Indian blood and you are white?" His hand drifted up into her silky hair.

"No, you would not be Windhawk if you were different, and if you weren't Windhawk, I would not love you."

"Since you have been away I have spent much time alone, Joanna. I began to examine the differences in our two worlds. I know your world is filled with marvelous things which I have never seen. I said to myself—I must learn about these things that touch Joanna's life . . ." He paused, as if trying to think of the right words to say. ". . . I reached for the moon and caught the sun, Joanna. You shine so brightly it sometimes hurts to look at you."

Joanna reached up and kissed his lips. "No woman ever had a more beautiful declaration of love than the one you have just given me, Windhawk. I admire you so deeply. You are truthful, honorable, brave, and so many things, that I could never name them all. I knew from the moment I saw you that you were someone special, but I didn't know how special until I really came to know you. You cannot know how honored I feel being your wife."

He crushed her tightly to him, thinking she was like no other woman. "Will you not miss your old life, Joanna?"

She heard the doubt in his voice and hoped she could wipe away any fears he might have that she would ever leave him again.

"Windhawk, I feel that I am where I belong. I love you so much it hurts. I will never want to go back to the life I had before I met you. I have no ties in the white world." She smiled against his face. "I am tied to the fierce, prideful chief of the Blackfoot. I yearn for the day when I can have your child. We will teach him the best of both worlds."

Windhawk touched her face lovingly. "I hope the seed has been planted that will put my child in your body. Then I will know you really are Windhawk's woman."

Joanna clamped her hands behind his neck and laughed playfully. "Perhaps we should make sure the deed is done."

He rolled her over on her back. "How will we do this thing," he said, smiling.

"If you don't know, perhaps I can show you. I had a very good teacher."

He laughed deeply. "I still have many things to teach you."

"Am I docile like the horse you once compared me to?" she asked lightly.

"No, my flaming-haired one, nor do I want you to be."

Outside, the wind howled and blew the snow into great snowdrifts. Inside the tent Joanna was warm and cozy, locked in the arms of her tall, dark husband. There were still many unanswered questions between them and Joanna knew that they must each answer to the other before they could find complete happiness.

"Windhawk, when I aimed the rifle at you, I would never have been able to pull the trigger."

"I know this."

"When I ran away from you I didn't really want to go, but felt I had to at the time."

"I know this also."

"Do you forgive me?"

"Joanna, as many times as you would come to me and ask forgiveness, that is how many times I would forgive you."

"I thought when you sent me away you no longer loved me."

He kissed her forehead. "I could easier stop breathing, than I could stop loving you, Joanna. The reason I sent you away was because I thought you never loved me. I was sorry for how cruelly I had treated you and I thought it was only right that I let you go. Had I known you wanted to stay with me, I would never have let you go."

She laid her head against his shoulder and traced the scar where the panther had clawed him. "I think we will hold our love all the more precious, since we almost lost it."

Windhawk buried his face in the thick curtain of red-gold hair. He was unable to speak past the lump in his throat.

"Windhawk, are you sure you never looked at another woman while I was away?"

"I could never be satisfied with the stars once I had touched the sun, Joanna."

She cupped his face in her hands and laid her cheek next to his. There were no more explanations that were needed between them. There was only one thing that puzzled Joanna.

"Windhawk, how did the bear-claw necklace get in my trunk?"

He smiled. "I put it there."

"But when? It wasn't in my mother's jewel case when I first went to the fort."

He raised her hand to his lips. "I came to the fort with the intention of finding out if you might still love me."

"Did you see me?"

"Yes, you were walking with that long knife. I wanted to kill him for touching you, but I did not."

"When was this?"

"Does it matter?"

"No, I suppose not."

"Joanna, what did the long knife mean to you?"

Joanna could hear the jealousy in Windhawk's voice. "Harland was no more than a friend. At one point he did ask me to marry him but I refused, telling him I was married to you."

"Did he ever touch you as I do?"

"I will be honest with you. I did allow him to kiss me, but the kiss meant nothing. I was too filled with loving you."

"I don't like it that he touched his lips to yours, Joanna," Windhawk said, rubbing his lips against hers, as if to erase any trace or memory left by the long knife.

"Windhawk, there will never be any cause for you to be jealous. I have never loved anyone but you."

His arms tightened about Joanna, and they both drifted off to sleep, knowing they had found a pure and lasting love.

The next afternoon when Joanna rode into the village beside her husband, she was quickly surrounded by happy, smiling faces.

Windhawk helped her dismount, and before she could turn around, Morning Song grabbed her and hugged her tightly.

"Joanna, I could not believe it when we heard you had returned," she beamed.

"I am home to stay, little sister," Joanna told her. Joanna's eyes moved to Sun Woman, who was studying her quietly. Everyone seemed to be waiting for Windhawk's mother's reaction to Joanna's return.

Joanna looked for some sign of welcome from Windhawk's mother. Suddenly, the old woman's face eased into a smile and she took Joanna's hand.

"It is good to have you home, my daughter."

Joanna slid her arm around Sun Woman's shoulder. "It is good to be home, my mother," she said, as happiness flooded her soul.

Amanda was overjoyed and her face declared her happiness at Joanna's return. Joanna noticed Tag was receiving the same warm welcome that she was. It was wonderful to see the genuine love reflected on the faces that surrounded them.

Suddenly Joanna could feel other eyes watching her. She looked over the head of Gray Fox's wife, White Dove, and saw an old Indian woman staring at her. The old woman had not come forward with the others to welcome her. The crowd opened up as Joanna approached the old woman. She looked at a face which was wrinkled with age, and hair that had long been gray. She noticed the gnarled hands that had so tenderly treated her when she had been so ill.

"She Who Heals, I would know you anywhere." Joanna reached out and lovingly touched the wrinkled face. She felt tears in her eyes when she saw the old woman's eyes moisten.

"Flaming-haired-one, my eyes tell me that you are no longer blind," She Who Heals said in a choked voice.

"That is true, my friend. I was told that it was because of your care, that I am able to see."

Windhawk came up and stood beside Joanna. She was his woman and they would start their new life together on a firm foundation. At last their love had breached the gap between their two worlds. There might be times in the future when they would have different views, but Windhawk welcomed that. Joanna would stand up for whatever she believed in, and he knew he would not want her to be any other way. She would walk beside him as his woman!

Joanna looked up into his face and could almost read what he was thinking. His midnight-black eyes caressed her face lovingly.

She Who Heals laughed. "I think it will not be long until there will be a little one around the chief's lodge."

Joanna's face flushed, and Windhawk's eyes flashed. Taking Joanna's hand, he led her to their tipi where they could be alone.

Inside the tipi, she went readily into his arms. Her heart was soaring as she saw the gleam in her husband's eyes. She had no regrets. She had tested fate and come out the winner. She had touched the wind and had been caught up in a whirlwind.

She would always be sad over the loss of her father, mother and Franny. There was a part of her that would always feel grief at their passing. They had each played a part in molding her into the woman she was today, and for that, she would always be grateful.

"I love you, Windhawk," she whispered. "I will always love you."

Windhawk's eyes flamed and he caught her close to him. He was a man who held the world in his arms. The tiny flaming-haired girl belonged to him. He no longer felt the restlessness within her. Today there would be a council meeting and Joanna's name would be changed to Flaming Hair, but in private he would continue to call her Joanna, as he was sure many of his people would.

Tag looked toward the eastern horizon. There was a restlessness deep inside him. He was not unhappy, but this unrest kept gnawing at his insides. He would tarry for a while with his sister and her husband, but someday he would return to Philadelphia.

He had an old score to settle. He wasn't impatient to grow up. What he had to do would wait until he became a man.

Tag heard Windhawk's voice calling out to him, and he returned to the present. Seeing Joanna and Windhawk were going for a ride, his face brightened.

"Can I go too?" he asked eagerly.

"Yes, come little brother," Windhawk told him.

Tag bounded onto his horse and rode beside his sister and her husband. He knew Windhawk could teach him many things. He could feel Joanna's and Windhawk's love reach out to him. The time to live was now; tomorrow would wait.

Joanna smiled as she rode beside her tall, handsome husband. Never had the future shone brighter. She felt his eyes on her and glanced up at him. The look he gave her spoke of his deep love for her. Her skin might be white, but inside she felt like an Indian. She was Windhawk's woman.

## MORE BESTSELLING ROMANCE BY JANELLE TAYLOR

**FIRST LOVE, WILD LOVE**  (1431, $3.75)

Roused from slumber by the most wonderful sensations, Calinda's pleasure turned to horror when she discovered she was in a stranger's embrace. Handsome cattle baron Lynx Cardone had assumed she was in his room for his enjoyment, and before Calinda could help herself his sensuous kisses held her under the spell of desire!

**GOLDEN TORMENT**  (1323, $3.75)

The instant Kathryn saw Landis Jurrell she didn't know what to fear more: the fierce, aggressive lumberjack or the torrid emotions he ignited in her. She had travelled to the Alaskan wilderness to search for her father, but after one night of sensual pleasure Landis vowed never to let her travel alone!

**LOVE ME WITH FURY**  (1248, $3.75)

The moment Captain Steele saw golden-haired Alexandria swimming in the hidden pool he vowed to have her—but she was outraged he had intruded on her privacy. But against her will his tingling caresses and intoxicating kisses compelled her to give herself to the ruthless pirate, helplessly murmuring, "LOVE ME WITH FURY!"

**TENDER ECSTASY**  (1212, $3.75)

Bright Arrow is committed to kill every white he sees—until he sets his eyes on ravishing Rebecca. And fate demands that he capture her, torment her . . . and soar with her to the dizzying heights of TENDER ECSTASY!